**Praise for the Novels of
Vicki Lewis Thompson**

"A sharp, sassy, sexy read. Stranded on a desert island? I hope you've got this book in your beach bag."
—Jayne Ann Krentz

"Wildly sexy . . . a full complement of oddball characters and sparkles with sassy humor."
—*Library Journal*

"A riotous cast of colorful characters . . . fills the pages with hilarious situations and hot, creative sex."
—*Booklist*

"Smart, spunky, and delightfully over-the-top."
—*Publishers Weekly*

"[A] lighthearted and frisky tale of discovery between two engaging people." —*The Oakland Press* (MI)

"Delightfully eccentric . . . humor, mystical ingredients, and plenty of fun . . . a winning tale."
—The Best Reviews

continued . . .

OVER HEXED

Vicki Lewis Thompson

AN ONYX BOOK

ONYX
Published by New American Library, a division of
Penguin Group (USA) Inc., 375 Hudson Street,
New York, New York 10014, USA
Penguin Group (Canada), 90 Eglinton Avenue East, Suite 700, Toronto,
Ontario M4P 2Y3, Canada (a division of Pearson Penguin Canada Inc.)
Penguin Books Ltd., 80 Strand, London WC2R 0RL, England
Penguin Ireland, 25 St. Stephen's Green, Dublin 2,
Ireland (a division of Penguin Books Ltd.)
Penguin Group (Australia), 250 Camberwell Road, Camberwell, Victoria 3124,
Australia (a division of Pearson Australia Group Pty. Ltd.)
Penguin Books India Pvt. Ltd., 11 Community Centre, Panchsheel Park,
New Delhi - 110 017, India
Penguin Group (NZ), 67 Apollo Drive, Rosedale, North Shore 0745,
Auckland, New Zealand (a division of Pearson New Zealand Ltd.)
Penguin Books (South Africa) (Pty.) Ltd., 24 Sturdee Avenue,
Rosebank, Johannesburg 2196, South Africa

Penguin Books Ltd., Registered Offices:
80 Strand, London WC2R 0RL, England

First published by Onyx, an imprint of New American Library,
a division of Penguin Group (USA) Inc.

First Printing, October 2007
10 9 8 7 6 5 4 3 2 1

 REGISTERED TRADEMARK—MARCA REGISTRADA

Printed in the United States of America

For Audrey Sharpe, because if you ever deserved exclusive billing on the dedication page of a book, this would be the one! Thank you for teaching me to believe in magic.

ACKNOWLEDGMENTS

From the beginning, this story has been touched by magic. The premise grew from a breakfast conversation in Sedona with my most excellent writing buddies, Rhonda Nelson and Jennifer LaBrecque. It sprang to full bloom with the support of my savvy agents at Trident Media Group. Many thanks to Robert Gottlieb for encouraging my new direction and to Jenny Bent for invaluable guidance and counsel. To my delight, the concept found a nurturing home with Claire Zion at New American Library. Claire, it's been a pleasure. Thank you all for making this a charmed experience!

Prologue

"For the crime of causing irreparable sexual mischief through magic, I hereby banish the defendants, Dorcas and Ambrose Lowell, to Big Knob, Indiana, until such time as they straighten out the dragon living there. So mote it be."

Dorcas lifted her head and looked at Cyril, the white-robed wizard who was about to ruin her life. "Cyril, are we talking about that dragon named George?"

"Yes, we are."

"But they say he's ADD!"

Cyril gazed down at her. "There's no medical evidence of that."

"Whatever. Nobody's been able to do a thing with George. We'll be stuck in that hick town, and you know it."

Ambrose nudged her. Defendants weren't supposed to speak during sentencing, let alone carry on a debate with the Grand High Wizard.

"But it's not fair," she muttered to her husband.

"Just accept it," he murmured. "Or it might get worse."

She didn't see how. And they hadn't screwed up *that* badly. For some reason, Cyril was trying to make an example of them, probably because the plaintiff, Thaddeus Hedgehump, was his brother-in-law.

Cyril gave her a stern look. "You're in no position to complain, Dorcas. Thanks to your untested potion, the plaintiff becomes aroused by *any* woman wearing support hose, not just his wife, as he requested. Restitution must be made."

"At least he can get it up now!" Dorcas felt completely unappreciated. "Before we came along, he was limp as a—"

Ambrose nudged her again, harder this time. "We understand, Your Honor."

"Good. Your belongings have been loaded onto a moving van, and the bailiff has your tickets for Indianapolis. We've arranged for a driver to take you from Indianapolis to Big Knob."

"What about Sabrina?" Dorcas wasn't going anywhere without her cat.

"Sabrina will travel with you on the plane. When you have something to report regarding George, you know where to find me. Court adjourned." With a sharp rap of his jewel-encrusted gavel, Cyril ended the trial.

Chapter 1

"I'm looking for an old-fashioned screw." Sean Madigan knew he was in trouble as soon as the words were out of his mouth.

Heather, the blond morning clerk at Big Knob Hardware and Camping Supplies, swooped into his personal space. "I can help you with that." Her double Ds brushed the front of his leather jacket.

Sean stepped back and cleared his throat. Better to pretend he didn't know what she was thinking. "It's longer than normal."

"I have no doubt."

Sheesh, he couldn't seem to say anything right. "About this length." He held his thumb and forefinger approximately five inches apart.

"Sean, don't underestimate yourself. According to the grapevine, it's *much* longer." As Heather moved in again, her perfume hit him like a blast of Mace. "No one's here but me. And forget the old-fashioned part, hon. Ever done it on Astroturf? Or cork?"

"No." Sean backed up some more and found himself trapped against the reels of ropes and chains. "Seriously, Heather, I'm not interested. I just came in here for—"

"Baby, you work too hard, always wearing that sexy

tool belt, always hammering something." Her blue
eyes burned with lust. "I'd love to get nailed."

"We're in the middle of the hardware store."

"I *know*. Think of the possibilities. How about a
little bondage action? I can tie you or you can tie me.
Whichever turns you on."

He could tell her that nothing turned him on these
days, but she wouldn't believe him. Nobody would.
Women craved him and guys envied him. They had
no clue the hell he endured with the catcalls, the groping, the leers.

It had been like this since puberty. In Big Knob,
Indiana, population 947, single guys were at a pre-
mium to begin with, so a green-eyed Irishman who
looked like Sean could name his price.

As a teenager he'd loved the attention. Nonstop
boinking was perfect when you were eighteen. Ten
years later, he could have any available woman in
town and probably a few who weren't, but he was
tired of their aggressive behavior, so pushy, so horny.
Unfortunately, none of the women in town seemed to
notice that he was no longer interested in sampling
what they had to offer.

At the moment all he cared about was finishing the
renovation of Calvin Gilmore's house. Once Calvin
paid him for that, Sean would have almost enough to
make a down payment on his childhood home. One
more job and he'd be ready to fulfill his dream and
buy the dilapidated old Victorian and the acreage that
surrounded it, assuming he could locate the owner.

"They say you're saving yourself for someone special, someone who'll keep you warm in that big old
house you have your eye on." Heather moistened her
lips. "Well, here I am, sugar." Without warning she
grabbed the zipper on his fly and yanked.

Sean caught her wrist before she could fondle his
privates. "I said *no*." He hated to push a woman, but

she gave him no choice. Shoving her aside, he left the hardware store, zipping his fly as he went.

"You're such a tease, Sean Madigan," she called after him. "But you don't fool me. Those bedroom eyes say you want me, baby. You want me bad!"

Bedroom eyes. He'd been accused of having bedroom eyes for years, and he'd never figured out what the hell that meant.

Once safely outside the hardware store, he turned up his coat collar against the biting November wind and glanced at the town's most obvious landmark: a chunk of granite that jutted 192 feet into the wintry sky. Rising from the forest on the northeast side of town, the prominent rock dominated the landscape. No wonder it had inspired the pioneers to name this place Big Knob.

Southwest of town nestled Deep Lake, also named by the pioneers. In the early 1800s, sexual symbolism hadn't been an appropriate topic of conversation. In some Big Knob households, it still wasn't.

But late at night, while enjoying a beer in the Big Knobian, some guys liked to speculate that if Big Knob ever buried itself in Deep Lake, the end of the world was at hand. Sean had always wondered if the combination of Big Knob and Deep Lake had a subconscious effect on the people in town, increasing their focus on sex.

Personally, he could testify that the women seemed quite focused on that topic, and they concentrated the bulk of their sexual interest on Sean. He would give anything to be less of a target.

For instance, instead of feeling compelled to jump in his old truck and leave, he'd love to grab a cup of coffee at the Hob Knob Diner. He'd appreciate the caffeine jolt if he could manage to order without being waylaid.

No such luck. Francine Edgerton, owner of the Bob

and Weave Hair Salon, came bouncing toward him, her multicolored hair dancing in the breeze. "Sean, you cutie patootie. Let me buy you a cuppa, cuppa, hubba, hubba." She closed one eye in a suggestive wink.

"Thanks, Francine, but I can't. I'm on my way back to the Gilmores'. Job's almost done, and I—"

"Don't be silly." She hooked her arm through his and tugged him in the direction of the diner. "Come play footsie with me under the table."

"Why, if it isn't Sean Madigan." A low female voice sounded in his left ear.

He turned. "Hi, Bet."

"Hi, yourself." She fluffed her bottle red hair and batted her fake eyelashes. Then she pinched his butt.

"Hey!"

"Hey, yourself." She laughed as she grabbed his other arm. "Come on, Francine. Let's share him."

Francine blew out an impatient breath. "Look, Bet, I realize you're a good customer and all, but I saw him first."

Sean held his ground. "As I keep saying, I don't have time for coffee." But how to escape? Aha. Dorcas and Ambrose Lowell, the new couple in town, were walking in this direction.

From his first glimpse of them, when they'd moved into the old Harrison place six weeks ago, Sean had wondered why they'd picked Big Knob. It was a nice enough town, all the lecherous women aside, but it wasn't the sort of location where you'd expect to find an attractive and fit middle-aged couple who looked like they'd stepped out of a Ralph Lauren commercial.

Today they both wore belted leather jackets and designer jeans. Sean pictured them strolling the wharf in San Francisco. Yet here they were in Big Knob.

Beside him, Francine stiffened. "Dorcas goes out of

town for her hair," she muttered. "Too good for the Bob and Weave."

"She says she does it herself," Bet said. "His, too."

"Yeah, and I'm Angelina Jolie. Nobody gets that natural brunette look from over-the-counter kits."

Sean made use of the distraction to yank his arms free. "Excuse me," he said to Francine and Bet. "I need to discuss something with the Lowells." Then he said the first thing that came to mind, "They have a problem with their porch."

He had no idea if their porch needed work or not. But the house was near the lake, which meant it was subject to damp fog most evenings. The porch might need work.

Both Francine and Bet backed off, because even they wouldn't stand in the way of a business opportunity, especially if the potential customers looked rich.

"I'll see you later, then," Francine said. "Don't do anything I wouldn't do, which leaves you plenty of room to maneuver."

"Francine, you're scaring the poor boy," Bet said. "Listen, Sean, I'll be up late tonight if you want to stop by. I make a great hot toddy."

Sean gave them each a wave and jogged down the sidewalk toward Dorcas and Ambrose. "I'm glad I ran into you. I wanted to discuss your front porch."

"You did?" Ambrose looked amused.

"Is this really about the porch?" Dorcas smiled at him. "Or is it that you need rescuing?"

"A little of both. Listen, I didn't mean to interrupt whatever you were doing, but—"

"Coincidentally, we were on our way to the hardware store," Ambrose said. "You must be psychic, because we just noticed a couple of loose boards on the front porch, and some warping going on. I wanted to fix that before the first snow."

"Seriously?" This was kind of freaky.

"Seriously," Dorcas said, and turned to her husband. "Unless you have your heart set on home repair, what do you say we hire Sean to do it for us?"

"Works for me. Let's take him back to our place so he can check out the job." Ambrose glanced at Sean. "Unless you have something else to do right now?"

"Nothing that can't wait." Sean had left his old truck parked in front of the hardware store, but he'd walk back and get it later, sometime when Heather was busy with a customer and wouldn't notice him.

"Then let's go." Ambrose turned back, taking Dorcas's hand as they started down the street.

The sidewalk was only wide enough for two, so Sean followed behind. Holding hands in public was another thing that made the Lowells stand out from your average Big Knobian. Someone had even seen them French kissing in broad daylight. They acted like teenagers, which many in the town thought ridiculous for a couple in their fifties.

The Harrisons' place, or what was now the Lowells' place, was at the far end of Fifth Street. The town's first residents, Ebenezer and Isadora Mather, had laid out the town's main streets in the shape of a five-pointed star. Legend had it that Ebenezer had intended the layout as a tribute to his wife, whom he called his guiding star.

Because of the shape created by these five streets, Big Knob boasted a town "square" with one extra side. Everyone still called it a square even though it wasn't. Businesses lined the square, and a five-sided gazebo in the middle was flanked by a life-sized statue of Isadora, a true heroine who had selflessly nursed the pioneers through a bout of smallpox. In another week or so, the gazebo would be decorated for the Christmas season.

"Hey, Sean!" Denise Woolrich ran coatless out of the Big Knob Realty office on the corner of Fifth and Third. "I think I've tracked down the owner of your family's old property!"

"Are you sure?" Sean had his doubts. He thought Denise might be drawing out the title search so she had a better chance of seducing him.

"This is it. I can feel it. Oh, hi, Mr. and Mrs. Lowell."

"Hello, Denise." Dorcas gave her the once-over.

Sean could imagine what a classy woman like Dorcas was thinking as she looked at Denise. Her red sweater was so tight it was in danger of unraveling any minute.

Eyes bright, Denise stepped in close and moistened her lips as she gazed up at him. "You need to come into my office, Sean."

He figured it was just another excuse to get him alone. "Couldn't you just tell me here?"

"I want to show you what I've found on the Internet." She lifted her dark hair from her neck as if dealing with a heat wave, despite the chill wind blowing across the square. The movement made her breasts quiver.

Instead of getting him hot, her behavior only annoyed him. "I'll come by a little later, okay?"

Denise pouted. "I thought you cared about this property, Sean. If you don't want me to track down the title holder for you, just say so."

As Sean was trying to decide how best to handle Denise, he heard a low whistle and a woman calling his name. He noticed a silver SUV gliding by with the window down and recognized Angie, an ex-girlfriend, behind the wheel. Not wanting to be rude, he waved at her.

"Sean, I'm trying to talk to you about this property." Denise sounded irritated.

He glanced back at her. "I do care about the property. But I'm kind of busy right this minute."

"If you're too busy to look at what I've found for you, then obviously your priorities have changed." Denise turned on her heel.

"I swear, they haven't." But it was too late. Denise had stomped back into her office.

Sean needed her help, so he'd have to go by later and soothe her ruffled feathers while trying to avoid ending up naked on her desktop.

He glanced over at Dorcas and Ambrose. "Sorry about that. Let's go."

They'd taken about three steps when another female voice brought him to a reluctant halt.

"Well, if it isn't Sean Madigan!" Candice, a woman he'd dated two years ago, came running across the square, plastic grocery bags in both hands, her short plaid skirt hiked up to reveal a shocking amount of creamy thigh.

Looking neither left nor right, she crossed the street, all her attention focused on Sean. Fortunately there wasn't much traffic. "What a coincidence! I just bought a package of those little cakes you like, the ones with the cream filling."

He panicked. Those little cakes had been part of some hot times. "That was quite a while ago," he said.

"Funny, it seems like only yesterday to me. We had such fun with those cakes, eating them in bed. Remember how I smeared them on your—"

"Gotta go!" Sean motioned to Ambrose and Dorcas as he took off down the street toward their house. "Emergency porch repair! Very critical!"

Within half a block, Dorcas and Ambrose had caught up with Sean, and they weren't even breathing hard. He couldn't help commenting on it. "You guys are in great shape for your . . ." He stopped short of saying *age,* which sounded insulting.

"For our age," Dorcas said with a wink as they reached the house, and she climbed the porch steps. "It's okay. Our secret is great sex."

Sean hadn't meant to let his jaw drop, and he snapped it closed the second he realized what he'd done. "That's terrific," he said quickly as they ushered him inside. The house smelled of incense, which confirmed his suspicion that they were from out west somewhere, probably California.

"Come in and sit down." Dorcas hung her jacket on a coat tree in the hall. Underneath it she wore a silvery silk shirt tucked into her jeans. "What would you like to drink?"

After the morning he'd had, he could use two fingers of Scotch, but it was a little early in the day to start knocking back hard liquor. "Whatever you have handy."

"I'll make some herbal tea. I'll only be a few minutes. Make yourself comfortable." She gestured through a doorway into a sitting room.

Definitely from California. If anyone in Big Knob drank tea, it was Lipton, hot in the winter and cold in the summer. Herbal tea sounded a little swishy to him, but maybe he'd like it.

He walked into a room filled with colored light, sort of like a church. Pretty soon he figured out why. Dorcas and Ambrose had hung stained glass in the windows—free-form designs of red, purple, blue, green and gold.

Or maybe they weren't so free-form. The one in the front window might be an angel or a fairy. The one in the side window looked kind of sexual, almost like a couple was about to . . . Whoa! Startled by the explicit picture now that he'd figured it out, he turned away. Definitely California.

"Let me take your jacket." Ambrose had already shed his coat. He was wearing a long-sleeved black

T-shirt with a picture on the front, a bumblebee wearing a halo. Underneath were the words BLESSED BEES.

"A band," Ambrose said by way of explanation. "I used to play guitar for them."

"Oh." Sean was having a tough time meshing the sexual stained glass with a religious-themed musical group. "You know, I didn't get a good look at that porch," he said. "Maybe I should go check it out." Come to think of it, he hadn't noticed any loose or warped boards when he'd walked in, but maybe they were off to the side.

"There's nothing wrong with the porch."

Sean stared at him. "But you said—"

"If I'd said that you looked as if you were having a problem and we could help, would you have gone along with that?"

Sean backed toward the door. "You're shrinks, right?" He might have a problem, but he didn't need a head doctor to solve it for him. He wasn't sure what he did need, but definitely not a session on the couch.

"We're not shrinks. We're relationship counselors."

"Same girl, different dress. And I have to say, I don't think you'll find much business in Big Knob. People around here don't go for that stuff."

"We're not really looking for business. We're taking a . . . a sabbatical."

"Oh." Sean wasn't exactly sure what that meant, but the Lowells looked like the kind of people who would be taking one, whatever it was. "The thing is, I don't need relationship counseling. I have more relationships than I can handle, and I wish they'd all go away."

"That's a problem in and of itself."

"Yeah, but unless you can change me into some kind of loser who doesn't attract women, you can't help."

Ambrose's gray eyes brightened with interest. "You want to change your appearance?"

"Come to think of it, no. I've tried gaining twenty pounds, and it made no difference. The women said they adored my love handles. I grew my hair out, and they said I reminded them of a sexy pirate. So physical changes don't work."

"Fascinating."

"Oh, I'm a regular science experiment. But since you don't have a porch that needs fixing, I should probably be leaving."

"Leaving? But I just made tea." Dorcas arrived carrying an enameled tray holding a flowered pot, cups and a bowl filled with lemon wedges. She was followed by a slender black cat who pranced over to Sean and rubbed against his legs, purring loudly.

When Sean reached down and scratched the cat's ears, she wriggled in ecstasy. "Let me guess," he said. "Female cat."

"She is. That's Sabrina." Dorcas set the tray on the coffee table in front of a plush-looking sofa upholstered in purple fabric.

Even the cat is fit, Sean thought as he stroked Sabrina's soft fur and listened to the deep rumble of her purr. "Ambrose just told me that you're relationship counselors." He straightened, and the cat strolled over to hop onto the windowsill under the explicit stained glass.

Dorcas frowned at her husband. "You did?"

"I also admitted there's nothing wrong with the porch. Sean was about to go look, and he would have found out right away that—"

"Maybe not," Dorcas said. "Have you checked the porch recently, Ambrose?"

Her husband lifted his eyebrows. "Did you—"

"Yes, but it doesn't matter now, does it? You've let the cat out of the bag, so to speak."

Sean wasn't following any of it. "Look, thanks for offering to help me, but I don't know what you could do."

"He says changing his appearance hasn't done any good," Ambrose explained to his wife.

"Really?" Dorcas surveyed Sean with amber-colored eyes. "We could try cutting off his phero-mones."

"Hey!" Sean backed up. "I don't want a sex change!"

"It's not that drastic," Ambrose said. "Pheromones are chemicals that attract the opposite sex. Yours might need to be toned down."

"Huh." Sean had never considered that he had a chemical imbalance.

"Can I take your jacket?" Ambrose held out his hand.

Sean hesitated. Nah, they couldn't do anything for him. No one could. "I'd better go."

"It wouldn't cost you anything except a little time," Dorcas said.

"I told him we were taking a sabbatical," Ambrose said.

Dorcas blinked. "Uh, right. That's exactly what we're taking. Anyway, you don't have to pay us."

"Thanks, but that feels like charity."

"Then we'll barter," Ambrose said. "We could use some carpentry work in the master bedroom. I've de-signed a sex bench, and I—"

"A *what*?" Sean couldn't believe what he'd heard.

"A sex bench," Dorcas said without blushing, not even a little bit. "And we don't have a lot of square footage, so we want it to fold out from the wall. It was actually my idea."

"But I came up with the design," Ambrose said.

"Yes, I have to admit you did, and I think the design's workable. Chairs are all well and good, but we've broken a few. We could use a nice firm bench."

"I see." Sean would bet no other house in Big Knob would require a fold-out sex bench. Even though sex wasn't a top priority with him right now, he was curious about the concept.

"So it would be our expertise in exchange for yours." Ambrose gazed at him.

He was tempted. It wasn't every day that a guy was handed plans for a fold-out sex bench. It would spice up his work routine considerably, and he did wonder what the thing would look like.

As he debated whether he could afford the time away from the Gilmore job, the cell phone clipped to his belt rang. "Excuse me a minute." He took out the phone and flipped it open. Speak of the devil; Calvin Gilmore was on the line.

But the connection was bad, which was weird. Big Knob had a lot of drawbacks, but cell phone coverage was usually great here.

He glanced up. "I need to take this call, and for some reason I'm not getting reception in the house. Can I get back to you about this later on today?"

"Absolutely." Ambrose smiled and wrapped an arm around Dorcas. "We'll be right here."

Sean gave them one last look before he walked out the door. They would be there, all right, and after hearing about the sex bench, he had no doubt what they would be doing with their time.

On his way across the porch, he tripped on a warped board. Funny, but he would have sworn it wasn't there when he'd gone in.

Chapter 2

Once Sean had left, Ambrose turned to Dorcas. "You really think this is a good idea?"

"Look, I don't know about you, but I'm getting sick of dealing with George's hyper behavior. We're relationship counselors. I miss doing the work I love."

"Dorcas, there's no way we can give up on George."

"Believe me, I'm well aware of that. I realize he's still our top priority. But I can't resist the challenge of a guy like Sean. We could have such fun with him!"

"Just to remind you, my love, we've never tried turning a sexy guy into a dud before."

She wound her arms around Ambrose's neck and kissed him on the mouth. "Trust me. We can do it. Besides, he's ripe for a soul mate. It seems as though he's had plenty of sex, but I doubt if he's had any deep relationships."

"Shouldn't we hold off on the soul mate part? He's burned out on women."

She shook her head. "No, he's burned out on meaningless sex. A soul mate is exactly what he needs. Let's find him one."

"But we haven't done any scrying for months, since before the trial. What if we're rusty?"

Dorcas smiled. Ambrose was so cute when he was

nervous. "We'll be fine. It's like riding a bicycle." She headed toward the door leading into the basement. Sabrina pranced after her.

"I still say we should wait until Sean agrees to let us change him. There's no point in bringing her here with the way he comes across now. All she'll notice is a hottie."

"I can guarantee that Sean is coming back tonight, and we'll have a head start on the project by the time he does." Dorcas grabbed a butane lighter from the table next to the basement door. Once she opened the door, Sabrina tore down the dark steps. Dorcas took it slower, lighting candles tucked into niches in the wall along the winding staircase, while Ambrose followed behind her.

At the bottom of the stairs, she turned to Ambrose. "You fill the cauldron while I light the gas logs."

"Okay. And I'll turn on the stereo."

She paused, suspicious. "What are you going to play?"

"What I always play when we're doing a soul mate search."

"Dear Goddess, tell me you're not playing Frankie Avalon."

"His music works for me. I hear 'Venus' and I'm in the groove."

"I hear 'Venus' and I want to kill myself."

Ambrose looked affronted. "Now, now, stop complaining. Negative energy screws up scrying." And off he went to turn on Frankie.

Dorcas stuck her tongue out at his retreating back. "Bossy pants."

"I heard that."

Dorcas grinned as she turned on the gas logs. It was good to be working again. She needed this desperately.

Puffing a little from the effort, Ambrose hauled over

the heavy iron cauldron filled with water and hooked it above the flickering flame from the gas logs. Dorcas sprinkled herbs over the inky surface as Frankie Avalon began to warble about Venus.

Dorcas glanced at Ambrose and Sabrina, who both stood beside her expectantly. "Ready?"

"Ready."

Sabrina meowed.

Drawing the magic circle, Dorcas closed them inside. As steam rose from the cauldron, Ambrose danced his jerky little cha-cha around the circle. He accompanied his shuffling movements with a rolling motion of his hands, punctuated with flinging each one alternately in the air. Sabrina followed behind, cha-cha-ing right along with him.

Dorcas bit her cheek to keep from laughing. It was like old times watching Ambrose and Sabrina dance while staring at the steam and waiting for . . . there!

"I see her." Ambrose stopped dancing and his voice quivered with excitement. Sabrina sat down and gazed upward at the steam, her tail twitching.

"I see her, too." Dorcas focused on the steam as the picture evolved and the voices became more distinct.

Ambrose leaned closer to the steam. "I think she's being called on the carpet for some reason. The nameplate on the desk says H. G. STACKHOUSE. Does that ring a bell with you?"

Dorcas shook her head. "Never heard of him."

"Her hair's a nice shade of red, and the freckles are cute," Ambrose continued, "but that's the ugliest navy suit I've ever laid eyes on. Doesn't she seem a little frumpy to you, with the glasses and everything? Maybe you forgot one of the herbs. What did you—"

"Hush." Dorcas concentrated on the scene in front of her. "I think she's going to be terrific. Just let me listen for a minute."

"Beat out again, Grady." The man named H. G.

Stackhouse steepled his fingers and gazed at the woman seated on the other side of the desk.

Ambrose made a sound of dismay. "I'm not sure about the name, either. A girl named Grady?"

"It isn't her first name," Dorcas said. "This is the kind of man who calls his employees by their last names. Be quiet so I can concentrate."

The woman sat straighter in her chair. "I will do better next time."

"I like you, Grady," H.G. said. "I liked you when I hired you and I like you now. You're a smart cookie."

"Patronizing SOB," Ambrose muttered.

"Shh." Dorcas put a finger to her lips.

"Thank you, Mr. Stackhouse."

"But this is no personality contest, and it sure as hell's no IQ test. It's business, darlin'."

Dorcas pegged him as a Texan from the way he pronounced *business* as *bidness*.

"You impressed me from the get-go, Maggie Grady, coming out of the gate with a plan and all those locations you'd researched. Mighty fine piece of work."

"Maggie's a good name," Ambrose said.

Dorcas shot him a quelling look.

"Unfortunately, we have nothing to show for that fine planning." H.G. adjusted his string tie and ran a hand over his bald head. "It's not enough to be a smart cookie, darlin'. You have to be a tough cookie, too."

"I am a tough cookie." Maggie's quick swallow revealed how upset she was.

Dorcas could tell this job was important, one Maggie didn't want to lose. On the wall behind H.G. was a citation of some kind, but she couldn't read it without her glasses, which she'd left upstairs.

She nudged Ambrose. "Can you read that framed thing on the wall?" she whispered.

"Yeah. It says COMMUNITY SERVICE AWARD PRESENTED TO SAVEALOT DEPARTMENT STORES."

"That helps. Thanks."

Maggie was speaking again and trying to look confident.

"This won't happen again, I promise."

"It better not." H.G. sighed. *"That New Mexico location was a honey. There would have been a promotion in it for you."*

"Don't worry, Mr. Stackhouse. I'll close the next deal."

Dorcas smiled and nudged Ambrose again. "Perfect. She's a location scout for SaveALot."

"What's perfect about that?"

"We have a location for her."

Ambrose looked at her. "We do? Where?"

"That property that Sean wants to buy."

"But it's right next to George!"

Dorcas tried to keep the smugness from her voice. "Of course."

"We can't have a SaveALot there. It'll be bad for Sean, and no telling what gonzo reaction we'd get from George. He could wig out completely."

Dorcas gazed at him indulgently. Sometimes he was slow on the uptake, but she loved him, anyway. "She'll fall in love with Sean and give up the location."

"You'd better hope to Hera that happens."

"It will. And as for George, we'll take credit for jinxing the SaveALot deal. A near disaster like that will be the wake-up call George needs to stop acting like a brat and buckle down to his responsibilities as the True Guardian of the forest. Then we'll get to leave Big Knob."

"Oh. Well, if you put it that way."

"But you have to remember to turn on the freeway exit sign so she can find us."

"I need to put it on tomorrow, anyway, remember? Jeremy Dunstan is going to Evansville to pick up supplies for the softball team."

"Oh, right."

Ambrose frowned. "It's damn hard to remember to turn it on and off whenever someone's coming or going. Maybe we should just leave it on and take our chances."

"No. Bespelling it so it appears and disappears on command was brilliant, so don't second-guess yourself. Unexpected people in the area are not good for George. He's too easily distracted."

"Yeah, but I really have trouble remembering about the sign."

Dorcas kissed him on the cheek. "Put a sticky note on the cover of your Book of Shadows and be done with it."

A major plumbing problem kept Sean at the Gilmores' until after six. He couldn't very well leave them with no bathroom facilities for the night, not when they were both pushing ninety. Rachel Gilmore was one of the few women in town who never made a pass at Sean, a feature of this job he treasured. Then again, she was legally blind and had no sense of smell.

Calvin Gilmore could see just fine, and he was a stickler for details. Calvin was the one who had insisted Sean had to match the old screws in the existing cabinets when he added the new storage space in the enlarged bathroom.

By the time Sean left the Gilmores', Denise had closed the real estate office and gone home. She was already pissed at him, so failing to show up as promised wouldn't make that situation any better. Damn it, he did care who owned the property, but she'd caught him at a bad time.

Sitting in his truck in front of the real estate office, he remembered the other callback he'd promised to make. He had no phone number for the Lowells, so he'd have to drive over there if he planned to talk to them again. Ah, he should forget it. He didn't have time for whatever they had in mind.

Then he saw Sylvia Hepplewaite leave the diner and catch sight of his truck. As she started toward him, he threw the truck in gear and headed for the Lowells'. Sylvia was more aggressive than all the other women he'd encountered today. He'd come out to his truck one morning and found her sitting naked in the cab, holding a box of condoms.

No doubt she would have come into the house, except for the skunks that lived in the crawl space underneath it. His landlord wanted those skunks gone, but Sean had stalled on removing them. They didn't bother him, and they were better than an alarm system when it came to women invading his privacy.

Sometimes he wished he was still a virgin, that he'd never given in to the temptation that had surrounded him all these years. Then he wouldn't have these women who remembered that he used to be eager for all the sex he could get.

He didn't hold out much hope that the Lowells could help him with the woman overload situation, but at this point, anything was worth a try. Arriving in the middle of what was probably their dinnertime wasn't cool, but he desperately needed to get away from Sylvia. She wouldn't follow him to the Lowells'. He hoped.

Five minutes later he stood on the Lowells' front porch, fog dampening his cheeks as he pushed the doorbell. It chimed some classical tune, one Sean had heard a million times but couldn't identify. He looked for the warped porch board he'd seen before. Even with the porch light on, the fog was so thick he couldn't find it.

A quick glance over his shoulder told him that Sylvia was walking purposefully down the street toward him. If the Lowells weren't home, he was dead meat.

Then Ambrose opened the door and the welcome smell of onions and garlic drifted out. Sean hadn't eaten since breakfast and he was starving. But his mother had raised him to have manners.

"I'm interrupting," he said.

"Sean!" Sylvia made a megaphone of her hands and called to him. "Wait up! I need to talk to you!"

"Screw the interruption," Sean said, and dove through the front door, almost knocking Ambrose down. "Sorry."

"No problem."

"If she comes to the door, tell her I'm handling some home repair emergency for you."

"She won't come to the door."

Sean ran a hand through his hair. "I don't know about that. She saw me come in here, and she's very determined."

"Don't worry." Ambrose smiled. "No one will bother you in this house. Won't you have dinner with us?"

Sean got over his panic enough to notice that Ambrose was wearing a long black bathrobe that looked like silk. Man, Sean had really intruded on their privacy. For all he knew, they ate naked. "You know, I should leave. If you'll give me your phone number, I can call tomorrow, and we can discuss—"

"Do I hear Sean out there?" Dorcas came from the back of the house wearing a robe similar to Ambrose's, only purple. "It is! You're just in time for dinner."

"You two weren't expecting company." Sean reached for the doorknob. "I'll come back tomorrow."

"Don't be silly." Dorcas hurried forward. "I cooked enough food for an army. We'll make plans while we eat."

Sean's stomach growled so loudly that he flushed. Come to think of it, this promised to be the first home-cooked meal he'd had in a while with no strings attached. Most women who cooked for him had ulterior motives.

Then he had a horrible thought. Surely not, but he might as well ask. In his experience, anything was possible. "Forgive me if I'm insulting you, but I hope you're not considering . . . a threesome."

Dorcas began to laugh, but then she put her hand over her mouth and fought to control herself. "Excuse me for laughing. You poor boy, always having to be on guard. Rest assured that Ambrose and I have no sexual interest in you whatsoever."

"Now I'm embarrassed that I even brought it up."

"I can see why you would wonder," Ambrose said. "There are some strange people out there. But Dorcas and I took a vow of sexual fidelity many, many years ago. It's . . . important to us."

Sean nodded. "I can see that, and it's inspiring. How long have you two been married?"

"If I told you that," Dorcas said, "then you could figure out how old we are. Let's leave some mysteries unrevealed, shall we?"

"Sure, sure. I just . . ." He paused, not willing to say that the two of them fascinated him and he wanted to know more.

"Hang up your coat and come on back to the dining room," Dorcas said. "I've made your favorite vegetable soup."

He could have sworn she'd just said she'd made his favorite, yet how could she know? His ears were still a little numb from the cold, so he probably hadn't heard her right. In any case, a bowl of home-cooked vegetable soup sounded like the best thing in the world.

Soon he was seated at a round dining table covered with a snowy white cloth that he hoped to hell he wouldn't drip soup on. Sabrina perched on a carpet-covered cat tree in a corner of the room and stared at him with green eyes. Red candles flickered on the table, and there were candles in other places, too—in sconces on the wall and in holders on the buffet up against the wall.

Dorcas must be one hell of a fast table setter, because that third place setting had appeared as if by magic. "This is great," Sean said. "Thanks."

"We always start a meal holding hands and saying a little something," Ambrose said.

"Uh, sure." Sean had been at several houses where they talked to their plates before eating, but hardly anybody held hands while they did that. Holding Dorcas's hand was no big deal, but he felt a little weird grabbing on to Ambrose. Oh, well. The soup smelled fantastic, and the blessing shouldn't take long.

Ambrose said something that sounded like a prayer, except it was in a language Sean didn't understand. It reminded him of the words on a dollar bill, *e pluribus unum,* so maybe it was Latin. Some sort of high-class prayer, obviously. Sean decided not to ask about it and show his ignorance.

"Have some wine." Dorcas didn't wait for a response before pouring him a hefty goblet of red.

"Thanks." Sean was more of a beer man, but he drank the wine to be polite. "Wow, this is good." He bet they'd paid at least twelve bucks for the bottle. He drank some more.

"Have you considered our proposition?" Ambrose asked.

Sean had never felt so relaxed in his life. This wine was outstanding. He discovered he really wanted to build their sex bench. If they thought they could help him in return, he'd give them a shot.

Gazing at them, he couldn't remember ever seeing two more beautiful people. "Let's go for it."

"Excellent." Ambrose beamed at him. "Dorcas, you

have that special brandy for toasting moments like this. I think we need some."

"Coming right up." She left the dining room and hurried into the kitchen. What a speedy lady. She had three tiny goblets and a dusty-looking decanter on the table before Sean could blink.

The brandy had to be really old because it looked like ink coming out of the bottle. Sean felt very sophisticated as he picked up his dainty glass.

"Before you take a drink," Dorcas said, "tell us again what you want out of this treatment."

"That's easy." Sean thought about the women that mobbed him at every turn, his lack of freedom to move around town without being pinched or whistled at, his complete disinterest in sex. He lifted his glass and candlelight bounced off the cut crystal. The Lowells wouldn't be able to do what he wanted, but what the hell, he'd ask.

"Turn off my sex appeal," he said. Then he laughed, because that sounded so impossible.

Ambrose continued to gaze at him. "You're sure?"

"Yeah. You can't do it, but it'll be fun watching you try."

"Yes." Dorcas smiled. "It will. Bottoms up!"

"Bottoms up." From the corner of his eye, Sean noticed Sabrina watching him. She blinked once, very slowly.

The brandy wasn't nearly as good as the wine. It tasted like used motor oil, not that Sean had ever tried used motor oil, but he could imagine how bad it would taste. He gulped the brandy, anyway, so he wouldn't offend anyone. Then he chased the god-awful stuff with another swallow of wine.

Between the shot of brandy and the wine, he was feeling no pain. He'd better slow down or he wouldn't be fit to drive home after dinner. Even his eyesight was affected. Dorcas, Ambrose and Sabrina all looked a little blurry.

Worried that he was getting seriously drunk, he picked up his soup spoon and started to eat. It was easily the best soup he'd ever eaten. He finished the bowl quickly.

"More?" Dorcas asked.

"Yes, please." He could have dipped his spoon into the big pot on the table and finished the entire batch. Instead he satisfied himself with polishing off the second bowl she served him.

"How are you feeling?" Dorcas sounded motherly.

That always affected him. His mother had died when he was eighteen, probably of a broken heart. His dad had run off several years before that after losing the entire family fortune.

"Sean?" Dorcas leaned toward him. "Are you okay?"

He swallowed the lump that always lodged in his throat when he thought of his mother's sad life. Never a strong woman, she'd miscarried several times before having him at age forty. "Sure. So how are you going to make me into a loser?"

"These should help." Ambrose reached into the pocket of his robe and pulled out the ugliest pair of black-framed glasses Sean had ever seen. "Try them on."

Good thing he was sort of drunk. Otherwise he might not have been able to make himself put on the glasses. When he'd asked them to turn him into a loser, he hadn't thought he'd end up looking quite this bad. He could wear them for now until he found something better.

But when he looked through what he assumed were clear lenses, the strangest thing happened. Dorcas and Ambrose went from blurry to sharp focus. The power of suggestion was amazing. He took the glasses off and everything got blurry again. Huh.

"The glasses are a nice touch," Dorcas said.

"Yeah." He put them on, and his vision cleared immediately. Bizarre. "Thanks."

"More soup?"

He was embarrassed to take thirds, but hunger won out over embarrassment. When the soup was all gone, Dorcas disappeared into the kitchen and came out with a huge chocolate cake and a carton of vanilla ice cream. He ate two large pieces of cake topped with ice cream.

By the end of the meal, he was sleepy. God, he was sleepy, but that stood to reason. Too much booze, too much food and a hectic day added up to exhaustion. But there was the sex bench to discuss.

"Did you want to show me the plans for your bench?" he asked.

"We can do that another day," Ambrose said. "You look tired. Why don't you stretch out on the sofa for a while before you drive home?"

The thought of stretching out anywhere sounded great, but he barely knew these people. "No, I should leave."

"I'm not sure that's wise," Dorcas said. "You have had a fair amount of wine. I would hate for you to be picked up."

"Me, too." He remembered that Judy usually drove the squad car on weeknights, and she was still mad at him for refusing to go along with her handcuff games two years ago. She'd write him a ticket for sure.

"Take the sofa," Ambrose said. "No point in pushing your luck."

"Okay, thanks."

They showed him back into the living room with its explicit stained glass, although it wasn't as vivid at night. Dorcas found him a pillow and Ambrose rustled up a soft blanket.

He took off the glasses and the contours of the room blurred. He must still be buzzed. "All you've done is give me these glasses," he said to Ambrose. "That doesn't seem like enough."

Ambrose gazed at him. "You'd be amazed at the difference they make. Keep wearing them and think unsexy thoughts."

Sean was too tired to argue. "If you say so." He settled himself on the purple sofa and pulled the blanket over him. At the last minute, Sabrina hopped up on the sofa and curled up at his feet.

Next thing he knew, faint light was coming through the stained-glass sex picture and Sabrina was no longer cuddled at his feet. He glanced at his watch and saw that it was almost seven. The house was quiet, but he wasn't about to go in search of his host and hostess. No telling what they were doing or if they were wearing anything while they did it.

His vision was still fuzzy, and he wondered if he might be in the grip of an extreme hangover. Once he put on the glasses, his vision cleared, and he didn't have a headache.

Time to head for home. Leaving the blanket and pillow folded on the sofa, he slipped out the front door, locking it behind him.

Dorcas overslept, and by the time she peeked into the living room, Sean was gone. She called out to Ambrose, who hurried down the stairs, tying his bathrobe.

"So he flew the coop," Ambrose said.

"Yes, and I so wanted to see what his physical transformation looked like."

"I still think we should have limited ourselves to altering his pheromones."

Dorcas rolled her eyes. "You're no fun. Besides,

now we can more easily monitor his progress. When he's acting heroic, we'll know because his hair will behave and his vision will clear up. And vice versa."

"That's assuming the potion works."

"It'll work." Dorcas gave him a kiss. "Let's make some coffee and plot our strategy for George. I'm on a roll."

Chapter 3

After getting no sleep the night before, Maggie knew she should be tired, but she was wide-awake as she drove her rented Escort toward Big Knob. The luck of the Irish had never worked for her before, but today was the day for four-leaf clovers and pots of gold. It was pure luck that she'd stayed an extra hour at work yesterday. If she hadn't, she would have missed the e-mail from the Realtor here telling her about a potential location for SaveALot.

In a deal like this, every hour counted. She'd learned that the hard way after MegaMart had beat her out on three different occasions. She couldn't say this to H.G., but there had to be a mole in the company, somebody who was getting kickbacks for leaking info. How else to explain that MegaMart had been a step ahead of her every damn time?

They wouldn't beat her out on this one, though, because no one, not even H.G., knew where she was. She'd flown out of Houston on the red-eye, leaving a message on H.G.'s private line that she was scouting a prime location and could be reached on her Black-Berry. But it was still too early for her boss to have received that message.

For now, it was just her and the location that would save her job. Jobs like hers didn't grow on trees these days, and if she lost this one, she'd lose the car and furniture she was still making payments on. Worse, she'd lose the feeling that she was bettering herself, climbing out of the muck of financial instability that had always been her parents' way of life.

The Realtor's e-mail had included a map, which Maggie had printed out. Strange pattern to the streets, but she could deal. Any kid knew the contours of a five-pointed star. Besides, she had the granite out-cropping of Big Knob itself to guide her. It should be coming up on her right any minute.

The area was perfect for a big-box store. The prop-erty values were low, so she could easily stay within her spending limit and still get the land. Prior to flying out last night, she'd Googled Big Knob and taken in-ventory of the retailers there. Typical small-town fare—grocery, hardware store, diner, hair salon, bar-bershop, gas station. There was a local dairy and one church, nondenominational.

Some of the businesses, like the Knobby Nook De-partment Store, might not survive after SaveALot opened its doors, but the days of such small shops were numbered, anyway. They couldn't carry the mer-chandise or match the prices of the bigger corpora-tions.

Before leaving for the airport Maggie had also spent time researching the small towns around Big Knob. No MegaMarts within a hundred miles. A new SaveA-Lot would pull in business from all the towns within driving distance. The area was crying out for SaveA-Lot bargains and an influx of jobs. She was the girl who would bring it to them.

At the edge of town, where the two-lane road turned into Fourth Street, she saw the old rural mail-box on the right, just as Denise had mentioned in her e-mail. There was NO FOR SALE sign because the prop-erty had simply been abandoned. Denise thought she'd found the owners and only needed to check a couple of things to make sure.

Although there was no traffic at this hour of the morning, Maggie put on her signal before turning onto the road that led to the property. She tried to avoid the potholes, but there were too many. Praying that the Escort's shocks could take it, she drove slowly along a drive lined with leafless oak trees and a few sycamores.

The road ended in front of the creepiest old Victorian mansion she'd ever seen. Gray clouds filtered whatever rays might be coming from the rising sun. In the murky light she had no trouble imagining ghosts and goblins hiding behind the sagging shutters, not to mention rats and big, scary spiders scurrying along the dusty floors. Bulldozing this place would be a service to the town.

Leaning against the steering wheel, she imagined the property cleaned up, with the trees cleared and a shiny new SaveALot replacing the dilapidated house. Huge improvement. Paving the parking lot would mean taking out more trees, but some could be saved to provide shade for the cars. There would be lots of cars. What a bonanza for her company, for the town . . . and for her.

She climbed out of the car and raised her arms, partly to stretch but mostly in jubilation. This would work! Then she checked her watch. Still too early to contact Denise.

Her black heels weren't designed for trudging around in the weeds, but she felt the urge to walk the property. She suspected that behind the house there would be a great view of Big Knob. SaveALot could put a hot dog stand back there, along with some picnic tables. Nice touch.

Belting her trench coat tighter, she grabbed her BlackBerry from the car so she could make a few notes. She walked around a sagging front gate that stood partway open and found a narrow path through the weeds. The path circled the house.

As she walked, little burrs stuck to her nylons. This walkabout was probably a dumb idea, but she had to do something with her excess energy, and she felt certain the view from the back would be worth the trip. The path seemed well worn, and she wondered why.

Maybe kids came out here at night on a dare. Or lovers used it as a rendezvous spot, although she couldn't imagine being able to have an orgasm while that spooky house loomed over her. A light rain began to fall, but she was almost all the way around the house, so she shielded her glasses and kept going. Her hair would frizz, but she wasn't here to win a beauty contest.

As she rounded the corner, she found a tire swing hanging from a tree in what used to be the backyard. On the other side of a rotting fence, what might have been a pasture was choked with weeds like everything else, and beyond that were the decaying remnants of a stable. At one time this must have been the most magnificent house in town.

It definitely commanded the best view. Rising on the far side of the property was the granite outcropping of Big Knob, looking craggy and phallic. Maybe the lovers who came out here concentrated on that big old rock instead of the house.

Maggie turned her back to the rain and made a note on her BlackBerry about extra security lights in the rear of the building. The SaveALot execs would have a cow if people continued to use the area behind the store for sex.

The rain started pelting her in earnest, and a cloud descended over Big Knob. *Like a condom,* Maggie thought with a little giggle. She had to get off this sexual kick. She was in Big Knob to close a deal, not get lucky. In fact, getting lucky was way down on her list of priorities these days.

Rain was running down her glasses, so she took them off and put them in her coat pocket. Time to get back to the shelter of the car before she ended up soaked. As she turned and started along the narrow path, she heard an approaching vehicle. It sounded more like a truck than a car, and sure enough, when she rounded the house again, her fuzzy vision revealed an old blue pickup parked behind her Escort.

She didn't expect Denise to drive an old rattletrap truck, but Denise was the only person who knew she was coming. The person who stepped down from the truck didn't move like a woman, though. Maggie grabbed her glasses from her pocket and put them on long enough to make sure that it wasn't Denise.

Nope, definitely a man dressed in jeans and a brown leather jacket. He wore ugly black-framed glasses and his hair was a wreck, as if he'd tried to cut it himself in a drunken stupor.

Quickly she became aware that she was alone in a deserted location and this guy might have followed her onto the property for some sinister reason. Just because a town was small didn't mean there were no vicious killers around. Look at *In Cold Blood*.

And here she was with no weapon and shoes that would be useless for running. He stood between her and the car, so she was trapped. She wondered how much damage a BlackBerry would do to an attacker.

"Can I help you with something?" he called out.

"Uh, no, thanks. I'm fine." She took off her glasses because she could actually see better without them in the rain. He hadn't done the same, so the rain on his glasses could work to her advantage.

"This is private property, you know."

"Do you own it?" If he did, she'd forgive him for scaring her to death.

"No."

She gulped. If he didn't own it, what reason could he have for being here other than to rape her and then cut her up into little pieces? She tried to think of all the ploys that she'd read on the Internet when faced with a situation like this.

He started toward her. "Not many people come out here."

Yikes. He was emphasizing how alone they were. "I'm meeting someone," she said. "I expect them any minute. Any second."

"Really?" He kept walking. "Somebody local?"

"Yes. Plus lots of people know I'm here. Tons of people."

He smiled. "This is a very small town. You'd have trouble rounding up a ton of people."

She noted that he had a nice smile, but then so had Ted Bundy. Other than the smile, he didn't have much else going for him. Plus he needed a shave. Not what you'd call an appealing character.

Maybe the direct approach would work. "If this is private property," she said, "then why are *you* here?"

"I saw you turn in and followed you." He smiled again. "You have really pretty hair."

She gasped and backed up a step. Anybody who would compliment her frizzed-out hair was seriously weird and quite possibly dangerous. "Okay, listen, whoever you are. I have an active case of genital herpes, and . . . and . . . I have my period right now . . . and . . . I'm coming down with stomach flu. If you have sex with me, I'll hurl all over you. See if I don't!"

His mouth dropped open. "You think I'm here to *rape* you?"

Her fear spiked into the stratosphere. "Oh, God, don't kill me. Please don't. I have some money in the car. Take it. Here, take my BlackBerry." She held it out with a shaking hand. "My rings are faux stones, but you can have them if you want."

"Hey, calm down." He started to reach for her. "I didn't—"

"Don't touch me!" She leaped back. "I just remembered. I know karate!" She crouched and held her arms at right angles the way she'd seen Bruce Lee do it in the movies.

The guy put up his hands as if she had a gun pointed at him. "Look, I have no intention of raping or killing you. I didn't mean to scare you, and I apologize."

She wasn't about to buy his story just like that. "Then why did you follow me?"

"I was on my way home from . . . Anyway, I was driving by. I saw you turn down the lane into this property, and I wanted to know who you are and why you're walking around it."

"What are you, some volunteer security guard?" The rain let up and she fished her glasses out of her pocket and put them on.

"I have . . . an interest in the property."

As her fear faded, a new suspicion took its place. "MegaMart sent you, didn't they?" If they had, she was beyond humiliated after spouting all that stuff about herpes and having her period. That story would make the rounds of all the MegaMart watercoolers, sure as the world.

"MegaMart?"

He was either not sent by her archrival, or he was very, very good. She'd believe the latter until proven otherwise. "Don't play dumb. I thought I'd covered my tracks, but obviously someone found out my travel plans and put it all together. They thought if they sent some ordinary local guy out to talk to me, I'd never suspect that he was a plant."

He stared at her. "I look ordinary to you?"

"Um, well, I didn't mean it in a bad way. But yeah. Pretty much."

"You don't find me . . . sexy?"

Her fears returned with a vengeance and she went into her fake karate crouch. "Stay back, bucko. I can break boards like they were matchsticks. I'll snap you in two before you know what happened."

"That wasn't a come-on. I honestly am no danger to you."

"So you say."

"No, really. It's just that usually women have a slightly . . . different reaction to me."

Slowly she straightened and took a deep breath. Okay, she had it now. He was the local Romeo, and in a small town, he might be the sexiest thing they had to offer, in which case she was in no danger of getting sidetracked on this trip.

Poor guy. She'd probably insulted him, but then again, if he was a paid spy for MegaMart, she shouldn't care.

He took off his glasses. "Do I still look ordinary?"

Men and their egos. But it wasn't in her to be deliberately cruel. "You know, have you ever considered contacts? You have very nice eyes, and the glasses sort of cover them up."

He nodded and put the glasses back on. "Okay."

Then she had another unsettling thought. "Don't tell me you were sent here to sweet-talk me out of closing this deal."

"What deal?" He looked uneasy.

"Of course you wouldn't admit it. Listen, just because I don't have a boyfriend right now doesn't mean that I'm desperate for male attention. But I wouldn't put it past MegaMart to try something sneaky like that."

"I have nothing to do with MegaMart."

"Maybe, maybe not. It doesn't matter, though. I

have the inside track on this one. Within the next six months there will be a SaveALot store right where we're standing. MegaMart can eat my dust." Or mud, in this case. The rain had turned the path under her feet into a squishy mess.

He looked as if he'd been hit by a cattle prod. "A SaveALot? You mean that big-box store?"

"The best of the big-box stores. And if you'll excuse me, I have some people to see." She fixed him with a determined glare, hoping he'd take the hint and move aside on the narrow path. Her nylons had gathered enough burrs and she'd rather not have to tromp through the thickest part of the weeds to get back to her car.

He didn't budge. "You want this property so you can put a SaveALot on it?"

So maybe he wasn't from MegaMart. That level of disbelief would be really hard to fake. "Yes," she said. "The location is perfect."

"This can't be happening."

"Sometimes you just have to pinch yourself, don't you? It will be an incredible boon for the area. If I close the deal quickly, before Thanksgiving, everyone in town will have something special to be grateful for."

"A SaveALot." He looked dazed, probably with happiness.

She thought of his battered old truck and his scruffy appearance. He probably needed work. "Unfortunately, I can't offer you a job. That's not my department. Once the deal is finalized, I'm sure a SaveALot personnel manager will visit the area and take applications. You could have the job nailed down by Christmas, although you wouldn't report to work until the facility's finished. Shouldn't take too long, though."

He continued to stare at her as if unable to comprehend his good fortune.

She realized that if he didn't clean up a little, he'd

stand no chance of getting that job, either. "I hope you won't take this the wrong way, but SaveALot tends to be on the conservative side when it comes to hiring. You might want to get a fresh haircut before you apply."

"But I just . . ." He shoved his fingers into his hair, and his eyes widened. "I just got a haircut."

"No kidding?"

"A week ago."

"Well, I hate to tell you this, but it looks as if your barber might be ripping you off. Now, if you'll please excuse me, I need to meet someone."

This time he did step aside, although she had to pass very close to him in order to avoid the weeds. Her shoes made sucking sounds in the mud, sounds that were almost sexual if your mind was drifting that way, and hers certainly wasn't.

His might be, though, because she could swear he caught his breath as she brushed by him. She hardly considered herself a bombshell, but maybe she would be in a town this size.

"What's your name?" he called after her.

She could see no harm in telling him. Everyone in town would know her name eventually, anyway. "Maggie Grady."

"That's a nice name."

She turned, feeling sorry for him again. He was showing signs of being attracted to her. Talk about hopeless. "I'll only be here a few days."

"We have no hotels in Big Knob."

"That's okay. A motel will work."

"No motels, either."

"Oh." She'd been in such a rush to get here that she hadn't checked that out. "I'll manage. I'm sure my real estate contact can help me find someplace to stay."

"Denise Woolrich?"

"Yes. Do you know her?" Of course he would. Everyone knew everybody in a small town.

"I know her." He didn't look happy about it.

Maggie wondered if Denise was an old girlfriend who'd done him wrong. "I barely know the woman," she said, "but she deserves a medal for contacting me yesterday afternoon. SaveALot will put Big Knob on the map."

Chapter 4

The minute Maggie's little Escort pulled out of the drive, Sean ran over to his truck and peered in the side-view mirror. The mirror was cracked, but he could see himself well enough to notice that his hair had never looked worse. Maybe he'd slept on it wrong.

Pulling a comb out of his back pocket, he tried to make his hair behave, but no matter how he combed it, pieces stuck out in all directions. No wonder she'd said he looked ordinary with hair like this. He climbed in the truck and started the engine. A shower and a shave, and he'd be back to his old self.

He needed his old self right now, for two reasons. First of all, Maggie Grady was a threat to his plan of buying this place and reclaiming his family home. Second of all, and this was an amazing revelation, she was the first woman in the past couple of years who turned him on.

From the minute he'd seen her standing there in the rain, he'd wanted her. And not just slightly, either. His skin had flushed like it was August, spit had pooled in his mouth, and his penis had expanded to the point that walking hurt. He hadn't had that kind of a reaction to a woman in ages.

If he could get her interested in him, he'd have a

chance to talk her out of this SaveALot deal. There
had to be other pieces of property in Southern Indiana
that would make a good location for her company.
He'd be happy to help her find them. He'd be happy
to help her do any little thing she wanted, except buy
this piece of property.

Just his luck he'd met her while sporting a bad case
of bed head and a day-old beard. Oh, and the glasses.
He still couldn't see shit without them. He'd never
had a hangover last this long, but his eyes should be
okay in a couple of hours. Then he'd ditch the glasses
and make his play.

He had to admit they'd gotten off to a really bad
start, with her thinking he was a serial killer. And his
one compliment, that she had pretty hair, had been
totally lame. He was generally smoother than that.
Maybe the wine last night had killed off a few brain
cells.

Funny, but he didn't have a headache. Taking the
dirt road leading to his house faster than normal
bounced him around some, but it didn't make his head
hurt. The little cottage where he lived belonged to
Clem Loudermilk, the richest guy in Big Knob. Clem
held the patent on a type of cleavage-enhancing bra
that had made him a fortune.

Fortune in hand, Clem had built a brand-new house
farther up the hill. It wouldn't do to have the access
road go past the old cottage, so Clem had paved a
new lane down to the main road with security gates
at the end of it. Then he'd put in a set of 106 steps
that descended the hill from his house down to the
cottage, so he could go check on how it was doing.

The cottage was doing great, because in exchange
for living in Clem's old house, Sean was gradually repairing everything and bringing it up to code. Clem
had obviously made the trek down the steps this
morning, because he was crouched down peering

through the latticework covering the crawl space when Sean drove up.

Clem stood with a groan of discomfort as Sean climbed down from his truck. Clem was a round little guy who didn't dress like a rich man and probably never would. He'd invented the bra as a service to his wife, and he was the first to tell anyone that it had been pure luck that some lingerie company had picked it up.

"We need to do something about those skunks," Clem said as Sean walked toward him.

"I will. Before I move out they'll be gone." And not one day sooner. He didn't want them hurt, so he planned to trap them and take them out to a part of the woods near the granite outcropping of Big Knob itself.

He'd picked out the perfect spot, in an area the pioneers had named the Whispering Forest. Everyone in town thought the place was haunted. There were tall tales about disembodied eyes, strange noises and the smell of smoke when there were no visible campfires.

Some claimed they'd heard the whispers that had given the forest its name. They swore it was *not* the sound of wind through the trees, but spooky words breathed into their ears. Although the state allowed hunting in Whispering Forest, hunters looking to bag a rabbit or a deer said their guns jammed whenever they tried to shoot anything.

Sean thought the stories were ridiculous, but the rumors made it the perfect hideaway for the skunks. No one would bother them there. They were a family, and he'd do his best to keep them together.

"I'm worried about them migrating up to the big house," Clem said. "Clara wouldn't like that. They might get tangled up with Bud." Bud was Clara's Chihuahua, and a tougher little cuss Sean had never met.

"They seem to stay close to home," Sean said. But if Clara was on a kick, he might have to relocate them sooner than he'd planned. Once Clara started pestering Clem, he was moved to action. That was how he'd ended up inventing the bra.

"Even so." Clem rubbed his chin and gazed at the roofline of his three-story house, which was barely visible through the trees. Then he took a closer look at Sean. "I hate to say it, but you look like hell, boy."

"I know. I'm headed inside for a shower and a shave."

"That would be a good idea. What's with the glasses? Some new fad I ain't heard about?"

"Oh." Sean took them off to see if the world still looked blurry without them. It did. Maybe they weren't clear lenses, after all, and they were screwing up his eyes. He'd leave them off for a while. "Just a joke. I forgot I had them on."

Clem nodded. "Must have been some night."

"Just dinner and drinks with a couple of friends. I ate and drank way too much, so they offered me the sofa and I took it."

"You gotta watch out for that stuff. You're at the age when your metabolism slows down and you start putting on weight. Before you know it, you'll look like me, and then it's hell to take it off again."

"I'll keep that in mind."

"And do something about the skunks. If they get tangled up with Bud, we got us a big problem. See you later." Clem started back up the steps to his house.

Sean watched him go. He wouldn't be surprised if Clem kept the cottage as his personal hidey-hole after Sean left. Clara had always been bossy, but once she got cleavage thanks to Clem's invention, she'd become unstoppable.

Sean called out a greeting to the skunks before he went inside. He had no idea if they understood or paid any attention, but he liked to think they appreciated being left alone. They'd never smelled up the place, not even slightly.

Inside the cottage he took a deep breath of freshly cut wood, thanks to the cedar wainscoting and cabinets he'd put in last month. His furniture was nothing to write home about, but the carpentry was primo, if he did say so himself. Someday he'd build himself some furniture, but for now he was too busy.

Shucking clothes as he went, he headed for the bathroom. He'd set up a mirror in the shower so he could shave and shower at the same time. He didn't realize until he was standing in the warm spray, ready to shave, that he couldn't see well enough to do it.

He stepped out of the shower and went in search of the glasses, shivering and dripping water on the floor. What a pain. Surely he wouldn't be forced to wear them much longer, but for now, seeing well enough to shave was a priority. He couldn't get anywhere with Maggie Grady if he looked like a homeless person.

Back in the warm shower, he lathered up and stroked the razor across his chin. The glasses kept fogging up, but eventually he got the job done. Then he washed his hair, which seemed much more coarse than usual.

At least his body was still fit . . . or was it? He gazed down at what he remembered as rock-hard abs. Now not so much. Farther down—now, this *had* to be an optical illusion—his dick looked smaller.

Getting out of the shower again, still dripping water, he tried to see himself in the medicine cabinet mirror. He didn't own a full-length mirror, had always considered that a vain thing to have. But without a full-length mirror, he was forced to climb on a stepstool so he could get the full picture, section by section.

The view wasn't encouraging. Surely he'd had more muscle definition yesterday. If not, why had six different women tried to hit on him? He'd been a stud muffin yesterday, but this morning, average Joe.

As he moved up and down the stepstool trying to decide if the mirror was flawed, his cell phone rang. He dried his hands, walked into the bedroom and picked it up off the dresser. He didn't recognize the number, but he answered, anyway.

Ambrose's voice came on the line. "How are you feeling?"

"Strange, if you must know. I can't see anything without the glasses you gave me, but that could be from a hangover. What I didn't realize is that I've apparently let myself get out of shape. On top of that my hair decided to go wacko on me this morning. . . ." A horrible thought came to him. But no, that was too wild.

"The herbal supplements must be working!" Ambrose sounded tickled to death. "Dorcas will be thrilled."

"You did this?" In a way he was relieved to know he wasn't slowly falling apart, but he didn't remember taking any herbal supplements. "What supplements?"

"Dorcas mixed a few things in with what you were eating and drinking last night. She thought that would be the easiest route to go. We expected that you'd stay around for breakfast so we could discuss the changes, but—"

"Hold on a minute. Herbs take a long time to work. This was overnight."

"The brandy acts as a booster. Also the cocoa in the cake."

"But you drank the brandy and ate the cake!"

"Just a little. But it's a peculiar thing with these types of herbs. They work differently depending on your body composition and your . . . well, your mental attitude. I'm sure you've heard about the mind-body connection."

It sounded like California woo-woo stuff to Sean. "You should have told me what you were doing."

"To be truthful, we didn't know if it would work. Dorcas had never tried this sort of po—uh, combination of herbs before. She was a little afraid that you'd actually end up looking better instead of worse. Thank goodness we lucked out and that didn't happen." He hesitated. "This is what you wanted, isn't it? I mean, you're not sexy anymore, right?"

"I guess so, but I didn't really imagine . . . My eyes are part of it, too, aren't they?" He tried not to panic. There was probably some antidote he could take.

"It's better if you really need the glasses than if you're faking it. People can tell if the glasses aren't necessary."

Sean rubbed his forehead. The headache he'd been expecting after drinking all that wine had finally arrived. "Okay, maybe I did ask for this, but something's come up, and I want the effects reversed. Mix up whatever you need to. I'll be over in fifteen minutes. I don't care what it tastes like, so long as it puts me back the way I was."

"Hey, Dorcas is good, but she's not *that* good."

In spite of standing there dripping wet in a cold room, Sean began to sweat. "What do you mean?"

"She made that concoction with some very rare herbs and she used up her entire supply. Gathering the herbs to reverse it would be next to impossible. She'd have to send away for some things, and a few of them might not be available this time of year. I'm afraid you'll have to let it wear off."

"And how long will that be? A day or so?" He could deal with twenty-four hours. Maggie would still be here, and he could take command of the situation then.

"Probably about two weeks, give or take."

"Two *weeks*?" Sean began to hyperventilate. "No, no, that's way too long. You have no idea what's on the line here. I just met someone."

"Really? Who?"

"You wouldn't know her, but she wants to buy my family's old property and put up a store. Plus she's really hot, and if I looked the way I used to, I'm sure I could talk her into dropping the whole idea."

"Man, I wish I could help you, but there's no way." Ambrose didn't sound as sorry as maybe he should have, considering. "I guess you'll have to work with what you have for the next couple of weeks."

Sean felt desperation clawing at his insides. "You don't understand. She's after the property I want. Ever hear that old song about paving paradise so they can build a parking lot? That's what she plans to do!"

"I'll bet you can change her mind."

"Not like this."

"Why not?"

"Because . . . because . . ." He couldn't bring himself to admit that sometimes he'd counted on his good looks to get him what he wanted. He'd asked Dorcas and Ambrose to transform him so he could be something besides a sex symbol. Obviously he was no longer a sex symbol, but who was he?

Maggie drove back into town and parked between the diagonal white lines in front of Big Knob Realty. Now that she'd achieved her first goal of inspecting the property, she became aware of other needs she'd shoved into the background. She could use a bathroom, a cup of hot coffee, something to eat and a place to sleep tonight. She hoped Denise decided to open up early this morning.

About twenty minutes later, a dark-haired woman in her forties parked next to her and walked toward the real estate office with a key in her hand. Maggie sighed in relief. Opening her car door, she called out to the woman. "Denise?"

The woman turned and smiled. "I wondered if you were Maggie. I didn't recognize you or the car. In Big Knob we know everybody and their vehicles."

Maggie got out of the Escort and locked it from habit. Probably didn't need to in Big Knob. "Then you must know a guy in his late twenties who drives an old blue truck."

Denise's smile turned to a scowl. "I do. That's Sean Madigan. *Very* full of himself, which comes from being a hottie all his life."

"Uh, yeah, I guess." Apparently Maggie would have to adjust to a different set of standards while she was here. If Sean was considered a hottie in Big Knob, she held out little hope for the rest of the male population.

Denise unlocked the office door and gestured Maggie inside, flipping on the overhead lights as she followed her. The lights flickered for a moment, and Denise paused to glance upward.

When they stopped flickering and stayed on, she took off her coat and hung it on the coatrack by the door. "Where did you meet Sean?"

"I drove out to the property, and he showed up soon after I got there."

"I'll just bet he did." Denise looked triumphant. "He wants to buy that piece of land."

"Really? But surely he doesn't have the money."

"Don't be fooled by the old rattletrap he drives. He doesn't buy new things because he's socking money away for a down payment."

"Oh." That explained a lot about his reaction to

her. She must be his worst nightmare. The comment about her hair must have been an attempt at flattery, in case he could woo her away from her plan. As if.

The information also cast Denise in an interesting light. "You know all this, and yet you e-mailed me late yesterday afternoon about buying the property."

"I most certainly did. It was serendipity. I just happened to see a pop-up ad for SaveALot on my computer yesterday afternoon, so I tracked you down through the SaveALot Web site."

"Why me? We have other location scouts."

"They were all men. I wanted a woman to have a crack at this."

Maggie didn't have to work very hard to figure out what was going on. She was part of a revenge plot, not that it was anything to her. She didn't care about Denise's ulterior motives, as long as the sale went through and Maggie got the credit for landing a prime location.

"Give me a minute and I'll have some coffee for us. I have a one-woman operation here. Don't even have a secretary."

"It's not all bad, being your own boss." Maggie could see the advantages. No H.G. breathing down your neck. She hung her trench coat on the rack alongside Denise's coat. "If I could use your bathroom, I'd be a very grateful woman."

"Sure thing." Denise filled the coffee carafe at the watercooler. "By the time you get back, I'll have coffee made and the computer up and running. I'm expecting an e-mail confirming ownership of the property."

In the bathroom Maggie turned on the light, which also flickered before coming on. The building had to be at least fifty or sixty years old, maybe more. No telling what shape the wiring was in.

Fortunately the plumbing worked fine. She took

time to repair her makeup and put her frizzy hair into a clip buried at the bottom of her purse. She needed a haircut, but she'd been putting it off, and now she wished she hadn't. Her hair looked like a rusty Brillo pad.

With a sigh, she cleaned her glasses and put them back on. She hadn't made a huge improvement, but that was as good as it was going to get today without a hair salon appointment.

As she reached for the knob on the bathroom door, she heard an argument start up between Denise and some man. The voice sounded familiar and she hesitated, trying to place it. Once she did, she felt like hanging out a while longer in the bathroom. She had no desire to meet Sean Madigan again now that she knew both of them were after the same piece of land.

She didn't care how long he'd been saving his money, or what his reasons were for wanting the property. He'd ticked off Denise for some reason, and he'd have to pay the price for that. She knew what it was like to have something you wanted taken away, but this time she wouldn't be the one dealing with failure. Let the other guy fail.

So what was she doing hiding in the bathroom? A tough cookie would go right out there and stare down this local Romeo. She'd let him know that he didn't stand a chance in hell of getting that property, so he might as well give up right now.

She opened the door, but she was still hidden by a partition that screened off the back area of the office.

"I got held up yesterday afternoon!" Sean said. "I would have come by, but—"

"You had your chance in the morning." Denise's voice was tight with anger. "I thought we were working together, but you blew me off. And by the way, I've never seen you in those glasses. Have you been wearing contacts all this time and nobody ever knew?"

"No. I—never mind the glasses. You have to squelch this deal you have going. You have to do something."

"Too late, buddy boy. And what's up with your hair? It's sticking out in ten different directions."

"To hell with my hair. Damn it, Denise, she can't get that property! It's not just me I'm thinking about—it's Big Knob. That SaveALot store will ruin—"

Maggie walked out into the office. "Hello, Sean."

He cleared his throat. "You . . . found out my name." He'd shaved and made some attempt to get his hair to behave, but until he got a decent haircut there was no hope for it. Of course, she should talk.

"Yes, I asked Denise who you were." *You are the enemy, and I will crush you like a bug.* "For your information, I am going to buy the property, and it will bring jobs and more tourist traffic to Big Knob. There may be a few people, like you, who aren't in favor of the project, but rest assured that many people will love the idea. So back off."

Chapter 5

Sean wondered how anyone as hot as Maggie could say such things to him. Women usually . . . but this wasn't usual. He didn't look the way he used to, and he had a hard time remembering that.

He glanced at Denise. No help there. She was convinced he'd snubbed her yesterday, and today he didn't have his macho sex appeal working to soften her up. She would be overjoyed to help Maggie buy the property out from under him.

That meant he had to work on Maggie . . . somehow. So far he was batting zero. First he'd scared her to death, and just now he'd dissed her pet project. "Tell you what," he said. "Let's get a cup of coffee at the Hob Knob and discuss this." Belatedly he remembered to tack on another inducement. "I'll buy."

Yesterday any woman he approached with that offer would have fallen all over herself snapping it up. Maggie seemed completely unimpressed with the invitation.

Behind her trendy little glasses, her blue eyes remained steely with resolve. "I'm afraid there's nothing to discuss. I'm planning to make an offer on the property as soon as Denise tracks down the owner."

Sean turned to Denise. "Have you done that?"

"I'm pretty sure I have."

Desperation gnawed at him. "Will you at least tell me who it is?"

"No. It would compromise my agreement with my client, SaveALot, Inc."

"Damn it, *I'm* your client, too!"

"We never had a client agreement." Denise lifted her chin. "To be honest, most of the time you did your level best to ignore my efforts."

"That's because you were stringing me along, hoping you and I would end up—" No, wait. He shouldn't say that. He needed to be charming to Denise if he wanted information. Too late. She'd already figured out what he'd almost said, and he could see the steam coming out of her ears.

"I think you'd better leave," she said.

This wasn't good. He needed to convince at least one of these women to support his cause, preferably the redhead with the drop-dead figure. He wanted her to give up on the property. He also wanted her to like him enough to go out with him.

He gazed into her eyes and almost lost track of what he'd been about to say. Finally he remembered. "Have you had breakfast?"

The question seemed to startle her. "No, but—"

"Then come over to the Hob Knob and let me buy you some. They make the fluffiest scrambled eggs in the world." He detected a spark of interest for the first time. "And cinnamon rolls to die for."

She ran her tongue over her lips.

He picked up his cue. "They serve them warm so the frosting melts and oozes down into the roll, which is loaded with butter, sugar and cinnamon. They use really fresh raisins, too, and they get all plumped up in the heat."

"No fair," Denise said.

Maggie swallowed noisily. "I'd love a cinnamon roll."

"Then let's go." He recognized Denise's coat, so the trench coat must belong to Maggie. He grabbed it off the rack and held it for her while he avoided looking at Denise, who was sending out waves of hatred.

"Maggie, do you have a cell phone?" Denise said out of tight lips.

"Yes." Maggie transferred her hold on her purse so she could shove her other arm into her coat. Then she rattled off her phone number.

Ordinarily Sean didn't have a good memory, but that phone number stuck in his brain as if it had been superglued there. He'd need the number as he navigated the next few days.

"I'll call you when I get the information." Denise's words had icicles dripping from them.

"Thanks, Denise." Maggie headed for the door. "I hope you'll excuse me, but I didn't have much dinner last night and I'm starving. Want me to bring you a cinnamon roll?"

"No, thank you." Denise made it sound as if Maggie had offered her a cow patty.

Sean held the door for her and followed her outside, where weak sunlight was beginning to dry up the puddles. Sean remembered hearing about a guy who'd thrown his coat down across a puddle so that the woman of his dreams wouldn't muddy her feet. That seemed a bit extreme, but he could at least take her arm and steer her around the worst parts.

She shook him off. "Thank you, but I'm perfectly capable of crossing the street by myself."

"I know that." He was so busy watching how the pale light touched her cheeks that he stepped in one of the puddles he'd been trying to help her avoid. He had work boots on so his feet didn't get wet, but the cuffs of his jeans did.

As they started across the street, he kept expecting

women to show up, begging for his attention. They always did when he was out in public. But nobody called out to him. Nobody drove by and propositioned him. He almost wished they would, because that might impress Maggie.

Maybe whatever had been in the brandy and the chocolate cake had messed with those pheromone things Ambrose had been talking about. Apparently without his full quota of sex chemicals, women weren't drawn to him like before. That was exactly what he'd asked for, to be left alone, but he didn't like it as much as he'd expected to.

Instead of attracting every female within his range of vision, he was the one feeling the heat every time he looked at Maggie. In a way, he hated to take her into the Hob Knob. Every guy in there would be gawking and hoping for a date. If Sean had anything to say about it, they wouldn't get the chance.

"Why didn't you tell me that you wanted to buy the property?" She sounded annoyed.

"I was too busy convincing you I wasn't an ax murderer." *And controlling my lust.* He was amazed at how much he wanted her. Helping her on with her coat had been like foreplay, at least for him. Obviously not for her.

"What do you do for a living?"

He took it as a good sign that she was asking personal questions. "I do renovation and restoration of houses."

"Then why don't you have some sort of sign painted on your truck?" That seemed to irritate her, too, as if she resented not being able to identify his job without asking.

"Don't need to in Big Knob. Since Abe Danbury retired, I'm the only guy who does that kind of thing. If anybody needs work done on their house, they call me." He tried to think of ways to make his job sound more interesting. "I was just asked to build a fold-out sex bench."

She stumbled while stepping up to the curb and he grabbed her arm, glad for the chance to play hero.

Instead of thanking him, she stared at him as if he were some kind of pervert. "What did you say?"

"I'm building a sex bench. It will fold out of the wall when needed, and go back in when it's not." He waited for the glow of desire to light her eyes, but nothing was happening. "See, it's better than a chair, because it's made specifically for—"

"Okay, okay. I get the idea." She sounded completely turned off. "Let's have breakfast."

He was so confused. Twenty-four hours ago a discussion of a sex bench with any available woman in town would have led to her requesting a similar bench, plus a demonstration of how it worked. He might need to reconsider his approach now that he looked less like a movie star and more like an extra.

At least she couldn't fault him on manners. He opened the door of the Hob Knob and let her go in first. She moaned softly as the scent of fresh cinnamon rolls and coffee rolled over them. That little moan was enough to fill his brain with X-rated thoughts and jack up his already excited penis.

He had to cool it, though, because he was about to face Abe's wife, Madeline, who waitressed most mornings at the Hob Knob. He'd apprenticed himself to Abe ten years ago when the old man had been close to retirement. While Abe had taught Sean all he knew about restoring houses, Madeline had taken every opportunity to lecture Sean about the evils of sex before marriage.

About a year ago he'd stopped sleeping with every woman who asked him, which meant he and Madeline got along much better. She and Abe were the closest thing to family Sean had, and Madeline would be very curious about why he was buying breakfast for the new girl in town.

"By the way, I'm paying for my own breakfast," Maggie said.

Well, that settled that.

Maggie was dizzy with hunger and it seemed she'd come to the right place to do something about it. A plump white-haired woman who radiated comfort showed them to a table by a window where red-checked curtains were tied back with white rickrack. Cream was on the table and coffee was poured the minute they sat down. The waitress didn't even ask, just poured.

Sean's description of fluffy scrambled eggs and cinnamon rolls had made such a vivid impression that Maggie ordered them without opening the menu. Sean did the same. Belatedly Maggie remembered she hadn't asked for separate checks. Oh, well. She had a company credit card, so she could pay for both. H.G. wouldn't care as long as she brought home the goods.

Maybe she'd looked as hungry as she felt, because the cinnamon rolls appeared seconds later. They were huge, the kind that required a fork and copious napkins. Maggie dug in with a sigh of pleasure.

"Was I right about the rolls?" Sean asked.

"Mm." Her mouth full, Maggie nodded. She was too busy wolfing down the roll to make conversation. Nothing had ever tasted this good to her, and she'd had some five-star meals, thanks to H.G. when she'd first hired on at SaveALot, back when he'd had more faith in her potential. Recently those invitations had dwindled.

While she ate, Sean tilted his head toward a table across the room. "Those two guys—Jeff's the owner of the Big Knobian Bar, and Hank's a mechanic over at the gas station. Horn dogs, both of them. If either one of them asks you out, say no."

She nodded, not wanting to stop eating in order to explain that she wouldn't be dating anyone on this trip, horn dog or not.

"And over in the corner is Johnny, who manages the Knobby Nook. He may look harmless, but I wouldn't want him dating my sister, if I had a sister."

She nodded again. Very strange that Sean would be so intent on warning her about the guys in the diner, as if they'd be ready to pounce on her at any minute. They'd given her a casual glance when she'd arrived, but not one had acted particularly interested. Long ago she'd accepted the fact that she wasn't the kind of woman who elicited wolf whistles and hot stares.

As she was polishing off the roll, the eggs arrived, paired up with fragrant hash browns and two strips of crispy bacon.

The waitress balanced the plates on one arm and held the coffee carafe in her other hand. She'd obviously been at this a long time. "Another cinnamon roll?" she asked as she poured more coffee.

Maggie swallowed the bite she'd been savoring. "They're fantastic, and I'd love another one. Somebody should franchise those rolls." She was already thinking there should be a cinnamon roll concession at every SaveALot in the country.

The waitress laughed. "I'll tell Joe, but don't hold your breath. He hates big business. He and Sherry moved here to get away from that kind of thing."

"Oh." Maggie decided she might not want to mention why she was in town to either Joe or Sherry. They might cut off her supply of cinnamon rolls.

"Madeline, I'd like you to meet Maggie Grady," Sean said. "Maggie, this is Madeline Danbury. I apprenticed with her husband, Abe, a few years back. Abe's also our mayor here in Big Knob."

"And doesn't he love the job," Madeline said. "Nice to meet you, Maggie. You here for long?"

"A few days."

Madeline nodded. "Staying with Sean?"

"No! I mean, uh, I'm staying . . . um, that is, I haven't—"

"We have an extra room you could use," Madeline said. "There aren't any hotels or motels anywhere close."

"Sean mentioned that." Maggie thought quickly. She'd hoped to get some housing help from Denise, but Denise obviously had a quick temper and was prone to revenge plots. Maggie decided she might do better with the woman who was in good with Joe and Sherry, keeper of the cinnamon rolls. "I'd be happy to pay rent," she said.

"Don't be silly. The room's going to waste. Our son's married and living in Indianapolis. They'll be down next week for Thanksgiving, but until then, we have the extra space."

"That's very kind of you," Maggie said.

"It's no trouble. Sean stayed with us for a while, but his extracurricular activities forced me to ask him to get his own place."

Maggie glanced over at Sean, who was turning red. "Boys will be boys," Maggie said, but she had trouble picturing this particular guy with his funny-looking glasses and his bad haircut cutting a swath through the female population.

Of course, looks weren't everything. Maybe he was an exceptional lover disguised as a loser without a clue. That thought gave her a twinge of sexual desire, but it was a controllable twinge.

"Fortunately he's not like that anymore." Madeline

patted Sean on the shoulder. "He's reformed the last year or so. I think he's saving himself for the right woman."

Sean looked embarrassed. "I've been concentrating on work, is all."

"Which is good." Madeline peered at him. "But I've been meaning to ask ever since you came in this morning, why are you wearing those glasses?"

"They're temporary. For some reason my eyes aren't focusing right, and a friend loaned me these. It's probably eyestrain. It'll go away."

So he hadn't worn glasses all his life. That made the lover-boy image a little easier for Maggie to imagine. When he was younger he'd probably been in better physical shape, too, and maybe he'd had a different barber.

"Eyestrain?" Madeline didn't look convinced. "That doesn't seem right somehow. I can't imagine how your eyes would suddenly go bad." Then she gasped and clapped a hand over her mouth.

Sean stared at her. "What's wrong?"

"Nothing." Madeline blushed and looked away. "Excuse me. I need to check on my other customers." She started to leave the table.

Sean caught her arm. "Hey, Madeline, you can't gasp like that and not tell me why."

"I most certainly can. It's too embarrassing to say out loud."

"What is?"

She leaned down and whispered in his ear.

Sean let out a bark of laughter. "Trust me, that's not the problem."

"You wouldn't tell me even if it was! I don't know which is worse: the way you were carrying on before or what you're up to now." Her color high, Madeline bustled away.

Sean laughed again and shook his head.

He looks good when he laughs, Maggie thought. And she was dying of curiosity as to what Madeline had said to him. She waited, hoping he'd explain.

Instead he picked up his coffee mug and drained it. Then he glanced out the window, obviously still struggling with his amusement. "It's raining again."

"You're not going to tell me what she said, are you?"

He looked at her, laughter brimming in his green eyes. "Probably shouldn't."

"Come on."

"She thinks my eye problem is related to the sort of activity that will make you go blind."

"Omigod." Maggie couldn't help laughing with him. "Nobody thinks that anymore."

"She does. I respect the hell out of her, but she's very conservative. According to her, nobody should have sex until they're married. She used to get so upset with me."

"I take it you were on the wild side."

"Wild by Madeline's standards, anyway."

She still had trouble imagining it, but not as much trouble as before. He did have great eyes and a good smile. "But Madeline said you've changed."

"Yeah. It was all just sex, which got old. I wanted . . . well, never mind. TMI, right?"

"No problem." Maggie's suspicion that he was a great lover increased, which gave her a stronger twinge of lust. She repressed it. She didn't need lustful twinges right now. What she needed was to buy this land and get out of Big Knob.

In the meantime, though, she had another cinnamon roll on order and she'd received no call regarding the property's owner. If she and Sean would be in the Hob Knob a while longer, they could use another topic of conversation besides sex. Only one thing came to mind.

"I assume you plan to develop the property, as well," she said.

"Not exactly."

She looked at him in surprise. "Surely you weren't planning to renovate that dilapidated wreck of a house?"

A shadow passed over his face and was gone. "I thought I'd try."

"Didn't you see that old movie *The Money Pit*? That's what that monstrosity would be. It's been sitting vacant for years, according to Denise."

"I know." He twirled his mug back and forth between his hands. They looked capable, adept at reshaping a house and giving it new life.

"I suppose you'd welcome the challenge." She thought about the spooky old house she'd seen this morning.

"I would, as a matter of fact. It has potential."

"And then what? Sell it?" She couldn't imagine what a single guy like Sean would want with a renovated Victorian that had to be at least three thousand square feet.

"No, I thought I'd live in it."

"Really? You and what army?"

"I hadn't gone that far in my thinking. I figured the house had to come first. Then I'd worry about the rest."

"A wife and kids." She could see that. He'd be the sort to help his kids build a tree house, and he could fix things around the house for his wife. If he happened to be good in bed, too, then he was excellent husband material. Maybe that explained the interest of the women in town.

He seemed uncomfortable with her *wife and kids* comment. "I don't know. Like I said, the house had to be the first step. Maybe you're right that it'll suck me dry and I'll have to unload it."

She leaned forward. "Count on it, Sean. This isn't a sensible move on your part. That thing could have structural problems, dry rot, faulty wiring, plumbing hassles, you name it."

"You sound as if you know something about that."

She threw her hands up. "Don't I ever! My parents live in a firetrap like that. It's not a Victorian. It's a two-flat brick albatross in Chicago that was built in the 1890s. They don't have the money to fix it, but they refuse to go anywhere else. I have to hope they don't die in their bed someday."

"Maybe they're attached to it."

"Sure they are. I can't pry them out with a crowbar, and I've quit trying. But you're not attached to this place yet. Let me do you a favor and buy that property so my company can bulldoze that house. Let SaveA-Lot save you from the biggest mistake of your life."

He was silent for a moment. "What if I found you some other property that was just as good? Maybe something out by Deep Lake."

"According to Denise, that's mostly state land out there. What's available is marshy and not suitable for building on. That's the beauty of this plan. If I nab the abandoned property, MegaMart won't be able to put up a competing store anywhere nearby."

A muscle twitched in his jaw. "I don't want you to have it."

"Why not?" The minute she asked the question, she didn't want to know the answer. It would complicate things.

"I grew up in that house."

Sure enough, she didn't want to know that. And there was no way she could unknow it now. If she took that place away from him, she'd be stomping on his dream to save his childhood home. If only she could convince him it wasn't a dream worth having.

Chapter 6

Sean hadn't meant to admit any sentimental attachment to the house. That made him vulnerable, and he already felt damn vulnerable with his newly acquired bad eyesight and bad hair. He wanted to impress Maggie, not make her feel sorry for him.

When compassion filled her blue eyes, he hurried to repair the damage he'd done. "That's only a small part of the reason I want to restore the property, though."

"But I get it," she said. "I grew up in a two-flat in Chicago, and I would *love* to make it look nice again, although I've never personally seen it looking good. It was already a wreck when they bought it."

"The Victorian was going downhill, too, but I've always had this image of what it could look like. My father—" He stopped himself from letting more personal information leak out. She didn't have to know his father had been a dreamer who'd promised to restore the property to its former elegance. In the end, he hadn't even been able to keep up the mortgage payments.

Many people in town still remembered that Patrick Madigan had left town the day after his family was evicted from the old house. Sean had spent years convincing everyone that he didn't give a damn what his father had done. If he wanted to buy the property and restore it, so what? He just hated to see a piece of architectural history disappear.

"I do understand the impulse," Maggie said. "Really, I do. But are you honestly prepared to devote years to some old building?"

He couldn't figure out how to explain his dedication to the house without sounding like an idiot, so he fell back on another argument. "It's not only the house. It's easily the best location in town. From the back you get a great view of Big Knob."

"I know. I walked back there. And you're right, somebody should be taking advantage of that besides the kids turning it into a make-out spot."

He sighed. "Yeah, I know they do that. I—" He paused as Dorcas and Ambrose, looking perky as hell, came into the diner.

They spoke to Madeline, who brought them over to a table right next to Sean and Maggie. Sean didn't think that was an accident. He'd bet they'd been looking for him all over town so they could get a good view of their handiwork.

He shouldn't be upset with them. They'd only done what he'd asked, but he wished they'd given him more warning about their program. He should have asked for references before he jumped into this deal. He should have allowed himself to think about it longer, should have asked a *lot* more questions about how everything worked. He should have asked if they were planning to shrink his dick, for crying out loud.

And the timing sucked. Right when he needed to charm the pants off a woman, he didn't have the goods. He could so easily save his property if he looked the way he used to. No woman had been able to resist him before, and Maggie would have been no different.

"Why, Sean!" Dorcas pretended that she'd just realized they were seated close to each other. "What a nice surprise."

He had no choice but to greet them politely and introduce Maggie. Of course, Dorcas asked what had brought her to town, even though she knew damn well.

"Business," Maggie said, as she polished off her second cinnamon roll.

Maggie is no fool, Sean thought. She'd already discovered that not everyone was in favor of her plan. Come to think of it, the property would have to be rezoned. Sean might be able to drum up some support for blocking the rezoning request. But that would be a last resort. He'd rather talk her out of it the old-fashioned way, while they were both naked.

"What kind of business?" Ambrose sounded as eager as a Chamber of Commerce representative, like he had no idea what was going on.

Sean made a mental note that Dorcas and Ambrose were sneakier than they looked.

Maggie still seemed wary. "I work for SaveALot."

"Is there a SaveALot around here?" Dorcas asked. "I don't remember seeing one."

"Not yet," Maggie said. "I'm scouting locations."

"Hm," Dorcas said. "Found anything yet?"

Maggie glanced at Sean. "There's a piece of property I'm very interested in. In fact, if you'll all excuse me, I need to go check with Denise at the real estate office." She stood and took her coat and purse off the back of her chair. "I'll settle the check on the way out. I can also make arrangements with Madeline about using her guest room."

Sean stood. "I'll take care of the check. After all, I invited you."

"Don't be silly. I'm on an expense account. Thanks for bringing me over here, by the way. The food was great." Her tone made it clear that their cozy little interlude was over.

Sean wanted to know what Denise had to say about the ownership of the property, but Denise had already said she wouldn't share that information with him, so there was no point in walking Maggie back over there. He needed another excuse to see her, though. He couldn't very well talk her out of buying the property unless they became closer . . . a whole lot closer.

"I have to get to work myself," he said. "I'll walk you out." Then he planned to walk right back in and have a talk with Dorcas and Ambrose. Now that they saw the problem, they had to help him out with it somehow.

Maggie turned to Dorcas and Ambrose. "Nice meeting you."

"Same here," Dorcas said.

Ambrose pulled something out of his pocket. "In case you need anything while you're in town, here's our card."

"Thanks." Maggie looked at the card and quickly shoved it in her pocket.

Sean remembered he still didn't have a phone number for Dorcas and Ambrose. He could get it off his cell phone, but he'd never quite trusted that option. "I wouldn't mind having one of your cards," he said.

"Sure thing." Ambrose produced another one and handed it to him.

Sean expected to find only their names and contact information, but no, they had a company name and a logo along with their current address. Suddenly they didn't look so much on sabbatical, or whatever the hell they'd called it.

The company was called Hot Prospects, Inc., and the logo was two intertwined gold rings. If Sean hadn't known better, he'd say they were in the matchmaking business. But that couldn't be right. They'd fixed it so that he was no longer attractive to women, so that was moving in the opposite direction from matchmaking, wasn't it? Nothing made sense.

As he glanced up, Dorcas mouthed silently, *We have to talk.* No shit. He was beginning to wonder if he'd been hustled. What if they had some scam going where they made people ugly and then charged them a fortune to find them a match? He only had Ambrose's word for it that he'd revert to his former studliness in two weeks. What if this change was permanent?

But he couldn't stand around worrying about it and let Maggie get away. He hurried over to the cash register where she was signing the credit card slip and discussing her rooming arrangements with Madeline.

"Come up to the house anytime you want," Madeline said. "I already called Abe and told him you would be staying with us. Supper's at five thirty."

"Oh, you don't have to feed me," Maggie said. "That's asking way too much."

"Abe and I would like the company," Madeline said. "Sean, you're welcome to come, too, now that I know you'll behave yourself and not be doing God knows what with a girl under the tablecloth. I'm fixing your favorite, meat loaf."

Sean sent Madeline a grateful smile. She'd just set him up with a semidate, one he needed desperately. "Thanks. I'd love to have some of your homemade meat loaf."

Maggie had a trapped-animal expression in her eyes, but she smiled at both of them. "Dinner sounds great. Well, I need to be going." She started toward the door.

Sean caught up with her. "Before you leave, I wondered if you'd like to set up a time today to tour the old house."

She looked at him as if he'd lost his mind, which most likely he had. Going through that dusty, dirty place was the lamest romantic idea he'd ever had. He couldn't even say why he'd thought of it, unless he now had a loser brain to go along with his loser looks.

"Why would I want to do that?" she asked.

He thought fast. "By going through it, you'll have specific information about the place—number of rooms, location of any plumbing fixtures, etcetera. I'm sure the demolition crew would appreciate having your notes."

"Well . . . you might have a point. This is the first time I've considered a property with a building on it. The other times have been undeveloped land." She paused. "I guess I should take a look. Is it open? Can anyone just walk in?"

"No." He'd made sure of that. Whenever a window was broken, he'd repaired it. And the lock on the front door worked as well as ever.

"Then what? We get a key from Denise? Because if that's the case, she and I can just—"

"Denise doesn't have a key. So far as she knows, or anyone in town, for that matter, there isn't one."

Maggie gazed at him. "But there is one, and you have it."

"Yep. How does one o'clock sound? I could pick you up if you want."

"That's okay." She kept her voice businesslike. "I'll meet you there."

Once she'd walked out the door, Sean pulled out his cell phone and called Calvin Gilmore. He was scheduled to spend the morning working at his house, but that wouldn't be happening.

First he had to have a chat with Dorcas and Ambrose and find out what their game was. And then he would spend the rest of the morning cleaning the old house. Inviting Maggie there might not have been the most brilliant idea he'd ever had, but maybe he could turn it to his advantage.

* * *

Maggie left the Hob Knob with the distinct impression that Sean was putting the moves on her. Of course he would try, because he didn't want her buying the property out from under him. Maybe he imagined he could seduce her so thoroughly that she'd agree to do whatever he wanted. If he imagined that, he must have incredible confidence in his sexual powers.

Damn it, now she was getting curious about those powers, which was not good. At least she wouldn't be tempted during the tour of that wreck of a house, and at dinner she'd be chaperoned by the ever-vigilant Madeline, who didn't allow any goings-on under her tablecloth.

Maggie had never been fondled under the table by any man. She projected the sort of no-nonsense attitude that discouraged groping, and she'd always been pleased about that. But hearing about Sean's checkered past gave her the feeling she'd been missing out.

As she crossed the street, her BlackBerry played the first few bars of "Yellow Rose of Texas," H.G.'s assigned ring. She stepped up on the curb before answering it. "Hello, H.G."

"Grady, you're pushing it, taking off without telling me where you were goin'."

"I wanted to surprise you with a really great location."

"And where is that?" Static crackled, disturbing the connection.

"I'll tell you soon, I promise."

"What's that? You're cutting out on me, Grady."

"I'll tell you soon!"

"Damnation, woman, why won't you tell me right now? Are you working for me or not?"

Maggie's heart rate picked up. She hadn't wanted to accuse anyone of anything, but now she had little choice. "I am working for you. But I think you have someone on the payroll who's working for Mega-Mart."

"What are you saying? I can't hear you worth a damn."

"Three times I've lost out to MegaMart, and each time they seemed to know all about SaveALot's plans to secure a particular location. That gave them an advantage."

"Say that again. I didn't catch it all."

"I think you have a spy!"

"The hell I do!" He sounded furious. "That kind of crazy accusation won't cover up your ineptitude, young lady."

Maggie took a deep breath to keep from saying something she'd regret. "Please let me work out this location on my own without anybody in the company knowing about it. I need the chance to prove myself."

The static crackled again, creating spaces in the transmission. ". . . tell . . . where . . . are."

She didn't want to. His son, Kyle, worked for the company, and H.G. told his son everything. Maggie had strong suspicions about Kyle, who smiled all the time but had the hardest eyes Maggie had ever seen on a human being. She thought Kyle resented his highly successful, workaholic father.

"I'll tell you soon," she said to H.G.

The reception cleared. "Tell me now if you value your job."

Maggie gulped. "Whoops! Gotta go! I'm late." And she hung up on her boss. Worse yet, she hit the off switch, blocking all calls. Well, he couldn't fire her if he couldn't get in touch with her. By the time she turned on her phone, she'd have a location that would make H.G. drool, and he couldn't very well fire her then, could he?

Slipping the BlackBerry into a pocket in her purse,

she walked into the real estate office to find Denise on her hands and knees under the desk.

Maggie cleared her throat. "Uh, Denise? Anything wrong?"

"Stupid computer! Stupid electricity! I was on the Internet, looking for that e-mail, and then I guess there was a power surge and the screen went blank. I've been trying everything, and just now I plugged into a different outlet, but that doesn't seem to make any difference. That's why I didn't call you."

About that time, the lights went out.

Denise groaned and crawled out from under the desk. "What next, a pipe giving way?"

"Believe me, I know about old buildings." Maggie was determined not to let this glitch hold her up. "I'll get my laptop out of the car. It has a good battery in it."

"Great."

As Maggie headed back out to her car, the office lights came on again. Good. She'd hate to depend entirely on her laptop battery. But at first, just to get the necessary e-mail, she wouldn't plug into the building's dicey wiring.

Back in the office, she took her laptop out of its case, opened it and pushed the power button.

"Here, use my desk." Denise gestured toward it. "I'm sure glad you brought a computer. I could have borrowed one from somewhere, I guess, although there aren't as many computers in Big Knob as you might think."

Maggie was beginning to get the picture that Big Knob was a decade or so behind the rest of the country. "Just hook me up to your DSL and we'll be good to go."

"I don't have DSL."

Maggie sighed. Keeping a positive attitude was becoming tougher by the minute. "Then who does?"

"Nobody. We just haven't felt the need for it in Big Knob. Dial-up works fine for us."

Maggie fought the urge to scream. She'd let go of dial-up ages ago, so her laptop was useless. H.G. was in a firing mood, and she needed to work fast to get back in his good graces. She pulled her BlackBerry out of her purse. "Then we'll try this."

Ten minutes later, she gave up on the BlackBerry. Although she could get her phone calls, an Internet connection was trickier, and it was obvious she wasn't going to access e-mail with her BlackBerry while she was in Big Knob. "How about looking for someone else with a working computer?"

"Let me think who has one we could borrow temporarily." As Denise stood tapping her finger against her mouth, the lights went out again.

Maggie groaned. "Denise, you need an electrician."

Denise glanced out the window. "It's not just me. The Hob Knob's lights are out, too."

A quick look confirmed that Denise was right. Maggie's tummy clenched. This was not going well. "What do you think is wrong?"

"There could be a line down somewhere. If the electricity's getting squirrelly, nobody is going to want to turn on their computer and risk frying it."

"So I guess you call the electric company."

"I will, but if there's a line down, it could take a while to get it fixed. We're off the beaten path here."

The lights came on again.

Maggie glanced across the street and the lights were back on at the Hob Knob, too. "I don't get it. How can the lights go on and off like that?"

"I'm no electrician, so I have no idea. Maybe the power line is making a connection only part of the time."

Although Maggie tried not to panic, her insides felt

like a cement mixer. "Let's call the electric company and tell them it's really, really important."

"We can try." Denise picked up her cordless phone and put it to her ear. Then she pushed the connect button a few times. "Something's wrong with the phone, too. I'm not getting a dial tone."

"Use my cell." Maggie grabbed her BlackBerry out of her purse and turned it on. There was a message from H.G., but she didn't plan to respond. He wouldn't call again. Men like H.G. didn't go running after people.

Denise punched in a number and put the phone to her ear. When a receptionist answered, she detailed the problem and handed the BlackBerry back to Maggie. "They'll look into it, but they're backed up and may not come out until tomorrow. They're short-staffed right now because they asked their employees to work extra hours Thanksgiving weekend, when people will be putting up Christmas lights."

"We need to regroup." Maggie took a deep breath. "Is there anyone who could work on your computer, so that when the electricity is stable you could be ready to use it?"

"Jeremy's the guy. He's a techno-wizard."

Maggie brought out her BlackBerry again and gave it to Denise. "How long before you could get him here?"

"Maybe ten minutes."

"That's not long." Maggie's shoulders relaxed a little. Maybe this place wasn't so bad. At least someone could be summoned.

"Oh, wait. He drove to Evansville today to pick up a bunch of cups."

"Cups? Drinking cups?" Maggie felt as if she'd fallen down the rabbit hole. Any minute the Queen of Hearts would come screaming down the street yelling, *"Off with her head!"*

"He's buying athletic protectors for the Knob Lobbers, our slow-pitch softball team. The team's on a budget, so when somebody heard about the sale in Evansville, he volunteered to pick them up today. I'm sure he's left by now."

Naturally they'd play *slow*-pitch in Big Knob. Maggie sighed. Apparently nothing happened fast in this town. "And he's the only person in town who knows computers?" Frustration had prompted the question. Maggie knew the answer. She was probably lucky that anyone in town was tech savvy, even if he had left to pick up a box of athletic protectors and wouldn't be back for hours.

"He's the only one," Denise said. "But if you want, I can call his cell and see how soon he'll be home again."

At least he has a cell phone, Maggie thought. That was something. But the call to Jeremy confirmed that he wouldn't be back in Big Knob until late in the afternoon, because he planned to stop and see his sister and her new baby while he was in Evansville.

Maggie was stuck with nothing to do until then. Taking another look at Denise, she evaluated her haircut. Not bad. Not bad at all. "Where do you get your hair done?"

"Right over at the Bob and Weave. Francine Edgerton is the owner, and she's pretty good with a pair of scissors."

"Think I could get an appointment this morning?"

"Shoot, yeah. The ladies who have weekly standing appointments all go in on Saturday morning, so it's slow on weekday mornings. Of course, they might be having electrical problems, too."

"I think I'll chance it. If everything magically fixes itself somehow and you're able to get on the Internet, you can call my cell."

"I'll let you know if anything changes, but I wouldn't bet on it."

Maggie wouldn't, either. Readjusting the clip holding her hair, she reached for her coat. "Then I might as well try to get a haircut. When it's humid like this, the frizz drives me nuts."

"Francine can help you. But be sure and ask for her. She's good and not too weird. The other operator, Sylvia Hepplewaite, is kind of a sex fiend, and she'll want to talk about her orgasms the whole time she's cutting your hair."

Chapter 7

After saying good-bye to Maggie, Sean watched her walk across the street to the real estate office. The rain had stopped for a minute, and one ray of sunshine had fallen on her hair, making her look like a model in a shampoo commercial. If only she'd come to town for some other reason than to buy the property he wanted. If only she'd shown up yesterday, when he was at full power.

Thinking of that reminded him of Dorcas and Ambrose, so he reluctantly stopped staring at Maggie through the window and returned to the table where they sat, munching happily on cinnamon rolls.

"Okay." He grabbed his chair from the other table, spun it around and straddled it. He needed something to grip so his frustration wouldn't get the better of him, and hugging the chair back helped. "What exactly is Hot Prospects, Inc.?"

Ambrose beamed at him. "Our new business name. Catchy, huh?"

"What happened to your sabbatical?"

Dorcas wiped a blob of frosting from the corner of her mouth. "Handling your case made us realize how much we miss working, so we've decided to run a little business out of our home."

Sean held up the card. "Matchmaking?"

"Something along those lines," Ambrose said. "We didn't want to put it so baldly on the card, but that's the general idea. With our experience in relationships, we're fully qualified to—"

"Wait a minute." Sean became more agitated by the minute. "You said my case inspired you to start working again. But mine is not a matchmaking case. In fact, the idea was to make me less appealing to the opposite sex. What's up with that?"

Dorcas swallowed another bite of cinnamon roll. "Sometimes you need a different perspective in order to be ready for the perfect partner."

Sean thought about that. "All right. I admit that I have a whole new perspective on what it feels like to not look sexy. I appreciate what I had before, and I'm ready to change back to being the way I was. ASAP."

They both looked at him with compassion but said nothing.

Sean shoved the card in front of them. "You're claiming to be matchmakers, right?"

"Right," Ambrose said.

"Then I need help with a match. I want to hire you. I'll pay actual money. We don't have to barter with the sex bench thing."

"You're already a client," Dorcas said. "And we really want that bench. Now that we're working again, the spark is back and we—"

"Okay, okay." Sean held up a hand to stop the flow of details. "I'll build you the bench. I might be able to get to it this afternoon. I'll have to put off Calvin Gilmore a little longer, but once I have the plans, I'll work it into my schedule."

"I brought the plans." Dorcas took them out of her oversized purse and slid them across the table toward Sean.

Just then the lights went out, which prompted a murmur of surprise from the customers.

"Oh, well," Dorcas said. "I like candlelight better, anyway."

"I'm sure this is temporary," Sean said. And sure enough, as Madeline bustled around making sure everyone was okay, the lights came on again.

Now that he could see better, Sean glanced at the so-called plans for the sex bench and barely kept from laughing. The drawing was crude, as if Ambrose had used the concept of a fold-out ironing board as his model. There were no dimensions, just the words *crotch high* and *sturdy enough for two people* lettered at the bottom. Sean would have to make all the calculations himself.

He folded the piece of paper and put it in his back pocket. "No problem. Like I said, I'll try for this afternoon."

"That would be wonderful." Dorcas squeezed Ambrose's hand. "Wouldn't it, darling?"

"Excellent." Ambrose gave her a fond smile.

The lights went out again.

"That's weird," Sean said. "Must be a short somewhere."

Madeline passed by. "It's not just here," she said. "The lights are off over in the real estate office, too."

Sean stood and looked out the window. Sure enough, they were. "I wonder if there's a line down somewhere."

"I wouldn't mind that," Dorcas said. "I think it would be fun to operate with candles and woodstoves for a while."

Sean had a sudden image of sharing that cozy situation with Maggie. He wondered if he'd dare use the fireplace in the old house. But as he considered that, the lights came on again.

He sat down and glanced over at Dorcas and Ambrose. "So what do you say? How about my matchmaking situation?"

They both stared at him. Ambrose was the first to respond. "You want us to find someone for you?"

"Nope. I've done that. I want you to change me back to the way I was so I can seal the deal with her. That's what I was trying to tell you on the phone this morning. The clincher is that if I can get her interested in me, I'm sure she'll give up the idea of buying the property I'm after."

Dorcas frowned. "You're talking about Maggie, right?"

"Sure am."

"You're in love with her?" Ambrose asked.

"Well . . . it's a little soon for that, but I think she's really hot. I could love her, I'll bet. She's beautiful and smart. I think we'd get along great."

"That's a long way from thinking she's your soul mate," Dorcas said. "We're in the business of soul mates."

"Okay, then, I think she could be my soul mate. Can you change me back?"

Dorcas shrugged. "Can't. I don't have the necessary herbs and it would take days, maybe weeks to get them. But even if I could, I'm not sure it's a good idea."

"Are you kidding?" Sean thought of how sweet it would be to have Maggie eager to spend time with him. And there was the added bonus of protecting his property from SaveALot. "Do you realize what's at stake?"

"Your whole future?" Ambrose suggested.

"More than my future! If SaveALot goes in, Big Knob will be changed forever. Maybe some people would be happy about that, but I'm betting most would rather keep it like it is."

Ambrose nodded. "Probably so. Good luck with that."

Disgusted with both of them, but mostly with him-

self for getting into something without checking it out
first, Sean left the Hob Knob to pick up cleaning supplies. If he couldn't make Maggie fall for him, maybe
she'd fall for the house.

Through the glass window of the Bob and Weave,
Maggie assessed the situation. More beauty parlor
than hair salon, the Bob and Weave was straight out
of the fifties. Maggie guessed that was the vintage of
the three hair dryers standing against the left wall,
their cracked vinyl seats and chrome hoods looking
well used.

On the opposite wall each of the two styling stations
had its own shampoo sink. No shampoo alcove separate from the stylist's chair. Once you plopped yourself in the chair, you were there for the duration,
unless you needed one of the hair dryers to complete
the process.

A woman with long tawny hair was getting an updo
at the far station from a blonde dressed in a tight
black skirt, a revealing black blouse and stilettos. Maggie guessed that was the stylist named Sylvia who liked
to talk about her orgasms. A woman with multihued
stripes in her hair stood at the front counter, rearrang-
ing a display of costume jewelry hanging on a revolv-
ing plastic rack.

She looked up when Maggie came through the door.
"Can I help you?"

"Are you Francine?"

"That's me."

Maggie heard murmured conversation from the
other stylist and her customer, but couldn't make out
what they were saying. "Have you had trouble with
your electricity this morning?"

"No. Why?"

"The lights have been going on and off at the real
estate office and the Hob Knob."

Francine shrugged. "The wiring in some of these old buildings is unpredictable, but so far today we've been okay."

"Do you happen to have a computer?"

"Nope. Don't have any use for the things. All that Internet and stuff—you can have it."

Maggie finally surrendered to the inevitable delay. "Then, if you have time, I'd love for you to cut my hair."

Francine gestured to the front chair. "Take off your coat and have a seat. My next appointment won't be here for another forty-five minutes, so I have time."

The other stylist laughed at something her customer said. "Oh yeah. Once with him and three times with the vibrator."

Yep. Definitely Sylvia.

"How did he like that?" asked the customer.

"Not much," Sylvia said in a throaty voice. "Can I help it if I'm multiorgasmic and he's not?"

Francine acted as if she hadn't heard a thing, so Maggie followed her lead and hung her coat on a row of pegs by the door. Then she sat in a chair molded by hundreds of fannies.

"So what's your name?" Francine fastened a towel around Maggie's neck and snapped a vinyl cape over it.

"Maggie. Maggie Grady."

"Just passing through, Maggie?"

"Actually, I'm here on business."

"Oh yeah? What sort of business?"

Maggie had a devil of a time concentrating on Francine's conversation with Sylvia detailing the difference between clitoral and vaginal orgasms. "I'm, um, looking at property."

Sylvia continued with her review of orgasm types. "Clitoral is like chocolate mousse and vaginal is like hot fudge," she said. "Depends what you're in the mood for, you know?"

"Property, huh?" Francine took out Maggie's hair clip and combed her fingers through Maggie's hair with practiced efficiency. "Whereabouts?"

Sylvia picked up a can of hair spray. "I'm mostly a hot fudge fan, though." She whisked the spray over the finished hairdo.

Maggie had never thought which kind of orgasm she preferred, but she hadn't had either in quite a while. Belatedly she realized Francine was waiting for a reply to her question about where Maggie was looking for property. "Oh, possibly that abandoned place at the end of town, the one with the old house on it."

"Huh." Francine twirled her around and tilted the chair back so Maggie's head was hanging in the shampoo bowl. "Sylvia, isn't that old house at the end of town the place Sean's after?"

"That's the one," Sylvia said. "Back in high school, me and Sean used to have some hot times on a mattress out behind that house. One of my clients said kids still go there to have sex."

"Sean Madigan," said the tawny-haired client as Sylvia unsnapped the cape around her shoulders and ushered her out of the chair. "What I wouldn't give to get my hands on that boy again. What a hunk."

"I wouldn't kick him out of bed." Francine ran warm water over Maggie's hair. "I've never had the pleasure, but I do have my Sean fantasies."

"The reality is ten times better," said the client as she walked over to the counter to pay. "I'm sure Sylvia would agree."

"Oh, Angie, you don't know the half of it. The last time Sean and I got it on was two years and six days ago." Sylvia wiggled her hips as she walked past Francine's station. "I could come just thinking about his naked butt."

"It was a year, two months and ten days for me," Angie said. "I've tried to get him interested since then, but no dice. Unless he's doing somebody who's not talking, he's taken himself off the market."

"I doubt he's shagging anybody in town." Sylvia opened the old-fashioned cash register with a clang. "Word would get out if he was. And he doesn't take many trips, so I think he's on hiatus for some reason."

"What a loss to womankind." Francine massaged shampoo into Maggie's hair. "An Adonis like Sean needs to be sharing his gifts."

Maggie listened in amazement. Didn't they see the bad haircut and weird glasses? Sean wasn't ugly, but he was no Adonis.

Sylvia bid her client good-bye and came back to straighten up her station. "Are you thinking of moving here, Maggie?"

"Uh, no."

"Just thought I'd ask, because I'm not sure Big Knob is the place to invest." Sylvia threw towels in a hamper and came back to sit in the vacated chair. "I know that's popular, to find land in some town that's about to boom, but I can't see Big Knob ever booming."

"Me, either." Francine rinsed conditioner out of Maggie's hair, wrapped a towel around her head and levered the chair upright again. "I'd try closer to Indianapolis or Evansville. We're really out of the way here."

Maggie had the oddest feeling they were discouraging her so Sean wouldn't lose the property he wanted. "So are jobs tough to come by in Big Knob?" She didn't have to have public support for her project, but it wouldn't hurt. And jobs were usually a hot button for people.

"Not really," Francine said. "It seems to work out. Like take Sean, for instance. He apprenticed himself to Abe, who was the only skilled carpenter in town.

So when Abe retired, Sean had plenty of work, and we still had someone who could do that kind of job."

"As if he needed a tool belt to make him look any sexier." Sylvia snapped her fingers. "Damn, why didn't I think of that? I need to find something for Sean to build for me, preferably in my bedroom."

"Forget it." Francine towel-dried Maggie's hair. "That's been tried. The boy has changed his ways, for some crazy reason. So, Maggie, what kind of haircut are you looking for? Just a trim, or something more drastic?"

Maggie looked at herself in the mirror, her hair a mass of ringlets that would turn to frizz the minute they dried. Her stylist in Houston kept urging her to keep it long, but Maggie was sick of dealing with it, especially when she traveled. She planned to get this promotion, which meant she'd be traveling even more in the future.

"I want it short," she said. "Really, really short."

Dorcas left Ambrose to pay the bill and stepped outside the Hob Knob to check for Maggie's car. It was still parked in front of the real estate office, but Dorcas couldn't tell from here if Maggie was in the office or not.

Ambrose came out, tying the belt on his leather jacket. "Ready to go home?"

"Not yet." Dorcas gazed at the real estate office. "I'm worried about the communication spell. The lights and phone and stuff were only supposed to go wacko at Denise's office, but the lights went out twice at the Hob Knob. What if we screwed up the spell? Maggie could already have the info she needs to close the deal. Denise could be on the phone with the property owner right this minute."

"I'm sure the spell worked."

"I don't know. We've never tried to bespell electricity and phones and computers before. Are you sure Mercury was the right god?"

"If he wasn't, they wouldn't put his image on the Teleflora ads, now would they? Teleflora is all about electronic communication. Her computer is out of commission, and Jeremy is in Evansville so he can't fix it yet. Everything's fine, so relax."

"Let's think of some excuse to go over there, so we can be sure."

Ambrose sighed. "Like what? We're not planning to sell the house. We just bought it, and besides, I don't like anything else we saw in Big Knob except that monstrosity Sean wants, which would take way too much work to fix up."

"We'll say we want to check the market value of our house." Dorcas started across the street.

Ambrose followed her. "That's a dumb question, Dorcas. It's only been six weeks."

"But if that computer's working, we have to take action." She stepped up on the sidewalk in front of the real estate office. "I admit to being a little worried. Sean is miles away from being ready for his soul mate. Did you hear him? *I think she's hot.* Nothing about feeling a psychic connection. It was all about sex, plus he thinks Maggie's a goddess."

"At least we jump-started his libido. That was good work on your part."

"Thanks, but he needs to get beyond that."

"Guys don't start out with a psychic connection. They start out wanting to get in a woman's pants."

Dorcas came to an abrupt halt. "Are you saying that's the way you felt when you first met me?"

"Pretty much." He gave her a cocky, purely male smile.

She skewered him with a look designed to wipe that self-satisfied smile off his face.

It worked. "But, hey, I felt that connection right afterward. Really soon afterward! Like almost immediately."

"Liar." She kissed him quickly on the mouth before taking his arm. "Let's go check on the current market value of our house."

Chapter 8

Sean soon realized he couldn't clean the whole house in the time he had left. Closing off the attic was a no-brainer, but he decided to close off three of the four upstairs bedrooms and leave only the master open. He put special effort into that because it had a small balcony opening off it and the balcony gave a view of Big Knob that wouldn't quit.

The balcony was safe to stand on. He'd kept tabs on structural details over the years. Any signs of termite damage or dry rot and he'd taken steps to correct the problem.

No one knew he had a key to the house and he'd been careful about his timing whenever he went in, making sure no one was around. He'd found the key by accident while cleaning out his mother's belongings after she'd died. Surprisingly enough, whoever had evicted them all those years ago hadn't bothered to change the locks, and the key still worked.

In the ten years since, Sean had kept the house from falling down and trapped the mice that had found their way inside, but he'd never bothered to clean. With no electricity he had to do it the old-fashioned way, with a broom and dust pan. By noon he still wasn't done, but he had a new idea.

Taking his phone from the pocket of his jeans, he

dialed Maggie. She seemed surprised to hear from him, as if he'd worked some kind of magic to get her number. She'd probably forgotten that she'd given it out to Denise in his presence.

"Have you had lunch?" he asked.

"Not yet. I was just about to—"

"Don't bother. I'll have something here for you."

There was a pause. "That's a nice idea, but the clouds have come in again and I think it's about to rain some more."

"That's okay." He'd noticed the clouds, too. "We'll eat in the house."

"Eeuuww."

"Trust me, there won't be a single thing *eeuuww* about it."

She didn't sound convinced. "Why don't I just grab a sandwich at the Hob Knob before I come over? I'll be there such a short time, anyway."

Not if I can help it. "Look, we didn't get off to a great start this morning, and you bought my breakfast, which I didn't mean for you to do. Let me take care of lunch."

"Well . . . okay." She sounded less than enthusiastic.

"Great. See you at one." As he flipped his phone closed he thought about how easy this would have been yesterday. He'd *never* had trouble talking a woman into a lunch date. Most times they'd asked him. As for the setting, any woman in Big Knob would have agreed to a picnic served in the middle of an anthill if that meant he'd be there.

The timing of this transformation was disastrous. But he'd have to work with what he had, and he had this magnificent house with its high tin ceilings and the massive staircase up to the second floor. He had a master bedroom with a view of Big Knob.

Because that rocky promontory obviously affected the women in town, he'd use that view to work on

Maggie's defenses. With less than an hour to get ready, he had to move fast. He had sandwich stuff at home, but what he really needed was a bottle of wine like the one Dorcas served last night.

He pulled out the card Ambrose had given him. If the Lowells were billing themselves as matchmakers, they couldn't very well turn down this request, especially because he was willing to pay for it. He dialed the number and Ambrose answered.

Sean didn't waste time on pleasantries. "Ambrose, this is Sean, and I need a favor. In exchange I'll install mirrors over your bed."

Maggie used the time after Sean's call to find Madeline's house. Her husband, Abe, a short man with a fringe of white hair wreathing his head, answered the door. A television blared in the background, so obviously nothing was wrong with their electricity at the moment.

"You're Maggie," Abe said.

"I am, and I hope this isn't too much of an imposition. I told Madeline I'd be happy to pay for my room, but she—"

"Of course you won't pay." Abe ushered her into the house, where the temperature was at least ninety degrees. "But you can help with my petition drive."

Maggie wondered if she'd have been better off with Denise. She unbuttoned her coat. "For what?"

"More like *against* what. Here, let me take your coat."

"That's okay. I won't be here long."

"Nonsense. You can't walk around the house with your coat on."

That much was true, considering they were living in a sauna. Besides, she didn't want to upset her host, so she took off her coat and let him hang it in the closet by the door.

"Now, then, Maggie." He clasped his hands and

gazed at her. "What is the single most detrimental element in our society?"

She considered the energy required to overheat this old house. "Our waste of fossil fuel?"

"Nope. I'll give you a hint. It's coming from that infernal box over there." He pointed to the TV.

She recognized an old episode of *Friends*. "Reruns?"

"Hell, no! Reruns are nothing compared to this. Dig deeper!"

She glanced at the screen. The story line had to do with Ross bleaching his teeth so much that they glowed in the dark. Okay, she had it now. "The pursuit of physical perfection?"

He waved a hand, dismissing her answer. "Chicken feed."

"Then I give up."

"Isn't it obvious?"

"No."

"Canned laughter! Fake yuks! Artificial guffaws!" As if on cue, a blast of that very thing came from the TV. Abe shuddered, ran over to the coffee table and made a note on a yellow legal pad. "The research is killing me, but it has to be done."

Then he grabbed a clipboard and shoved it at Maggie. "Sign here."

She read the petition, which claimed that canned laughter was rotting the brains of everyone within range of a television signal. Underneath were two signatures, Abe's and Madeline's. Figuring it couldn't hurt anything, Maggie signed.

Abe beamed at her. "Excellent." He unclipped the petition from the clipboard. "Now you can take it around."

Instantly on the defensive, she raised both hands. "No, no. I'm not good at that. You should be the one. You'll bring more passion to the effort."

"I don't have time, what with all the documentation. When I testify before Congress, I'll need ammunition!" He rattled the petition. "Take it. I want two hundred signatures by Christmas. Do your best."

"Okay." She took the paper, figuring she didn't have to do anything with it. In a couple of days she could give back his petition with its three lonely signatures and be on her way.

"Good. Your room is up the stairs and to the right. I'd take you there, but— Oops!" He leaned down and made another notation on his pad. "Can't leave my research."

"No problem. I'll find my own way." Maggie hauled her suitcase up the stairs and into their small guest room on the second floor of their hot little house. Once there she changed into jeans, a black sweater and running shoes. A bikini would be more appropriate for the temperature, which was even more sweltering upstairs.

As she began to sweat, she hurried back down to retrieve her coat. She still wasn't looking forward to spending any time in that spooky old Victorian Sean loved, but it would be a relief to be out of this heat. She'd never been a sleep-in-the-nude person, but this oven of a house could drive her to it. She gave Abe a quick wave as she went out the door.

"Get signatures!" he called after her.

Rain spattered her windshield as she drove back to Sean's house. *No, not Sean's house.* Just because everyone else in town thought of it that way didn't mean she had to. Soon it would belong to SaveALot, and within six months it would be gone, replaced by a store that would bring dozens of job opportunities to the town, whether they thought they needed that or not.

Parking behind Sean's battered truck, she climbed the wooden steps, which had been swept free of leaves, and walked across the wraparound porch, also swept. She wished he hadn't done that. If he thought cleaning up this old relic would sway her, he'd wasted his time. He might be hopelessly sentimental about the place, but she wouldn't let herself fall into that trap.

She'd scraped for a living all her life because that's what her parents had done. It had been the only reality she'd known until she'd finally understood that her parents' miserable and bitter existence stemmed from bad choices, not the bad luck they constantly blamed for their problems. Maggie intended to make her own luck, starting with this piece of property.

The brass door knocker was an elegant lion's head, tarnished from years of neglect. In a more urban setting, the knocker would have been stolen a long time ago. Maggie had never lived in a place where you didn't triple-lock the doors. She doubted Big Knob residents locked theirs at all.

Miraculously, the frosted glass insets in the heavy door weren't cracked, either. She'd been so busy noticing the peeling paint and the weeds out back that she'd missed seeing some of the nicer features. Maybe the demolition team could take this door off before bulldozing the house. The place needed to go, but that didn't mean a few things couldn't be salvaged.

She used the tarnished knocker, relieved that Sean hadn't polished it. Knowing he'd swept the steps and the porch was bad enough. Maybe she shouldn't have accepted his invitation to revisit the house.

No, it was a good idea. H.G. would be impressed that she'd taken time to give a complete report about the structure to be demolished. She'd get points for that, and she needed all the points she could scrounge.

No one came to the door, so she banged the knocker again, louder this time. Finally she heard Sean calling out, telling her to come on in. With mice and spiders a distinct possibility, she wasn't all that eager, but she opened the door and cautiously stepped into the entry hall.

A crystal chandelier hung overhead. She didn't inspect it too carefully for fear of what might be living in it. The place smelled musty, especially on a rainy day like this, but there was no dirt on the floor as she'd expected. Nothing scurried away from her or swung down from the chandelier overhead. Sean had been a busy guy.

"I'm upstairs," he called out. "Go through the door on your left and you'll see the staircase."

The door on her left stood open, and she walked into a room with a marble fireplace on the outside wall. A fire would be nice right now. The house was chilly, although she'd rather have that than the overheated situation at Madeline's. Here she could keep her coat on while she ate lunch.

A staircase stood at the far end of the room. She steeled herself against falling in love with that staircase and its graceful wooden banister. The space underneath the stairs had been lined with bookshelves and would make a cozy library.

At the top of the stairs, the railing continued along the hallway, giving her a view of the second floor. This would be where children could peer through the spindles and spy on their parents tucking presents under the Christmas tree.

Reality-check time. All of this was going down. No children would ever again peek through the railing to the living room below. No one would fill the bookshelves or decorate a Christmas tree placed perfectly in front of the corner window. Maybe the wood from the staircase could be salvaged. She could ask H.G. about that.

The tall windows, which would never again be decorated with tissue-paper snowflakes or reflect the lights of a Christmas tree, looked out on the front porch and the trees surrounding the house. The branches were bare now, but with spring and clean windows, the view would be lovely.

Besides the grimy windowpanes, the windowsills and the mantel were covered in dust, which made her smile. Men paid attention to floors, but they usually forgot about the other surfaces.

Sounds of banging and the scrape of metal came from over her head somewhere. "What are you doing up there?" If he was killing rats, she was leaving.

"Trying to get the balcony doors open."

"Sean, it's raining." She started up the steps, which creaked. Instead of being annoying, the sound sent warm memories swirling through her.

Her parents' old two-flat had creaky stairs, and she'd played on them as a kid. Life hadn't been so bad then. But eventually she'd become old enough to get a part-time job and was ordered to turn her earnings over to her parents. They'd squandered the money the way they'd squandered everything else.

The banging and scraping continued on the second floor. "I know it's raining," Sean said. "But it might stop, and the view from the balcony is great."

She climbed the stairs, determined to set him straight. "Look, it's obvious what you're trying to do, but it's no use."

At the top of the stairs she glanced down the hall and found the only open door. The sounds of Sean working on the balcony door were coming from there, so she headed toward it. "You can clean up this house and show me views until the cows come home, but I'm still going to buy this property for SaveALot. The location is excellent and the customer base is—"

She reached the doorway and stared in speechless fascination at the setting he'd prepared. A quilt had been spread on the floor of what she guessed might be the master bedroom. On top of that sat a wicker chest holding two candlesticks and red tapered candles—both lit to chase away the gloom of a rainy day.

In addition to the candlesticks, the chest held two plates complete with sandwiches and covered with wax paper, and two wineglasses. A bottle of red wine and a bowl of potato chips sat on the floor next to the quilt. In the corner of the room stood a small heater, which had to be fueled by propane since there was no electricity.

Sean was on his knees next to the French doors leading out to the balcony. Wielding a mallet and chisel, he worked at the rust coating one of the hinges. He wore a tool belt, and Maggie had to admit that added to his Romeo potential. Or maybe she'd been influenced by all the talk in the Bob and Weave this morning.

No matter. This kind of seductive behavior on his part just wouldn't do.

He glanced up from his work. "You cut your hair."

"Uh, yes. It was driving me nuts." She ran her fingers through her shorn locks and wished she didn't feel self-conscious. She shouldn't care if he liked her hair or not, but he'd made a comment about it this morning. Ridiculously, she seemed to want his approval of the change, and that was not a good sign.

He studied her for a moment and nodded. "Nice."

"Thank you." She took a deep breath. "Sean, this is all very inviting." She swept her hand to encompass the carefully prepared setting. "But I'm sure it's calculated for maximum effect, so I can't stay, knowing what you have in mind."

He put down the mallet and shoved his glasses up against the bridge of his nose. "What do you think I have in mind?"

She had a sudden vision of rolling naked with him on the quilt. "Convincing me to give up on this purchase."

"You just said it wouldn't make any difference what

I did. That you won't change your mind under any circumstances."

"That's right. I won't." Even if she had sex with him, which she had no intention of doing, her decision would be the same. But she was hungry and she couldn't remember the last time a man had set up such a romantic meal for her. Maybe this was how he'd charmed all the women in Big Knob into thinking he was some sort of love god.

"If nothing will change your mind, why not sit down and eat? Unless you don't like chicken salad."

Naturally, she adored chicken salad. He couldn't have chosen a sandwich filling she would have craved more. After eating eggs and two cinnamon rolls today, she shouldn't be hungry, but something about this town made her famished for food and . . . other things that she'd best not think about right now. Until today she hadn't realized how much her sex life sucked green bananas.

Sean gazed at her a moment longer. "Go ahead and think about it. I've almost loosened this hinge." He went back to his pounding.

He did look manly doing that. In the MBA world she inhabited, the guys wore conservative suits and had their nails manicured every two weeks. Maybe that was another reason her libido had gone into hiding. The men she came in contact with didn't inspire damp undies.

To be fair, they might all look as sexy as Sean if they dressed in jeans and picked up a couple of tools. Using them with Sean's level of finesse would be even better. That kind of expertise wasn't usually called for in the corporate headquarters of SaveALot, Inc., though. She'd been free to concentrate on her career.

She would still do that. Eating a chicken salad sandwich wasn't likely to derail a tough cookie like her. And she was *very* hungry.

"Got it!" With a smile of triumph, Sean laid down his tools. Then he stood, reached for the handle of the door he'd been working on and opened it with only a faint creak. "Still needs WD-40, but at least the hinge isn't stuck anymore."

There was no mistaking the pleasure in his expression. Maggie knew that feeling of getting something right, and it was a feeling she had yet to experience on the job at SaveALot.

Cold, damp air made the candles flicker, and Sean closed the door again. "If it stops raining, we can go out there. I want you to see the view."

"Why?"

"Because you're right about my plan. I want you to rethink buying the property and leveling the house."

"I won't rethink it." She glanced at the chicken salad sandwiches with regret. "And because I won't, I would feel guilty eating your sandwiches. I'd better go."

"Please don't."

"I have to. I'm afraid you went to all this trouble for nothing."

He shook his head. "Not for nothing. I haven't had a meal in this house since I was seven years old. That makes eating here special, but I'd rather not mark the occasion by myself. You'd be doing me a favor if you'd take off your coat and stay."

She didn't believe that for a minute. "From the conversation I heard in the Bob and Weave today, you could pick up your phone and have any number of women here within three minutes, all of them eager to share your lunch." *And your quilt later on.*

"But then it would be all over town that I have a key to this place. Technically, I'm trespassing by being here. I've been trespassing for years. I'm counting on the fact that you won't want to advertise that."

Her glance strayed to the chicken salad sandwiches.

Even covered in wax paper, they looked plump with filling. Ruffles of fresh lettuce peeked out from under the bread. Her mouth watered.

"It's only a sandwich," Sean said. "That's not much of a bribe."

Hunger overcame her better judgment. She'd always heard that the way to a man's heart was through his stomach. The same thing seemed to be true for her. "Okay." She took off her trench coat, folded it, and placed it on a corner of the quilt. "But no wine."

"It's amazing wine. I got it from the Lowells, the couple you met at the Hob Knob. I'm not a wine drinker, but I love this stuff. You should at least taste it."

She gazed at him. "You don't take no for an answer, do you?"

He looked startled by that. "I haven't had much practice hearing it, I guess."

"No, I guess you haven't, judging from the way Sylvia, Angie and Francine talked today."

"Mm."

She shouldn't have brought that up, because now she was thinking about the fantastic sex Sylvia and Angie had raved about. She needed to eat her sandwich, partly to prove she could do it without compromising her principles, and then leave before she compromised something else.

She started to step onto the quilt and thought better of it. "That looks like an antique. I'll take off my shoes."

"It is an antique, but it washes."

"Even so, it's muddy out there." She nudged off her running shoes before positioning herself cross-legged on one side of the wicker chest.

"Yeah, you're right. No point in getting the quilt dirty." Sitting on the quilt, he unlaced his work boots and pulled them off.

The work boots were sexy, too. And he wore clean white socks under them, which was also kind of— *Oh, come on, Maggie! You must be seriously deprived if you find clean socks sexy.*

She was seriously deprived, but she'd chosen to focus on her job. She happened to have a little downtime right now, so her unmet sexual needs were popping up like dandelions in her carefully groomed lawn of disinterest. Considering the stakes—a lucrative career versus unemployment—she had to rip those little dandelions out by the roots.

Sean settled down on the opposite side of the chest, picked up the wine bottle and poured some into her glass.

"Sean, I'm not drinking it." Wine was liable to make her dandelions grow.

"Then don't. I am." He poured his own glass full and set down the bottle. Then he picked up his glass and touched it to hers. "To friendship."

She left the glass sitting there untouched. "I don't see how we can be friends. We're both after this property, and we can't both have it."

He smiled at her. "I'm beginning to think that being hungry makes you grumpy."

That made her laugh, because it was right on target. No man had ever noticed it before, not even the guy she'd seriously considered marrying. Henry's work had taken him away from Houston, and he'd assumed she'd leave with him.

The timing had been lousy. She'd just landed the job with SaveALot and had been amazed Henry would expect her to abandon it. She realized now that he hadn't known her at all, including how much she needed regular meals.

"I suppose I am grumpy when I don't eat," she said. "Thank you for making the sandwiches." Taking off the wax paper, she picked up the sandwich and took a bite. Heaven.

If he'd made this chicken salad, she didn't care about his dopey glasses or his wacked-out hair. A guy who made chicken salad this yummy didn't even have to be good in bed. If he was good in bed *and* good in the kitchen, he deserved all the women he could get.

Just not her.

Chapter 9

Sean took heart from the expression of bliss on Maggie's face when she tasted the sandwich. He was definitely making progress.

"Chips?" He held out the bowl to her.

Still working on her first bite, she nodded and took a handful for her plate.

He tried not to stare, but he'd never seen anyone look so cute while they ate, and he'd shared plenty of meals with plenty of women. Behind her little wire-framed glasses, her blue eyes shone with pleasure and her freckles seemed to dance with enjoyment as she chewed. He liked that she didn't try to cover her freckles with a lot of makeup.

A dab of mayonnaise escaped from the corner of her mouth. Instead of using her napkin, she flicked the mayonnaise back in with her tongue, as if she didn't want to miss a single bit of this food. She'd been the same way when she'd devoured the cinnamon rolls at the Hob Knob, and he'd been fascinated then, too.

She swallowed and picked up the sandwich to dive in again. "This is incredible chicken salad. Did you make it?"

"No." No use pretending he could cook. "It came

from the Big Knob Market's deli counter. I always keep a container of it in my fridge."

"I would, too, if I lived here. I wonder if they ship."

Sean laughed. "You could ask, but I doubt it. We're not very up on that kind of thing in Big Knob." Then, because he was afraid she'd catch him staring at her like a lust-crazed idiot, he unwrapped his own sandwich and bit down.

Man, it was good. He'd been eating a chicken salad sandwich on unseeded rye a couple of times a week for seven or eight years, ever since Bradley had taken over the deli counter. It was always great, but today it was incredible. He couldn't explain the difference, because this was from the same batch he'd eaten a couple of days ago.

Maybe it was the wine. That wine seemed to make everything taste like it came from a five-star restaurant. Then again, he'd never eaten at a five-star restaurant, so he wasn't much of a judge.

Maggie probably was, though, and she was obviously enjoying herself. That was even without the wine.

"You should take a sip of the wine," he said. "It makes the sandwich even better."

"Not possible." She'd finished half of her sandwich and started munching on the chips. "That chicken salad is so yummy that I'm pacing myself, making myself wait to eat the second half, so I can draw out the experience."

He wondered if she knew how sexy that sounded, or if she realized that having an appetite for good food usually translated into an appetite for good sex, too. His hormones kicked in. "I'm glad the sandwich is a hit."

"It's a complete hit. And there's no way a little glass of wine could improve on perfection."

"I'm telling you, it will. Last night's meal at the Lowells' blew me away, and now I'm thinking it might have been the wine that made it all taste so amazing. It's like a flavor booster for whatever you're eating."

Her eyes narrowed. "Is this a trick just to get me to drink the wine so it will lower my resistance?"

"No." He hated to admit to her that he wasn't that tricky. He'd never had to resort to wine to lower a woman's resistance. No woman had ever resisted him.

She continued to regard him with suspicion. "You're sure?"

"Honest. You don't have to try it if you don't want to. Maybe you're not much for wine."

"I am. I love wine."

"Then you'll be missing some outstanding stuff if you don't drink at least a little bit. I have no idea how expensive it is, but I need to find out."

"You didn't buy it?"

"I did, in a way. I bartered for it. I guess they have a bunch in their basement. God knows what it costs a bottle, but if it's less than twenty bucks I might splurge on it once in a while."

Maggie sighed. "Oh, all *right*. Sheesh. If it's that big a deal, I suppose one little taste isn't going to kill me."

"You'll thank me for it." He waited as she picked up her wineglass. Watching her drink was as much of a turn-on as watching her eat.

She rested the rim of the glass against the curve of her lower lip and took a tentative sip. Then her eyes drifted shut, and she took another sip. "Mm."

His mouth grew moist from wanting to kiss her. "Told you."

"Didn't believe you." Eyes still closed, she tipped the glass and drank again. Then she lowered the glass, opened her eyes and gazed at him. "They have a bunch of this in their basement?"

"That's what they said."

"Let me see the bottle."

He handed it to her and she studied the label. He hadn't paid much attention, figuring he wouldn't recognize it, anyway, not being a wine person.

"It's a malbec," she said, "from Mystic Hills Winery, which is in Sedona, Arizona. I didn't know they made wine there, let alone fantastic wine." She handed the bottle back to him. "What did you barter for it?"

He regretted telling her about the sex bench earlier, even though he hadn't said whom it was for. Telling her about the mirrored ceilings would be an even worse breach of client privacy. "I promised to do some carpentry work for them," he said.

"They have a matchmaking business, don't they?"

They do now, thanks to me. "Something like that."

"I'm going to take a wild guess and say that the Lowells are the ones you're constructing the sex bench for." She drank the rest of her wine. "So now you're building them something else besides the bench, something that's also sexually oriented."

The fierce pang of want grew stronger. "I shouldn't have said anything about the sex bench."

"Aha! So I'm right! Hey, don't worry. I won't rat you out."

"I appreciate that." He loved the way her black sweater draped over her breasts. He wondered if she had freckles on her breasts, too.

"No problem. Now let's test your theory that the sandwich will taste better after drinking the wine." She picked up the second half of her sandwich and took a bite. "Mm-*mm*!"

"I was right, wasn't I?" He guessed that she had freckles on her breasts, freckles everywhere. He wanted to lick each one.

She nodded vigorously and gestured for him to pour her some more wine.

Hey, he couldn't very well turn down a lady's request for more wine. That would be rude. He refilled her glass.

"So they're matchmakers," Maggie said when she took a break from her sandwich to have some more wine. "Pardon my saying so, but they don't look as if they belong here."

"Yeah, I know what you mean." He felt sure she was a natural redhead, which meant she'd have downy red hair . . . in one strategic spot. Even though he'd had lots of experience, he felt seventeen again, as if he'd never seen a naked woman before.

"It's not just how the Lowells look, but how they act. I'll bet nobody else in town has commissioned a sex bench."

There was no reason he couldn't build a sex bench for himself and Maggie. "I'm not sure why they picked Big Knob, but they're taking a sabbatical." He hoped she wouldn't ask him what that was.

Maggie chewed her last bite of sandwich. Then she swallowed and looked at him. "I know what's going on. They're on the lam."

"In Big Knob?" His hot thoughts about Maggie were temporarily derailed by the concept of Dorcas and Ambrose as Bonnie and Clyde. God, he hoped not.

"Makes sense to me. Sleepy little town in Southern Indiana. Nobody asks any questions. Maybe they're not even using their real names."

"I don't think they're running away from anything." Sean thought about their expensive wardrobe and their pricey wine and wasn't all that sure. Maybe they were con artists who came into town, took everyone's money, and left.

They hadn't exactly taken his money, though. Maybe they were running from some terrible thing they'd done. What if they had used the wrong combination of herbs on someone and killed them? What if he was their next guinea pig, and they had no idea whether he'd survive this transformation or not?

"Sean, I didn't mean to upset you."

"I'm not upset." He slugged back some more wine. "Dorcas and Ambrose are just a normal, upscale couple who enjoy the atmosphere of a small town. Besides, they can't be fugitives."

"Why not?"

"They have a cat."

Maggie giggled. "Well, that certainly settles it. Anybody with a cat has to be on the up-and-up."

"Think about it. Cats don't like to move around. A dog is one thing, but you don't drag a cat with you if you're on the run." He'd cling to that belief until he could question the Lowells some more. He'd been way too trusting.

"Maybe you're right about the cat. Can I have a wee bit more of that wine?"

She wanted more wine. He shut out thoughts about the Lowells and emptied the last of the bottle into her glass. As she picked it up, he noticed she was looking at him differently than she had at the beginning of the meal. Her gaze was warm and open. Someone might even describe it as inviting.

He knew exactly what he wanted to do about that, but he wasn't quite sure how to go about it. In his past experience, the woman in question would be sitting on his lap by now, French kissing him and trying to get his zipper down. He'd never had to make the first move in his life.

Right away he could see that this setup, one he was responsible for creating, didn't make things easy for them to get together. He was on one side of the wicker hamper and she was on the other side. Somehow they needed to end up on the same side for anything good to happen. And they needed to do it without knocking over the candles and setting the quilt on fire.

How had the women he'd dated accomplished that? He'd never noticed. One minute they'd be talking, like he and Maggie were doing now, and the next minute the woman would be all over him, removing clothes and getting down to it.

He sensed that crawling around the hamper and grabbing Maggie wasn't going to impress her, plus no doubt he'd knock over the candles in the process. He glanced out through the French doors to see if it was still raining, and it wasn't. Not much, anyway.

"Come on." He shoved his feet into his work boots. "Let me show you my Big Knob."

Maggie grinned as she reached for her shoes. "I don't think I know you well enough for that."

"Bad choice of words." He tied the laces on his boots. "I meant the rock outside."

"I know. I couldn't resist teasing you." The dynamic between them had changed, and she blamed the wine. Correction, she blamed herself for drinking the wine, but it was easily the best she'd ever had, and she couldn't regret having some. The problem was she'd had more than *some*. Her skin felt hot and other, more internal parts of her body were warming up rapidly, too.

"I suppose I do feel possessive about that hunk of granite." He stood. "I was only four when we moved into this house, and my mother let me think it was my own private mountain." He held out his hand to help her up.

She took his hand, which felt way too warm and wonderful, so she released it the minute she was upright. "Have you ever climbed it?" The wine was affecting her eyesight, too, because Sean grew better-looking by the second. His haircut wasn't nearly as bizarre. Even his shoulders appeared broader.

He opened the balcony door and held it for her. "I was too young to climb it while I lived here. But once I was old enough, yeah, dozens of times. All one hundred and ninety-two feet of it."

Passing by him, Maggie caught a whiff of his cologne mixed with the tang of sweat from the work he'd done today. It had been long months since she'd allowed herself to get sweaty with a man, and she hadn't thought she'd missed it. Wrong.

She stepped out on the wet balcony with a relieved sigh as the cool air touched her hot skin. A fine mist fell, but she could see that jutting rock perfectly from here. The rain had given it a dull sheen, and from this angle it looked even more like . . . yes, it certainly did. It was even more erotic wet.

Parts of her that had been dormant for a long time woke up and stretched as she gazed at Big Knob. Belatedly she realized her awkward position. She was alone in a deserted location with a man who was becoming increasingly appealing to her wine-soaked libido. And because her judgment and her reflexes were clouded by wine, she couldn't drive away from here, at least not right now.

Sean came out on the balcony and stood behind her, the warmth of his body inviting her to lean back and let him wrap his arms around her. She had no doubt he'd do that if she made the slightest move in his direction. She grabbed the railing, its peeling paint rough under her hands, and held on for dear life.

"Nice view," she said in a hoarse voice.

"I love this view." He was silent for a moment. "Did Denise find the owner?"

"I don't know." *And right this minute I don't care,* whispered a traitorous voice in her head. She cleared her throat. "Something went weird with the electricity and her computer is on the fritz."

"Yeah, the lights were going crazy over at the Hob

Knob, too. It happens with old buildings, especially when it rains."

"I'm hoping the electric company comes out this afternoon and the computer guy shows up." At least she should be hoping that. Instead she was hoping Sean would touch her.

"That would be Jeremy. He went to Evansville."

"That's right. How did you know?" His voice worked on her, making her long to hear him murmuring something sweet in her ear as he held her close.

"Everyone knows everything in this town. But I would know that, anyway, because I'm the pitcher for the Knob Lobbers and he was collecting money from each of us for the . . ."

"Yes, I know." Protective cups for the valuable equipment she was busy trying not to think about. With Sean right behind her and Big Knob looking wet and very erect in her immediate field of vision, she couldn't seem to think of anything but firm penises.

She was standing on this romantic balcony with the town's legendary lover, and yet he hadn't made a move. Maybe he was more ethical than she was giving him credit for. Or maybe he didn't really want her and he was forcing himself to follow through.

Now there was a truly depressing thought. Come to think of it, that made more sense than anything else. She'd never been a man magnet—too driven and too intellectual to appeal to the majority of guys.

"Let's go in." She turned, expecting him to back up in relief and let her pass by.

Instead he blocked her way. Interestingly, he'd taken off his glasses. Apparently he'd left them in the house in preparation for the kiss fest that he hadn't been able to stomach.

"Hold on a minute," he said.

She couldn't bear to continue looking into his eyes as he struggled to hide his distaste at the idea of kissing her. So she ducked her head and talked to his third shirt button.

"Sean, it's obvious you brought me out here to kiss me, but you can't make yourself do it, not even to try and save your house. Kissing me isn't going to work, anyway, so let's go back inside and save both of us some embarrassment, okay?"

He gripped her shoulders. "You have no clue how much I want to kiss you, Maggie. I'm scared to death I'll do it wrong and spoil everything."

"What?" She glanced up in surprise. "How could you possibly do it wrong? When it comes to sex, you're the talk of the town!" But sure enough, he looked uncertain as he gazed down at her.

"I never had to do anything to get girls," he said. "They came to me. They begged me to have sex with them, so I did. They kissed me before I could kiss them. They did everything, and all I had to do was go along with it."

"Because you gave them wine?"

He shook his head. "No alcohol was involved. They just . . . wanted me. They all wanted me."

"Are you saying I'm the first girl who hasn't thrown herself at you?" She was dangerously close to doing that. Without glasses, he'd become a green-eyed love god, and his touch burned through her sweater. She hadn't quite believed in his powerful mojo before, but she believed in it now.

"That's what I'm saying."

She reached deep and salvaged enough pride to resist the pull of his sexuality. "Well, that's not how it will be with this chick. I've never thrown myself at any man, and I'm not about to start with you."

"So it's all up to me." He surveyed her, his gaze smoldering.

She began to tremble. "Of course not. You can let me go and we'll forget this moment ever happened."

"What if I don't want to?"

"It's for the best, Sean. Once I feel sober enough to drive, I'll leave."

"And what will we do until then?" His voice became soft and silky.

She would *not* kiss him, would not become another in the long line of women who begged him for sex. So what if her panties were damp and her heart thumped like a jungle drum?

She cleared her throat. "Well, I realize there's no coffee, but maybe I can run up and down the stairs to work the cobwebs out of my brain. Meanwhile, you can tidy up the—" She gasped as he dragged her up against his taut body. He had more muscles than she'd expected, and they were all rigid, especially the one pressing against her belly.

"Like hell," he muttered. Then his lips came down on hers.

Like heaven, she thought dreamily. Then she became one pulsing mass of lust and couldn't think at all.

Chapter 10

Sean discovered something in the moment that he decided to take action and kiss Maggie. Being in control of the situation got him hot, hotter than he'd ever been in his life. She tasted like the wine he loved so much, and when he'd indulged himself thoroughly there, he moved on, kissing her cheeks, her chin, her throat.

Her glasses got in the way and he took them off with one hand while he continued kissing every inch of freckled skin available to him. There wasn't nearly enough of that. He dropped her glasses to the floor of the balcony and reached under the hem of her sweater.

His goal was the back clasp of her bra. He'd never had to take one off before—women generally came to him braless—but he thought he could handle it. Her skin was so soft, and the clasp was so . . . so damn hard to unfasten!

He groaned in frustration, and then the clasp seemed to magically come apart. Ah. Returning to kiss her mouth, he cupped one breast with the same pounding excitement he'd felt the first time he'd touched a woman. Brushing her tight nipple with his fingers seemed like a brand-new experience.

She trembled and moaned, the sound muffled

against his mouth as their kiss grew wetter and deeper. But she didn't start ripping at his clothes. She didn't fondle his crotch or back him up against the balcony railing and give him explicit instructions as to what she wanted him to do to her.

For the first time in his life he could savor the softness of a woman's breasts without being pressured to get on with it. What a concept. Now the pressure was all on his side. He was the one who wanted more, wanted her sweater and her bra gone so he could map all her freckles with his tongue.

But when he stopped kissing her long enough to pull her sweater over her head, she backed up against the railing. "Whoa, big boy!"

Instinctively he moved toward her, and heard the sickening crunch as he stepped on her glasses. He closed his eyes. "Shit."

"Oh."

He opened his eyes. Amazingly his eyesight had improved. He could see that she was still quivering and her pupils were dilated with lust. "Don't worry. I'll replace your glasses." Intent on getting her back in his arms, he reached for her.

"Stop." She put a hand on his chest.

"Stop?" He frowned. "What do you mean, *stop*?" He gazed longingly at her tender lips, the ones he'd just been caressing with his mouth and tongue. They were temptingly parted as she struggled for breath. He wanted to thrust his tongue into her mouth again.

And she wanted it, too. He could feel it. He could smell it.

She swallowed. "I mean halt, quit, cease and desist."

"But you liked it." He was thoroughly confused.

She crossed her arms over her chest. "I admit that kiss and . . . everything . . . felt good, but—"

"Especially the *and everything*."

She had the decency to blush a little at that. "Yes, okay, but—"

"Then why are you telling me to stop?"

"Because when you progressed to removing clothing, my brain kicked into gear and reminded me that I was here on business, not pleasure."

"So I must have tried to remove it wrong." Damn his inexperience at seduction, anyway.

"That's not it."

"Sure it is. Usually when I have sex with a woman, she takes everything off before I have a chance to. I never have to undress her. I never have to undress myself, either. I was clumsy, and that distracted you."

She stared at him as if he'd stepped out of a spaceship. "So when you get involved with a woman, she always takes over?"

"It probably sounds crazy." It would to her, considering his altered appearance. But he felt stupid trying to explain his involvement with Dorcas and Ambrose. It was such a weird story that she might think he'd made it up.

"I have no reason to doubt you," she said. "And after listening to the women in the Bob and Weave, it all makes sense. I don't mean to insult you or anything, but are there . . . other single guys in town?"

Sean nodded. "Yeah. There's Jeremy, who went to get the cups today. Bruce is single, and so is Jeff. Then there's Hank and Johnny and Bradley, although there's some question about Bradley. He's never dated girls, but we don't want to hang a label on him or anything. I mean, there's no proof."

"Are these guys somewhat attractive?"

"Hey, I'm a man. I'm not the one to ask." But he knew what she was getting at. "They date, if that's what you mean. I'm not the only choice around here, but for some reason, I'm just—"

"Catnip."

"I guess." He paused. "Except for you."

"Oh, I'm not immune, obviously. But I have other priorities."

"That's too bad." He rubbed the back of his neck in frustration. Once aroused, he'd never been denied. Not ever. This was new territory for him, and he didn't like it.

She took a deep breath. "I can see you're not used to having a woman call a halt."

"Can't say I am, not once we get to this point. You were moaning."

Her freckled cheeks grew pink. "I suppose I was."

"And kissing me back. Really kissing me back."

"I . . . I know."

"So I thought you'd want me to take off your sweater." He had another thought. "Do you . . . is there some problem with your breasts?"

"No, there's no problem with my breasts!"

"Because I like freckles. I like freckles a lot, and I was hoping—"

"My breasts are fine. I just don't think going topless on this balcony is a good idea right now." Her voice quivered the tiniest bit, as if she might be losing some of her self-control.

"Then let's go inside."

"Not in there, either. None of this is a good idea."

"I think it's a great idea." He couldn't think of anything he'd rather do than go inside and get rid of her sweater. Oh, maybe one thing would be more fun than that, but he hadn't brought condoms, and he was willing to bet she hadn't, either. Every other woman he'd kissed had come packing, but this one wasn't anything like the other women.

"Well, I have a reputation to protect, and you don't. Then again, I suppose getting naked with me would keep your reputation going strong, wouldn't it?"

"I don't care about that. I've never cared about that." She gazed at him. "For whatever reason, I believe you." Kneeling down, she picked up her crumpled glasses. The glass was shattered and the frames hopelessly bent. "This presents a problem, though."

"I said I'd replace them." He was discovering something else. Lack of food made her slightly grumpy. Lack of sexual satisfaction, once he'd felt the urge to merge, made him *extremely* grumpy.

"No, you won't."

"I dropped them on the deck and then proceeded to step on them, so that makes me responsible. I'll replace them." He looked at the crushed glasses, which could very well be designer frames for all he knew. "But it will take some doing. We don't have any place that sells glasses in Big Knob, except those magnifiers for reading."

"I was afraid of that, which brings me to the next problem. I can't drive without glasses."

So she was at his mercy, which did him absolutely no good at all, because she didn't want to cozy up with him. Well, she did, but she wouldn't let herself. He still couldn't get used to the idea of rejection.

"I'll take you wherever you need to go," he said.

She sighed. "That's nice, but it doesn't solve my other problems, like any reading I have to do to finalize this deal."

"I can't promise to help you with that."

"I wouldn't expect you to." She glanced at her watch and then muttered a swearword. "I can't even see what time it is."

He looked at his watch. "Two thirty."

"Wait a minute. You're not wearing your glasses, either. How can you read your watch?"

"I guess my eyes have improved."

"In the past *hour*?" She shook her head. "Let me see your watch. I'll bet the numbers are bigger." She grabbed his wrist and peered at the face of his watch. "Not that much."

He couldn't help himself. He reached up and trailed a finger along the line of her chin. After all, she'd touched him first.

Her breath caught. "Don't do that."

"How about this?" He leaned down and ran his tongue around the edge of her ear. He was acting on pure instinct, because he'd never needed moves before.

"Don't do that, either." But her voice was soft and yielding, and she hadn't let go of his wrist even though she'd admitted she couldn't see the numbers on his watch any better than hers.

"Then maybe this." He drew the neck of her sweater aside and nuzzled the curve of her shoulder.

"Sean." His name came out as a sigh as she turned her face up to his. "You're making me crazy."

"Good." Amazed at the effect such small caresses had on her, he cupped her chin and ran his thumb lightly over her cheek. "Let me make you even crazier."

She held his gaze. "I shouldn't."

That didn't sound like a definite *no*, so he kissed her. The minute he did, he knew that there hadn't been a bit of *no* in her answer, but there was a hell of a lot of *yes*.

He might not have experience in engineering these moments, but he was a quick study. Out on the balcony was not the place to continue. Other women might not have cared about appearances, but this one did.

Reaching behind his back, he found the doorknob. Without breaking the kiss, he opened the door, drew her inside, and closed the door again. He couldn't have done that if she'd resisted him, but incredibly, she went along with the whole maneuver.

He must be doing something right, because she was kissing him like there was no tomorrow, opening her mouth and angling her head so they could turn this into a very French experience. She released his wrist so she could bury both hands in his hair.

He backed her up against the wall and pressed his aching body against hers. She pressed back with a groan. He had the despairing thought that if he'd been smart enough to bring condoms, he could have her right here, right up against the wall.

Reaching between them, he found the button on her jeans. He expected her to stop him, but she didn't, so he unfastened it and pulled down the zipper. Still no protest, just heavy breathing and little whimpers of need.

Okay, then. He slid his hand inside her panties and nearly came himself from the discovery that she was drenched. Somehow he'd found the override switch on her self-control. He couldn't believe a gentle touch on the cheek could result in this level of excitement, but there it was.

If she stopped him now, then he didn't understand the first thing about a woman. She didn't stop him. She kept on kissing him fiercely as he thrust two fingers deep inside her. Her orgasm didn't take long to show up. She must have been wound tighter than a spring-loaded tape measure, because she snapped in seconds.

Wrenching her mouth away from his, she cried out as she arched against the wall. He'd long ago lost count of the number of climaxes he'd given women over the years. Not a single one had affected him with this kind of rush—part tenderness, part triumph and part incredible joy.

Suddenly he was jealous of every man who had ever made her come. From now on he wanted to be the only guy with that privilege, which was insane. He'd never wanted exclusive rights to a woman, especially one he'd known a matter of hours.

Slowly he eased his fingers free and wrapped his arms around her. Holding her gently, he dropped kisses on her eyelids, her nose, her parted lips. Gradually the tension left her body and she slumped forward, resting her forehead on his chest.

He couldn't believe how happy he felt, considering his dick was still in his pants and was going to stay there. Ordinarily he also cared about his own satisfaction. Self-sacrifice hadn't been much a part of his sex life.

But at this moment, even though he ached and would love to get some relief, he was more than willing to give up on it for now. If only one of them could know the melting pleasure of gratification, let it be her. He loved knowing he'd given her that gift.

She lifted her head and looked into his eyes. He waited, expecting her to smile and thank him for what he'd done.

Instead she sighed and shook her head. "My God, that was such a mistake."

"It was not!" No woman was going to call her orgasm a mistake, not when he was the instigator of said orgasm. "Your body was crying out for that, and you know it."

Her blue eyes grew stormy. "B.S. I'm in charge of that body, and I can muzzle any crying out that's going on. I allowed myself to get worked up. I have to take responsibility for behaving like a complete idiot."

"I don't see it that way."

"Of course not. You're the one with the piece of property to protect. Anything you can do to distract me from my plan is—"

"No, damn it." His grip tightened. "That was not about me trying to distract you."

"No? Then what was it about?"

She had him there. His original goal had been to get friendly and persuade her to lay off the property.

He'd made obvious progress in the getting-friendly department, so why wasn't he pushing his advantage?

"Sean, I concede that you're attracted to me, although why that is I don't know."

"You don't?" He stared at her in astonishment.

"No, I don't." She moved away from him and buttoned her jeans. "I'm not the kind of woman who incites men to lust."

"That's where you're wrong."

"At least have the decency to be honest with me." She zipped her jeans. "I figured out that you wanted to seduce me to get some leverage, and then you started enjoying the seduction for its own sake, I suppose because you're oversexed."

She was starting to make him mad. "If I'm so oversexed, why haven't I slept with anyone in almost a year?"

"Oh, that's easy. You've been through all the women in town, and you're bored. I'm a novelty."

"That's not true, Maggie." God, he hoped it wasn't true. That wouldn't say much for his character.

"Besides that, I'm a challenge. I don't fall at your feet like all the women in this town. I think the challenge excites you."

He wouldn't accept that. He couldn't be that shallow. "I wanted you the first time I saw you, before I knew you'd be a challenge."

"Because I was new in town."

"No, damn it! It was your hair, and your freckles, and your mouth."

"Arranged in a particular combo that you hadn't seen on the women you've dated in Big Knob. And it was convenient to be attracted to me, because then you could use sex to get what you want."

There was some truth to that, but his gut told him it wasn't the whole truth. He remembered how happy he'd been to make her come and how little he'd cared for his own satisfaction. That had never happened to him before and he thought it was significant. Something more than sex might be going on.

But he wasn't about to discuss that now, with her standing there looking so righteous. She wouldn't believe him, anyway. She'd only think he was trying to justify his behavior.

Her expression softened. "I'm not judging you for what's happened. If anything, I'm judging myself for falling in with your plan. My boss said I have to be tougher if I plan to make it in this business. I'm embarrassed to discover that he has a point."

"What do you mean, tougher?" He'd thought she was plenty tough, coming here by herself to negotiate this deal.

"I have yet to close the sale on any property I've tried to buy for SaveALot." She reached under her sweater and arched her back so that she could fasten her bra.

The motion stirred him up again, but he clamped down on his reaction. He had bigger fish to fry. "What happens if you don't get the property this time?"

"Simple." She leaned down to pick up her coat. "I lose my job."

Sean felt like punching something. He didn't want her to lose her job, but he didn't want her buying this property to put up a big-box store, either. If Denise didn't hate him right now, he could ask her to hunt for some other piece of property that would work for Maggie. There had to be *something*. But Denise wasn't in a mood to help him.

Well, he'd have to fix that. His eyesight had improved, so maybe the effect of the loser herbs was wearing off a little. He didn't want to go to bed with Denise, though. Maggie was the only person who fit that description. This had become so damn complicated.

Maggie leaned down toward the wicker chest. "We might as well blow these out."

"No, wait!"

She glanced up. "Why?"

"These are special candles. You don't just blow them out."

"What do you do, squirt them with water? Dunk them in wine?"

"You do this." Sean licked his thumb and forefinger and pinched the candle wicks, extinguishing the flame.

"Ouch. Didn't that hurt?"

It had, a little, but he wouldn't say so. "Nah."

"What kind of candle has to be put out like that? I've never heard of such a thing."

"I haven't, either. I borrowed these from Dorcas and Ambrose, and they told me not to blow them out. You can use a snuffer, but I don't have one."

"I'd like to take a look at them. But without my glasses, I might as well not bother. Couldn't see anything unusual even if it was there."

"You could try mine." He picked up the black-framed glasses from the top of the wicker basket where he'd laid them earlier.

"I doubt they'll work, but thanks." She took them and put them on.

He caught his lower lip between his teeth to keep from laughing. Her delicate features, the freckles sprinkled on her nose and those oversized glasses made quite a combination.

She popped a candle out of its silver holder. The holders were also borrowed. Ambrose had brought over the wine early this afternoon, and then he'd handed Sean the candlesticks and candles, along with instructions on how to put them out.

Sean had been in too much of a hurry to ask him why the special instructions. He figured they were some kind of California candles that needed more

TLC. Many things about Dorcas and Ambrose were strange. Added to everything else was Maggie's suspicion that they were fugitives. He and the Lowells needed to have another conversation.

Maggie turned the candle this way and that. "Looks like an ordinary red candle to me."

"I'm taking them back this afternoon." He had a sex bench to build, for one thing. "I'll ask what the deal is."

Still holding the candle, Maggie gazed at Sean through those ridiculous glasses. "So the Lowells bartered for the wine, but they loaned you the candles and holders, which is going above and beyond."

"I guess you could say that." He struggled to keep a straight face, but she looked like such a little geek.

"It's obvious they're trying to match us up. Did you hire them to do that?"

"No! Swear to God. I didn't even know until today that they had a matchmaking business. They told me they were relationship counselors, but they said they were taking a sabbatical." He didn't mention that he'd *tried* to hire them and they'd refused.

"I assume they realize we're after the same property?"

"Yes. I told them."

Maggie tapped the candle against her palm. "Then I guess they don't want me to have it, either. I'm beginning to think the only friend I have in town is Denise."

"You have me."

She laughed, but it wasn't exactly a happy sound. "You're not a friend, Sean."

She couldn't have said anything that would have cut him deeper. But he supposed he had it coming.

Chapter 11

Telling Sean he wasn't a friend might have been un-kind, but Maggie needed to put distance between them. She had only herself to blame for this messy situation, and she had to be the one to clean it up. From now on she'd be a tough cookie, no matter what.

No more wine from the basement cache of Dorcas and Ambrose, no more candlelight or plump and juicy chicken salad sandwiches. And definitely no more orgasms courtesy of Mr. Sean Madigan. She would have a hard time forgiving herself for that indiscretion.

At least she was stone-cold sober now. She laid his glasses on the wicker chest. "Thanks."

"If you're going to drive, you should keep them."

"I'll be fine." When she started putting on her coat, he made a move as if to come over and help her, but she waved him away. "Thanks. I've got it."

"Seriously. Take the glasses."

She picked up her purse from the floor where she'd left it. "I can manage. It's not as if Big Knob has a freeway running through it."

"I don't think driving without your glasses is a good idea. It's Friday afternoon."

"What, you have rush-hour traffic?"

"No, we have Edith Mae Hoogstraten. She's eighty-seven, and she heads into town right about now on

Friday afternoons. Her old Buick is in mint condition, but her vision isn't what it used to be and her driving is a little . . . crooked."

Maggie was scandalized. "You let somebody drive who shouldn't have a license?"

"We do. She only goes from her house to the Hob Knob. We always leave three parking spots open for her, and she hasn't hit anybody's vehicle yet."

"I can't believe someone hasn't taken her license away." Maggie figured that when SaveALot came to town, traffic would increase exponentially and Edith Mae's driving days would need to be ended.

"Nobody can bear to take it away because she loves her independence so much. Besides, she owns a shotgun and has threatened to shoot anybody who tries to pry that license out of her hands."

"Good grief." Maggie had been living in cities so long that she had no frame of reference for such behavior.

"It's okay. She drives slow, and everyone recognizes her old Buick. We work it out."

"Well, all I need is to wreck the rental car, on top of everything else. H.G. would have a royal fit." But she didn't want Sean driving her, either. What a sticky situation, and she wasn't just talking about her panties.

"H.G. is your boss?"

"H. G. Stackhouse, regional manager for SaveALot, a kindly old Texas gentleman who used to like me. Now I'm not so sure." She gazed out the French doors toward the balcony.

She really couldn't see worth shit without her glasses. Even the French doors were fuzzy. She imagined that outside she saw a blurry scrap of rainbow, but it could be her imagination. She didn't believe in superstitious signs, anyway.

"Did this Stackhouse guy send you here? Are you supposed to buy this property on his orders?"

She glanced back at Sean, who was slightly more in focus than the French doors. "No. I didn't tell him where I was going."

"How could you get away with that? I thought you said something about an expense account."

"I do have one." Come to think of it, she might not have the expense account anymore. H.G. might have been angry enough to cancel her company credit card. At least breakfast would have gone through. She'd use the card for some small purchase next, to test whether it was still valid.

Sean blew out a breath. "You're not making much sense. How can you be the only person at SaveALot who knows about this potential property? I don't understand exactly how these things work, but I sure didn't think there was this kind of secrecy involved."

She would love to be able to confide her suspicions about H.G.'s son to someone, but Sean wasn't the guy. He didn't have her best interests at heart, meaning that he might use anything she said against her. Then a horrible thought came to her.

Thanks to her big mouth, he knew the name of her boss. He could very easily figure out how to make a call to H.G. and report Maggie's whereabouts. He could also let H.G. know that she'd behaved unprofessionally and should be fired. She might be fired already, but if not, Sean could see to it.

Whether all that would save his precious property was another question, but he could dynamite her plans to buy it for SaveALot. She felt sick with dread. She'd given him so much power over her.

"Maggie, what's wrong? You just turned white."

"I'm . . . not feeling well."

"Damn." He started toward her. "I hope it wasn't the chicken salad."

She held up a hand to stop him. "Not that kind of sick. I won't upchuck or anything." She wondered if he had any idea that he held the tools for her destruction—or if he'd use them. "I haven't had much sleep recently, that's all. A little rest and I'll be fine."

"Let me take you to Madeline's."

His image was blurry, so she couldn't read his expression that well, but he sounded concerned. That was a good thing, because she had to count on his common decency not to torpedo her with H.G.

"No, thanks," she said. "I can get myself there. I promise to watch out for Edith Mae Hoogstraten in her old Buick. But first I need to check with Denise and see whether her computer's up and running." She dug in her purse and pulled out her BlackBerry. That needed recharging, too, but she had enough battery life to make one call.

Denise answered right away. "Hey, Maggie. I thought I'd hear from you before now."

Maggie turned her back on Sean, as if that would shut out the memory of what had happened here this afternoon. "I was checking out the property." She squeezed her eyes shut, wishing she could rewind the clock.

"Jeremy called and he's on the road, heading back here. He'll be at my office in about thirty minutes. He's brilliant, so I think he'll find the problem in no time. The electricity seems to have settled down, too, so if you want to stop by, we could have the information within the hour."

"Thanks, Denise. I'll be right there." She ended the call and glanced at Sean. "I'll be on my way, then."

"Jeremy's fixed it?"

She couldn't afford to give him any more information. "Thanks for lunch." She walked out the door.

"Wait!"

"Gotta go." She hurried toward the stairs. Because she couldn't see where she was going, she stumbled on the second step and had to grab the banister for support.

His long legs ate up the space between them and he grasped her arm. "Take my glasses."

God help her. The jolt of excitement when he'd touched her had destroyed all her vows to stay away from him. She'd wanted him to haul her back upstairs and kiss her until they both went crazy.

He didn't pull her close, much to her traitorous body's disappointment. Instead he released her and held out those ugly glasses.

She glanced back at him. He was fuzzy, but she could tell he was frowning at her.

He shook them at her. "Take the glasses, damn it."

"Why would you want to help me?"

"I don't want to help you get the property, but I don't want to see you get hurt because you can't see your nose in front of your face." He sounded angry. "And don't deny it. You almost fell down the stairs."

"Are you sure you don't need them anymore?"

"Apparently not. I thought it was a temporary thing, and sure enough, it is."

"Then I'll borrow them for a little while." She took the glasses and put them on. His image snapped into focus and he looked mouthwateringly good to her. From this angle his chin looked strong and masculine and his hair fell in a gentle wave over his forehead. His frown of irritation didn't detract one bit from those magnetic green eyes.

Then his frown began to disappear, and his eyes sparkled with laughter.

"What?" She dipped her head and the glasses slid down her nose. Naturally they were too big.

"Those glasses on you. They're—"

"Funny-looking." She could imagine. And that was good, because the weirder she looked, the less likely he'd want to kiss her again. She pushed them firmly in place.

"I was going to say cute. Prim." The laughter faded

and something hotter crept into his expression. His gaze grew more intense. "Maggie." His voice was hoarse with frustration.

Longing bloomed within her, a kind of deep ache that she hadn't felt in ages. She swallowed.

"Get going," he murmured.

"Right." Tearing herself away, she held the glasses against the bridge of her nose as she ran down the stairs. She didn't look back.

Sean braced his hands against the railing and watched her go. The joke was on him. He'd finally found a woman he craved beyond reason, and all she wanted to do was run away.

Once she was out the door and he heard her car start, he relaxed his grip on the railing. He'd always loved this feature of the house. Being able to creep out of bed at night and spy on the grown-ups having a party on the main floor was a kid's dream.

He realized now that his father hadn't been able to afford the liquor and the food, but he'd been the kind of guy who would put off paying the electric bill so he could throw a party and invite most of the town. Sean wondered if anyone remembered those parties.

He'd never forget them. Such happy things, those parties. Watching them take place from upstairs, he'd imagined that his parents had the world by the tail. He'd believed in his father right up to the moment they'd been kicked out of this house and his dad had left town, never to be heard from again.

Sean sighed and pushed away from the railing. He wanted this house back, damn it. Maggie made it sound as if this property was her only hope for saving her job, but he couldn't accept that. There had to be other locations she could choose that weren't either state land or marshy, and he'd do what he could to help her find one.

In the meantime, he had to cover his ass. Unclipping his cell from his belt, he speed dialed Jeremy. "Hey, bud, I hear you're headed back into town."

"I'm about ten minutes away," Jeremy said. "You got a problem, or are you just eager to have me deliver your cup?"

"A problem." Sean wandered back into the bedroom and gazed out the French doors. A rainbow arched over Big Knob, giving a glow to the rock and the trees below, a mixture of pine, oak and sycamore. Anyone who believed those woods were haunted had never seen it like this, looking almost magical.

"What can I do for you?" Jeremy asked.

"I was wondering . . . is there any way you can stall off fixing Denise's computer?"

"Why?"

"Thanks to Denise, there's someone in town trying to buy the property I'm after. They want to build a SaveALot there."

Jeremy whistled under his breath. "That's big stuff. I can't imagine a SaveALot in Big Knob."

"Me, either, and I especially don't want the old house destroyed so they can put up a store." As he watched, the rainbow lost some of its brilliance.

"I'm sure not."

"Denise has finally tracked down the property's owner, and once her computer is fixed, she'll be able to get that info and give it to the SaveALot rep."

"I see." Jeremy paused. "Denise really must be pissed at you to do something like this."

"I guess. Anyway, if you could stall until tomorrow, maybe I can come up with an alternate location for Maggie."

"Who's Maggie?"

"The SaveALot rep."

Jeremy began to laugh. "Are you shittin' me? The rep's a woman? Is she terminally ugly?"

"No."

"Older than Edith Mae Hoogstraten?"

"No."

"Then what's the deal, buddy? Turn on that famous Madigan charm. Problem solved."

Sean thought about explaining his unfortunate transformation, but decided against it. His eyesight was better already, so the other effects might be fading, too. Jeremy probably wouldn't even notice, and Sean would rather not have to confess that he'd done something so ridiculous.

"I sort of tried that," he said. "But she's really focused on getting this property. You know the type— it's all about the promotion." The rainbow grew fuzzy. The tree branches became less distinct, too.

"I don't know the type," Jeremy said. "Not too many like that around here. And I've never met the woman you couldn't have on a silver platter."

"That's because you haven't met Maggie Grady. She's tough as nails." He blinked, trying to clear his vision. "So can you stall the repair for me?"

Jeremy cleared his throat. "You know I'd do most anything for you, buddy. But you're asking me to lie to my customer. That goes against the grain."

Desperation curled in Sean's gut. "I'm not asking for much time. Just the rest of this afternoon, so I can scout out some other locations." How he'd accomplish that, plus build a sex bench for the Lowells and keep Calvin Gilmore happy was anybody's guess. But he had to try. If Maggie got her information this afternoon, she'd do her best to contact the owner today.

Whoever that person was, they couldn't care much about Big Knob or they'd have put in an appearance before now. They might think the place had little or no value. Sean had been counting on that to keep the price in a range he could afford.

But once the owner found out a big company like

SaveALot wanted the land, Sean wouldn't have a prayer of getting it. He needed to keep the owner and Maggie far, far apart. Jeremy was his only hope.

"I wish I could, Sean." Jeremy sounded unhappy.

"But you can't." Sean ran a hand through his hair, which seemed coarser than the last time he'd touched it.

"It doesn't feel right."

"Okay, I understand."

"I hope so. Listen, if there's anything else I can do . . . I'll be glad to talk to this Maggie person and tell her how much the house means to you."

"That's okay. She knows." And he didn't want Jeremy, or any other guy, getting into deep conversations with Maggie. "One other thing, though."

"What's that?"

"She's pretty hot, so I wouldn't blame you for asking her out."

"And you don't want me to," Jeremy said.

The words tasted like sawdust in his mouth. He'd never had to ask this of any man before. "I'd count it as a favor if you wouldn't hit on her or anything."

"Wow, I never thought I'd see the day."

Sean winced. Here it came. Jeremy was going to rub it in, and Sean couldn't blame him. Jeremy wasn't the smoothest guy in the world, and he'd struggled to get dates, while Sean had been awash in women. It must have been tough to put up with that all these years.

Jeremy chuckled. "I can't believe it. Sean Madigan is worried about a computer geek like me."

"It's not that I'm worried, exactly." But he was. Without his normal looks he was extremely worried.

"Yeah, you are, and forgive me if I savor it for a minute. But I won't horn in on whatever you have planned." He laughed. "As if I could."

Sean ran his hand through his hair again, which

seemed to have grown longer in some places just in the past few minutes. "You might be surprised. Anyway, see you later, buddy." Sean closed his phone and glanced around the bedroom. Was it his imagination, or was everything in here sort of fuzzy?

Surely his eyesight wasn't going bad again. One way to tell for sure. He walked over to pick up the empty wine bottle. Earlier he'd been able to read the label just fine.

He stared at the label and could barely make out the Mystic Winery part of it, which was in big type. *Shitfire.* The smaller print was out of the question.

He carried the bottle over to the French doors, where the light was better. The lettering was still blurred. Damn! What was in those blasted herbs that his eyesight would fade in and out? That could be dangerous!

So here he was, stuck with the same situation he hadn't wanted Maggie to have, forced to drive back into town without being able to see past his nose. At least he knew the road and could almost drive it blindfolded. Almost.

He couldn't very well ask Maggie to give his glasses back, so he had to make it over to see Dorcas and Ambrose without running into anything or anybody. They had to fix this. They had to have some antidote he could take.

Maybe it would be crude. Maybe they'd have to substitute something for one of the herbs they didn't have time to order. But they should have backup plans if they were as professional as they'd seemed. Unfortunately he had a bad feeling that they weren't.

Chapter 12

Maggie repaired her makeup before she walked into Denise's office, but there wasn't much she could do about the glasses. She might be able to get away without them for part of the time, but eventually she'd have to read something on the computer screen and the glasses would need to come out. Might as well wear them into the office and hope Denise wouldn't notice they were exactly like Sean's.

No such luck.

Denise turned from the filing cabinet and caught sight of Maggie. "Those look exactly like Sean's glasses!"

"They are his glasses."

Denise shoved the filing cabinet drawer closed with a hollow clank. "Really."

"Clumsy me, I managed to break mine. His temporary eye problem seems to have gone away, and these are close enough to my prescription, so he loaned them to me."

Irritation tightened Denise's expression. "How handy that he was nearby when you broke yours." She flipped open the file in her hand and studied it, as if she had no more interest in the matter.

Maggie didn't buy Denise's disinterest. "It *was* handy." She chose her words carefully and hoped she wasn't blushing. "I decided to meet him out at the old house. He knows more about the property than anyone, things like the stress points, the best way to approach taking it down." She had no clue what she was talking about. Was *stress points* even the right term to use?

Denise walked over and sat at her desk. "Makes sense, I guess, although I can't imagine Sean pointing out the best route for the bulldozer to take." She sat rigidly in the chair. She obviously wasn't happy that Maggie had been spending time with Sean.

Maggie decided to address the problem in case it could cause complications later. She didn't need any more than the ones she'd already created. "Go ahead and tell me to mind my own business if you want, but did you two, uh, date or anything?"

Denise's laugh sounded forced. "Heavens no. He's too young for me. We were just friends."

"But you're not friends anymore?"

"Not really. He didn't appreciate my efforts on his behalf, so who needs that kind of friend?" Denise tried to sound casual, but there was nothing casual about the hot anger in her dark eyes.

"I understand."

"If you must know, he was more interested in getting into my pants than having me handle his business needs."

"Oh. That's not good." Now Maggie didn't know what—or whom—to believe. The women in the Bob and Weave had complained because they couldn't have more sex with Sean, but Denise was saying she'd had to fend him off. Then there was Maggie's own experience today. She didn't dare think about those hot moments for fear her expression would give her away.

"I wasn't about to become another notch on his

tool belt." Denise pierced Maggie with a look. "And if you're smart, you won't, either."

Maggie was saved from having to respond by a tall, lanky man coming through the door with a metal briefcase in one hand. He wore wire-rimmed glasses, jeans, running shoes and a faded navy sweatshirt with MIT on the front. His dark hair was short but still managed to look unruly.

"Hey, Jeremy." Denise smiled at him. "My savior."

The praise seemed to make him uneasy. "No guarantees, Denise."

"When it comes to computers, you're a god and you know it. Jeremy, I'd like you to meet my client, Maggie Grady, from Houston. Maggie, this is Jeremy Dunstan, the smartest man in Big Knob."

This time Jeremy blushed. "Hey, cut it out. You're going to jinx me."

"Not possible." Denise turned to Maggie. "This guy thinks like a computer. If it's fixable, he'll fix it."

"That's good." Maggie couldn't imagine anything she'd rather have right now than a working computer and an e-mail revealing the contact point for the property's owner.

"Nice to meet you, Maggie." Jeremy shook her hand.

She might be getting paranoid, but she thought he studied her with more than idle curiosity. "Has Denise told you why I'm here?" she asked.

"Denise didn't tell me, but I have heard that you want to put up a SaveALot in Big Knob." His tone was carefully neutral.

"That's right." Either word was getting around or Sean had talked to Jeremy. "And I sure hope you can fix Denise's computer."

Jeremy smiled at her. "I'll do my best."

*   *   *

Sean couldn't believe it. He'd sideswiped Edith Mae Hoogstraten's vintage Buick. He'd tried to be so careful. Edith Mae had been stopped in the middle of the street, ready to make her turn into the parking area in front of the Hob Knob, and Sean had thought he could go on by her without a problem.

He hadn't seen the pothole until the last minute, and then he'd overcorrected. He leaped out of the truck and ran around to make sure Edith Mae was okay.

She climbed out of her old car and stomped toward him. He couldn't see her all that well except to notice that the funny little cylinder of a hat she always wore was tipped sideways and she was shaking her fist. She wasn't very big, barely over five feet, but she still scared the shit out of him.

"Sean Madigan, you hooligan! You hit my car!"

"I know. I'm sorry, Edith Mae. I miscalculated." From the corner of his eye he could see the curiosity seekers arriving. Francine and Sylvia from the Bob and Weave showed up, along with Clem Loudermilk's wife, Clara. Clara wore a purple plastic cape with a towel tucked around her neck. The cape cantilevered out at almost a ninety-degree angle, thanks to Clem's patented cleavage bra. Clara's hair was wrapped in tinfoil and she held Bud, the killer Chihuahua, in her arms.

Heather came out of the hardware store, and Madeline hurried over from the Hob Knob, still clutching her order pad.

"Is anybody hurt?" Madeline called out.

"I'm perfectly fine." Edith Mae marched around to the passenger side of the car where Sean's truck had scraped it. "It's my car that's been violated! Only fifteen hundred and sixty-three miles on it, and not a scratch, until this irresponsible hoodlum ran into me."

"I'll pay to have it fixed." Sean wished the pothole beside him would open up and swallow him.

"Bah! It'll never be the same." Edith Mae glared at Sean. "And look at you! You've let yourself go to rack and ruin. You used to be such a handsome young man. Now you look like the devil, and you're driving recklessly and running into innocent people."

Heather sidled up next to him. "You do look a little rough around the edges, Sean," she said. "When was the last time you had a haircut?"

"Last week," said Walt, the town's only barber, who walked out to the street, carrying his scissors. "What've you been doing, boy, using that Rograin on yourself?"

"Just a bad hair day." Sean tried to toss it off with one of his winning smiles, but he could sense the reaction to him was totally different from what it would have been twenty-four hours ago. Yesterday he would have been able to charm Edith Mae out of being upset. He could have made the rest of the onlookers laugh at the joke. Today they all seemed to be out for blood.

He was almost glad he couldn't see very well, especially when he glanced around and noticed, on the fringes of the crowd, Maggie's red ringlets. She was blurry, but after what had happened recently between them, he would recognize her anywhere, even blurry. Then again, if he had been able to see, this wouldn't have happened in the first place.

"I called Bob." Jeremy stepped forward and put a hand on Sean's shoulder. "He was out checking on your skunks, but he'll be here in a couple of minutes to make out a report for the insurance company."

Sean squinted at Jeremy. "What's he doing with the skunks?" He hoped to hell Bob wasn't out there trying to poison them. Damn it, why did everything have to happen at once?

Clara spoke up, her tinfoiled hair making her look like a science experiment gone wrong. "I told him I wanted those skunks G-O-N-E, gone! He said he'd handle it. I can't have those skunks around. They scare Bud." At the sound of his name, Bud started yapping.

"See?" Clara stroked the Chihuahua lovingly. "Just mention skunks and Bud gets upset. Clem came down this morning to tell you to get rid of them, but he said you'd made no firm commitment, so I had to act."

"He did mention it." Sean's patience was being severely tested. "And I plan to do something about the skunks." If it wasn't too late.

"When?" Clara tapped her expensively booted foot. "Next month? Next year? Next century?"

"I'll get started tonight." He'd have to build several traps and prepare a hiding place for them in the woods. Maybe this accident had happened in the nick of time to pull Bob off of skunk detail.

"If everybody's okay, I need to get back to the diner," Madeline said. "Edith Mae, why don't you come with me and have a nice cup of calming tea? I'm sure Bob will be happy to move your car into your usual spot once he's finished making out his report."

"I don't need tea at a time like this," Edith Mae said. "I need gin."

"Now, Edith Mae." Madeline put an arm around the woman's narrow shoulders. "You know we don't have hard liquor at the Hob Knob. We leave that to Jeff over at the Big Knobian, and they won't open for another hour."

"Should've brought my flask," Edith Mae said.

"I understand this is upsetting," Madeline said. "Maybe I can find you a small glass of cooking sherry."

"Can't abide the stuff," Edith Mae muttered, but she allowed herself to be led away.

Francine moved closer to Sean and spoke in an undertone. "If Walt cut your hair a week ago, then maybe he's losing his touch. Come on over to my shop after this is over and I'll trim you up."

Sean glanced at Francine. "Thanks, but my hair should be okay in a few days."

"Doesn't look like it from where I'm standing. Some places are long, some short, and in spots it's sprouting out of your head like crabgrass. Did you start using a cheaper shampoo?"

"No, I—"

"Well, well!" Bob Anglethorpe's voice boomed out, and he strutted over in his khaki police chief's uniform. "Have a little fender bender, there, Madigan?"

"Minor problem, Bob." Sean hoped it was minor. He couldn't see well enough to determine that. "I hear you were out investigating the family of skunks under my porch." It wasn't technically *his* porch, which was why he couldn't dictate what went on under it.

"Yeah, I left some poisoned bait out for them. That should take care of the problem."

Sean thought quickly. The skunks wouldn't come out for at least another two hours. That gave him enough time to go home and gather up the bait, once he'd paid a quick visit to Dorcas and Ambrose. But the sex bench would have to wait.

"How many packets did you figure it would take?" he asked, pretending he didn't much care.

"I set out eight. Now let me take a look at this wreck you managed to have with Edith Mae." Clipboard in hand, Bob started walking around both vehicles.

"Looks like things are under control, buddy." Jeremy slapped Sean on the shoulder. "I'd better get back to work."

"Have you fixed it?"

"Not yet. It's taking longer than I thought it would."

Sean lowered his voice. "On purpose?"

"No, not on purpose. I told you I wouldn't do that. There are some electrical issues, too. The power's cut out twice since I've been there."

Sean couldn't tell if Jeremy was really having problems or secretly trying to help him out. "Well, thanks."

"I swear I'm not stalling."

"Okay, okay."

"And I have to agree with Edith Mae that you look like hell. What's the deal?"

"Jeremy, if I told you, you wouldn't believe me."

"Now you've made me curious. How about meeting me for a beer later on at the Big Knobian?"

"Man, I would love to, but I don't think I have the time." *Skunks to save, sex benches to build, Maggie to distract, not to mention the job to finish over at Calvin Gilmore's house.*

"Maybe later, then. I want to know what's going on with you."

You're not the only one. Sean bid him good-bye and turned back to Bob, who was ready to ask some questions about how this had happened. Sean only hoped he'd be able to see well enough to sign his name on the report.

The day had been a series of disasters, but he couldn't write it off as shitty all the way around. There had been that one shining moment when, thanks to his intervention, Maggie had enjoyed an orgasm. As far as Sean was concerned, that balanced out everything else.

Maggie was convinced Sean had run into Edith Mae Hoogstraten because his eyesight hadn't improved the way he'd imagined it had when they were at the house. If he hadn't loaned her his glasses, this wouldn't have happened. She didn't want to feel guilty about that, but she couldn't seem to help herself. He'd looked so miserable and embarrassed standing there in the middle of Fifth Street.

"I can't figure out what's happened to Sean," Denise said as the three of them walked back to her office and Jeremy returned to the malfunctioning computer.

"Yeah, it's weird." Jeremy had removed the computer's casing and was fiddling with its insides. "He doesn't look like himself. It's almost like his ugly twin showed up and took his place."

Maggie continued to gaze out the plate glass window at Sean, who was still talking to the sheriff. "Does he have a twin?"

"Nah." Jeremy continued to tinker with the computer. "He's an only child, which is too bad, considering that his dad left town when Sean was seven and his mother died when he was eighteen. So far as I know, he doesn't have any other family. I think that's why he's so protective of the skunks."

Maggie turned. She'd heard something about skunks while they were all standing in the street, but she hadn't been able to follow what was going on. "What's happening with the skunks?"

"Oh, it's ridiculous," Denise said. "Nobody in their right mind harbors skunks under their house. I'm not a big Clara Loudermilk fan, but in this case, I think she's right. They need to go."

"Plenty of women in this town wanted the skunks out of there long ago, but Sean insisted they kept him from being mobbed," Jeremy said. "Nobody would sneak up on him at night, for fear they'd get sprayed."

Denise pulled out a file drawer with enough force to make it clang. "He couldn't install an alarm system? If you ask me, he's too lazy to get rid of them."

"No, I think he's actually attached to them, believe it or not," Jeremy said.

Maggie's picture of Sean was changing rapidly. She'd never known a man with sympathy for skunks. Being a city girl, she didn't know much about skunks, either. Her only experience came from Disney cartoons, where the skunks were cute.

She glanced out the window again. Sean climbed back in his truck, and Bob moved Edith Mae's Buick. Neither of the vehicles seemed the worse for the collision. In Houston no one would take any notice of such a minor accident, but here it was front-page news.

If everyone got so worked up about a little fender bender, she could just imagine their reaction to a SaveALot being built on the edge of town. It would be the topic of conversation for months. Her decision to locate the store here would have a huge impact on Big Knob and its inhabitants.

She'd known that intellectually before, but now she understood it on a gut level. The impact on the town would be considerable and could end up being very positive for many people. Just not Sean. As she watched his pickup move carefully down the street, she felt an intense pang of regret. Whether she meant to or not, she was about to smash his dreams to bits.

Chapter 13

Sean parked in front of the Lowells' house. Carrying the silver candlesticks, he navigated the wooden steps leading up to the front porch with great care. All he needed was to trip and fall on his face.

Then again, nothing could be more embarrassing than sideswiping Edith Mae Hoogstraten. In all the years she'd been weaving down Fifth Street, not one person had run into her. He was the first idiot to accomplish it.

Dorcas and Ambrose had to do something about his condition. His bad eyesight would keep him from finding the poison set out for the skunks. The Lowells might not care about that, but if he couldn't see, he couldn't work, so if they wanted their sex bench, they'd better cough up an antidote.

The oh-so-classy doorbell chime set his teeth on edge. Everything had seemed wonderful last night, with the great wine and the delicious food. He'd had no idea they were planning to mess with him like this.

Dorcas answered the door wearing a soft blue sweater and jeans. And she was blurry, of course.

"Sean! Come in, come in. We've been expecting you. How did your rendezvous go?"

"Never mind that." He could hear some fifties music in the background, some singer his mother used to like. "I need you to reverse this thing. I can't see worth a damn, and I—"

"But we gave you some glasses." She took hold of his arm and drew him inside. "What happened to them?"

"See, that's what I don't get. This afternoon my eyesight started getting better." The music seemed to be coming from the basement, of all places. Maybe they had a rec room down there with a pool table.

"When did you notice your eyesight improving?"

"When I found out I could read the label on the wine bottle without them."

Dorcas nodded. "I see. And did you enjoy the wine?"

"Yeah, sure, but that's not the point. The point is that I need an antidote to whatever you gave me last night. Ambrose said you don't have the right herbs, but can't you substitute something else? Something that's close?"

The basement door opened. "Sean!" Ambrose came striding down the hall in a green plaid shirt and cords. He was also blurry, but his out-of-focus face was ruddy, as if he'd been exerting himself. Sabrina trotted after him. "I was checking out the pipes," Ambrose said. "Good to see you!" He stretched out his hand.

Sean shook it out of politeness. "I would say it's good to see you, too, except that's the problem. I can't see."

"Where are your glasses?"

Dorcas turned to him. "His eyesight got better this afternoon." She said it with pride, as if she'd somehow accomplished that herself.

"Did it?" Ambrose rubbed his hands together. "That's great news, just great."

"But now it's worse than ever," Sean said. "Because of my eyes, I ran into Edith Mae Hoogstraten's Buick."

"Oh, my," Dorcas said. "From what I hear, no one's ever done that. Is she okay?"

"Physically she's fine, but she's mad as hell, and there was a big scene in the middle of the street, and I'm sick of this and I want you to fix me."

"Come into the parlor," Ambrose said. "We'll talk." He sounded so irritatingly genteel.

Sean's anger built. "I don't have time to talk. I have a family of skunks to protect."

"A *what*?" Ambrose stared at him.

"Skunks. They live under my house, or I should say it's Clem Loudermilk's house, and his wife, Clara, wants them out, so Bob set out poison this afternoon."

"That's terrible," Dorcas said. "You have to gather up the poison before night comes."

"I can't because I can't see it." Music still wafted up from the basement. Sean found himself trying to identify the singer. Bobby Darin, maybe? "I want to trap the skunks and take them out into the woods where they'll be safe, but I can't do any of that with my eyes like this."

"And you don't want to ask Maggie to give back your glasses?" Dorcas asked.

"No, because she needs . . . Wait a minute. I didn't tell you Maggie had them. How did you know that?"

"Come in and sit down," Ambrose said. "Dorcas, don't you have something you can give Sean?"

"Let me go look."

Sean agreed to go into the parlor and sit on the sofa, but he didn't sink back onto the purple cushions. He remained stiff and determined, ready to fight for what he needed. Sabrina followed them into the room and rubbed against his leg. He stroked her soft black fur, but he kept his gaze on Ambrose, who lounged in a wingback chair next to the sofa.

"Who's that singing on the CD you have going?" Sean asked.

"Frankie Avalon."

"Oh." Sean remembered now. His mom used to love that guy. But just because Ambrose and Dorcas liked him, too, that didn't mean Sean could trust them.

"It's admirable that you want to save the skunks," Ambrose said.

"Whatever." Unwilling to be flattered out of his bad mood, he skewered Ambrose with a look. "Dorcas talked to Maggie this afternoon, didn't she?"

"I don't think so."

"Come on. That's the only way she'd know that I gave away my glasses. Whatever game you're playing, I want it to stop. If you'll just change me back the way I was, I can handle this situation without any interference from you."

"Hostility isn't going to help, Sean."

"I'll bet if you had this happen you'd be cranky, too. The changes went way too far. Nothing's the same, not even my privates."

Ambrose pressed his lips together, obviously trying to hold back a smile.

"Go ahead and laugh. Wouldn't be so funny if it was your dick that had shrunk, now, would it?"

"I'm sure not." Ambrose cleared his throat. "But you have to admit you got what you wanted. Women leave you alone now."

Sean scowled at him. "Some consolation. Now I'm helpless to stop Maggie from buying that property."

"I wouldn't say that. I think you have many— Ah, here's Dorcas."

Dorcas walked in carrying a plastic shopping bag, which was a good sign. Sean assumed the antidote was in there. No matter how obnoxious the stuff was, he'd take it. He'd eat rabbit turds if they would do the trick.

Sabrina bounded over to the bag and danced around it, reaching up to bat it with her paw.

"It's not for you," Dorcas said to the cat. "It's for Sean." She handed him the bag. "Let me know if these work."

Sabrina hopped up on his lap as he peered into the bag, which contained several little packets tied with purple ribbon. *Finally.* Sabrina kept trying to get in the bag, and he had to keep nudging her back.

On top of the packets lay another pair of black-framed glasses. They were even uglier and in worse shape than the first pair. The nosepiece was held together with white adhesive tape.

Sean pulled out the glasses and held the bag closed so Sabrina couldn't climb in. "These are to tide me over, right? Until the antidote works?"

"What antidote?" Dorcas said.

"Isn't that what's in the packages?" Still holding Sabrina away, he took one out and held it up. It smelled funky, like last week's garbage. Sabrina started to meow.

"That's skunk bait. It will attract the skunks into the cage you build, and once they eat it, they'll become mildly sedated, so they'll be easier to transport."

Sean stood to get away from Sabrina, who was going a little crazy wanting whatever was in the packet. "These are *all* skunk bait?"

"Yes. I put in four, which should be enough."

"I thought you were getting something to help me!"

Sabrina put her paws up on his leg and meowed again.

"This will help you."

"Not with Maggie, it won't!" Sean felt panic set in. "You have to give me some herbs to reverse this condition, at least a little bit. You have to."

Dorcas folded her hands in front of her. "Sean, I would if I could, but it's not possible. You'll have to deal with this for the next two weeks."

Sean stood there a moment, stunned by his incredible

bad luck. In two weeks his plans would be wrecked. He wanted to lash out at Dorcas and Ambrose, but this was his own damn fault. He'd rushed into something he knew nothing about, and he was about to pay the price.

He put on the taped glasses. At least now he could see. Then he looked at the two people who had helped him trash his future. He couldn't protect himself, but he would protect the skunks. "How do I know this bait won't hurt them?"

"Open a packet and give a little to Sabrina. She loves it. When we travel, I give her some, which keeps her calm for the trip."

That reminded Sean of Maggie's suspicion that the Lowells were on the run. "I don't remember hearing where you moved from."

"Sedona," Ambrose said.

"That's in Arizona, isn't it?" Sean had been so sure they were from California, but the wine label had been from Sedona, so apparently he'd been wrong.

Ambrose nodded. "Red rock country."

Sean remembered seeing pictures of the place on TV, and he could imagine Dorcas and Ambrose there. "You didn't like it?"

"It was fine," Ambrose said.

But something went wrong there. Sean couldn't explain why he knew that, but he would have bet all his carpentry tools that Dorcas and Ambrose had been forced to leave. The police chief could do a background check on them, but Sean didn't want to stir things up, at least not yet.

He decided to let the subject drop for now. Sabrina was still going nuts trying to get to the packets, so he looped the handles of the plastic bag over his arm so he could untie the ribbon on one packet and give her a little of what was inside.

The packet was full of brown pea-sized nuggets that looked like granola. "How much should I give her?"

"Two or three pieces is plenty," Dorcas said. "You can't overdose an animal on this, but you might as well not waste it."

Sean crouched down and held out the nuggets. About that time Frankie Avalon started singing his mother's favorite song, "Venus." He told himself not to get sentimental about it.

Purring loudly, Sabrina ate the nuggets before he could blink. Then she rubbed against his hand. He petted her for about five seconds and then she did the strangest thing. He could swear that she was moving her feet in rhythm to the song coming from the basement. She was doing a cha-cha just like the cats in an old cat food commercial. Except this wasn't trick photography.

He was about to comment on it when she stopped dancing and hopped up on the purple sofa. After a big yawn, she curled up and closed her eyes.

Sean glanced at Dorcas. "Was she dancing the cha-cha?"

"No. Just happy to get a treat."

Ambrose laughed. "Don't I wish she could dance. We'd put her on Letterman."

"Right." He must have imagined it. "She seems relaxed now." He walked over and sat beside Sabrina. He stroked her fur and her eyes opened a slit before closing again. She looked as if all she wanted to do was sleep.

"I guess I'll try the tranquilizer for the skunks." He stood. "Thanks."

"You're welcome." Dorcas smiled at him. "Let us know how it turns out."

At the door he turned. "Isn't Sedona kind of a woo-woo place?"

"Some people think so," Ambrose said.

"I'll bet somebody there could overnight the herbs to fix me up."

Dorcas shook her head. "It's not that simple."

Sean didn't believe her. He thought it might be that simple if she felt free to contact someone in Sedona. But then they'd know where she was. Dorcas and Ambrose were definitely hiding from something, which meant he wouldn't be getting any help for his condition, damn it.

With a sigh, he took his skunk bait and left.

By five that afternoon, Maggie had to accept the fact that she wouldn't be contacting the owner of the property until at least the next morning. When Jeremy couldn't get the computer to work, he'd tried to figure out what was wrong with the office's electricity, but he'd had no luck there, either. As predicted, the electric company hadn't shown up, so business was at a standstill for Denise.

Maggie left Denise and Jeremy to battle with the situation and drove to Madeline and Abe's house for dinner. The thought of seeing Sean there made her jumpy. It wouldn't be easy to sit across the table from him and try to act normal when earlier today he'd had his hand inside her panties. She still couldn't believe she'd allowed that.

Maybe Abe would be on his rant about canned laughter and she'd be spared the need to make idle conversation. One thing she'd do for sure—return his glasses. She couldn't have him running into people on account of her.

She knocked on the front door and Madeline opened it this time. The television was still going full blast in the living room.

"I don't know what I'm going to do with that boy." Madeline ushered her inside.

Maggie saw Abe parked in front of the TV with his notepad, but she didn't think Madeline was talking about him. "Who?"

"Sean! He turned down a home-cooked meal so he can build a cage to trap that family of skunks. I've never seen the like!"

"So he's not coming to dinner?" Maggie made the unwelcome discovery that she was disappointed.

"No, he's not, and I'm worried about him." Madeline wiped her hands on her apron, as if needing something to do with them. "That fender bender today was a shock. Sean drives fast sometimes, but he's never been careless."

"It's my fault."

"Yours?" Madeline glanced at her.

Maggie took off the black-framed glasses. "These are Sean's. Mine got broken, and so he loaned me these. That's why he sideswiped Mrs. Hoogstraten."

Madeline flushed. "So his eyes really are going bad? I was hoping it was temporary, like he said."

"He thought they were getting better today, but I guess not." Maggie remembered Madeline's theory about why Sean's vision was deteriorating. "But I really don't think . . ." What an awkward topic. She wasn't sure how to proceed.

Madeline wiped her hands on her apron some more. "I've been too hard on him. I don't want that boy going blind."

"He won't. At least not because of . . ." Try as she might, Maggie couldn't make herself discuss the harmless nature of masturbation with Madeline.

"I'd hate to chance it. He needs to find a nice girl and settle down. That would solve everything." Madeline gazed at her for a moment. "Tell you what. Why don't you take dinner out to him? I'll give you directions to his place."

"Madeline, are you trying to fix me up with Sean?"

Madeline's round cheeks turned pink. "Well, you seem like a really nice girl, and—"

"I'll only be here a few days. I have a career in Houston." At least she hoped she did. "If you really want to find a woman for Sean, you'd better look closer to home."

"He's not interested in anybody here. If your job is a problem, I could find you one. Joe and Sherry are always looking for more help at the diner. It's a real good place to work."

"I'm sure it is." Maggie suppressed a laugh. She didn't want to insult Madeline's choice of employment by saying that there was no way she'd be happy waitressing at the Hob Knob. "But I like the job I have."

"I don't think I caught what job that was. Sean didn't mention it."

Maggie hesitated. But she couldn't keep it a secret forever, not in a small town like this. "I'm a location scout for SaveALot."

"That big discount store?" Madeline's eyes widened. "Are we getting one in Big Knob?"

"I hope so. It depends on whether I can find the right property."

"I've only been in one of those stores a couple of times, but oh, the bargains!"

Maggie was encouraged. At last, someone who was excited about SaveALot moving to town. "That's what people like about them," she said.

"But if they build one here, why couldn't you work out of that store? That would solve everything."

"I, um, no . . . I need to be at the corporate headquarters in Houston."

Madeline smiled. "Things have been known to change. We won't worry about that now. Just take Sean's dinner out to him. I'm sure the poor boy's not eating right."

"Okay, I can do that." Maggie could see there was

no point in trying to pry Madeline away from her matchmaking plans, and refusing to take him dinner would make her look mean-spirited. The trip would be harmless enough if she kept up her guard. She'd have a chance to return his glasses and check out the skunk situation, which intrigued her.

Ten minutes later, she was back in her car with a grocery sack on the seat next to her. Madeline had packed everything in Tupperware. Maggie decided she'd be safe with this meal because there wouldn't be any wine involved.

The rain had stopped, leaving the pavement shiny in the beam of her rental car's headlights. Once she returned Sean's glasses, she would have some trouble getting back to Madeline's house, but she'd go slowly. She had to solve this glasses thing, though, or she wouldn't be able to drive back to the Indianapolis airport. First thing in the morning she'd call her optometrist in Houston and ask him to overnight her a new pair. Tomorrow was Saturday, but the office would be open until noon.

Following Madeline's directions, she found the turn-off to Sean's house. He lived on the outskirts of town, not far from the property she was after. If—no, when—she bought it for SaveALot, Sean would be able to hear the noise of construction.

Damn it, she had to stop feeling guilty. She was saving him from making a terrible mistake, because that house would bankrupt him if he tried to restore it.

Sean's truck was parked in the gravel driveway in front of a one-car garage next to a small bungalow. Maggie stopped behind the truck. Pulling the bag across the console, she got out of the car and immediately heard the whine of a saw coming from the garage. Sean must be working on his trap in there.

Her footsteps crunching on the gravel, she walked toward the door on the side of the garage, all the while watching out for skunks. She knew enough to realize that startling one would be a bad thing.

Knocking on the door did no good. Sean was making too much noise with the saw and a nail gun to hear her. Finally she twisted the knob, opened the door and stepped inside. Just to make sure no skunks got in, she closed it behind her right away.

Sean was so engrossed he didn't notice that she'd come into the garage, so she had some time to watch him at work. A pair of safety goggles covered what looked like another pair of black glasses. She wondered where he'd picked those up.

But she was more interested in the way his T-shirt stretched across shoulders that seemed broader than she'd remembered. And his jeans revealed a really nice ass. How had she missed that before?

Yes, his hair was still messy, but that made sense when a guy was embroiled in a construction project. As he nailed another board in place on the large trap he was building, his muscles flexed under the white cotton T-shirt. The scent of fresh sawdust mingled with the aroma of the hot food she held in the bag, but that wasn't what made her mouth water.

Maybe Sean wasn't the sexiest guy on the planet, but at this very moment, he was the sexiest guy in Big Knob. He was more of a temptation than she'd expected when she'd agreed to drive out here with his dinner. Once again, they were alone in a secluded spot. She would have to watch herself.

Chapter 14

Sean smelled meat loaf. At first he thought it was his imagination, wishful thinking considering that he could be sitting down to one of Madeline's meat loaf dinners right about now. But the scent stayed in the air to the point that he stopped working and turned around.

Seeing Maggie standing there holding a paper sack startled him so much he dropped his nail gun on his foot. Fortunately it didn't go off and shoot a nail into his leg.

"I'm sorry!" She rushed forward, bag and all. "Are you hurt? I should have called out."

Although he was wearing his work boots with the steel-tipped toes, his foot still smarted, but he wasn't going to let her know. He picked up the nail gun. "I'm fine." He liked the way she'd hurried over when she thought he'd been hurt, though.

An arm's length away from him, she stopped. "That's good."

Once the shock of seeing her had worn off, he realized why she might be here. She'd probably talked with the property's owner and wanted to give him the bad news in person.

He took off his safety goggles and laid them on his

work bench. "I'm assuming you're here to tell me you had a successful afternoon."

"Unfortunately, I didn't."

Tension eased from his shoulders. "Why not?"

"The electricity kept acting up in Denise's office, and besides that, Jeremy couldn't figure out what was wrong with her computer. We'll have to try again in the morning."

Good old Jeremy. Sean would have to call and thank him for doing him that favor after all. "I can't say I'm sorry that you didn't get the information."

"I'm sure you're not." She shifted the bag in her arms. "But I didn't come to talk about that. I brought dinner. Madeline thought you should eat."

Maybe having a reprieve was affecting his libido, or maybe the smell of meat loaf was an aphrodisiac for him, but he'd never had such an urge to strip a woman naked and make love to her. He realized that she was the first woman he'd ever had standing in his garage. The skunks had worked wonders to keep women from bothering him here.

He was curious as to why the idea of skunks hadn't kept Maggie away. "Weren't you worried about coming over here, knowing I have skunks living under the house?"

"I probably should be, but I'm a city girl. I've had limited experience with skunks."

Just listening to her talk got him hot. It was the damnedest thing, after going all those months not being interested in sex at all. He remembered the way he'd touched her this afternoon and wanted to do that again. . . . But only for starters.

He wondered if that box of condoms was still in his bathroom cabinet. Sylvia Hepplewaite had thrown the box at him when he'd refused to have sex with her in the cab of his truck. He'd picked up the box from the driveway and kept it, figuring there was no point in pitching it out.

But now wasn't the time to be thinking of such things, damn it. He had a skunk trap to build, and he couldn't expect Maggie to hang around while he finished it. "I really appreciate the food," he said, "but I need to get this trap finished and set before I eat. I can take the bag and heat up everything later."

When he stepped forward to take it, she moved back and her cheeks turned pink. "Madeline sent enough for both of us."

That surprised him, Madeline arranging a cozy meal like that. She must approve of Maggie. "So you haven't eaten yet?"

"No, but I—"

"Then let me set you up in the kitchen. You can eat while I finish here."

She shook her head. "That's silly. I can wait."

"Can you?" He couldn't resist teasing her to see how she'd react. "You know how you get when you're hungry."

She blushed. "I'm not starving. I had . . . plenty for lunch."

He thought it was a very good sign that talking about their lunch made her flustered. "Then let's put the bag on the work bench and you can take off your coat and help me."

"I know *nothing* about building things."

"That's okay." He stepped forward to get the bag, and this time she let him take it from her. The transfer involved him touching her, and the connection jacked up his heart rate.

He set the bag on a clear space on his bench. The food smelled great, but she smelled even better. "I just need someone to help me hold the chicken wire while I staple it in place."

"What if I hadn't come along?"

"I could do it alone, but it'll be faster with an extra pair of hands." He turned to find she was still wearing her trench coat. "But you don't have to help if you don't want to."

"I'll help." She started unbuttoning her coat.

He discovered he couldn't watch her do that without wanting to move in and do it for her. And he wouldn't stop with the coat, either.

So he walked over to stand beside his trap, which was framed and ready for the chicken wire. "I'm later than I wanted to be getting this built. First I had to pick up all the poisoned bait packages Bob left around."

"I can't believe someone would deliberately try to kill them. Hasn't he ever watched Pepe LePeu?"

Sean thought of the burly chief of police watching cartoons and had to laugh. "Probably not. He was doing what he thought was right, I suppose." He glanced over and saw her standing there with her coat, obviously wondering where to put it.

"I'll take that." He reached for the coat, which meant touching her again and getting another jolt that traveled straight to his privates.

"Where did you find another pair of glasses?"

"Borrowed them." He didn't want to think about Dorcas and Ambrose right now. Every time he did think of them, he got mad at himself all over again.

After laying her coat across a pair of sawhorses next to the bench, he searched through a pile of cotton gloves and found a clean pair. He gave them to her. "These will be big, but they'll protect your hands."

She put them on. "I look like Minnie Mouse."

"Yeah." He couldn't help grinning. He'd never known a woman who took so few pains to look sexy yet ended up looking superhot, anyway.

He'd precut the chicken wire, so he picked up a

section and stretched it over one side of the cage. "If you can hold the two ends, I'll staple it on."

She pressed her gloved hands down on the wire, but as she leaned over, her glasses started to fall. "Hold on a minute. I need to take these off."

He put his hand where hers had been and she took off the glasses, tucking the earpiece in the back pocket of her jeans. "Okay." She put her gloved hand back on the section of wire. "This is a big trap you're building."

"I'm going to try to trap all of them at once." He had to lean in close to staple the wire into place, close enough that he could feel her heat and hear her breathing. Being this near, within kissing distance, was so excellent that he hated to change positions. He put in twice as many staples as he needed.

"How can you get them all in at once?" Her warm breath fanned his cheek.

He closed his eyes and fought the urge to turn his head and plant one on her. Without her glasses she might not even see it coming until it was too late. "I have some bait that will tranquilize them."

"But it won't hurt them, right?"

"Nope. I checked that out." Reluctantly he stood and backed up. "You can let go. I'll turn it around and we'll do the other side."

She moved back a couple of steps.

He lifted the cage as carefully as he could, but it was awkward. Along with losing his eyesight, he hadn't been his usual coordinated self all day, either. As he moved the cage, he jabbed her thigh with one corner. "Oh, God, I'm sorry!" Dropping the cage, he reached for her.

She jumped back. "It's fine." But she rubbed the spot even as she said that.

He felt terrible. "You could be bleeding."

"I doubt it."

As far as he knew, he'd never injured a woman, and now he'd probably left a mark on that soft freckled skin. "I think you need to ice it."

"Seriously, I'm okay." She stopped rubbing her leg as if to prove it to him.

He picked up her coat. "Let's go inside and make you an ice pack."

"Sean, that's ridiculous! I'm not hurt."

"I think we should see how bad it is." He held out her coat. "A little ice could keep you from bruising."

"A bruise isn't life threatening."

"No, but I hate to think of your skin turning black and blue."

"Look, if this is some tactic to get me to take my pants off, it isn't going to work."

He went very still. He'd been so focused on tending to her injury that he hadn't thought of what she'd have to do so they could inspect the damage. But he thought about it now. Imagining her taking off her jeans in his kitchen turned his brain to mush.

Kitchen sex had a lot to recommend it. There were sturdy counters available and various condiments right at hand. One of his girlfriends had demonstrated to him that certain kitchen appliances could double as vibrating sex toys.

Until Maggie had arrived in town, that kind of adventure had ceased to matter. He'd lost all interest in kitchen sex or hallway sex or even his favorite, shower sex. But here came this freckled redhead, revving up his sex drive.

Maggie cleared her throat. "We need to get something straight. What happened this afternoon at the old house was not the beginning of anything."

"I understand." And he also recognized that she was the one bringing it up now. She was the one who'd figured out that examining her bruise would require taking off her pants. He might be guilty of thinking of having sex with her, but she was equally guilty of thinking about having sex with him.

"I only came out here tonight because Madeline asked me to," she continued.

Calling her a liar wouldn't help his cause, so he stayed silent.

"I also thought it would give me a chance to return your glasses." Her breathing was uneven. "That's it. End of story."

His heart hammered as he gazed at her. Her words seemed to leave no room for interpretation, but her body language and the catch in her breathing communicated something else entirely. He wasn't very good at reading subtle signals. All the signals he'd ever received had been of the sirens-and-flashing-lights variety.

Did she want him to kiss her, even though she was saying the opposite? He wasn't absolutely sure. Her color was high and her eyes were bright, and in his experience, that usually meant a woman was worked up about something. With him around, that something usually involved getting naked.

She groaned. "Why do you have to look so damned appealing? Why?"

Green light. Tossing her coat and his glasses onto his work bench, he closed the distance between them and pulled her into his arms.

"No," she whispered.

He ignored her.

Maggie thought about pushing him away . . . For a nanosecond. But then his mouth covered hers, and her brain took a vacation. The rest of her followed right behind, sinking against him with an abandon that should have been embarrassing, but she was too busy snuggling close to be embarrassed.

Kissing him felt so damn good. Apparently practice made perfect, because this was a guy who could make a fortune in a kissing booth. Or as a gigolo. He knew exactly how to wrap his arms around her to make her feel desired yet cherished at the same time.

The pressure of his hand at the small of her back was just right. And when he fit his hips against hers, she wanted exactly what he was suggesting with that slight rocking motion.

She didn't care if she was another notch on his tool belt. In fact, she'd be delighted to be there, because the way he kissed made it clear that he'd know how to put a smile on her face in no time. She'd already had a taste of his abilities, and now she wanted the entire meal.

Sliding both hands under his T-shirt, she found more muscle than she would have expected. Oh, God, that mouth of his. He was turning her inside out with a kiss that was so French she wouldn't be surprised to open her eyes and see the Eiffel Tower.

But she didn't open her eyes. She kept them closed and wiggled against him, letting him know that whatever he had in mind was A-OK with her.

He lifted his mouth a fraction from hers. "Maggie, I want you."

His low, husky voice sent shivers through her. "I want you, too," she murmured. "I shouldn't, but—"

His hold on her loosened. Air moved as he backed away from her, but she kept her eyes closed for a moment longer, in case he planned on coming back.

When she heard his deep, heartfelt sigh, she opened her eyes and discovered him looking at her, his expression troubled.

"What's . . . what's wrong?"

He massaged the back of his neck and glanced at her. "I don't want you to be sorry afterward."

Absorbing that took a moment because she was still vibrating with so much sexual excitement. But as that calmed some, she realized he had every reason to think she would be sorry. She'd just said she shouldn't want him.

On top of that, she'd called their afternoon session a mistake. No man would like that, but Sean would hate it more than most. She doubted any woman had told him such a thing before.

She took a deep breath. "You're right. I need to decide what I want and take some responsibility for my actions. I need to get clear about you."

"You probably still think I'm trying to seduce you so you'll forget about the property."

"Are you?"

His smile was tinged with sadness. "I'd be lying if I said that had nothing to do with it, but it's not the main reason. See, for me, it's win-win. I want you, and maybe if we have sex, you'll start seeing things my way. You can't blame a guy for thinking like that."

"I guess not."

"But I don't want us to have sex and then have you proceed to beat yourself up about it."

He was protecting her from herself. What a concept. "But you're the best lover in Big Knob. Why not take the risk that your strategy will work like a charm and I'll become putty in your hands?"

He gazed at her. "I'm not sure. It's probably the smart way to go. You wouldn't have stopped me just then."

Heat surged through her again. "No." And she might not have the self-discipline to stop him now if he followed up on that good beginning. In spite of being afraid that he actually *would* affect her decision about the property, she still wanted him. She was in a dangerous spot.

"I guess it's because I've never had sex with a woman who had reservations. If you're not with me a hundred percent, a hundred and ten percent, then we're both settling for less. Does that make any sense?"

She clenched her hands in front of her to keep from reaching for him. No man had ever cared whether she was with him 110 percent. As a result she'd never been that committed. She wondered what it would feel like to be that into sex with a man. *This* man. She wondered if she dared find out.

Chapter 15

Sean told himself he was a fool not to push her. From the way she'd kissed him, he thought she'd be willing. But he couldn't do it, not when she might regret it later. Man, this was the most complicated sex had *ever* been.

"Tell you what," he said. "Let's bag this subject for the time being."

"Good idea." Her shoulders relaxed. "Listen, why don't I just leave the food with you and head back to town? I'll grab something at the diner."

Automatically, Sean glanced at his watch to check the time, and only afterward realized he could see the damned thing perfectly. His eyesight was improving again. He didn't get it.

"The diner's not a good option," he said. "The kitchen's about to close."

"You're kidding."

"Most people eat at home in the evening. Joe keeps the kitchen going until six for the few who go out to dinner, but after that, there's only the Big Knobian, and they don't serve actual meals." Besides, he didn't want her to leave. But he decided to use logic instead of admitting to that.

"Okay. I'll pick something up from the deli in the grocery store."

"That'll be closed, too. You'd be stuck with pretzels and popcorn at the Big Knobian."

She looked flabbergasted. "Are you telling me you can't have dinner out after six at night around here?"

"That's about the size of it."

"I've never heard of such a thing. Big Knob needs a SaveALot, if for no other reason than the snack bar that's open twenty-four/seven."

He decided not to mention that people liked the town this way or they wouldn't have continued to live here. Natural selection had weeded out the ones who wanted that kind of convenience, and sent them off to Indianapolis or Evansville. A few adventurous souls had made it as far as Chicago, and one highflyer lived in New York, where the whole damned town was open twenty-four/seven.

The way he looked at it, if you kept a store open twenty-four/seven, that meant someone had to work the graveyard shift. That might be worth it for emergency services like police and fire, but for a hot dog? He didn't think so, and neither did most of the people in Big Knob.

"So how does the meat loaf sound to you now?" he asked.

She gazed at him. "Like my only choice." Then she caught her breath. "That sounded incredibly rude. I didn't mean it that way. I just—"

"Don't trust yourself."

She flushed. "That's one way of putting it."

"Then trust me. Nothing will happen that will make you hate yourself in the morning. I don't operate that way." He'd never had to, and he wasn't about to start now, even with his beloved property at stake.

"I believe you, and I'd love to stay for dinner." She studied him more closely. "I wish I could figure out what's going on with your hair, though."

"I know, it's a mess."

"Sometimes it is. Like this afternoon when you had that accident with Edith, it looked terrible, like you'd washed it with Elmer's Glue and then hacked at it with a table knife. It was too short in some places and too long in others."

The image made him wince because he figured it was pretty accurate. "Yeah, I've been having some trouble getting it to behave lately." Understatement of the century.

"Except now it looks pretty good. It's all about the right length, and it's not sticking out in every direction."

He ran his hand through it, and sure enough, it felt normal. He shrugged. "Who knows what's going on?" But he had an idea. The herbs Dorcas had given him seemed to work differently depending on the time of day. Maybe sunlight had one effect and darkness another. Or mealtimes. What else could it be?

"Your hair reminds me of a doll I used to have. You could pull her hair out to make it longer, or you could push a button in her back and the hair would retract inside her head again."

"I promise you my hair doesn't retract into my head. That's something a guy would notice."

She grinned. "Guess so."

"Tell you what. Let's take the food into the kitchen. I'll show you where everything is and you can start reheating it while I finish the trap and set it up outside. Those skunks will start moving around any minute, and I want to be ready for them."

"Then get busy on the trap." She seemed more at ease than she had been since she'd arrived. "I can find my way into the kitchen, and I'll bet I can even recognize a stove when I see one."

He hesitated a fraction of a second only because

he'd never had a woman in his house before, and it felt strange to just send her in there. "Sure. That's fine."

She must have caught that slight hesitation, because she immediately started backpedaling. "On second thought, you'd better show me where everything is. I'm sure you don't want somebody poking through your cupboards."

"I don't mind." The more he thought about it, the more he liked the idea of her in his house. After all his efforts to keep women out of it, he'd found one he'd love to have hang around.

"You're sure? After all, you kept those skunks so you wouldn't have to deal with women invading your privacy."

"Who told you that?"

"Jeremy."

He wondered what else Jeremy had told her. Over dinner he might ask. "Well, I used to feel that way, but things change."

She pulled her glasses out of the hip pocket of her jeans and put them on. Then she walked over and picked up her coat. "So I'll get started." She shook out the coat and started to shove one arm into the sleeve.

His response was automatic. "Here, let me help you with—"

"That's okay." She stepped out of reach. "I've got it. The less touching, the better."

"All right." He backed off and let her put on her coat and pick up the bag holding their dinner.

"I'll see you soon." She went out the door.

He sucked in a breath. What had he gotten himself into? Not five minutes ago he'd promised he wouldn't coax her into doing anything she would regret.

That might be easier said than done. His kitchen was so tiny that two adults would have a tough time moving around in it without bumping against each other. The next hour could get very interesting.

"There goes another chair." Dorcas heard the tell-tale crack right after she and Ambrose had achieved simultaneous orgasms, one of their specialties. How irritating. She would love to slump against her husband and enjoy the glow of predinner sex, but if they didn't move the operation somewhere else, they could both end up in a heap on the floor.

"Don't worry. I have you." With amazing strength for a man his age, Ambrose cupped her bottom and lifted her at the same time as he rose from the damaged chair. It crashed sideways, one leg destroyed by their antics.

"I love you." Dorcas wrapped her arms around his neck and nestled her cheek against his shoulder as he carried her to the bed.

"I love you, too."

"Before I forget, we need to head for the Whispering Forest after dinner and pay George a visit."

Ambrose deposited her gently on their feather bed and stretched out beside her. "What are you planning to say?"

"Just that SaveALot is coming, and we're doing all we can to stop it."

"So we masquerade as his savior."

"It's not a masquerade. We are saving him. Unless he transforms into the True Guardian of Whispering Forest and earns his gold scales, he'll never be happy." She molded herself against her husband and noted with satisfaction that his penis began to rise again. Ambrose had the sexual reactions of a seventeen-year-old, but then again, he should. She'd been lacing his coffee with yohimbe for years.

"And unless he earns his gold scales, we won't be allowed to leave Big Knob," Ambrose said.

"Exactly. But I do appreciate that he's a little bit bored out there. I ordered him an iPod and it arrived in the mail today. We'll call it an early Christmas present. He should like that."

"Are you sure he deserves a present? Last I noticed he was blowing off his forest-patrol chores so he could teach the raccoons to play Texas Hold 'Em with those cards he stole."

Dorcas sighed. "I know. Filching things from people who wander into Whispering Forest is a bad habit. But he's done well with that whispering trick to make them believe the place is haunted, and his gun-jamming skills are excellent."

"He's whispering to people because he loves scaring the living daylights out of them, and he's jamming guns because he doesn't want to get shot. Sorry, I'm not impressed. He's guarding the forest by accident, not design."

"I guess." Dorcas snuggled closer. "I was trying to look on the positive side. Can't you think of one thing he's doing right?"

"He makes awesome smoke rings, which is a talent good for . . . let me think . . . absolutely nothing. Face it, Dorcas, he's a screw-off who isn't taking the job seriously."

"You're right, you're right. But I'm hoping an actual present will demonstrate that we value him as an individual and he should value himself and the forest more."

"Or it will demonstrate that we're condoning his bad behavior."

"Maybe, but I think it's worth a shot. Anyway, enough about George." She curled her fingers around her own personal phallic treasure. "Have you noticed that Big Knob looks a lot like this?"

Ambrose lifted his head and looked down the length of his body. "Big Knob looks like my penis?"

"Not yours, specifically, but like a generic version."

"That must be why there are all the rumors about this place. Somehow that granite outcropping radiates sexual potency."

"That would explain Sean." She stroked him gently and was encouraged by the firmness of his response.

"Sean could be the tip of the iceberg. I'm betting this is one lusty town."

"Could be. Right now I'm only interested in one lusty wizard." Satisfied that he was prepped for another adventure, she levered herself to a sitting position and climbed aboard. Ah, that was good.

Ambrose cupped her breasts in both hands. "Wish we had our sex bench."

"Me, too." She began to ride him slowly. At their age, they could afford to take their time. "But Sean has other things on his mind right now."

Maggie closed the side door into the garage and started toward the small house. About that time something darted across her path. She noticed a streak of white, but the rest of the creature melted into the darkness.

Without being a wildlife expert, she could only guess, but she'd probably seen her first live skunk. It paused at the corner of the house, tail raised.

She didn't think a raised tail was a good sign. "Nice skunk," she said. "Good little skunk. I'm not going to hurt you, sweet little skunk." Calling a skunk *sweet* might be going a bit far, but she wasn't above flattery if it saved her from being sprayed with some noxious liquid.

Keeping an eye on the mostly invisible creature, she edged toward the bungalow's back door. What in hell was she doing out here, anyway? She was a city girl, out of her element in the woods with skunks and a small-town loverboy who probably wouldn't live up to his press.

Yeah, right. He was guaranteed to be good in bed, and she knew it. She'd never been kissed like that, even by sophisticated guys who drove Jags and flashed their no-limit American Express cards. Well, so she'd only dated one of those, and he'd been a self-important jerk. Sean could kiss rings around him.

As a result of Sean's talented mouth, she was currently dodging a skunk and climbing the steps to his back door so she could set up a homey little meal for the two of them. It wasn't exactly in line with the image she'd tried to cultivate for the past six months at the corporate offices of SaveALot.

In spite of that, she was having a good time. Helping Sean rescue a family of skunks from being poisoned felt right to her, even though she'd never met a skunk in the flesh, or in the fur, until a minute ago. Maybe this experience in Big Knob would provide her with anecdotes she could tell at the SaveALot Christmas party.

Or not. She'd been in this town less than a day, and she was already feeling protective of its backward ways and colorful residents. Edith Mae Hoogstraten and her old Buick might make a good watercooler story back in Houston, but Maggie didn't think she'd be telling it.

When the SaveALot corporate machine moved in, they wouldn't take any notice of people like Edith Mae, anyway. They'd be looking for cheap labor and cooperative building inspectors. Once the store was in place, the Edith Maes of the town would be categorized as potential customers, not individuals who had lived a lifetime in this area.

And that was as it should be. A company couldn't offer the kinds of bargains that SaveALot provided unless they dealt in volume sales. The people of Big Knob would have more choices at a lower cost. Most of them would be pleased about that.

Maggie opened the back door and stepped into

Sean's dark kitchen. After fumbling around on the wall beside the door, she located a light switch and flipped it on. Then she let out a sigh of pleasure.

The kitchen was small, but every nook and cranny had been lovingly utilized for storage. Maggie had never met a man who understood the need for storage, and here was one who not only understood it, he'd created it with his bare hands. Or his gloved hands, which was even sexier.

In any case, she was positive he'd built the handsome birch cabinets lining the kitchen walls. To her surprise, she liked knowing a guy was handy with tools. She'd had no clue that cabinetry could get her hot.

In her imagination she watched Sean building these cabinets, his gloved hands steady on the power saw, his eyes focused on the whirring blade. No doubt about it, he had a sexy job, far sexier than the corporate hotshots she'd spent the past six months with.

She wasn't here to admire the cabinets, though. She'd offered to get dinner on the table, and even a kitchen klutz like her should be able to reheat food and serve it up on a plate. Taking off her coat, she draped it over one of the chairs surrounding the oak table. Then she pulled out all the Tupperware containers and got to work.

Ten minutes later, she had places set and food steaming. She'd never felt so domestic in her life. It wasn't a realistic perception, because someone else had cooked the food and this wasn't even her kitchen. If she was feeling all *Little House on the Prairie,* she needed to realize it was an illusion.

Everything about Big Knob seemed surreal, now that she thought about it. If she wasn't careful, she'd fall in with their time-warp mentality and start imagining that closing up all businesses except the local tavern at six on a Friday night was perfectly normal.

The back door opened. "Sure smells good," Sean said as he hung his coat on a peg by the door.

Maggie blinked. His comment was straight out of a suburban sitcom, ranking right up there with *Honey, I'm home!* Except no guy in any sitcom she'd ever watched kissed like Sean.

They didn't do passionate lip-locks in family shows. No matter what illusion she was working with here, it was definitely R-rated, maybe even bordering on X. Instead of sitting down at the oak table with Sean, she wanted him to shove her onto its smooth surface and unzip her jeans.

"Your timing's good." She kept her tone light, as if she weren't having thoughts of wild sex on the kitchen table. "Everything's ready." *Me, too, in case you were wondering.*

"Great." He moved to the sink and turned on the water to wash his hands. "I set the trap. In an hour or so I'll go check and see if it worked."

"Good. By the way, I really love your cabinets."

"Thanks. Me, too." He lathered up.

Judging from their sedate conversation, they might as well be an old married couple who shared the evening meal every day of their lives. She prepared the food and he trapped the skunks and built the cabinets, a neat division of labor. She should be horrified to find herself in such a clichéd situation. Instead the pit of her stomach grew warm with happiness, and her sexual needs simmered below the surface, ready to burst into flame at the slightest provocation.

Maybe this was how life was for those who were well matched. But other than the obvious sexual attraction, she and Sean were polar opposites. He would hate living in her world and she'd have to give up all her ambitious dreams to live in his. Giving up dreams was never a good idea.

But giving up the potential for great sex didn't seem

too brilliant, either. As Sean grabbed a towel and dried his hands, she found herself watching those hands and imagining them stroking her naked body.

He turned and caught her staring. "What's up?"

"I want to make sure we understand each other." She wondered how she'd ever thought he was homely. For some reason he'd left his glasses in the garage, and without them, he was looking superhot again.

"Understand each other about what?"

"I'm here to buy that property for SaveALot." She thought of him naked and almost forgot to breathe. "Once I do, I'm heading back to my life in Houston."

"Yeah, you keep saying that."

"Because I mean it." She tried not to look at the crotch of his jeans, but her glance kept straying there. "Sex between us would change nothing." But discussing it made her quiver so much she could barely stand.

"Okay." Holding her gaze, he reached behind him and laid the towel on the counter.

"So I don't see what's in it for you."

He studied her, as if hesitant to say. Finally he took a deep breath. "Look, I haven't had sex in almost a year. Until you showed up today, I had no interest in it. I was beginning to wonder if that was the end of my dream of having a wife and kids. If so, then I sure as hell wouldn't need that big old house."

"Whoa." She backed up a step and clamped down on her libido. Going to bed with a guy who was wife hunting would be cruel and unfair. "If you're thinking that I might—"

"No way. I'm not a complete idiot. But if sex with you is good, then I'll know I'm not dead inside."

The blowtorch of lust fired up again and her panties grew damp. "So I'm like therapy?"

He smiled. "I think we'd have more fun than that. But I don't want you feeling upset about it afterward."

She began to tremble. "I won't if we're clear about our motivation."

His voice softened. "I just gave you mine. What's yours, Maggie?"

She knew it, but she wasn't sure she could say it. She gathered her courage. "I want you. I'm going crazy from wanting you."

His green eyes glowed with heat. "I like that motivation."

"But we're supposed to have dinner."

He reached for her, pulling her tight against his hard body. Gently he took off her glasses and laid them behind him on the counter. "Dinner can wait."

Chapter 16

He could have her. Here, in the kitchen, exactly as he'd fantasized. And it was his fantasy for a change. In the hundreds of times he'd had sex with a woman, he'd always been a part of *her* fantasy. Now Maggie was giving him a chance to act out his own.

Cradling her cheek in one hand, he gazed down at her, savoring the picture of what would happen between them very soon. The kitchen smelled of meat loaf now, but soon it would smell of meat loaf and sex. He couldn't think of a better combination than that. Down-home cooking mingled with down-home loving.

Leaning toward her, he touched his mouth to hers, putting all his gratitude and anticipation into that kiss. Then he released her and stepped away. "Stay right there. Don't move." He hated to leave and take a chance on breaking the mood, but if he wanted condoms, he had no choice.

She gazed up at him, her blue eyes bright. "We're not going to the bedroom, then?"

"Maybe next time."

Her mouth curved in a secret smile. "Okay."

"But I have to get something." Hurrying down the hall, he ducked into the bathroom and wrenched open the cabinet. Ah. The box was where he'd remembered.

He opened it, pocketed one foil packet and headed back down the hall.

God, he hoped she hadn't changed her mind in that short time. When he walked into the kitchen and found her topless, he decided she hadn't. If anything, her mind was completely made up.

But her mind wasn't the focus of his attention right now. He gulped as she cupped her breasts in both hands.

"Earlier today you asked me if there was anything wrong with these," she said.

His tongue stuck to the roof of his mouth. "Mmph." He'd never seen such beautiful breasts in his life— so pale, so perfectly formed, so sweetly dusted with cinnamon freckles. Her rosy nipples puckered as if begging for a kiss.

"As you can see, there's nothing wrong with them." He shook his head.

She let her hands fall to her sides as she walked toward him. "Touch me, Sean. I've been wanting you to ever since this afternoon."

His hands trembled as he came in contact with her silky skin. A groan slipped out. She was so soft, so very warm. And his fantasy was about to come true.

Sliding both hands to her waist, he lifted her and turned, positioning her in front of him on the granite counter. Then he lowered his head and proceeded to enjoy the bounty she'd offered him.

She seemed happy about that. Bracing her hands behind her on the counter, she leaned back, lifting her breasts in an erotic move that drove him wild. The kitchen filled with the sounds of his mouth and tongue, blended with her soft moans of delight.

He licked and sucked until her skin gleamed with moisture. He gave thanks for the return of his eyesight, which allowed him to trace each freckle with the tip of his tongue until she began to writhe against the granite counter.

Her breathing became labored. "Sean . . . I need . . ."

Filling in the blanks took no imagination at all. He knew exactly what she needed. He slipped off her shoes but didn't bother with her socks. Her jeans and panties took more effort, but she helped, lifting herself off the counter so he could pull them off.

"You, too," she murmured, her gaze hot as it swept over him.

He had one uneasy moment as he worried about whether his body would be less than studly. He'd never had to think about that before, and it was a little unnerving. His eyesight was better, though, and so was his hair. Maybe his dick was its usual size, too.

If not, he'd keep her too busy to notice. Vowing not to let that kind of nonsense affect his enjoyment of the moment, he shucked his clothes. As he tossed them aside, he noticed a stick of butter sitting on a saucer on the counter nearby.

Normally he wasn't inventive when it came to sex. He'd left that to the women who worked so hard to seduce him. But this time when he saw that butter, he became inspired. It had been placed too close to the stove and was losing its shape. Perfect.

Plunging his fingers into it, he turned back to Maggie. All along he'd planned to butter her up, but until this moment, he hadn't thought he'd be doing it literally.

Her gaze traveled over him, pausing when it reached his erect penis. He fought the urge to look down and see if it measured up. When her mouth curved in a smile of appreciation, the small knot of anxiety in his chest relaxed. The getting naked part would be okay.

Then she glanced at the butter on his fingers and sucked in a breath.

"Hold still," he murmured. Moving between her thighs, he began smearing the butter on her breasts.

"Ahhhhh." Leaning back, she closed her eyes and ran her tongue over her mouth. "Incredible."

The sensation of rubbing the creamy butter over her warm skin nearly sent him over the edge. If her rapid breathing was any indication, the buttery massage was having the same effect on her. His oiled hands slid over her breasts in long, sensuous strokes, as if he were molding her, shaping her for the sex they would soon have. In the light spilling from the overhead fixture, she began to gleam like polished marble.

Scooping more butter from the dish, he extended his range, covering her rib cage and moving down over her flat tummy. Skirting his ultimate goal, he rubbed the butter over her thighs.

He paused when he saw the faint bruise where he'd rammed into her with the skunk trap. "I did hurt you, after all."

Her voice was low and throaty. "Kiss it and make it better."

Falling to his knees, he kissed her there, gently, with a slow sweep of his tongue at the end. From the way she caught her breath, he imagined he could read her mind. Slowly he began massaging butter onto her inner thighs, making circles that brought him ever closer to his final destination.

The scent of her drew him, made his cock throb with wanting her. But first . . . his oiled fingers thrust deep, sliding effortlessly inside her wet channel as she arched upward and groaned. Leaning forward, he used his tongue in rhythm with his fingers, while his senses filled with the aroma of warm butter and hot woman.

She whimpered and braced her feet on his shoulders. As she began to thrash about on the slippery counter, he grasped her hips with both hands and pressed his mouth fully against her heat. With a strangled cry, she came, her body quaking in his grip.

He nearly came himself, but managed to control the pounding need in his groin. As the urge to climax ebbed, he held her, kissing her damp curls until she grew still and her breathing slowed. Still on his knees, he dragged his jeans over with one hand and found the condom in his pocket. He put it on while kneeling there, afraid if he stood, his legs might not hold him. He'd never been so dizzy with lust.

Using the support of the counter, he pulled himself to his feet. Her head was thrown back, her eyes closed, her oiled breasts quivering with every breath. Her sexy vulnerability gave him new strength.

She was perched a little too high for him to take her while she sat on the counter. "Wrap your legs around my hips," he murmured.

Her eyes fluttered open, and they were darkened by the same needs flowing through him. Wordlessly, holding his gaze, she clutched his shoulders and circled his hips with her legs.

Sliding her slick body off the counter, he lowered her just enough. . . . Right *there*. With a guttural sound of satisfaction, he pushed home.

Her eyes widened and her lips parted. The flame flickering in her blue eyes ignited as his fingers dug into her soft bottom, holding them both steady. If he came now, they would collapse onto the floor. And he was so close.

Thank God for a small kitchen. Turning away from the counter, he eased her to the table. Silverware clattered to the floor as he swept it aside. Then he lowered her to the smooth surface. Keeping his feet on the floor, he leaned forward, rubbing his chest against her gleaming skin.

The sensual friction, made even more erotic by the

slickness of the melted butter, wiped out what was left of his control. Easing his hips back, he began pumping hard and fast, sliding back and forth across her belly and her breasts with each rapid movement of his hips.

She stayed right with him, clutching his arms and begging for more. Their pace grew more frantic, until the table rocked and the wooden legs thumped the floor with each thrust. He meant to wait for her, meant to make sure that she came again, but his climax would not be denied.

The impending force of it wrenched a groan from him that filled the tiny kitchen. As he drove into her, the spasms ripping through him, she lifted her hips and cried out his name. Her orgasm rolled over his penis, intensifying his contractions until he wondered if he would disintegrate from the power of it.

Finally there was no sound but their ragged breathing. He rested his cheek against her shoulder and shifted his arm position. In the process he brushed against something, and the last piece of silverware fell to the floor with a tinny clang. He smiled. End of Round One.

Chapter 17

Maggie had promised herself she wouldn't regret having sex with Sean, and it was going to be an easy promise to keep. As she lay stretched out on his kitchen table in a stupor of satisfaction, she couldn't imagine regretting the most uninhibited experience of her life.

She didn't recognize this Maggie Grady. The person she'd thought she was would never be caught naked and smeared with butter in the kitchen of a man she'd met twelve hours earlier. Could that possibly be right? Had she only met Sean this morning?

Of course, that was the point of uninhibited behavior. You didn't assess the situation for days before you took action. You seized the moment. Which she had pretty much done when she'd started taking off her clothes.

Sean nuzzled her ear. "You okay?"

The warmth of his mouth made her shiver with pleasure. "Couldn't be better."

"That wasn't too wild?"

"It was the wildest thing I've ever done." She ran a finger up his backbone. "And I loved it."

"Good to know. So did I."

"Good therapy?"

"The best." His breath tickled her neck. "But I haven't fed you yet."

"I just found out something. Climaxes make me forget about food."

"Me, too." He lifted his head and brushed his lips across hers. "How do you feel about shared showers?"

"Think we need one?"

"Nah." He nibbled on her lower lip. "I just want the pleasure of lathering you up."

That one little suggestion was all it took for her to start feeling achy and liquid again. After this session in his kitchen, she had no trouble believing Sean was the toast of Big Knob's female population. Stupid as it was, she was feeling a little jealous about that.

She pinched his firm butt. "I'll bet you say that to all the girls."

Propping himself on one elbow, he looked down at her. "You probably won't believe this, but I don't say that to all the girls."

She gazed back at him. He was a little blurry, but she could make out the sparkle in his green eyes. "Okay, then, most of the girls."

He kissed the tip of her nose. "None of the girls."

"C'mon. I'm not that naive. I know you've had a lot of sex."

"Yeah, but as I've explained before, I was never the instigator."

She rolled her eyes. "Poor you. Suffering through all those horizontal tangos."

"I didn't suffer, but I didn't make sexy suggestions, either. Didn't need to."

"So they'd be the ones dragging you into the shower with them?"

"Pretty much." His eyes crinkled at the corners as he smiled. "But I like this way better. Let's go."

Before she quite knew his intention, he'd slid off of

her, leaned down and hoisted her over his shoulder in a fireman's carry.

"Hey, I can walk!"

"But isn't this more fun?"

"I'll let you know when it's over. You might bang my head against the doorjamb on your way to the shower." Yet she was secretly thrilled with his take-charge attitude.

No man had ever hauled her off to the shower, where he intended to have his way with her. And there was no doubt that Sean intended to have his way with her. She planned to let him, too.

Moments later she was leaning against the tiled wall of Sean's shower because the way he was soaping her up had turned her legs into wet noodles. Who knew her belly button was a pleasure point? She'd heard that some women liked having the backs of their knees stroked, but she'd never understood why until Sean did it with soapy hands.

Then he showed her how much she loved having someone rub the inside of her elbows and the arch of each foot. She seemed to be chock-full of erogenous zones, not even counting the obvious places, like her breasts.

Naturally, when he finally slipped his hand between her thighs, she went crazy. But he stopped before she was able to come, which was slightly frustrating.

Then he turned on the handheld shower, and she understood his evil plan. "I get that next," she said.

"You get it now." He began running the spray over her body.

"No, I mean I get to use it on you."

"Maybe." He trained the spray on her nipples until they tightened into hard little buds. "If you're good."

She sank back against the tile as she began to tremble from the effects of the water. "And what does that mean?"

"I want you to come for me."

She gasped as he brought the pulsing jets down over her belly. She knew exactly where he was going with that thing, and she could hardly wait. "I don't think that will be a problem."

He handed her the showerhead. "Then it's all yours."

She almost dropped it. "But I thought you . . . I thought you were going to . . ."

"So did I." His eyes glowed with hunger. "That was my original idea. But I seem to be getting more creative in my old age. I'd rather watch you do it."

"To myself?" she squeaked.

"Uh-huh." His gaze taunted her. "Think you can?"

"I don't know." But there was a vixen inside her clamoring to get out. That vixen had loved having sex on the kitchen table. She would probably also love masturbating with the showerhead in front of this extremely sexy man.

Maggie swallowed. Then she took a shaky breath and spread her legs. "Okay. Watch this."

Sean had thought he knew what good sex was all about. After all, until about a year ago he'd been having it constantly, and he'd felt satisfied after every episode. Turned out he'd been clueless.

He'd allowed his partners to have all the ideas, and naturally they'd done what turned them on. He was beginning to understand what turned *him* on, and watching Maggie work with the showerhead was definitely high on his list.

She was tentative at first, whisking the spray over that triangle of red curls as if she were washing a car. She wouldn't look at him, either. He waited, waited for her to get serious about giving herself an orgasm. Surely she'd done that before, but maybe not with an audience.

Gradually her movements became more focused.

Then she glanced up at him, ran her tongue over her lips, and pressed that nozzle tight against her crotch. He trembled in a sudden rush of adrenaline, as if he were about to come instead of her. Maybe he could, just as a not-so-innocent bystander. But he wouldn't. This was all about her.

He knew the moment she abandoned her shyness, the moment nothing mattered but what was going on in her hot little body. Her eyes got very bright and she began to breathe quickly through her mouth.

Then she leaned against the shower wall and lifted herself so the showerhead gave her maximum stimulation. She moaned and shifted her position again, gaining even more access to the pulsing jets. Sean wondered if he'd be able to stand there without touching her. He ached unbearably.

But he'd asked her to do this, and he wouldn't interfere. He just . . . wished . . . she'd . . . come. Then she did, gasping and writhing against the slick tile as she clutched the showerhead so tightly that her knuckles showed white.

She let it go and it whipped around, blasting him and the rest of the shower stall as it twirled on its connection. She didn't seem to notice. She was lost in the grip of her climax, and he was right there with her, experiencing the spasms as if they were his own.

But they weren't, and he was stiff as a Jedi light saber. He wouldn't blame her if she was ready to call it quits for now, though. She was panting like a long-distance runner, and her cheeks were the color of ripe strawberries.

She turned her gaze on him, as if asking what next.

"We can get dressed now, if you want," he said.

She surveyed him, her attention lingering on the light saber look-alike that was pointed straight at her. She cleared her throat. "You might . . . you might have trouble getting that out of sight."

If he hadn't been so damn aroused he might have laughed. "A little cold water should do the trick."

"I have a better idea." Grabbing the dangling showerhead, she walked over toward him and sank to her knees.

He wondered if her idea had any similarity to his. He sure hoped so.

Slowly she worked him over with the pulsing jets, making sure to hit his penis and his balls with equal accuracy. He couldn't decide if it felt good or if she was only taking him higher with no relief in sight.

Apparently that was only her warm-up exercise, because next she filled her mouth with warm water from the showerhead. Holding it there, she took his penis in her mouth without spilling hardly any of that water. He knew because he was watching her, which only added to the pressure building in his groin.

When she began to swish that warm water around so it rippled over the sensitive underside of his shaft, he lost the battle in two seconds. He had no time to think of whether this was cool, or whether she'd storm out of the shower in protest afterward. He just came because that was all he could do under those conditions.

And she . . . swallowed.

He'd tried so hard to stay neutral on the issue of Maggie, knowing she'd leave town soon, knowing she had no plans for a future with him. But when he heard the soft sound of her throat moving, he knew he'd been kidding himself. He was in up to the hilt of his cock. When it came to Maggie Grady, there was no easy way out. Not anymore.

Maggie wasn't used to offering blow jobs, especially this early in a relationship. But apparently all her usual behavior had gone out the window when it came to Sean. Somehow he'd flipped the switch from *Be*

Cautious to *Anything Goes*. She couldn't turn back now.

Truth was, she didn't want to turn back. They laughed and kidded like old friends as they toweled each other off. Then they found their clothes, struggled into them, and ate a little cold meat loaf and congealed mashed potatoes before they bundled up in their coats and headed outside to check on the skunks.

None of this seemed the least bit strange to her. Someday it might, but for now, she was going along with the program. She was having too much fun to question whether she was being foolish or wise.

"Stay by the front corner of the house," Sean said as they descended the back steps. "Let me see if they're in there or not." His breath made little clouds in the cold air.

Maggie paused where she'd been instructed to wait, and put on Sean's glasses. The night seemed sort of glittery, like the lighting in an Italian restaurant, so she looked up to see if the clouds had moved away. They were gone, but omigod, the *stars*. She'd never seen so many.

"Is this normal?" she whispered.

He turned back. "Probably not, but I'm doing it, anyway."

"No, I mean the stars. Are we having a meteor shower or something like that?"

Sean glanced skyward. "Not that I can see."

"But they're *everywhere*."

He smiled. "Yeah, I know. That's why I could never live in the city."

That was certainly pointed. He'd almost come right out and said that if she'd had any idea that he'd follow her like a puppy dog back to Houston, she might as well kill the thought. So she would. Thoughtful of him to remind her that this canoodling, though delicious, was temporary.

Crouching beside a pile of evergreen branches, Sean turned his flashlight beam to low and swung it over the ground. "Paw prints," he murmured. "Good deal."

"Is the trap closed?" Maggie called out softly.

"Not yet." He reached under the branches.

Maggie held her breath. Belatedly she remembered that skunks had teeth. They could bite the hand that was trying to save them.

Then she heard some soft murmurs and realized that he was talking to the skunks. Now, that was seriously weird, but touching, too. His voice was low and soothing, and his words simple, as if he were consoling a child.

"You're okay," he said. "I'm closing this now, but I won't hurt you, I promise. You need to find a new home, and I'm going to help you. Take it easy. Don't be afraid."

After snapping something metal into place, he stood. "Now I'll see if they're all inside or not. I was afraid to shine the flashlight in for fear I'd startle them."

"Can I come over there now?"

"Sure. They're either in there or they're not. Let's find out." Slowly he removed one of the pine branches covering the trap.

She walked cautiously over the soggy ground toward him, her running shoes making a squishing sound. "I didn't know I was hanging out with the Skunk Whisperer."

"Yeah, well, that's probably dumb, but I've gotten in the habit of talking to them." He moved another branch and peered through the wire mesh. "Wow, they really are snoozing in there. Dorcas was right about the effects."

"Dorcas? What does she have to do with this?"

"She gave me the bait and said it would have a

tranquilizing effect. It works on their cat when they travel."

"And where does she get this stuff?" Maggie's suspicions about Dorcas and Ambrose were growing with every new bit of information. Now she was adding *drug runner* to the potential list of their crimes.

"She makes it."

"I see."

"She makes all kinds of herbal things." He leaned closer to the trap. "I'm trying to count them in there, but they're all lumped together in a pile. I think there's five, though. That would be right. Two adults and three babies, although the babies are pretty big by now."

"Sean, have you ever considered that Dorcas and Ambrose put something in that wine they gave you?"

"Like what?"

"An aphrodisiac."

He looked up and gazed at her a moment. Then he shook his head. "Nah. It was sealed and everything."

"Maybe they bottled it themselves." From his silence she could tell he was thinking about it. "If it was a strong enough aphrodisiac," she said, "then we could still be feeling the effects."

"So what you're saying is that instead of us having natural chemistry, we're under the influence of some substance Dorcas put in the wine?"

"You have to admit that would explain a lot."

He sighed. "I don't like to think that's what's been going on. I'd rather believe this was our idea, not the result of some artificial stimulant."

"Me, too." Thinking they'd been manipulated like that did take some of the joy out of their romp tonight. "Maybe I'm wrong. Didn't you say you were attracted to me this morning when we first met? That was before you'd had any wine."

"No, it wasn't. Not really. Don't forget I had it the night before. That's how I knew it would be great stuff."

"Well." She took a deep breath. "I guess we'll find out, won't we? It should wear off by tomorrow. If we see each other tomorrow and there's no spark, we'll know it was the wine."

"That's a depressing concept. That would mean my sex life is still down the tubes."

"And I'm not as uninhibited as I thought."

He put his arms around her and drew her close. "I think you are. And if we didn't have the skunks to worry about, I'd prove it right out here in the front yard."

Just like that, her libido spiked. "By doing what?"

"We have pine boughs." He reached in his coat pocket, pulled out a packet and rubbed it over her nose. "I have a condom."

"We'd freeze our tushes off!" But the idea had her juiced up and ready to go.

"I might, being the one on top, but you wouldn't." He pulled her in tight against his crotch. "I'd keep you warm. Very, very warm."

She moaned softly. "No fair. Now I want to."

"After we take care of the skunks, we can see about having some outdoor sex."

"If the wine hasn't worn off."

"If it's the wine, then we might as well make the most of it until it does wear off." He kissed her swiftly. "Let's move the skunks so we can start having more sex."

Sean carefully loaded the trap into the back of his pickup, expecting at any moment that the skunks would wake up and start spraying everything in sight. Fortunately for him and Maggie, that didn't happen. He covered the trap with the pine boughs and put a shovel and a tarp in the back so he could create a home for them in the woods. Then he helped Maggie into the passenger seat, and they were off.

The wine situation was bugging him, though. He would love to call Dorcas and Ambrose on his cell and ask them flat out if they'd spiked it, but he didn't want to do that with Maggie there. He might slip up and say something he didn't want her to hear about the herbs they'd given him. For now, they seemed to be a nonfactor.

No, that wasn't really true. His brain was working much more creatively than it had yesterday, especially when it came to sex. He'd started planning ahead, which was why he'd brought along a condom, even though he'd had no idea when and where he'd use it. He'd never made love to a woman on a bed of pine boughs before, either, and yet the thought had come to him so easily.

He wouldn't mind hanging on to the creative ideas that seemed to be part of his transformation. Maybe Dorcas could isolate that particular ingredient and give him more. That would be awesome.

"Your friend Jeremy seems like a nice guy," Maggie said as they drove down the dark, deserted highway.

Sean went on alert. "He didn't ask you out, did he?"

"No, of course not."

"Why say *of course not* as if you didn't expect him to?" Sean needed to talk to Jeremy and make absolutely sure he had no designs on Maggie.

"Because if he's like most men, he was warned off by my attitude."

"I don't know what you mean." Sean thought she was totally hot and Jeremy would see that, too.

"When I'm on the job, which I was this afternoon, I'm all business. That usually scares men away."

"It had zero effect on me."

"But that could have been the wine."

"I don't think so." At least he didn't want to think so.

They reached the dirt road that led off into the forest on the north side. Sean slowed the truck and crossed the road with care. He didn't want to jostle the skunks unnecessarily. That meant taking the dirt road slow, too.

"It sure is dark out here," Maggie said. "I don't know if I've ever been in a place where there are absolutely no lights."

"I wanted to release them where they wouldn't bother anybody. And nobody comes out here."

"Looks like the perfect teenage make-out spot to me. Much better than the area behind your house, especially when it's so cold out." She paused. "Um, I meant to say, the area behind *that old* house."

"I heard you the first time. It is my house. You just haven't admitted that yet."

"Let's not talk about it tonight."

"Okay, let's not." Sean eased the truck down the dirt road at a pace slower than he could have walked it. But he couldn't very well carry a cage full of skunks, so driving was the only option.

"So how come there aren't kids out here parking?" Maggie asked. "It's Friday night. Or don't kids park in Big Knob?"

"Oh, they park. Just not in this part of the woods."

"Why not? They'd have all the privacy in the world."

"Oh, you know. Silly rumors."

"Sean Madigan, if this is the place where the guy with the hook for a hand is supposed to hang out and prey on teenagers making out in the woods, we're leaving."

He laughed. "Where did a city girl like you hear that story?"

"Every teenager in America has heard that story,

whether they've ever gone parking in the woods or not."

"There's no guy with a hook out here." Watching the road in the truck's headlights, he found the spot he'd located some time ago. Back in the trees a little ways was a hollow log that would make a good hiding place for the skunks, in addition to the cage, which he planned to leave out here for them to use as home base.

"You still haven't explained why nobody comes out here."

Sean pulled the truck to the side of the road and shifted into neutral. "Well, the pioneers called this section Whispering Forest."

"That's kind of cool. Trees do seem to whisper when the wind blows."

"Yeah, but apparently some people hear actual words. They say the place is haunted."

"What?"

He glanced over at her. "Don't worry. It's not."

"Of course it isn't. That's crazy." In the glow of the dash lights her freckles stood out as if she might really be scared. "But just for kicks, is there anything besides the whispering going on?"

"Oh, you know. People let their imagination run away with them and think they see and hear things."

"Such as?" Her voice sounded a little higher than usual.

"Oh, strange noises. Roaring and grumbling, mostly."

"Are there bears in these woods?"

Sean shook his head. "Not for years."

"Then the noise could be a plane going overhead."

"Yeah, or a semi driving by on the road."

Her voice steadied. "Right. Out here you could dream up all sorts of things that weren't real. So, what else?"

"The usual spooky stuff—disembodied eyes."

"For heaven's sake. Talk about ridicu—" Suddenly she gripped his arm and pointed a shaky hand at something over his left shoulder. "L-like that?"

Chapter 18

Sean looked out his window. "I don't see anything."

"They're . . . they're gone." Maggie stared at the spot, her heart racing. "But I swear to you, I saw *eyes*."

"I believe you. Probably an owl."

"No. I've seen owl eyes, and these were no owl eyes. They were *red*."

"You've seen owl eyes? I thought you were a city girl."

"I saw them in the movies, okay? And they were yellow, not red."

He turned back to her. "Was this in a cartoon?"

"Yes, but don't go all Davy Crockett on me and act like I don't know what I'm talking about. Owl eyes are big and round, like this." She held circled fingers up to her eyes. "These were oval, like this." She shrank the circle.

"So it was a bobcat or a raccoon."

"Six feet off the ground?"

"A bobcat or a raccoon in a tree."

She didn't believe that for a minute. "Shine your flashlight over there."

He did, sweeping the beam over a bunch of leafless

trees with a few evergreens mixed in. No eyes showed up. Nothing showed up except the trees.

Maggie was starting to feel like a wuss, except that she had seen *something*. He was right, though. Her knowledge of wildlife was pretty much confined to the zoo and whatever Disney had to say on the subject.

"You can stay in the truck with the doors locked while I take care of the skunks," he said.

"No, I want to help." A tough cookie like her couldn't let a pair of red eyes scare her off. Besides, Sean had put a shovel in the back of the truck. A shovel made a decent weapon. She wasn't sure how well it worked against a ghost, but she didn't believe in those. Much.

"If you're sure." His gaze was gentle. "I can handle it if you'd rather not get out."

"Yeah, but would you respect me in the morning?"

He smiled. "I don't blame you for being spooked. You're not used to the woods at night."

She didn't point out that the entire town, with the exception of Sean, Mr. Ghost Buster, was spooked by Whispering Forest. She didn't want to align herself with that superstitious lot. She wanted to align herself with Sean. Preferably naked and horizontal.

But she did have one concern. "When you talked about having outdoor sex, did you mean here?"

His smile widened. "Would you do it?"

No, and hell, no! "Absolutely." She tried to keep her teeth from chattering. "If you're game, so am I."

"I wasn't planning to have outdoor sex here," he said. "We might scare the skunks."

She relaxed. "Well, there's that."

"I meant back at my place, and maybe we shouldn't even do it then. The bed's more cozy."

"Well, just so you know, I could get it on right out here in these dark woods. I could do that."

"I'm sure you could." He leaned forward and kissed

her firmly, then released her and opened his door.
"But we need to stop talking about sex, because I
can't carry a skunk trap when I have an erection."

"Are you going to leave the motor running?"

He glanced over his shoulder. "Mine or the
truck's?"

"Good one." She laughed, feeling braver by the second. "I meant the truck's."

"I'm leaving the truck running so I can use the
headlights to see where we're going. As for my own
personal motor, I can't seem to find the off switch
where you're concerned."

Maggie savored that for a minute. She couldn't recall any man ever saying that he was overcome with
passion whenever he was with her. Now that one had,
she felt a new image coming on, one that involved
living lusty and living large. She was definitely getting
out of this truck and helping Sean with the skunks.

The air was cold after the warmth of the cab. She
belted her trench coat more tightly and walked to the
back of the truck, where Sean had lifted a pine bough
to check on the skunks.

"Still asleep," he said. "Let's leave them there while
we dig a pit for the trap."

"Right." Maggie rubbed her hands together. "I'm
good with a shovel." *A snow shovel, that is,* and she
hadn't wielded one of those since leaving Chicago.

"Then let's do it." He handed her the shovel. "You
can carry that and I'll take the tarp." He gathered the
folded blue vinyl into his arms. "This way."

In the glow from the headlights, she followed him
into the forest, being careful to step over tree roots
while she watched for red eyes. Ahead of them lay
the hollow log Sean mentioned. Something could be
in that hollow log. She hoped nothing was.

Little puffs of fog came out with each exhalation.
"I feel like a fire-breathing dragon," she said.

"I'm really glad you're not," he said. "I'm not into interspecies sex."

"I thought we weren't going to talk about sex anymore."

"I can't help myself. You're walking along beside me through the woods, so naturally I keep thinking of your warm, silky body and how much I want to touch you again. Nobody else is around, so we could do anything we wanted to. It's tempting."

She was tempted, too, at least as much as he was. But Red Eyes was out there somewhere, and she thought that might prevent her from totally enjoying the experience. "We don't want to risk scaring the skunks," she reminded him.

"They'd probably sleep right through it."

Maggie sucked in a deep breath, hoping the extra oxygen would give her courage. She'd already announced her willingness to have sex in the woods, so she couldn't back out now without looking like a chicken. The air smelled like the bag of potting soil she'd bought last summer when she'd had the urge to grow some houseplants. It also smelled like something burning.

"Sean, do you smell smoke?"

He stopped to sniff the air. "A little. Probably drifted here from someone's chimney."

"We seem like a long way from the nearest chimney."

"I suppose. Maybe somebody's camping on the other side of the highway." He shrugged. "At least I know we don't have to worry about a forest fire. Everything's so wet it would never burn."

They reached the hollow log and Sean laid down the tarp. "I'll take the shovel now."

"But I want to dig."

"Really?"

"Really. I'm invested in this project." She hefted

the shovel, ready to jab it into the wet dirt. "Give me the plan."

He sent her a glance that warmed her in places that had nothing to do with sex. She had the fleeting thought that if they started liking each other a lot, that would be inconvenient. She could give up the sex, but she'd hate to lose a friend, too.

He drew a square in the dirt with the toe of his boot. "We need a pit about this size, so the trap will fit down in it. Once it's dug, we'll lay the tarp in the hole so they won't be on wet dirt to start with."

"That's sweet."

"It's probably totally unnecessary. But they have a dry place under the house, so I wanted them to have a reasonably dry place out here, at least to start with."

Yep, she was really starting to like this guy. Jabbing the shovel into the damp dirt, she shoveled until she was breathless.

When she paused, Sean came over. "Let me take a turn."

"If you insist." She hated to let him know that her arm muscles quivered from the effort. And she'd made a hole about the size of shoebox. As Sean went to work on the hole, she saw immediately that her technique had been flawed. After sticking the shovel partway into the ground, he stomped on the flat edge, forcing it another six inches in.

He'd probably noticed that she wasn't doing it right, but he hadn't said a word. She gave him points for that. Not every guy would have been able to resist instructing her in the proper way to wield a shovel.

When he was about half finished, she asked for the shovel back. This time she did it his way and it went faster, but her muscles ached, anyway. She tried not to show it, but eventually he tapped her on the shoulder.

"I think you need another break," he said.

"Maybe." She gave up the shovel and dragged in

air. She was turning into quite the sissy. She shouldn't care, but something about this place made her want to show that she had the right stuff, that she could do her share.

Something about this place also made her want to grab Sean and shove him up against the nearest tree so she could have her way with him. He was breathing heavily from the shoveling, which made her remember how it had felt the last time she'd heard him panting like that.

He had a wonderful natural rhythm for that activity. She closed her eyes and allowed herself to relive the feel of that delicious friction as he'd thrust deep, sending the kitchen table rocking. Maybe outdoor sex right here and now wasn't such a bad idea, especially if the skunks were still sleepy-bye.

Maybe they should make use of the tarp before setting it up for the skunks. Oh yeah, the tarp would work fine. It would be smooth under her bare bottom, allowing her to slide a little, rise to meet him as he entered her.

The scene felt so real that she could hear him whispering in her ear. . . . *Hey, hot mama, whatcha doin' out here in the forest?* Wait a minute. That didn't sound like something Sean would say.

"Maggie, are you okay?"

She opened her eyes immediately, embarrassed that he'd caught her fantasizing. "Sure! Fine! Why do you ask?"

"Your eyes were closed and you were moaning and rocking a little bit. You looked sort of—sort of possessed."

"Uh, I was—" She cast around for an explanation that wouldn't sound ridiculous and couldn't find one. "Wow, look at that! The hole's finished!"

"If you can give me a hand with the tarp . . ."

"Sure thing." Fantasizing about making out on the

tarp was one thing. Having the nerve to suggest it to him was a whole new level, and she wasn't there yet. Then she thought about the words whispered in her ear, the words that hadn't sounded like ones Sean would use. Had it been the ghost of Whispering Forest?

No, definitely not. If she didn't watch out, she'd spook herself and end up looking like a fraidy-cat in front of Sean. She vowed to concentrate on helping him with the tarp and forget about whispers and disembodied eyes.

They positioned the tarp so it was lining the hole, but they left a section free that they could wrap over the top of the cage. These skunks would be cozy.

"I'll get the skunks if you'll bring the branches."

"Let's do it." On the way back to the truck she smelled smoke again. "I have to wonder who'd be camping in the woods on a cold night like this."

"It's not so bad if you have a thick sleeping bag and a good tent."

Instantly she imagined them inside a thick sleeping bag, naked and sweating. When they reached the dirt road, she realized that she could glance up through the opening in the trees and see the bulk of Big Knob rising into the night sky like some ancient fertility god.

Tomorrow she'd have to refocus on her goal of buying the property for SaveALot. But tonight, her job was the last thing on her mind. With that hunk of granite rising from the forest floor, who wouldn't think of sex?

Sean lowered the tailgate slowly, with as little noise as possible. Then he peered in at the skunks. "They might sleep until morning. That would be just as well. If they start roaming around in a strange place at night, they could get separated."

Maggie thought about what Jeremy had told her—that Sean's dad had left when he was only seven and his mother had died when he was eighteen. Apparently Jeremy was right about Sean's protective feeling about the skunks. He wanted to keep the little furry, stinky family together. She was touched by that.

He lifted the pine branches one at a time, checking to make sure the skunks still slept. They hadn't moved.

"They're alive, right?" Maggie asked as she took the last branch.

"Oh yeah. I can see them breathing." Sliding the cage slowly toward the edge of the tailgate, he lifted it. "Let's go."

Maggie led the way, cautioning him about tree roots or dead branches in his path. He settled the skunks into their new home without incident. Maggie helped him pull the tarp over the cage and lay the branches on top of that. At last Sean leaned down and unlatched the door and secured it with a piece of wire.

Then he reached into his jacket pocket and took out some chunks of carrot, which he scattered just inside the cage. "That should do it. I'll probably come out tomorrow and leave a little more food, to tide them over until they find their own source."

"It's a great setup."

"It's the best solution I could come up with. That's it, then." He picked up the shovel in one hand and wrapped his other arm around her shoulders. "Time to go back."

"Sounds good." It sounded more than good. It sounded fantastic.

He gave her shoulder a squeeze. "Thanks for your help."

"It was fun. I—"

A roar ripped apart the peaceful silence.

Maggie leaped at least a foot and then grabbed hold of Sean. "Wh-what was *that*?"

"Easy." Holding her close with one arm, he

changed his grip on the shovel. "I'm sure there's an explanation."

"Yeah, but do we want to know what it is?" She tried to stop shaking, but it was no use. City girls weren't used to hearing roaring noises in a dark forest. Personally, she preferred whispers.

"We have to find out what it is. The skunks are still in a helpless state. I can't leave them out here if there's a predator around."

"R-right." She peered into the darkness beyond the truck's headlights. "I told you I saw red eyes. Do bears have red eyes?"

"There hasn't been a bear in these woods for at least fifty years, maybe longer. Or a mountain lion, either. The biggest thing we have is bobcats, and that wasn't a bobcat."

"Maybe a lion escaped from the zoo. Or the circus."

He shook his head. "I don't think so. Someone in town would have heard about it on the news, and everyone would have been on the alert. Nothing sneaks up on us in Big Knob."

"Then what made that noise?"

"I don't know. Maybe just teenagers having fun on a Friday night."

"Yeah, this is a real blast."

"You're shaking like a leaf." He started forward, his arm still around her. "Let's get you into the truck. Then I'll go investigate."

"Hold on." She dug in her heels. "I have a better idea. Let's load the skunks back into the truck and then we can all skedaddle."

He turned to her. "That's a lot of work."

"I know, but then we'd be sure nothing would happen to them." *Or him.* But she figured he wasn't as worried as she was that he'd get mauled and eaten by some wild animal.

"Okay, if I can't figure out what made that noise,

we'll get the skunks. But I hate to disturb them again, now that they're all tucked in, especially if it's only a couple of teenage boys playing a prank."

"Sean, I really don't want you running around in the woods armed only with a shovel. Let's get the skunks and go home."

"Not yet. We— Yikes!"

Dorcas and Ambrose stepped into the beam from the truck's headlights.

"Don't worry," Dorcas said. "The skunks will be fine."

Chapter 19

The jury was in, Sean decided. Dorcas and Ambrose were weird. He could understand teenagers running through Whispering Forest on a Friday night, trying to scare themselves and anybody who happened to be around. He couldn't think of a single reason why Dorcas and Ambrose should be wandering through the woods tonight.

Besides that, he hadn't heard another car. Then again, he wasn't sure that Dorcas and Ambrose owned a car. Come to think of it, he'd never seen them driving one.

"Didn't mean to startle you," Ambrose said.

Sean remembered that he still had his arm firmly around Maggie. He let her go. No point in creating gossip. "It's just that I didn't hear a car."

"We walked," Dorcas said. "Great night for it."

"All the way from your house?" Sean noticed they were both wearing velour warm-up suits—purple for her and black for him—and high-end running shoes, but still. They had to be a good five miles from home, ten if you counted the return trip.

"Sure," Ambrose said. "We can always use the exercise. But I'll bet you wonder why we chose this place as a destination."

"It's crossed my mind," Sean said.

"And there's something out here," Maggie added. "I'm sure you heard that loud noise."

Ambrose laughed merrily. "Yes, yes, and we thought we needed to come by and explain."

"It was Ambrose," Dorcas said.

Sean stared at them as he tried to connect that roar with mild-mannered Ambrose. "I'm sorry, but that wasn't Ambrose."

"It was." Ambrose looked slightly embarrassed. "I was goofing around. You know there's a popular therapy where guys go out in the woods and beat their chests and declare how manly they are. I was trying that out."

"That didn't sound like a person," Maggie said.

Ambrose glanced at her. "Then I'm flattered. I was trying out my lion imitation, so I must have succeeded. It's amazing what you can accomplish if you open up your chest and bring the sound up from your diaphragm."

"So you came out here to roar like a lion?" Sean had decided he didn't really want to know the details, which could very well involve sex. It was one thing to consider having outdoor fun and games with Maggie. It was a whole other thing to imagine Dorcas and Ambrose out here doing it. They were both old enough to be his parents.

"The roaring was an afterthought," Dorcas said. "We came out looking for mushrooms," she added, as if she'd peeked into Sean's mind. "There's a particular kind that needs to be harvested at night."

"Right," Ambrose said. "Mushroom harvesting. It's a delicate job."

Sean didn't believe them for a minute. He didn't think two people qualified as an orgy, but Dorcas and Ambrose had been up to some sort of hanky-panky out here. "Any luck with the mushrooms?"

"Unfortunately not," Dorcas said. "The soil must not be quite right in this area."

Maggie cleared her throat. "As long as we're talking about mushroom gathering and stuff like that, I have a question about that Mystic Hills wine."

Here we go. Sean had wanted to ask them about the wine privately, but Maggie obviously wanted an answer now. He didn't blame her. He just wasn't sure whether Dorcas and Ambrose would start blabbing about the herbs they'd given him. That would be embarassing.

"If you want another bottle," Dorcas said, "you're welcome to it. We have quite a bit in the basement."

"Did you make it?" Maggie asked.

Ambrose's chest lifted in obvious pride. "We did. And it's at its peak right now, so we need to drink it up."

"It's great wine," Maggie said. "Is there anything special in it?"

"Oh, the usual," Ambrose said. "Grapes, yeast."

Dorcas gave Maggie an assessing look. "What makes you ask?"

"I told her you gave me the bait for the skunks," Sean said. "That had such an amazing effect on them that she wondered . . . we both wondered . . . if there was something unusual in the wine."

"After all, you have that business that looks a lot like a matchmaking setup," Maggie said.

"So you *are* attracted to each other." Dorcas looked pleased.

Maggie stepped a little farther away from Sean. "Well, I wouldn't exactly say that we're—"

"I would." Ambrose looked from Sean to Maggie. "There's definitely some sparks between you two."

"Which could be because of the wine," Sean said.

"Ah." Dorcas smiled at them. "You think the wine

might be drugged in some way, like in that Sandra Bullock movie. What was it called, Ambrose?''

"*Love Potion Number Nine.* What an off-the-wall concept. That's Hollywood for you."

"But you haven't exactly answered the question," Maggie said.

And she wasn't giving up, Sean noticed. If he thought he could distract her from buying the property out from under him with a little bit of sex, he was wrong.

"If you two are feeling attracted to each other, it's not because of the wine," Dorcas said.

"I didn't think so," Maggie said. "That would be a little too hocus-pocus."

"Exactly." Dorcas pulled the zipper tight on her warm-up jacket. "Anyway, the skunks will be fine. I'll bet if you check them you'll discover they're waking up."

"Okay, I'll do that," Sean said. "Put my mind at ease."

"You did well to relocate them, and Whispering Forest is a nice, safe place. Well, Ambrose, my love, it's getting late. We'd better start for home."

"I can give you a ride," Sean said. "But somebody will have to sit in the back."

"Don't worry about it." Ambrose took Dorcas's hand. "We love to walk. You two have a good evening."

Sean watched them start off down the dirt road until they disappeared in the blackness. "Do you suppose they even brought a flashlight?"

"Doesn't look like it." Maggie gazed after them. "Oh, wait. There's some kind of light. That green spot flickering through the trees must be them."

Sean saw it, too, a greenish circle of light that kept appearing and disappearing in the shadows. "They must have one of those Glo-Sticks. I can't imagine why they wouldn't use a plain old flashlight, though, especially if they're taking a ten-mile hike."

"Do you believe what they said about the wine?"

Sean turned to her. "Not particularly. Do you believe Ambrose made that roaring noise?"

"Nope. They know what did, though, and for whatever reason, they don't want us to find out about it."

Dorcas held a faintly glowing orb in her free hand as she and Ambrose walked quickly down the dirt road. "This fairy light is losing power, Ambrose. You should have brought your staff along so we could recharge it."

"Yeah, right. Walk down Fifth Street with my wizard's staff. Are you nuts?"

"You could say it's a walking stick."

"I could say it, but anybody who's seen *Lord of the Rings* would know it's a wizard's staff. It looks exactly like the one Gandalf uses. It was so much easier to maintain secrecy before those movies came out. Thank you, Peter Jackson, for blowing our cover."

"So get yourself a staff that looks like a walking stick," Dorcas said. "They were on sale last month in the W and W catalog. I even showed them to you."

"I know, and they look dorky. I *like* my staff. It's just too blasted obvious these days."

"Then I hope you enjoy walking in the dark, because this light is fading fast."

Ambrose picked up the pace. "Walk faster."

"If I walk faster, I'm more likely to trip on something." Dorcas jiggled the green fairy light to see if she could coax a little more power from it. "If I had my broom we'd be home in no time."

"If you had your broom, Officer Bob would slap us in the pokey. My staff is a hundred times less conspicuous than your broom. Talk about gaudy."

"Gaudy?" She leaped to the defense of her beloved

broom. "That shaft was painstakingly hand carved and hand painted."

"With Kama Sutra positions! I begged you to buy the plain one, but noooo. It had to be the Kama Sutra broom or nothing."

"You're just intimidated because you can't do all those positions."

He blew out a breath. "Like you can."

Dorcas started to throw back another barbed comment, but stopped herself. "You know why we're snarling at each other, don't you?"

"Yes. Because ten miles is too far to walk and our fairy light is going out. Maybe we should buy a scooter for tootling around town."

Dorcas sighed. That was so Ambrose, to try and solve a problem by buying a gadget. "We don't need a scooter. We won't be here long enough to justify the expense."

"I've always wanted a scooter."

"Focus, Ambrose. Our problem is George. He didn't sound too worried about SaveALot. In fact, I think he likes the idea of it going in next door."

"Yeah, he does. I guess you decided against giving him the iPod."

"I couldn't justify it in light of his attitude. He's still not taking his guardianship seriously if he's willing to have a huge department store next to the forest he's supposed to be protecting."

"No kidding," Ambrose said. "The impact on the wildlife in Whispering Forest would be significant."

"I know." Dorcas shook her head in frustration. "On top of that, when I dared suggest that he should be worried about the store moving in, he roared at me. Not good."

"Not good for many reasons. I don't think Sean and Maggie bought our story about the mushrooms and me trying out my lion imitation."

"It was sort of lame." Dorcas jiggled the fairy light again. "But what else could we say? If the good people of Big Knob find out there's a dragon living in their woods, they'll call out the National Guard."

"So what now?"

She thought about that for a few minutes. "We need some uninterrupted time with him, when we're sure nobody else will be around. We'll come back later, like two in the morning."

"On foot? I don't think I'm up to that."

"Me, either, but everybody will be asleep. It should be safe to ride my broom."

Maggie watched the little green light until it disappeared. "That is the strangest couple I've ever met in my life."

"They're different, all right." Sean glanced over at the spot where they'd left the skunks. Then he took Maggie's hand. "Come on. Let's check out the skunks and see if Dorcas is right about them waking up."

"I wish I'd asked her about the red eyes." Maggie had a feeling Dorcas and Ambrose knew a lot about what was going on in these woods. How they knew was a mystery, though.

"I still say it was some animal, and a trick of the light made the eyes look red."

"And the roar came from?"

"God only knows." About twenty feet from the skunk lair, Sean squeezed her hand and let go. "You stay here. I'll check. No point in both of us taking the risk of getting sprayed."

"I'll go along with that." She waited while Sean crouched down and peered into the space under the tarp and pine boughs.

"Whoa!" He scrambled backward. "They are definitely awake in there. Let's go." Grabbing her hand, he pulled her back along the path they'd come in on.

Moments later they were in the truck, and Sean had it in gear. "Mission accomplished." He turned around on the dirt road and started back toward the highway.

Now that the skunk situation was under control, Maggie's thoughts turned to the sexy guy sitting beside her. Her thoughts had never quite left him, but with red eyes and something roaring in the woods and the sudden appearance of Dorcas and Ambrose, she'd put her sexual urges on hold.

Now those urges had returned, and it seemed as if the short break had only made them stronger. She'd had more orgasms in the past eight hours than she'd had in the past eight months. Shouldn't she be over the impulse after all that? Well, she wasn't.

She still wondered if the wine was responsible. Thinking of the wine made her remember Dorcas and Ambrose. She watched for them on the road, but they must have cut through the forest, because they were nowhere to be seen.

As Sean pulled the truck into his driveway and shut off the motor, his cell phone rang. He unclipped it from his jeans and checked the number. "It's Madeline."

Maggie clapped a hand to her mouth. "I should have called her. She must be wondering where in the world I am."

"Want me to answer it?"

"Um, well . . ." This was awkward. Sean had talked about coming back here and having more sex, but he hadn't mentioned it recently. She also hadn't stopped to think about having to answer to anyone about spending the night here.

"I'll let it go to voice mail."

She glanced at him. "I feel as if my mother just called to check on me."

"Believe me, I know what you mean." He leaned

an arm over the steering wheel. "What do you want to do?"

Make love to you all night. But she didn't have the guts to say so.

"You must be tired," he said. "You've been through a lot today."

She had the horrible thought that he'd reconsidered asking her to come inside. Suggesting a woman might be tired could be a polite way to get her out of his hair. Maybe the effects of the wine had worn off for him. He had more body mass, so that made sense.

"You must be tired, too," she said, steeling herself for him to agree, preparing herself to climb back in her rental car and go back to Madeline's house. "You had that fender bender to deal with today, on top of everything else." *Like having sex with me.*

"For some reason, I don't feel tired at all."

Her hopes took an upward swing. "Really?"

"Really." He glanced over at her. "Look, I have no right to expect anything. You probably need your rest."

"Probably." If she wanted him, she'd have to say so, but she wasn't used to being assertive when it came to personal relationships. Business was different, but this wasn't business. Her heart raced as she gathered her courage.

He opened his door. "Then let me get the Tupperware so you can—"

"But I don't want to go back to Madeline's."

He glanced back in her direction, his eyes shining in the overhead light in the truck's cab. "You don't?"

"Nope." The triumph of going for it gave her a jolt of adrenaline. "But I have to let her know I'm okay. How do I accomplish that?"

"I'll take care of it. But are you sure you want to—"

"Yes." Her blood pumped heat through her veins. "Yes to whatever you have in mind."

Sean flipped open his phone and punched in a number. "Madeline? It's Sean. Yes, she's fine. We didn't want you to worry, but . . . she'll be staying with me tonight." He paused. "Uh, okay. Talk to you later." He closed the phone.

"Was she scandalized?"

He clipped the phone back onto his jeans and looked over at her. "No."

"But you said she was superconservative."

"She is. It's the darnedest thing. I thought she'd ream me out for keeping you here and corrupting you with my wild ways, but she didn't."

"Then what *did* she say?"

"Just one word. *Good.*"

Chapter 20

Once Sean knew Maggie was back in the game, he didn't waste any time hustling her inside and getting her naked. Although he'd considered the idea of outside sex, it was way too cold to be fun. Besides, having a naked woman in his bed was novelty enough. He'd never allowed that to happen before.

Maybe that explained Madeline's reaction to the news that Maggie was sleeping over. Madeline might have figured this situation was different from his other sexual escapades. Either that or she'd do anything to keep him from going blind.

As he tumbled to the mattress with a very warm and willing Maggie, he realized he might be crossing into commitment territory. He might be able to forget that he'd had sex with her on his kitchen table, but he'd never forget this picture of her lying beneath him in the glow of the bedside table lamp, her head resting on his pillow.

A condom lay ready on the table and Maggie had wrapped both hands around his eager penis. Knowing it was long enough to require two hands reassured him that the herbs were no longer messing with his appearance. She was doing wonderful things down there in his southern hemisphere, stroking his cock and fondling his balls.

He ached from wanting her and was almost ready to use that condom. Almost.

She rubbed her thumb over the moistened tip of his penis. "Let's get you into your party clothes."

"In a minute." Her caresses were heaven, but if she kept them up, he wouldn't be able to ignore the pressure building in his groin. He didn't want to hurry this time.

Sitting back on his haunches, he gently took her hands in his. Leaning forward, he raised them over her head and pressed them into the pillow. "Let me look at you."

She blushed. "I'm just an ordinary girl."

"Not even close to ordinary." He'd never appreciated twenty-twenty eyesight more than now, when he could use it to gaze at Maggie. Everything about her fascinated him—her milky skin dusted with pale freckles, her wide blue eyes and up-tilted nose, her breasts tipped with taffy-colored nipples, her slender waist and the inviting flare of her hips.

As he studied her, she began to squirm on the mattress. "You're making me self-conscious."

"A woman who looks like you should never be self-conscious." Soon he would be rocked in the cradle of those hips. Soon he would thrust past the soft curls guarding the entrance to his own personal paradise. Soon their passion-slick bodies would writhe on this mattress and send the headboard banging against the wall.

He'd never had the luxury of anticipation before, and it was sweeter than he could have imagined. He allowed his glance to roam slowly back up to her face. "You're beautiful," he said.

"I'm not, but thank you."

"You are, and thank *you*." He kissed her mouth, her throat, her breasts. He could spend forever on her breasts. They were the nicest size—not too large and not too small. Perfect for nuzzling, licking, sucking. He took his time, savored the feel of her nipple rolling between his tongue and teeth.

She began to breathe faster and struggled half-heartedly, as if to break free of the grip he had on her wrists.

He'd never held a woman prisoner like this, and his heart hammered with the excitement of it. He lifted his head to gaze into her eyes. His voice was thick with lust. "Do you want me to let you go?"

She gulped and shook her head.

"Good." He lowered his head to her breasts again.

She continued to struggle, and her breathing grew ragged. As he sucked rhythmically on her breast, she tensed. He used his teeth, just a little.

"I'm coming!" Arching her back, she gasped and trembled beneath him.

He waited until she sank back to the mattress before he released her and scooped the condom off the table. Trembling himself, he had to concentrate to get it on. Finally he managed it.

Her skin was flushed from her orgasm, her channel hot and wet as he slid deep inside her. Instantly she began to tighten around his cock, and he rocked forward, making her come again.

As she shuddered in his arms, he began to thrust, first slowly, and then faster until the headboard slammed against the wall exactly as he'd imagined it would. What a beautiful sound. When they climaxed together, his surge of joy told him what he already suspected. It might be inconvenient, but there it was. Maggie was the one.

"I'm too old to be pulling an all-nighter," Ambrose grumbled as they sailed over the leafless trees on Dorcas's Kama Sutra broom.

"It's not my fault dragons sleep during the day."

Personally, Dorcas was thrilled with that particular behavior. She was loving this nighttime ride.

She didn't dare fire up her broom in broad daylight, so visiting George in the dead of night was the perfect excuse to fly. Steering was a little trickier with Ambrose adding extra weight on the tail section, and she couldn't do any barrel rolls or he was liable to puke. Even with those disadvantages, it was great to be back on her broom again.

Sabrina had wanted to come, but Dorcas had made her stay home. George didn't need an extra distraction like Sabrina around when focusing was already a problem for him. Dorcas had promised to give Sabrina a ride another night. That kitty loved feeling the wind through her fur. She could hold on like nobody's business during the barrel rolls, too.

This particular flight was over way too soon. Dorcas took a spin around Big Knob for the hell of it before setting the broom down in a small clearing in the trees.

Climbing off, she glanced back at Ambrose, who was holding the gift-wrapped iPod. "Good. You didn't lose the present."

"It's a wonder you didn't lose me. When you buzzed Big Knob I almost fell off."

"Sorry about that. It's just that I miss flying so much."

Ambrose's expression softened. "I know. We need to convince George to assume his duties so we can move back to Sedona and get on with our normal lives."

"Let's hope tonight is the beginning of that." Dorcas leaned her broom up against a tree. Then she pulled a recharged fairy light out of one pocket and a small wooden flute out of the other. She set the fairy light on a stump.

"I'm still not sure about the iPod, Dorcas. We have no way of knowing if the Perpetually Charged spell worked or not. What if the thing has to be charged on a regular basis? That could cause more problems."

Dorcas glanced at him. "It's the thought that counts."

"It feels like a bribe."

"Well, it's not. It's a gesture of friendship and goodwill." Dorcas lifted the flute to her lips and played the summoning tune that would bring George out of his lair deep under Big Knob.

Drawing him out of the lair was no problem. George was always up for a distraction. Dorcas knew he might not even be in his lair. He could be off somewhere playing poker with the raccoons. The flute would bring him, though. Dragons were powerless to resist the lure of this type of flute.

For a dragon weighing two thousand pounds, George was amazingly light on his feet. She didn't realize he was approaching until she saw his red eyes hovering about eight feet off the ground. The wind must have been blowing away from him, because she didn't smell smoke yet.

For the second time tonight, he'd decided to pull his invisibility trick, so that all anyone could see were his eyes. He'd done that earlier and scared poor Maggie half to death. Dorcas was used to it.

She lowered the flute. "Hello, George."

"Good evening, George," Ambrose said. "How's it going?"

George blew a smoke ring in the shape of a heart. "Pocket aces, that's how it's going, and then, bam! you do the flute thing. Those raccoons cheat, so I go, 'Don't you dare switch those cards, because I'll be right back.' But I know them. They'll switch 'em. This better not take long, because they'll steal my chips, too."

Dorcas vowed to stay calm. "So you must have already made your rounds tonight."

"Making rounds is lame, man." His next smoke ring was in the shape of a diamond. "Nothing ever happens in this freakin' forest. Total waste of time to go around checking it out like a dweeb. Besides, I'm ADD."

"That's never been ascertained medically," Dorcas said.

"Who cares? I totally fit the profile, dude, 'cause I can't concentrate." He blew a club-shaped smoke ring at them. "If I can't concentrate, I'm, like, crappy at doing rounds, so why bother?"

Ambrose cleared his throat. "Because it's your job. Because it's the only way you'll earn your gold scales."

"Gold scales are for losers. Brownish-green is camouflage, man. It's cool." He finished his playing card smoke rings with a spade. "So what's that on the stump? Looks like a present." His eyes lowered until they were even with the wrapped box. "Or a bomb. A bomb would be cool."

Dorcas picked up the package. "It's a present. But before I give it to you, I want your word that you'll start making rounds every night."

"What is it?"

She wrapped her hands around it. "You won't find out unless you give me your word about making your rounds."

"Sheesh! Okay, okay, I'll do the dumb-ass rounds! Give me the present."

"Reveal yourself first," Ambrose said.

"Or . . . I could just *take* the present." George's eyes hovered closer.

Dorcas stepped back. "I wouldn't do that if I were you. You're dealing with a fully functioning witch and wizard."

"Blah, blah, blah. Oh, all right, don't have a coronary." Suddenly George stood before them in all his scaliness. He had a horn in the middle of his snout, ears that flopped sideways and wicked-looking teeth.

Because he was still young, only about three hundred years old, those teeth were razor sharp. "Now give me the present."

"And you *will* do rounds?" Dorcas asked.

"Yeah, yeah. Whatever. I'll do the rounds. Give it here."

Dorcas handed over the package with more than a few misgivings. She had no real confidence that George would keep his promise, but she had to start somewhere.

He tore into the package and had the iPod out in about two seconds. "Word! Perfectamundo!" In another two seconds he had the earplugs in and was gyrating in time to the music only he could hear. "Oh yeah. I'm bad."

Ambrose glanced at Dorcas. "Great. Now we can't talk to him."

"I have to admit I didn't think of that. But I did get him to say he'd do his rounds."

"Uh-huh. And you believe him?"

Dorcas took a deep breath. "Yes, I'm going to choose to believe him."

"Dreamer."

About that time George became invisible again, so all they could see were his eyes and the iPod jiggling around. "Catch you later, dudes. Rock on." He blew a smoke ring in the shape of a guitar. Then the eyes and the iPod bobbed off through the trees.

Ambrose sighed. "That went well."

"One night at a time, Ambrose. One night at a time."

Maggie woke up to sunshine coming through a completely unfamiliar window. Besides that, she was naked, and she never slept naked. As memory returned like a slap to the head, she rolled over and confronted an equally naked Sean lying next to her, his green eyes filled with welcome and his smile promising immediate seduction.

There was a reason why she couldn't give in to the lust that washed over her as she looked at him, but what was it? She had to do something today, something very important. But as Sean pulled her close, damned if she could remember what it was.

From across the room, her BlackBerry played "The Yellow Rose of Texas" and she remembered. She wiggled away from Sean and climbed out of bed. "Sorry. I have to get that."

"Are you sure?" His voice was deep and sensual, his gaze hot. "Doesn't that thing take messages?"

As she turned to gaze at him lying in the rumpled bed where they'd made love six ways to Sunday during the night, she realized why she couldn't get back into that bed. For all she knew, he'd be willing to keep her occupied there all day. It could be his tactic for making sure she didn't contact the owner of the property.

The knowledge that she was tempted to ignore H.G.'s call and climb back in bed with him scared her. Sweet as it was to have sex with him, he could be using it as his ultimate weapon. After all, that had been his goal in the beginning.

"It takes messages," she said. "But that's my boss calling. If he's calling, that means he hasn't fired me yet. If I get him his location today, I might still save my job. I can't afford to ignore him right now."

Moving quickly, she located her BlackBerry in the tumble of clothes on a chair. She managed to connect with H.G. before the phone switched to voice mail. "Hello, H.G." She turned her back to the bed.

"Grady, you're getting on my very last nerve. Why haven't I heard a blessed word from you?"

"I had some difficulty locating the owner of the

property yesterday. I should be able to do that today. I'll call you this afternoon once I've closed the deal."

"You can close the deal on a Saturday?"

She'd temporarily forgotten what day it was. She wasn't surprised that H.G. was working on Saturday. He always did. But she might not find other key people available. Damn it.

She took a breath. "I realize it's Saturday." *Now.* "It might take me until Monday to finalize the paperwork, but I'll get it started this morning, and I'll let you know before you leave the office today what kind of progress I've made."

Sean came up behind her and slipped both arms around her waist. She was trapped between him and the chair. He began to nibble on her ear.

H.G.'s drawl sounded in her other ear. "Tell me where you are, Grady. Maybe I can help expedite things."

It took all her concentration to ignore Sean's tongue outlining the contours of her ear. "I'll tell you this afternoon," she said. "Once everything is wrapped up. See you later, H.G. Gotta go!" She broke the connection.

"Now can you come back to bed?" Sean murmured in her ear.

"No." She put down the BlackBerry and pried his arms away from her body. Then she grabbed her clothes and moved to the other side of the room.

Sean followed. "Maggie . . ."

She held up one hand like a traffic cop. "Stay away. I have work to do, something you know very well. You shouldn't have tried to interfere with that phone call, and you know it."

"I was only—"

"You were trying to distract me so I'll forget about Denise, forget about locating the owner of the property, forget about keeping my job." She dressed quickly. "It won't work, Sean."

He found his briefs and put them on. "Stay for breakfast. Another thirty minutes won't matter."

"It might." She peered at him. "Your hair's going all funny again."

"Probably slept on it wrong."

"No, it's more than that. Go look."

With a sigh, he walked into the bathroom and flipped on the light over the sink. "Damn Dorcas and Ambrose!"

She had no idea what he was talking about and wasn't going to take time to find out. She picked up the black glasses and grabbed her coat. "I'm off!" she called as she left the bedroom.

"Wait!" He came after her, hopping on one foot as he tried to shove his other leg in his jeans. "Let me put some clothes on. I'll walk you to the—"

"Sorry, have to leave!" Practically running, she made it out the kitchen door and down the steps. He was not going to derail her. No way.

Chapter 21

Sean was not in a good mood as he showered and dressed for the day. Everything had been going so well. Having Maggie in his bed this morning had given him a terrific idea. They could spend all day there, and maybe she'd forget about trying to buy the property. The plan was simple and elegant.

If his conscience bothered him a little for manipulating the situation, he remembered how happy she seemed to be when she was with him. At times, when they were both naked and sweaty, she acted positively ecstatic. All he wanted was to keep that smile on her face . . . and a grip on his property.

Why couldn't he have both? The longer Maggie was in Big Knob, the more she seemed to like it here. Between cinnamon rolls and skunks, she seemed to be having a pretty good time.

He was counting on that, because she might be right about losing her job if she went back to Houston empty-handed. With enough good sex, she might not care about losing her job. She might start thinking of relocating to his neck of the woods.

And wouldn't you know it, right when he had that strategy all mapped out, his hair had gone wacky again. The herbs Dorcas had given him must be activated by daylight. That was the only explanation for

why he looked worse this morning than he had last
night. No wonder Maggie had run away.

He felt helpless to stop her from getting a lead on
the property. Dorcas and Ambrose were his only
hope, and they kept saying they couldn't do anything.
Maybe if he built the sex bench he'd promised them,
they'd be more cooperative. If he showed that he was
holding up his side of the bargain, they might try
harder to find a solution for him. He'd have to make
another excuse to Calvin Gilmore, though.

While in the kitchen brewing coffee, he glanced at
the Big Knob Hardware calendar on the wall and noticed with surprise that it was Saturday. He'd been so
preoccupied with events that he'd forgotten what day
it was. Calvin wouldn't expect him to work on Saturday, so he was free to build the sex bench and take
it to the Lowells.

After putting on a sweatshirt, he stuck his cell
phone in his pocket, poured his coffee and started out
to work. He'd barely stepped inside the chilly garage
and turned on the space heater when his cell phone
rang. Maggie with a change of heart? Adrenaline
pumping, he checked the display. Jeremy. Well, that
was okay. He needed to talk to Jeremy, anyway.

He flipped open the phone. "Hey, buddy. I meant
to call you and thank you for not fixing Denise's computer yesterday. I owe you."

"You don't owe me anything. Like I said, if I'd
been able to fix it, I would have. Between the hinky
electricity in that office and some internal problem I
couldn't figure out, it was DOA."

"Then she may be out of luck, huh?" Sean tried
not to sound too happy about that.

"Not really. I'm hauling my laptop over there. She
can run it on batteries for close to four hours, so if
the phone line isn't compromised, she'll be fine."

"Oh." Sean's black mood descended again.

"But that isn't why I called. I just heard something that you probably should know about. How's the medical coverage on your car insurance?"

"Why?" Uneasiness settled in the pit of his stomach. "Is something wrong with Edith Mae?"

"I hope not, for your sake. I suppose she could have bumped her head on the steering wheel. Anyway, according to Denise, Edith Mae's gone a little bonkers."

"That's nothing new. She's always been nuts."

"Yeah, but not like this. Claims she got up in the middle of the night to go to the bathroom, looked out her window and saw two people flying overhead on a broomstick."

Sean laughed. "Did she happen to mention how much gin she'd been sipping prior to this broomstick sighting?"

"I thought of that, too, but Denise doesn't think that's it. I guess Edith Mae made an unexpected trip down to the Hob Knob this morning just so she could tell everyone about what she saw. Swore she was sober as a judge last night. Some people are thinking she might have a head injury from yesterday."

Sean groaned. "So where is she now? Still at the Hob Knob?"

"I'm not sure. You could call over there and find out."

"I will. I need to talk to her. Hell, I'll take her to Doc Pritchard myself if need be. I personally think it's the gin talking, but I probably shouldn't assume that."

"Probably not. Even though she's a pain in the butt, she's our pain in the butt and we all love her."

"Right. Thanks, buddy."

Five minutes later Sean was on his way into town, driving with the aid of the taped-together glasses.

Once again, his eyesight had gone from twenty-twenty to shit, and he couldn't afford to be running into anything this morning.

He'd learned from Madeline that Edith Mae was still ensconced at a table in the Hob Knob. He'd deal with that situation, and once he had Edith Mae under control, he'd go over to the Lowells'. He wouldn't have the sex bench in tow, but surely they would see that his life was spinning out of control and something had to be done. Pronto.

As she drove to Madeline and Abe's house for a shower and a change of clothes, Maggie longed for the anonymity of a hotel room. When you'd spent the night doing something you probably shouldn't have, there was nothing like melting into an urban crowd to ease the guilt.

Instead she had to face Abe as he opened the front door. She felt like a kid caught out after curfew.

Fortunately, Abe seemed to have bigger fish to fry. "Hurry up and come in." He pulled her inside and shut the door. "I'm busy working. Did you get Sean's signature?"

"On what?" For one wild moment she imagined Sean scrawling his name over her naked body, but that couldn't be what Abe meant.

"On my petition."

The blast of laughter coming from the TV reminded her. He was watching a rerun of *Dharma & Greg*.

Snatching up his legal pad, he made a note before looking at her again. "Did you get it?"

"Not exactly."

"What, he wouldn't sign? I'll have to talk to him. That's the problem in this country—public apathy. And what causes public apathy?"

"Let me guess. Canned laughter."

"Bingo!" Abe spun toward the TV and made another note on his legal pad. "Wish I could talk, but I need to catch this while it's available."

"Have you ever considered recording these shows, so you could do your research at your leisure?"

Abe whirled back to her. "And that's *another* thing poisoning the minds of the masses! VCRs, TiVo, video rentals! Nobody has to *plan* anymore. It's all handed to them whenever they crook their little finger. I won't stoop to recording these shows and become part of that mentality."

"Oh, okay." Maggie started backing toward the staircase. "I'll leave you to your work, then."

"Right." Abe scribbled on his pad. "Somebody has to be the pioneer, so I guess it's up to me. Next time you see Sean, tell him that if he isn't part of the solution, then he's part of the problem."

"I will." And she thought truer words had never been spoken.

The advantage to short hair, she quickly learned, was being able to shower and shampoo in no time. She dressed in jeans and a cream-colored sweater and scooted out the door in such record time that she decided to reward herself with a cinnamon roll. She'd order it to go and take it with her to Denise's office. In fact, she'd buy three so she could share with Denise and Jeremy.

But the minute she stepped into the fragrant interior of the Hob Knob, she realized her mistake. Sean was there, a look of concern on his face as he talked with Edith Mae Hoogstraten. Maggie recognized her as the same woman involved in Sean's fender bender yesterday. Today she wore a different pillbox hat to match her outfit.

So Sean was still trying to make amends. That was sweet. And damn, he looked good doing it. His hair was behaving again, so maybe he had slept on it wrong, like he'd said. He'd also ditched the glasses, and his green sweatshirt picked up the color of his eyes.

As if he had radar, he glanced up and saw her come through the door. She still might have been able to turn around and leave, except that Madeline bustled over, all smiles.

"Maggie! I'll bet you're here to meet Sean for breakfast."

"Well, actually, I'm getting some cinnamon rolls to go."

Madeline shook her finger at Maggie. "Now, now. That's no way to keep yourself healthy, wealthy and wise. Sit down and have a real breakfast. How about a stack of pancakes with lots of butter and syrup? Doesn't that sound good?"

If Maggie hadn't been so focused on avoiding Sean, she might have laughed. Many more meals at the Hob Knob and she wouldn't be able to zip her jeans. "I'm in a bit of a hurry," she said. "And the cinnamon rolls would be quick."

"So will the pancakes." Madeline turned toward the kitchen and hollered out the order. "Sean's right over there, talking to Edith Mae. Come with me."

Arguing with the woman who was giving her a free room didn't seem like the best idea, so Maggie followed Madeline over to where Sean sat talking with Edith Mae.

"Look who I found!" Madeline said.

Sean's chair scraped on the wood floor as he pushed it back and stood. "Hi, Maggie."

"Hi, Sean." He looked even better up close. Her heart thumped in happy recognition of the pleasure he'd given her only hours ago.

"Who's this?" Edith Mae scrutinized her from head to toe.

"A friend of Sean's," Madeline said proudly.

"Never seen her before in my life," Edith Mae said.

"Where've you been keeping her, boy? In your closet?"

"She's a new friend." Sean came around the table and pulled out the empty chair next to Edith Mae. "Maggie, this is Edith Mae Hoogstraten. Edith Mae, this is Maggie Grady from Houston."

"Is that so?" Edith Mae gave her another once-over. "Did you bring any other Texans with you?"

"No, just me." Maggie had little choice but to take the chair Sean offered. As he scooted her closer to the table, her senses registered warm skin and the scent of soap. The last time she'd smelled that fragrance she'd been in his shower, naked and extremely orgasmic.

Her body had total recall of that moment, and was currently demanding an instant replay.

As if he knew that and was ready to capitalize on it, Sean leaned closer. "You look great," he murmured.

So did he, but she wasn't about to say so. "Thanks."

Edith Mae turned to peer at Maggie. "Are you into witchcraft down there in Houston?"

"I beg your pardon?"

"Edith Mae, what you saw last night wasn't—"

"Hush, Sean." She waved a hand at him. "Witchcraft, Maggie. You know, brewing potions and riding on broomsticks. That kind of thing."

Maggie glanced at Sean for some signal that this was a joke.

He wasn't smiling. "Edith Mae says she saw two people on a broomstick last night. Of course, that's impossible. I'm trying to convince her to let me take her to see Doc Pritchard for some X-rays. She might have hit her head yesterday and not realized it."

"I did *not* hit my head, and you're not dragging me in for some procedure I don't need, young man."

"It might be a good idea to get checked out, Mrs. Hoogstraten," Maggie said.

Edith Mae looked her in the eye. "I'll thank you not to call me that. My mother-in-law was Mrs. Hoog-straten, and she was hell on wheels. I prefer to go by Edith Mae."

"All right, then, Edith Mae." Maggie met her direct gaze. "Even minor accidents can affect a person. You might have detached a retina or you could have jostled your brain somehow."

"My retinas are firmly attached and my brain hums like a top. I saw what I saw. Two people—I think a man and a woman—riding a broomstick across the night sky, just like in *The Wizard of Oz*."

Sean leaned across the table. "You might have been dreaming. That can happen to anyone. You have a dream and swear you're awake and it's real."

Edith Mae glared at him. "In my dreams I never get up to take a pee." Then she turned back to Maggie. "Since you're new in town, I thought you might have been one of the people on the broom."

"No, it wasn't me." She almost added that she had an airtight alibi and he was sitting across the table from her, but thought better of it.

"I believe you." Edith Mae pushed away her empty plate. "Too bad nobody believes me."

"It's not that I don't believe you," Sean said. "I'm sure you think you saw something, but there has to be a logical explanation for it."

"The logical explanation is that we have a witch, maybe two, in Big Knob." Edith Mae stood and re-trieved her purse from where it hung on the back of her chair. "And I intend to find out who it is."

After Edith Mae left, Sean focused on Maggie. For some reason, ever since he went looking for Edith Mae to try and take care of her problem, his eyesight and his haircut had improved. So daylight had nothing to do with the herbs Dorcas had given him. The effect must be completely random.

In any case, he felt more confident that he could distract Maggie from her plan now that he looked more like himself. "It's good to see you," he said.

"I only came in for a couple of cinnamon rolls." She glanced up as Madeline approached with a tray.

First Madeline put down a stack of three pancakes with ribbons of creamy yellow butter running from the center and spilling over the sides. Then she set a ceramic pitcher of syrup next to the plate.

"That's pure maple," she said. "I heated it up." Last she placed a cup of steaming coffee on the other side of Maggie's plate. "Enjoy."

"Thank you." Maggie glanced at the pancakes, then looked out the window of the diner, as if checking to see if Denise's car was parked in front of Big Knob Realty. "But I really do have to get going."

"Just try a bite," Madeline said. "They're buttermilk." Then she winked at Sean. "I notice you aren't wearing your glasses this morning."

"Uh, no." He picked up his coffee mug and took a swig to avoid looking at Madeline. Sure as the world, she thought his eyesight had improved because he was having sex with Maggie instead of going solo.

"Just one bite, then," Maggie said. She poured syrup over the entire stack, though.

Sean had eaten those pancakes before, and he knew they melted in your mouth. Between using so much syrup and loving her comfort food, Maggie would probably eat everything on her plate, which was good news for him. He'd stay and talk to her, maybe convince her to take a drive and look for other locations. He knew some great parking spots out in the woods, woods that had no reputation for being haunted.

Madeline stood by, the serving tray propped against her hip, and waited for Maggie to take that first bite. "I just know you'll love those pancakes."

"I doubt they can beat the cinnamon rolls." Maggie cut a little wedge out of the pancake stack, ran her fork through it, soaked up a little more of that warm syrup, and put the fork in her mouth. Then she closed her eyes and moaned with delight.

Sean clutched his coffee mug tighter as desire rolled through him, leaving him shaking in the aftermath. He had a bad case of the hots for this woman, and he wondered if that would ever happen again with someone else. He hated to think it was Maggie or nobody, because he wasn't the least bit certain he could have her.

"Good, aren't they?" Madeline beamed at the two of them.

Maggie swallowed and cut another wedge out of her stack. "They're fantastic. Light as a feather."

Madeline nodded. "It's because Sherry beats the egg whites separate. And getting the butter and milk fresh from the Big Knob Dairy makes a difference, too. Stay right there, Sean. I'll get you a fresh cup of coffee."

As if he had any intention of leaving. Watching Maggie eat was almost as exciting as having sex with her. He'd never known a woman who practically made love to her food.

Once Madeline left, Maggie glanced at Sean. "I shouldn't be having these, but they are sinfully good."

"I'm guessing they don't make pancakes like this in Houston."

"Not at any place I've found."

He wanted to reach across the table and touch her hand, but he didn't dare in front of all the people in the Hob Knob. Rumors were probably flying already, without having him add more fuel to the fire.

"Maggie, I hate that you felt you had to run out this morning."

She paused in the middle of cutting another bite of pancake. "If I hadn't, I might never have left."

That encouraged him. "So you had a good time?"

"Too good." She finished slicing off her next bite and swirled it in a puddle of syrup. "But I'm determined not to let that derail me."

"Let me show you some other locations today. We'll take a drive and—"

"No way. You'll try to seduce me somewhere out in the woods."

"No, I won't. I swear."

She glanced up, syrup dripping from her fork. "Yes, you will." She popped the bite into her mouth.

"Maggie, we wouldn't do anything you didn't want to do. I promise."

She finished chewing and swallowed. "That's the problem. I would want to. Once you had me in your truck, I'd be thinking about sex instead of my job."

He was thinking of sex right this minute and trying to figure out how to get her alone. He ached for her in a way that he had never ached for anyone before. It was almost like coming down with a disease.

Taking a sip of her coffee, she studied him over the rim of her coffee mug. "Your hair is going funky again."

This time he could feel it happening, a prickling in his scalp. What was worse, her features were growing blurry. Muttering an oath under his breath, he stood. "Excuse me, but I just remembered that I have to be somewhere."

Madeline tried to stop him on the way out. "What about your coffee?"

"I need to see someone. It's urgent. Very urgent."

She lowered her voice. "Mark my words, Sean Madigan. If you let this one get away, you'll be sorry."

"Don't I know it." He left the diner, his strides lengthening as he hurried down Fifth Street toward the refurbished Victorian on the southwest side of town. Dorcas and Ambrose had to help him.

It wasn't only about the property anymore. It was about Maggie. He needed her more than he needed the house. And he didn't know how to get her.

Chapter 22

When Maggie tried to pay for her pancakes, Madeline wouldn't take the money, so Maggie left a generous tip on the table. Obviously the poor woman was trying to be a matchmaker, and Maggie felt sad that all that effort would go to waste. But strong sexual attraction didn't necessarily lead to a commitment, and besides, Sean primarily wanted to distract her from buying the property. He'd never said a word about undying love.

She hoped he wouldn't. That would be embarrassing when she had no intention of staying in Big Knob, no matter how much fun she'd had in bed with Sean. She'd also have to question his sincerity; pledging his undying love could be just another tactic. She didn't fully trust him.

Out on the street, she noticed Denise's car parked in front of Big Knob Realty, along with Jeremy's truck. Surely she'd get what she needed this morning so she could put an end to this roller coaster she was on. She couldn't avoid Sean in a town this size, and every time she saw him she wanted to jump his bones.

She also thought about him way too much, even when he wasn't around. Like now, as she crossed the street to Denise's office, she wondered where he'd gone in such a hurry this morning, and why his hair had started looking weird all of a sudden. She hoped he didn't have a health condition. Although she wasn't ready to change her whole life in order to hang out with him and have lots of sex, she wished him well. She didn't want him to be sick or anything.

Denise was at her desk, a laptop open in front of her and a promising expression on her face. Jeremy was on his knees on the floor, boxing up her monitor.

When Maggie walked in, Denise glanced up. "I was just going to call you."

"New laptop?"

"Jeremy's."

Still on his knees, Jeremy folded the flaps on the box. "I'm loaning it to her until I can figure out what's going on with this baby." He stood and hoisted the box into his arms. "See you later."

"Bye, Jeremy," Denise said. "Thanks."

"Yes, thank you so much." Maggie gave him a smile before she walked over to Denise's desk. Anticipation churned in her gut. "Can you get on the Internet, or is the phone still out?"

"Phone line's good to go. At first the server was giving me some grief and I couldn't sign on, but I've got it now. Keep your fingers crossed I can access my e-mail."

"I'm crossing everything that can be crossed, including my eyes." Watching the screen over Denise's shoulder, she unbelted her trench coat and took it off.

"Get some coffee if you want it," Denise said.

"Thanks. I . . . I've had some." Better not mention whom she'd had it with. The way gossip traveled in this town, Denise would find out soon enough. She'd probably also find out that Maggie had spent the night at Sean's. Someone would have noticed the rental car sitting out there until morning, or else Madeline would let something slip.

Maggie hoped to be in contact with the property

owner before that information made the rounds and filtered down to Denise. Once Maggie knew how to contact the owner, she wouldn't need Denise's good-will quite so much.

"We're in!" Denise scrolled through her list of e-mails. "And there it is!"

Maggie's heart thumped as she stared at the screen. *At last.* Denise opened the e-mail, and miracle of mira-cles, it contained the name of the person on record as owning the property at 609 Fourth Avenue. Harold Pierpont lived in Evansville. And he had a phone number.

Denise reached for her desk phone and punched in the number. Maggie resisted the urge to pull the re-ceiver out of her hand so she could talk to Harold herself. But Denise was the real estate agent. She should handle this part.

Maggie walked back around the desk and sat in one of the two chairs positioned in front of it. She would trust Denise to do her job. From the way Denise was shouting into the phone, Maggie guessed that Harold Pierpont had a hearing problem.

"I have an offer on your property in Big Knob!" Denise said for the second time. "B-I-G K-N-O-B. That's right. 609 Fourth Avenue." Then she quoted the amount Maggie had authorized.

In the long silence that followed, Maggie stared at Denise so hard it was a wonder the woman didn't spontaneously combust.

Finally Denise spoke again. "Mr. Pierpont? Are you there?" Then she covered the mouthpiece with her hand. "I think he passed out. Or had a heart attack."

"Don't say that."

Denise uncovered the mouthpiece and tried again. "Hello? Mr. Pierpont? Can you hear me?"

Maggie pictured the phone dangling by a cord and Harold Pierpont stretched out on the floor, unconscious or worse. She chewed on her fingernail and willed him to say something, anything.

"Oh! You are there!"

Maggie slumped against the chair. She couldn't take this. Correction—she certainly could take this. She was a tough cookie.

"I'm not sure," Denise said. "Let me check with my client." Denise covered the mouthpiece again. "He wants to meet with you at the property tomorrow at ten. Do you want to do that?"

"Is he selling it to me or not?"

"I don't know. I think so. But he wants this meeting. He sounds really old."

"Okay. I'll meet with him." Maggie fought disappointment. She'd hoped to have this finalized today, or at least have a verbal agreement so she could complete the paperwork on Monday. Nothing about this deal was turning out to be simple.

"Fine! Tomorrow at ten!" Denise hung up the phone. "I hope he has all his marbles."

"Denise! You're giving me ulcers!"

"Well, his voice was pretty quavery. And you'd think if someone owned a piece of property, he'd remember it. From the sound of him, I hate to think he'll be driving on the freeway. Maybe he'll have somebody bring him. I hope so."

While Denise started checking her other e-mails, Maggie couldn't sit still, so she left the chair and paced the office. This arrangement made her more than a little nervous.

Finally inspiration struck. "Okay, here's an idea. I could drive over and get him to make sure he arrives safely. Why don't you call him back and suggest that?"

Denise didn't answer right away as she scrolled through an e-mail. "Okay," she said at last. She punched in the number again and cradled the phone against her shoulder. A few moments later she took the receiver away from her ear. "No answer."

"Let it ring. If he's hard of hearing or slow on his feet, answering could take a while."

"Or if he's dead, it could take forever." Denise sounded amazingly cheerful about that possibility.

"Will you stop? Whose side are you on, anyway?"

"Yours, of course." But Denise had a strange expression on her face. "But I might ask you the same thing."

"What do you mean?"

"Oh, a little e-mail birdie just told me your car was parked outside Sean's place all night. Sleeping with the enemy, are we?"

Sean had to ring the doorbell three times before Ambrose answered it. He was wearing his black silk bathrobe and he looked sleepy.

Sean didn't care. "We have to talk."

Ambrose peered at him. "You don't look so hot."

"Neither do you, but at least you can shave and shower in order to look decent. I have no control over what I look like, and it's driving me nuts."

"Hm. I guess you'd better come in." Ambrose opened the door wider and stepped back. "Dorcas! Sean's here!"

"I know." Dorcas came down the hall barefoot and wearing her purple silk robe.

Sean wasn't surprised to notice that her toenails were painted purple, too, and she wore a silver toe ring. Her hair looked mussed, as if she'd just crawled out of bed, too. Sean thought middle-aged people got up early.

"Hello, Sean." She covered a yawn with her hand. "You're wearing your glasses again."

"That's because my eyesight went bad in the middle

of breakfast at the Hob Knob. I never know when my eyesight will turn crappy or my hair will start growing in strange directions."

Dorcas nodded. "That's normal. Come on back and I'll make us some coffee." She turned and walked down the hall to the kitchen.

"There is nothing *normal* about this." As Sean followed her, Sabrina came trotting down the stairs and pranced over to rub against his leg. He paused to pet her and noticed a broom leaning up against the wall.

Sabrina walked over to sniff it, which was when Sean noticed it was no ordinary broom. The handle was carved into shapes of people. Sabrina batted at the broom. Then she looked up at Ambrose and meowed loudly.

"I guess she likes that broom." Sean leaned closer, trying to decipher the carvings.

"Here, let me get that out of your way." Ambrose snatched it out from under Sean's nose, opened a closet and tossed the broom inside. After he closed the door, Sabrina scratched at it as if wanting to get at the broom.

"She *really* likes that broom," Sean said. Edith Mae's words came back to him—*two people riding on a broomstick.* Nah. There was no such thing.

"We picked it up in Peru," Ambrose said. "I swear the straw is laced with catnip."

"I couldn't help noticing the fancy handle."

"Yeah, Dorcas hates the sound of a vacuum cleaner, so we use a broom. I could have bought a top-of-the-line vacuum for the price of that broom, but it makes Dorcas happy so I go along."

Sean nodded. Dorcas and Ambrose were the kind of people who would buy a hand-carved broom to sweep their hardwood floors. "You're going to laugh at this, but Edith Mae Hoogstraten swears she saw two people riding a broom last night."

Sure enough, Ambrose laughed. "When was the last time she got a new prescription for her glasses?"

"She doesn't wear glasses since her cataract surgery, but I think she was either sipping gin or dreaming."

"Or both. Come on. I can smell coffee."

As they walked into the kitchen, three mugs of coffee sat waiting on the kitchen table.

"That was fast." Sean estimated no more than two minutes had gone by since Dorcas offered to make the coffee.

"I have this special European pot," Dorcas said. "You set it up the night before and then hit a remote control from the bedroom."

Sean glanced around, wondering if he'd find some kind of space-age brewing system on the counter. "Where is it?"

"Tucked inside a cupboard. I like to keep my countertops clear. Sit anywhere you like."

"Thanks." Sean pulled out a chair and sat down.

"Hey, Dorcas, you'll never believe the latest Big Knob gossip," Ambrose said. "Edith Mae Hoogstraten says she saw two people riding on a broom last night."

"She must have watched *The Wizard of Oz* one too many times," Dorcas said. "I'll bet it was an owl carrying a mouse with a long tail."

"Nobody believes her, anyway," Sean said. "Seeing your broom in the hallway made me think of it."

"Oh yes." Dorcas laughed merrily as she sat across from Sean at the small marble table. "The one Ambrose didn't want me to buy when we found it in Switzerland. But it sweeps like a champ."

"It was Peru, dearest," Ambrose said. "We bought it in Peru, remember? From the family that raised llamas."

Dorcas blinked. "Oh, right. Oh, well—the Andes, the Alps—who can keep them straight?"

Sean had never seen either one, but he thought he'd remember whether he'd been on one particular continent or another. Still, he didn't care where the damned broom came from. He had more important issues to address.

He ignored the coffee sitting in front of him. "About my appearance. If you can't change me back the way I was, at least tell me how these herbs work, so I know what to expect."

Dorcas poured cream into her coffee. "Everyone's case is different. Cream?"

"No, thanks. Look, you must have some general description. You can't go giving someone a bunch of herbs and not have some idea of how they'll work."

Dorcas stirred her coffee and glanced up at him. "You're the first person we've tried this combination on."

"What?"

She took a drink and put down her mug. "Usually people want to be better-looking and sexier, not the opposite. Yours was an unusual request."

"Are you saying I'm some kind of guinea pig?" The more he heard, the more he cursed himself for getting into this. What an idiot he'd been.

"I wouldn't put it that way," Ambrose said.

"Oh yeah? Then how would you put it?"

"I would call it a learning experience for all of us." Dorcas sipped her coffee. "How are you coming along on the sex bench?"

Sean gritted his teeth. "I have no time to work on the blasted sex bench because I'm busy fighting for my life. I'm sure Maggie has the information on the property by now. She may even be in touch with the owner and making an offer."

"What will you do about that?" Ambrose asked.

"There's nothing I can do. I don't have the money to make a counteroffer. I don't have the looks to charm her out of buying the place. Worse than that, I can't figure out any way to make her fall in love with me."

Dorcas cradled her warm mug in both hands. "You want her to do that?"

"Hell, yes, I want her to do that! She's everything I need, but I'm not what *she* needs, so I'm dead in the water. If I had my looks and sexiness back for good, I could convince her to give up her job and move here so we could get married."

Ambrose cleared his throat. "You haven't said anything about being in love with her."

"Well, I . . ." Sean thought about that. "I think I am."

"Thinking you are and actually being in love are two different things," Dorcas said. "Personally, I'm glad you don't have your old self to work with. You might trap that poor girl into loving you when you only *think* you love her. That would be cruel. You have to know without a shadow of a doubt that you're crazy in love with her."

Sean gazed at her. "How will I know that for sure?"

"Trust me." Dorcas smiled at him. "When it happens, you will know."

Sean's cell phone rang. "Excuse me a minute." He checked the display and discovered it was Clem Loudermilk, probably calling because Clara was bugging him about the skunks. He could answer it later.

"I think you should take that call," Ambrose said.

"It can wait. I still want to know if you can help me predict when I'll change from looking good to looking bad."

"Take the call," Dorcas said. "Then we'll talk."

"I can't get good reception in this house."

Ambrose waved a hand in the air. "That may have changed. You know how those transmissions vary."

With a sigh, Sean answered his phone, expecting

static and breaks in the conversation. To his surprise, Clem came through loud and clear.

"Sean, Clara took a notion that she wants a sunroom. A big sunroom. I want you to build it, and because of my tax picture this year, I want to pay you now, before you do the work." Then he named a figure that made Sean gasp. "Can we make a deal?"

"Uh, sure, Clem. I'd be happy to do that work for you."

"Can you come up here this morning and talk to Clara about it? She's real anxious to start the planning."

"All right. I'll be there."

"And don't park by your place. Come up the main road to the big house. I just went down to the cottage, looking for you, and the place is crawling with women. I guess the word's out about your doings last night."

Sean groaned. "Thanks for the warning."

"No problem. See you soon."

"Right." Sean closed the phone and stared at it, still not quite believing the offer Clem had made. The women converging on his little place would be a hassle, but it might not be his place much longer, anyway, if he bought the house.

"Good news?" Dorcas asked.

Feeling a little dazed, Sean glanced at them. "I guess you could say that. Clem Loudermilk is about to give me a chunk of money. I might even be able to make a counteroffer on the property Maggie wants."

Chapter 23

Maggie should have known that her night with Sean would be all over town first thing this morning. She'd done the crime, so she'd have to do the time, or, in this case, brave the embarrassment.

Her cheeks felt hot, but she made herself look Denise in the eye. "He's not the enemy. He's just a guy who wants to buy his childhood home."

"And he's using sex to try to get it?"

"Maybe, but as you can see, I'm still planning to buy the property for SaveALot. If that was his plan, it failed."

"If he was his old self, it wouldn't have failed. I don't know what's happened to him, but he's lost that extreme sexiness he used to have."

Maggie didn't think he'd lost anything. Sure, his hair misbehaved sometimes and his glasses weren't very attractive. But she had a vivid picture of how he'd looked last night, his biceps taut as he braced his arms on either side of her, his eyes bright as emeralds as he thrust deep. She'd never seen a sexier man in her life.

"So you're planning to love him and leave him?"

Denise's question interrupted her brief fantasy. "That's a little harsh, don't you think? We're both consenting adults. We can choose to have a little sex for its own sake."

Denise's gaze filled with envy. "You know, he's never had a woman at his place. Never. Some have tried, but he wouldn't invite them inside."

"He probably feels safer with me because I'm from out of town. For all you know, he's relieved I'll be leaving soon."

"He's not the only one. Now that the women in town know he's back in the game, they're lining up to take advantage of that."

Which irritated the hell out of Maggie. The thought of a parade of women cycling through Sean's bedroom put her in a foul mood. She wondered if he'd allow that, now that she'd broken the ice by being the first girl in his bed. Would he have kitchen table sex with them, too? She could still feel the smooth surface of the table against her bare back, still hear the thump of the table legs keeping time with their heavy breathing.

"So it was good."

The best. "I don't think you and I know each other well enough for me to answer that."

"It was good. I can tell from the way your eyes glazed over a second ago. I suppose it doesn't matter what he looks like if he still has the moves."

"I really don't want to talk about this anymore." No, she wanted to do it, which was insane.

"Okay, but are you thinking of spending any more time with him while you're here?"

"No, not really." She was meeting Harold Pierpont in the morning to close the deal, assuming the old guy arrived in one piece. Sean couldn't change the course of events now.

Because of that, he might not want to have anything to do with her. That was a depressing thought. She might as well stay away from him and avoid a potential rejection that would crush her ego.

"I wouldn't try to see him if I were you," Denise said. "It could get dicey."

"In what way?"

Denise gestured to her computer screen. "There's an e-mail loop in town called *Sean Watch*. It's been inactive for months because he wasn't dating anyone. This morning I have ten e-mails with the subject line *Sean's back*! I predict you'll have to fight through the crowd to get to him."

"No, thanks." Battling other women to see Sean didn't appeal to her. Besides, it wasn't as if she couldn't control her craving for him. She had twenty-four hours before she would see Harold. Surely she could stay away from Sean that long.

"So what are you going to do with yourself until tomorrow at ten?"

"Go back to Madeline's."

"Not much to do there."

"Sure there is. I can help Abe document his laugh tracks."

But ten minutes later as she climbed into her car, she found herself driving back to the property. Her excuse was that she wanted to see it when the sun was shining. Her reason was that Sean might be there.

Sean stopped by Denise's office on his way to Clem's. If he had the money to bid on the property, then she had to allow him to do that.

She glanced up from the screen of a laptop, a laptop that was obviously working. If he'd had any hope that Jeremy hadn't come to her aid, that was gone. Jeremy must have loaned her the laptop.

Denise regarded him with narrowed eyes. "She's not sticking around, you know."

He didn't have to ask whom she meant. "I know." If he thought he could change that, he would try, but the herbs Dorcas had given him could sabotage that effort.

"Why her? Why go all this time not dating, and then end up with her?"

"I didn't come in here to talk about that." He couldn't answer the question without sounding like a dope, anyway. There was something about Maggie that stirred him up, something he couldn't quite put his finger on.

"You want to know if I've found the owner."

"That's part of it, and I—"

"What's it worth to you?" Denise gave him a once-over.

That slow scan was enough to remind him of the horrors he'd faced before taking Dorcas's "cure." He didn't want to resume that life. He only wanted to look good for Maggie.

He cleared his throat. "I'm not going to play games. Clem Loudermilk just hired me to do a major addition to his house, and he's paying me in advance. I want to bid on the property."

Denise's eyebrows rose. "I see. What kind of money are we talking about?"

Sean named his figure, which included all he'd saved, the money Calvin Gilmore owed him, and the advance from Clem. "And I can go higher. That's what I'll have in cash, but my credit's good. I should be able to borrow more if necessary."

"I'll call Harold Pierpont and let him know we have another offer. Maggie needs to know, too." Denise picked up the phone and punched in a number written on her memo pad. After a minute, she put the phone down again. "No answer from the seller."

"This Pierpont guy doesn't have a machine?"

"Not unless it's a defibrillator. The guy sounded ancient on the phone. I'll be surprised if he shows up at ten tomorrow, like he said."

"He's coming here?"

"Supposedly. Let me try Maggie."

"Wait."

Denise paused, her hand on the receiver. "You want to reconsider?"

"No, I want to tell her myself."

"That's not how it's done. You don't have the competing buyers notifying each other. It has to go through me."

"Oh, for crying out loud, Denise. This is Big Knob, not Chicago. Let me call her. I need to be the one to break the news."

She studied him for a moment. "I'm beginning to think you actually care about her."

He shrugged, unwilling to comment one way or the other.

"I never thought Sean Madigan would be in danger of having his heart broken."

"It's not like that. Telling her myself is the decent thing to do, considering . . ."

"Considering you've slept with her, you mean." Denise scowled. "I don't know what's wrong with you. You could have most anyone in town—or you could before you started losing your looks. Maybe that's it. You took stock and decided you'd better grab the first available woman."

Sean pulled out his cell phone. "I don't have to listen to this. I'm calling her." He punched in the number he'd memorized yesterday.

"I'm warning you, she'll be outta here by Monday, with or without buying the property. If you want my opinion, you'll settle for someone else, someone who doesn't mind so much if you have weird hair."

Sean ignored her and waited for Maggie to answer.

When she did, she sounded out of breath . . . and wary. "Hello?"

"I got a sudden influx of money," he said. "I'm in Denise's office and I just told her I'm bidding on the property."

Silence.

"Maggie, are you there?"

"Yes, I'm here. Did MegaMart get to you? Is that who gave you the money? Please have the decency to tell me if it is."

"It has nothing to do with MegaMart. It's my money. Clem Loudermilk's paying me in advance for a construction job."

There was a sound as if she'd swallowed hard. "Sean, you're making a huge mistake. This place will be a horrible drain on your time and money. It looks as if it could have a ton of hidden defects."

"It sounds as if you're out there right now."

"I . . . I am. I decided to take another walk around the place."

To hell with his lack of sex appeal. He needed to convince her that her future was here, with him, in that house. "Stay there. I'll be right out."

He snapped the phone closed and glanced at Denise. "Let me know if you get in touch with Pierpont."

"If you don't hear from me, just meet Maggie and me out at the house at ten. I guess we'll be doing this the old-fashioned way, face-to-face."

"Fine with me." If he had any luck with Maggie, she'd withdraw her bid.

As he drove toward the property, he remembered promising Clem he'd come up there and discuss the addition. Without Clem, he had no prayer of outbidding Maggie. Driving one-handed, he called Clem.

"I'm running into a little situation," he said. "Can I come up there in about an hour?"

"Better not make it any longer than that," Clem said. "When Clara takes a notion, she wants action. I convinced her to use you instead of some big outfit from Indianapolis, but if you don't jump right on it, she might change her mind."

"I'll be there in an hour." Sean closed the phone and tucked it back in his pocket.

On the way past his little cottage he glanced over and saw several vehicles parked there. About five women stood in the yard, talking. He recognized all of them. He should. He'd seen every single one naked.

Apparently the news that he'd slept with Maggie had been like throwing chum in the water. The sharks were circling and eager to leap in the boat. The women all remembered what he used to look like, though. They might scatter once they saw the loser he'd turned into.

Unfortunately one of them spotted his truck. Good Lord. They were piling in their cars and coming after him. He grabbed his phone from his pocket and dialed Maggie. "Change of plans. I've picked up an escort. I need to lose them."

"Who?"

"Some women." He glanced in the rearview mirror and saw the first vehicle, Angie Jankowsky's silver SUV, was gaining on him.

Maggie drew in a breath. "So Denise wasn't kidding about that."

"Guess not." He stepped on the gas. "Listen, I really want to talk to you."

"That doesn't seem possible."

"It is, but I need to handle this, and I really have to talk to Clem and Clara. How about if I meet you in two hours out in the Whispering Forest where we left the skunks? I wanted to check on them, anyway. You can drive there, but I'll be on foot."

"On foot?"

"Yeah. It's the only way I won't be spotted." Closing the phone, he floored the gas pedal. As a guy who'd had countless make-out sessions in the woods, he knew the back roads better than anyone in Big Knob. He was as good as gone.

Maggie spent most of the next two hours wandering around the old house and wondering if she dared meet Sean. On the one hand, she might be able to talk him out of throwing away his money on this rickety old place. On the other hand, he would have an opposing goal, to talk her out of buying it for SaveALot, and she didn't want to take a chance on losing her focus.

On the third hand—and she ignored the logic that there was no such thing as a third hand unless you were an alien—she might never have another chance to be alone with him. She wasn't fooling herself, either. If they were alone, they'd have sex. Whichever way things went tomorrow, she doubted there would be sex after the deal was closed. One of them would not be feeling charitable enough toward the other to get sweaty and naked together.

Before the deal was closed, however, was a whole different thing. There was wiggle room before the deal was closed. She would love to do some more wiggling with Sean before she had to give him up forever. But she couldn't let it influence her decision.

In the end, she let curiosity about the skunks tip the scales. The Whispering Forest didn't seem scary in broad daylight, and she'd like to find out if the skunks were sleeping quietly in their den. She thought she'd be able to peek in without disturbing them.

And because she didn't know what kind of evasive action Sean had been forced to take, she drove back to the Hob Knob and picked up two orders of home-made vegetable soup and two coffees. The sun might be shining, but the air was still brisk. If Sean was on time, the soup would still be warm.

She found the road leading into the forest without

much trouble, but the trees and underbrush all looked different during the day. One wide spot in the road seemed like the right one, but after tramping around in the woods nearby she found no fallen log with a skunk family living under it.

What she found was a stump with footprints around it. Maybe this was where Dorcas and Ambrose had been before they'd appeared so suddenly the night before. Maggie wandered around the clearing, curious whether she'd find any clues as to what Dorcas and Ambrose had been up to out here.

Eventually she came to a print in the moist earth that made her pause and study it. It was the sort of impression that would be made if someone had a large claw-footed table out here. That was unlikely, unless Dorcas and Ambrose had set up a banquet. But if they had, where was this table? Where were the chairs, the plates, the knives, forks and spoons?

Searching the ground nearby, she found more of the same impressions. Strange, very strange. She'd have to bring Sean here and see what he made of it. He knew the residents better than she did. He could probably come up with an explanation.

She drove farther down the road and ended up at the base of Big Knob. She'd gone too far. Turning around wasn't easy, but finally she managed to point herself in the right direction. Then she retraced her path past the area where she'd seen the large impressions and finally found another wide place in the road that she'd missed the first time through. This had to be it.

A quick check of the surrounding woods proved that she was in the right spot. She found the fallen tree and the den she and Sean had created. Crouching down, she peered into the dark little cave.

"I wouldn't startle them if I were you."

Gasping, she leaped to her feet and turned to find Sean standing there, a backpack slung over one shoulder. For some reason he'd ditched the glasses again.

She didn't notice whether his hair was messy or not. She was too busy looking into his eyes, which burned with the same lusty intent she felt racing through her body.

"I'm here to talk you out of buying the property," he said.

"What a coincidence. I'm here for the same reason."

He unhooked the backpack from his shoulder and set it on the ground. "Then let's get to it." He stepped toward her.

Her heart hammered with anticipation. "Yes, let's." She tucked her glasses in the pocket of her trench coat.

A split second, a blink of an eye, and they were on each other.

Chapter 24

Thank God I brought condoms. Sean hadn't been sure what kind of a reception he'd get, hadn't even known if Maggie would show up. She'd shown up all right. In spades.

He'd wondered if he'd ever kiss her again, and here she was opening her mouth for him, using her tongue, moaning as if she couldn't get enough. Metal rasped as she unzipped his leather jacket so she could get her hands under his shirt. He'd already untied her coat and unfastened the buttons.

Lifting his head, he caught her face in both hands. "I'm ready to come right now."

"Me, too." Her breath was quick and shallow. "Right now."

"But we have to move away—" He groaned as she fondled his crotch. "Away from the skunks."

"How far?" She sounded as desperate as he felt.

"This way." He caught her hand, grabbed up his backpack and pulled her farther into the woods. "Here." Dropping the backpack, he unzipped it and pulled out a soft blanket.

"I thought we'd do it up against a tree." Her voice was low and rich, the voice of a woman who'd lost her inhibitions.

The blanket fell from his shaking fingers as he envi-

sioned bracing her against the nearest evergreen and
pushing in deep. Glancing at her, he saw both need
and boldness in her expression. Bold women had
turned him off before, but on Maggie, boldness
looked good.

Taking her by the shoulders, he kissed her hard as
he maneuvered her toward a sturdy pine. Then he
released her long enough to take off his jacket and
drape it around her shoulders. He needed padding for
what he had in mind.

Getting her out of her jeans seemed to take forever.

"Hurry," she murmured.

Finally he had her free, and when he reached between her thighs, he understood why she was begging
him to be fast. She was so wet, so hot, and seconds
away from coming. Pushing her against the tree, he
kissed her again and drove his fingers into her slick
heat. She erupted, her cries muffled against his mouth.

Somehow he held himself in check as he stroked
her, drawing out the pleasure. His tongue mimicked
the movement of his fingers, which made him long to
finish this in the way nature intended it to be finished.
The scent of her climax drifted up to him, driving him
crazy with lust.

When he felt her begin to relax, he let her sink back
against the tree, eyes closed, while he unbuckled his
belt, wrenched open his jeans and rolled on a condom.
God, she looked sexy leaning against the tree, fully
clothed from the waist up, completely naked from the
waist down. He'd bundled her jeans at the foot of the
tree so her bare feet wouldn't touch the ground.

But now it wouldn't matter. "Take—" He had to
stop and clear his throat, which felt thick from the
urges pulsing in him. "Take hold of my shoulders."

Her eyes opened, and lust burned there. "Yes." She
clutched his shoulders. "I still want you. You made
me come, but it's not enough."

"I'm glad." He grasped her hips. "When I lift you, wrap your legs around me."

Wordlessly she followed his directions. He sought her heat with the tip of his penis. "Tighter."

She locked her ankles behind his back and he thrust in and up. Oh *yes*. Closing his eyes, he fought for control. He didn't want it to be over that fast.

"You just found where I live," she whispered.

Opening his eyes, he held her gaze as he withdrew a fraction and pushed home again. "There?"

She licked her lips. "Uh-huh. Right . . . *there*." She tightened around him, giving him a jolt of pleasure.

He almost lost it, but by clenching his jaw, he was able to hold back his climax. "I like it there." That was the understatement of the year. Being this deep inside her felt incredible, as if he'd just unlocked the secrets of the universe.

Her grip on his shoulders intensified and her voice was breathy. "Then by all means, make yourself at home."

"I believe I will." The sensation of pulling back and rocking forward into that sweet spot was like nothing he'd ever known before.

Instinctively he recognized that except for the latex between them, he could make her pregnant right now, this very minute. He wasn't sure how he knew that, but he was absolutely sure of it. It would be easy. He wondered if she knew how open she was, how ready to be filled with his eager sperm.

Instead of the usual panic at that thought, he felt a glow of excitement. So this was what it would be like to make a baby. For the first time in his life, that's exactly what he wanted to do.

But he wouldn't. Instead he would begin a steady rhythm that would give her another climax before he claimed his. At least that was his conscious plan. But somewhere along the way, staying steady lost out to driving urgency. He stroked faster, propelled by the fire in his veins and the lush sensation of thrusting into her hot body.

His belt jingled as his movements grew more frenzied. His cries mingled with hers.

"Now," she said, gasping.

Yes, now. His fingers digging into the soft skin of her bottom, he shoved hard and deep. A second after her keening cry of release, his orgasm ripped through him with a force that left him stunned and breathless. Sex had never been this good. Never. Then the thought tickled his mind, *This isn't just sex.*

Although Maggie felt hot enough to tear off the rest of her clothes and run through the woods naked, she decided that might not be a prudent plan. Instead she put her clothes back on while Sean tried to help. He wasn't much help, but she enjoyed the touching and the playful kisses as she pulled on her panties and jeans.

"I want to do it all over again," he murmured, nuzzling her earlobe.

She found herself back in his arms, her body melting against his as he kissed her in earnest. When he came up for air, his hands were under her sweater and he'd unhooked her bra. They were both breathing hard.

He cupped her breast and she moaned.

His voice rasped in the stillness of the forest. "I want you naked." He nibbled on her lower lip as he fondled her breast. "But you'll be cold."

"That's what you think." She'd never been so hot in her life. Any minute Smokey the Bear would arrest her as a fire danger.

He pressed his mouth to her throat. "The car."

She sighed. "The soup."

"The what?" He worked his way back to her mouth.

"Soup. I brought soup."

"That's nice." He ran his tongue over her lips. "But if it doesn't taste like you, I don't want it."

"We should eat something."

Without warning, he stopped kissing her and swung her up in his arms. "Maybe I will."

He was true to his word. Inside of five minutes, she was sprawled naked in the backseat of the car as he gave her incredible oral sex. They wouldn't both fit in the car, at least not in this position, so he'd had to leave the door open. Kneeling on a bed of pine needles, he was at the perfect height to drive her insane.

One deeply satisfying orgasm later, she divested him of his pants and directed him to lie on the seat, his legs dangling out the door, while she climbed on top. She was so wet that she slid onto his penis in record time.

He groaned. "Good."

"Yeah." She couldn't believe how much she craved this sensation. It wasn't only the delicious friction as she rode him. It wasn't only the climax she could feel building in her and knew must be building in him. It was about the joining, the connection, being as close to him as she could get. A warning bell sounded in her brain.

He cradled her jiggling breasts. "I love this."

"Me, too." Bracing her hands on his broad shoulders, she moved faster.

"I mean, I *really* love this."

"So do I." She gazed into his eyes as her movements brought her closer and closer still.

He gasped and clutched her hips. "Maggie, slow down."

"Don't you want to come?"

"Not yet." His jaw muscles clenched. "I love being inside you. I want . . . to make it last."

"All right." She began an easy rhythm, rising and descending gently. As she held his gaze, the connec-

tion grew stronger. The warning bell sounded again.
"Like that?"

"Mm." His expression changed from the fierce intensity of lust. His mouth curved in a tender smile.
"Maggie," he murmured. "Oh, Maggie."

She swallowed. Such sweetness between them might not be a good thing. Wild sex was okay. They could deal with that. But this . . . this was dangerous. She picked up the pace.

"Don't."

"Yes." She moved faster.

"Please . . . I can't . . ." He came.

So did she, and it was wonderful but sad. She knew what he wanted from her. But she couldn't give it to him.

Before they ate the soup, Sean went to get the backpack he'd left in the woods so they could have the crackers and cheese he'd smuggled out of his house. He picked up the soft blanket, too, in case they had more car sex and Maggie needed it to stay warm afterward.

He would have liked some cuddle time after the last round, but with the door open, it was too chilly for cuddling. They'd had to get dressed.

The shadows were already lengthening, and soon it would be downright cold out here. Maybe after it got dark they could chance going back to his house. They could hide her car in the trees next to his truck and walk in.

He wanted to spend as much time as possible with her. Although he couldn't complain about the sex they'd had so far, he couldn't pretend it had any particular significance, either. She might be willing to get naked with him, but she didn't want it to be meaningful. He'd never cared about meaningful before, but now that he wanted her to stay in Big Knob, meaning-ful sex was everything.

He wasn't giving up on that, though. He'd seen glimmers of deep feeling in her eyes, whether she wanted him to notice or not. A woman like Maggie wouldn't stick around just for the sex, but if she started to care about him, she might.

She could also be playing him for a fool, as Denise had predicted. Maybe she wanted only a few more orgasms before she bought the property and left town. If that was her plan, he intended to stop her by out-bidding her.

And he could do it, too. Thank God he'd decided to confide in Clem, who had pulled some information off the Internet. SaveALot had a track record of pay-ing very little for property in rural areas like this. Mag-gie wouldn't be authorized to spend as much as Sean could raise.

Clem and Clara didn't relish a SaveALot messing up the view from their front porch, so Clem was will-ing to back Sean on the purchase. Sean now had the resources to take her down, but he didn't want it to be that way. He hoped she'd make the decision herself, because she cared about him. If he crushed her dreams, they'd have no future.

On the way back to the car, he used the flashlight tucked in his backpack to check on the skunks. Near as he could tell they were all in there, sleeping in a pile as they usually did. A few sets of tracks indicated they'd ventured out during the night. He scattered some carrots around the den's entrance so they'd have another snack, although eventually they'd have to find their own food.

Maggie was leaning against the car's fender when he returned. She set two Styrofoam containers on the hood and turned on the engine. She'd put on the ugly black glasses again, which made her look cuter than the dickens. And she smiled at him. "I'm heating up the soup."

That smile warmed him more than any bowl of soup ever could. He was beginning to realize how much he needed to see that smile on a regular basis. "Clever idea."

"Just trying to keep up with you. How did you get away from the women following you?"

"Took some back roads." He opened his backpack and pulled out a sleeve of Ritz crackers, only slightly crushed, and a package of sliced cheese.

"How many were there?"

"Five."

"That sounds like a posse. What would have happened if they'd caught you?"

"I don't know." And he hadn't wanted to find out, either. Years ago he would have laughingly made dates with all of them for different nights. Switching partners every night hadn't bothered him then. Now he'd have to turn them all down flat. He'd rather avoid a scene like that.

"So where's your truck?"

"Once I lost them, I doubled back, left the truck on a side road and hiked to my house so I could talk to Clem about the remodeling job. Then I picked up a few things and came here." He laid the crackers and cheese on the fender and opened them. "Want some?"

"Sure. Thanks." She took a couple of crackers, folded a slice of cheese and made a little sandwich. But before she took a bite, she looked at him. "Is there any way I can convince you not to bid on the property?"

He shook his head. "How about you? You still in?"

"Yes."

They eyed each other for a few seconds.

"Maggie, do you love your job?"

"I like it."

Which wasn't the same as loving it, but he let that pass. "Why do you like it?"

"It makes use of my economics major, and if I succeed with SaveALot, I can make very good money. Very good."

"I guess money's important to you."

She sighed. "It is, only because there was never enough of it growing up, and I'm really sick of that feeling. I've seen what poor money choices have done to my parents and I won't live like that."

"I can relate." His father's poor money management had cost his family dearly, too. He gazed at her. "We're not solving this, are we?"

Her smile was sad. "Not exactly."

"Well, since we're at a stalemate, and you were nice enough to bring food, we might as well eat it."

"Might as well." She gestured toward the Styrofoam cups. "Help yourself. I don't know if they're much warmer, though."

"Doesn't matter. It's not like we've never eaten cold food after having sex."

Her cheeks grew pink. "True."

He liked knowing he had that kind of effect on her. She wasn't totally cool about this relationship. Picking up one of the containers, he took the plastic spoon she handed him. "Thanks."

"I thought we'd need something."

He looked into her eyes. "You knew we'd have sex, didn't you?"

"I thought we would. Didn't you?"

"I hoped we would. I had no idea, especially after you found out that I'm bidding against you."

She held his gaze a moment before turning away. "I should shut off the engine."

While she was doing that he ate a cracker, just to give his jaw something to crunch on. If they didn't have this issue between them, life could be so sweet.

When she came back, she took the top off her soup and used it as a plate for her cracker sandwich. "Bidding against me is pointless, you know."

"Maybe, maybe not."

"Sean, you don't want to go up against a big company like SaveALot. They have deep pockets."

But you're not authorized to dig very deep. He wasn't going to tell her he knew that, though. Maybe, just maybe, they wouldn't get to that stage. He had until ten tomorrow to change her mind.

"I'm sure they do." He popped the lid off his soup. "But I'm highly motivated."

She paused, her spoon halfway to her mouth. "So am I."

"Then may the most deserving person win." He took a mouthful of lukewarm soup.

"It's not very hot," she said.

"It's fine. The flavor's great. I love this kind." He was touched that she'd thought to bring it in the first place.

"I'm glad. I took a guess."

"And if it's not real hot, that's my fault, anyway."

Framed by the big black glasses, her blue eyes sparkled. "Not completely your fault."

No, not completely, he thought with a smile. She'd been all too willing to suggest sex up against a tree. And she hadn't argued about having more sex in the back of the car, either. He didn't think she'd argue if he suggested they go back to the same activity after they finished their delayed lunch.

He was used to sexual enthusiasm from a woman. It was the sort of reaction he generally expected. But in this case, it wasn't exactly the reaction he wanted. Because he'd never gone beyond sexual enthusiasm in his dealings with women, he wasn't sure how to make true affection happen. Maybe as the afternoon wore on, he'd figure it out.

Chapter 25

Maggie was making little progress talking Sean out of bidding on the property, but she still had several hours to work on him. She wanted him to give it up willingly because he realized the place would suck him dry. She could see him wearing himself out and going deep into debt to fix and maintain such a monstrosity.

Strangely enough, she was more worried about that than her job. But if she could get him to see reason, then everything would work out. He'd avoid making a huge mistake and she'd get back in H.G.'s good graces and finally claim her rightful place in the company.

The soup tasted okay lukewarm, but not the coffee, so they poured that out. While they were eating more crackers and cheese, Maggie remembered the strange impressions she'd seen in the dirt farther up the road.

Dusting cracker crumbs from her hands, she turned to him. "Let's take a walk. I want to show you something I found earlier today and see what you make of it."

"Okay." He fell into step beside her. Then, as if they'd been walking together like this for years, he took her hand.

She couldn't remember the last time she'd walked

hand in hand with someone. Funny how you could have wild sex with a guy and still keep a certain emotional distance. But let that guy hold your hand while you're walking down a country road, with late-afternoon sunlight filtering through the treeless branches and a hint of smoke in the air, and suddenly there was an intimacy between you that all the sex in the world couldn't create.

She had to be careful, or she'd start getting sentimental about Sean. Maybe the best tactic was returning to their area of disagreement. "Haven't you ever wanted to build your own house, design it from the ground up?"

"It's crossed my mind." He stroked his thumb against hers. "But I love a place with history."

"Create your own history." The lazy touch of his thumb lit a fire under her. She was set permanently on simmer whenever he was around, and the slightest touch cranked her up to the boiling point.

"The truth is, I want to rewrite history."

"How?" She started thinking of the stump in the middle of the clearing and wondered if it would work as a sex bench.

"I want to turn that house into the warm, welcoming place I remember. I want to do it for me, and maybe a little bit for my mother."

That comment touched her more than she wanted him to know. She had to give herself a few moments before she could say anything. "I don't think your mother would want you to sacrifice yourself to that house."

"I wouldn't. I have the skills to bring it back. If I happened to be a computer guy like Jeremy, I'd be a fool to buy that house, but restoration is what I do. I'm good at it. It might take me a while, working nights and weekends, but I can restore that place without bankrupting myself."

She didn't want to picture him working on the house, but she couldn't help it. She imagined a light burning in an upstairs window late at night, after the rest of the town had gone to sleep. Sean would be up there sanding floors or scraping off paint, probably whistling to himself. He'd be loving every minute of it.

The first crack in her certainty appeared. She'd been so convinced that he would make the worst mistake of his life if he bought that old house. She'd been going on her parents' experience, but they knew nothing about repairing and restoring old places. For them, owning an old house had been a self-defeating nightmare.

No, she couldn't kid herself that she'd be rescuing Sean if she bought the property. She'd be saving her own ass, and that was all. That was a worthy goal, but she didn't like knowing she'd be taking something away from a guy she . . . liked a lot.

They reached the second wide spot in the road. "This is where I came first when I was trying to find the skunk den." She led him into the woods. "Come over here and take a look at this."

He squeezed her hand. "You bet. I'll take a look at anything you want to show me out here in the woods."

Her libido snapped to attention again, reminding her of the smooth stump that might be exactly chair height. It had definite possibilities, and yet the light was much dimmer now than when she'd first found the clearing, and the air colder. The scent of smoke was stronger, too.

She couldn't shake the feeling that they weren't alone out here. Maybe it was campers and maybe it wasn't. Soon it would be dark, and she wasn't crazy about sticking around after dark. She decided they wouldn't be here long, even considering the available stump.

The clearing looked about as she remembered it, with the stump in the middle. "First of all, I found footsteps all around this stump."

"Are you thinking Dorcas and Ambrose spent time in this clearing before showing up by my truck last night?"

"It's possible."

"It's more than possible, considering I haven't built their sex bench yet." He caught the collar of her trench coat in both hands and drew her close. "Looking at that stump gives me a few ideas of my own."

His suggestive tone and heated glance created quite a stir in her significant parts. "We can talk about that, but—"

He brushed his lips over hers. "I'd like to do more than talk." He reached to take off her glasses.

"Wait." She caught his hand. "First you have to see something."

"If it's more footprints, forget it. I'm more interested in kissing you." He dipped his head toward her again. "And your glasses are in the way."

"No, seriously." She wiggled out of his arms. "Tell me what you think this is." She walked to the edge of the clearing and searched for the impressions she'd found.

Because the light was becoming so dim, she had more trouble locating them, but finally she found one. "Here." She crouched down and pointed to it. "What made that?"

Sean glanced at the ground. "Huh." Then he hunkered down next to the impression and poked at it. "It looks like someone had a huge antique table out here, the kind with those big claw feet."

"That's what I thought. But why? And don't you think it was recent?"

"Probably, considering the rain we just had." Sean

traced the impression with one finger. "It had to be heavy, too. These are deep."

"There are more." Maggie studied the ground and found another one, then two more. "They're not in the sort of pattern that you'd expect from a table with four legs."

"So somebody had one table leg out here, for some reason." He sniffed the air. "Maybe the same campers who have that fire going again."

"Sean, people think the Whispering Forest is haunted, right?"

"Some do. I don't."

"What if there's a hermit living out here, and he wants to scare everybody off so he won't be discovered?"

He nodded. "I guess that's possible, but he'd have to be a really old hermit. I've been hearing stories about these woods ever since I was a kid. My mother forbade me to play in here, but I did, anyway. It was right next door."

"Did you ever smell smoke?"

"Maybe, but I thought it was from our chimney. It's only now that I realize it's coming from somewhere else."

"How about whispered words?" Maggie remembered that she'd imagined someone whispering to her the night before.

"Hey, when you're a kid, you always imagine stuff like that. It's not real."

The whisper was soft, barely audible in Maggie's ear. *That's what you think, dude.* "Sean, did you hear that?"

"Hear what?"

"I heard someone whisper."

"You're scaring yourself, Maggie. Nothing's here."

She wanted to believe him, but the whisper had

been very distinct. She shivered. "Maybe we should go back to the car."

"We can do that." Sean gazed around the clearing. "I'll come back another time. If someone is living out here, I'd like to know about it. I—" His darting glance froze on a spot at the edge of the clearing. "Maggie," he said in a low voice. "Get behind me."

She began to tremble. "What is it?"

"I don't know. *Get behind me.*"

She didn't like to think of herself as a coward, but she did what he said. Her legs felt rubbery, but she stumbled over and stood behind him as she stared hard at the same place where he was looking with such intensity.

Something moved. Something *huge*. The hairs prickled all over her body. "Is it a bear?" she whispered. Frantically she tried to remember what a person did when confronting a bear. You didn't run. You rolled into a ball and pretended to be dead.

Yeah, right. Forget that. She would run until her legs wouldn't carry her or the bear caught up, which was supposed to be quick. They could run faster than a human.

Then the creature stepped into the clearing, and she opened her mouth to scream, but nothing came out. She must be dreaming this. She was having some horrible nightmare, and any minute she would wake up in a cold sweat and be grateful that such things didn't really exist.

But she couldn't seem to wake up. She had to be dreaming, though. The thing was wearing . . . *an iPod?* It reared on its hind legs and blew a star-shaped smoke ring at them. *Please let me wake up! Now!* But when the smoke ring cleared, she was still standing there, her fingers digging into Sean's leather jacket.

And in the clearing stood a dragon. A smoke-ring-blowing dragon wearing a white iPod.

"Damn," Sean muttered, his voice shaking. "Guess it was no table leg."

"I think it's time we admitted that we've lost control of the situation." Ambrose paced the living room with Sabrina pacing behind him, whiskers twitching.

"Not at all." Dorcas sat in the wingback chair, paging through a manual titled *True Guardianship: The Dragon Transformation Process*. "With a little more time, Sean and Maggie will fall in love. Then they'll sort out this business with SaveALot."

"I'm not convinced they'll fall in love soon enough. And there's George. I don't like how that's going at all. I'll bet we'll get out to the Whispering Forest and find him grooving with his iPod, oblivious to his duties."

"I'm betting he's done his rounds." Dorcas flipped another page of the manual. "It says here that once a dragon assumes his True Guardianship duties, he can earn his gold scales within a month of constant application to the job. That's encouraging."

Ambrose continued to pace. "I hope you're right that he's making rounds. I hope that's what we discover when we get out there."

"We will."

"You do realize that we can't take the broom. And I'm worried that Sean's seen it and might start getting suspicious. We need a less conspicuous model."

"Then buy one. But we can't chance using it so soon, no matter what it looks like. We'll have to let a few months go by before we take another ride."

Sabrina stopped pacing and meowed at Dorcas.

"I know you're disappointed, sweetie, and I apologize. If I can get Edith Mae Hoogstraten over here for a cup of tea, I'll give her something to muddle her memory."

Sabrina began to purr.

Ambrose glanced at Dorcas. "That could make things worse. The last time you attempted to wipe out someone's memory they sprouted hair on the end of their nose. You haven't perfected that potion yet."

"If you say so." She smiled sweetly at him. "But it's a long walk out to George's lair."

"Exactly. Which is why we need to buy that used scooter Bradley has for sale. I saw the notice on the deli bulletin board this afternoon. It's cheap. And it's red."

"As if *that* won't attract attention! We can't be seen buzzing out to the Whispering Forest every night on Bradley's red scooter. If we're walking, then we don't seem to have a particular destination. We're simply out for a stroll. On a scooter, a *red* scooter no less, we'd look as if we're definitely going somewhere."

Sabrina came over, propped her front paws on Dorcas's knee and made a little chirping sound.

"See, Sabrina wants the scooter," Ambrose said. "And *I* want the scooter. That's two to one."

"Oh, for goddess' sake, buy the scooter, then."

"I was hoping you'd say that."

"Why?"

Ambrose started toward the front door. "Come with me."

Dorcas followed him out to the front porch, and there stood a shiny red scooter resting on its kickstand. She groaned. "This scooter is so not me."

"But it's me."

She gazed at her husband. "That's what I'm afraid of."

"We can take it tonight, at least. One trip won't be a problem."

"I suppose not." But no matter what Ambrose said, she was going to try to get a memory loss potion down Edith Mae Hoogstraten one of these days. A scooter did not replace a broom, and she was itching to take another broom ride.

"Can we go now?" Ambrose eyed the scooter with longing.

Dorcas shuddered. "Let's wait until it's darker. Maybe then nobody will see me on that thing."

Chapter 26

If Sean hadn't been so afraid for Maggie, he would have been petrified for himself. He didn't know what the hell this thing was or where it had come from—maybe some DNA experiment gone wrong—but no matter what it was, he was keeping it away from Maggie.

"Here's what we'll do," he murmured. "I'll distract it, and you take off. Run for the car and go for help."

"I'm not leaving you."

"Don't think of it like that. You're not leaving me. You're going for help."

"And let you get mauled by the dragon? No way."

"It's not a dragon. Dragons don't exist."

The creature pulled out its earphones. "Dude, I was reading your lips just then and you are totally wrong."

Sean nearly leaped out of his skin. The thing *talked*. Then he began to relax. It only looked like a monster. Some kid was in there pulling strings and talking for it. This was nothing more than a giant Halloween costume.

He leaned down and picked up a stick. "Okay, whoever you are inside there, you're coming out, and you're coming out now. This has gone far enough."

The creature blinked. "Say what?"

"Come on, joke's over. I don't know who the hell you are, but you have plenty to answer for, scaring us to death."

Maggie tugged on his sleeve. "Sean."

"Not now, Maggie. I want this yahoo to show himself."

"But I think it's really a dragon."

"There's no such thing and you know it."

"Oh yeah?" The creature reared on its hind legs. "Check this out." Its roar echoed through the trees.

"Yeah, yeah." Sean tapped the ground with the stick. "Very impressive. You've built yourself quite a machine. Why aren't you working for Disney instead of hanging out in the woods, terrifying the locals?"

The creature dropped to all fours. "Looks like you got a fair maiden there." It took a step closer. "I've been looking for one."

Sean raised his stick. "You make one move toward that fair maiden and you'll wish you hadn't."

"And I'm not a maiden," Maggie added. Her voice quivered a little, but she sounded as if she was trying to be brave.

"Oo, oo, he's got a *stick*!" The creature drew back in mock dismay. "Gonna hit me with that big stick, macho man?" He began hopping from side to side. "Are ya? Huh? Huh? Take your best shot, dude."

"I'm warning you, stay away from her," Sean said.

"I'm *so* scared."

"You'll be plenty scared once I haul you out of that animated suit."

Maggie tugged on his sleeve. "Sean, take a good look at those scales. They're real."

"They just *seem* real, but they're—" He stared at the spot where the dragon had been standing. "Where'd he go?"

Vroom! The dragon reappeared several feet closer. "Right here, buddy boy."

Sean's heart rate picked up considerably. He backed up, pushing Maggie behind him again. "Neat trick."

"I'm taking the fair maiden. Dragons totally do that kind of thing."

Sean gulped. Whatever was going on here, he might be at a slight disadvantage, seeing as how he was armed with a rather skinny stick. "Run, Maggie," he murmured.

"No." She cleared her throat. "Look, Mr. Dragon . . ."

The creature's ears perked up. "Hey, there, hootchie mama. You can call me George."

Sean stared at him. "You have a freaking *name*?"

"George," Maggie said, "you don't want to capture me. What you want is a virgin. That's the way it goes in all the fairy tales."

"I don't feel like waiting around for a virgin, okay?"

Maggie's voice grew stronger. "But you have to. Those are the rules."

"I hate rules!" Smoke billowed out from George's nostrils.

"Don't blame me. I didn't make them."

"Maggie," Sean said. "Don't get into a debate with—"

"I don't have to follow no stinkin' rules because I'm ADD." George's chest swelled.

"Oh, really?" Maggie blew out a breath. "And who, pray tell, told you that?"

"Maggie, stay back." Sean grabbed her as she started edging around him.

George lowered his head in a menacing gesture. "Nobody. I just am. Deal with it."

"Like hell." Sean raised his stick. In the real world there shouldn't be a dragon in this forest, but something had gone very wrong with the world he knew. Now it was up to him to protect Maggie at all costs.

"Move aside, dude." George took another step forward.

"You'll have to go through me to get her."

"I can totally do that. Prepare to die, loser."

Maggie dashed out from behind him. *"You will not kill Sean!"*

"Maggie, no!" He made a grab for her with his free hand and missed.

Before he could stop her, she stomped straight up to the dragon and smacked him on the snout. "You spoiled brat! You're no more ADD than I am. What's wrong with you, running around scaring people like this? Dragons are supposed to be noble creatures. You're a disgrace to your kind, and I have half a mind to— Sean, let me go!"

He wasn't about to. Dragging her with one arm, he pulled her back, brandishing his puny stick at the dragon. She might have a death wish, but he wasn't going to stand by and let her get killed.

Amazingly, George didn't move. He stood in apparent shock and stared at Maggie.

Sean figured he'd snap out of it any second, though, and when that happened, Sean would be ready. In the movies, the guy won the day by driving a spear through the dragon's neck. Except he didn't have a spear. He had a crappy stick that would probably splinter on impact.

He had to go with it, anyway. Yeah, he was scared. He was deafened by the sound of the blood rushing in his eardrums. But he was out of options for evasive action. Pointing the stick at the dragon's neck, he waited for his moment.

"George!" Dorcas's voice rang through the forest. She strode into the clearing, a purple cape billowing around her. "Just *what* do you think you're doing, George?"

George pointed a claw at Maggie. "She hit me!"

"Because you're spoiled and selfish!" Maggie yelled back. "And you were ready to kill Sean."

"That was totally a joke."

"It's not funny, George." Ambrose drove up on a red scooter, with Sabrina riding in a little carrier on the back fender. "Nobody's laughing."

Sean slowly lowered the stick as he tried to get his mind wrapped around what was happening. Nothing in his experience had prepared him for this. He kept a protective arm around Maggie as he turned to Dorcas and Ambrose. "Okay, who the hell *are* you two?"

Dorcas glanced at him. "Your friends."

"That remains to be seen." He pointed his stick at George. "What's with this guy?"

Dorcas folded her arms and glared at the dragon. "According to what I've heard, George has been a problem since he was born. Whether it was nature or nurture, we don't—"

"I'm ADD!"

"Oh, give it a rest," Maggie said. "You're just using that as an excuse to be a pain in the ass. You should be ashamed of yourself. You've been scaring people out here for years, haven't you?"

"It was something to do." George fiddled with his iPod earphones. "It's *boring* out here."

Maggie blew out a breath. "Cry me a river. What do you expect, a career on Wall Street? You're a dragon. You're supposed to . . ." She turned to Dorcas and Ambrose. "What is he supposed to do?"

"He's supposed to be the True Guardian of the Whispering Forest," Dorcas said. "That means he watches out for all the creatures in it, checks that no trees are smoldering if there's a lightning storm, things like that."

Maggie glanced back at George. "That's a *wonderful* job. You should be so grateful for a job like that."

"Wait a minute, Dorcas," Sean said. "How do you know so much about this True Guardian stuff?"

"If there's a problem with a dragon, as in this case, the wizard world is put in charge of straightening it out."

Maggie gasped. "Did you say *wizard world*? So you're wizards?"

"Technically, Ambrose is the wizard. I'm a witch."

"Omigod, you put a love spell on us, didn't you? That's why we can't seem to stay away from each other and why we're constantly—"

"No." Dorcas shook her head. "We didn't put a love spell on you. We would never do that. Whatever you're feeling is real. The wine might have jump-started things a little, but it won't work unless there's actual chemistry."

Sean kept quiet. Obviously they'd put a spell on him in order to turn him into a toad. He didn't want to mention that in front of Maggie and risk looking stupid for letting himself get involved in such a crazy thing. Besides, he didn't want to draw attention to whatever unattractive thing he had going on right now.

But at the same time, everything was starting to make sense. The two people flying over Edith Mae's house, the incense, the special herbs, even the black cat. He'd heard about such things, but he'd never believed they were real. Unless he was hallucinating, he couldn't very well doubt it now.

"Hel-*lo*, people." George leaned toward them. "We're here to talk about the dragon, remember?"

"I do believe that's right," Ambrose said. "So let's talk about you, George. We're all sick of your behavior and we want it to stop."

George smirked at him. "Dude, you can't make me do anything."

"Want to bet?" Ambrose reached inside his coat and pulled out something that was in two pieces. He screwed it together like a pool cue, but this was no pool cue.

"You totally won't use that on me. I know about wizards, man. You're all *with harm to none.*"

Dorcas stared at her husband. "You made your staff collapsible?"

Ambrose shrugged. "I worked on it this morning. Transports easier this way." He glanced back at George. "As for that *with harm to none* vow, yeah, I took it. But that means protecting others from being harmed by the likes of you. Don't push me, *dude.*"

Sean wasn't eager to witness a showdown between a wizard and a dragon. In the movies, that usually turned nasty and flaming stuff flew everywhere. Innocent people could get hurt. "Maybe I'll just take Maggie and go home," he said.

Maggie shook her head. "You can go if you want, but I'm staying. I'll never see something like this again in my lifetime."

George blew out a series of ragged smoke rings in quick succession. "You won't use that staff on me, man."

Ambrose muttered a phrase in Latin and the tip of his staff glowed bright enough to light the entire clearing. "Everyone, get back."

Sean didn't need to be told twice. He drew Maggie into the trees. "Don't be stubborn. This is our chance to leave."

"No way. I'm staying."

He sighed. "All righty, then. Me, too, I guess."

"But don't you think this is fascinating?"

"I'm too busy dealing with the adrenaline rush. I'm still worried that we'll both end up dead."

She nestled her head against his shoulder. "You were really brave."

"I was really scared shitless."

"That's what bravery is—being scared shitless and doing it, anyway."

He thought about that and felt sort of proud of himself. "Thanks. So were you scared shitless, too?"

"At first I was. But when he threatened to kill you, I just got mad."

"Huh." He liked thinking of her going into a rage on his behalf. He also liked standing here with his arm around her. There was nothing sexual or suggestive going on, just two people holding each other.

Even with an impending wizard/dragon battle, he wouldn't trade places with anyone in the world. Something warm and intense made his chest tighten up. He'd never felt anything quite like it, but he had a pretty good idea what it was.

·

Chapter 27

As unsettling as this whole episode had been, Maggie had never felt as secure as she did standing in the protective circle of Sean's arm. She marveled that he'd been willing to give his life to save her. Equally significant, she'd been willing to challenge the dragon to save him.

Some heavy-duty emotions were rocking and rolling inside of her. She could use more time to sort them out, but time was in short supply right now. And then there was the whole dragon issue. Building a SaveA-Lot next door to George might create some unexpected complications.

The appearance of the dragon had brought up long-forgotten fantasies from her early years, when she'd believed in such things. Then reality had turned her into a logical, career-focused adult. Discovering that witches and dragons actually existed was like traveling back to her once magical childhood.

Ambrose lifted his staff. "Well, George? Ready to duke it out?"

"Uh, you know what? I was just kidding. Let's totally forget about it."

"Oh, no, we won't," Dorcas said. "I want your

promise right now that you will begin assuming your guardianship of the Whispering Forest."

George looked uneasy. "Like when? Because I have this hot poker game I have to get back to, and—"

"Immediately!" Ambrose lifted his staff. "Do we understand each other?"

"Sheesh. Yeah, okay! Man, you don't have to go all postal on me. I'll do the True Guardian thing."

"Glad to hear it." Ambrose lowered his staff and mumbled another Latin phrase. The light winked out.

Dorcas took a deep breath. "Great. We'll be off, then."

"Us, too," Sean said.

Dorcas turned to him. "Why don't you ride back behind Ambrose on the scooter as far as the rental car? Maggie and I will follow along behind. It'll give us a chance for some girl talk."

Maggie was game. She'd never shared any girl talk with a witch. "All right." She took the car keys out of her coat pocket and handed them to Sean. "You can start the motor and turn on the heat. It's chilly out here."

He didn't seem at all sure about the idea as he glanced from Maggie to Dorcas. "I think maybe—"

"I'd like to talk with Dorcas," Maggie said.

"Okay, then." He climbed on the scooter behind Ambrose and the two of them drove out of the clearing with Sabrina sitting proudly in her basket on the back fender.

As Maggie fell into step beside Dorcas, she took a last look behind her. Without Ambrose's staff to light the clearing, she couldn't see as well, but it seemed as if George was still sitting there, thinking about things.

Maggie lingered, wondering what would happen next, but Dorcas took her arm and hustled her down the narrow path to the road. "We need to leave him alone and let him show some initiative," she said.

"What if he doesn't do as he's told?" Maggie had to walk fast to keep up. When Dorcas walked, she didn't piddle around.

"He will, now that Ambrose threatened him with his staff. I was hoping that wouldn't be necessary and George would develop some internal discipline, but that wasn't happening, so external discipline will have to be applied for a while. Ambrose and I will monitor the situation."

Maggie was puffing, but determined to satisfy her curiosity. "How powerful is that staff Ambrose has?"

"Quite powerful if he keeps it tuned up. Unfortunately, he tends to be lax about that. And I have no idea whether making it collapsible had a negative effect. It's probably good that it didn't come to an actual battle with George."

"Yikes. He could have lost?"

Dorcas nodded. "Maybe. He should have checked with me, but that's Ambrose for you. Always messing with something."

"Why did you and Ambrose come to Big Knob?"

"We've been assigned to George, but let's not talk about him. Let's talk about you."

"Oh, let's not." Maggie gulped for air. "I'm not interesting."

"From the expression on Sean's face every time he looks at you, you're the most interesting person in Big Knob."

"Which I don't get." Maggie skipped to catch up. "No man has ever looked at me like that. I think you enchanted him somehow." The sound of an engine starting in the distance indicated the guys had reached the car.

"There was no enchantment involved. That's the real deal you're seeing." Dorcas stopped and turned to her. "I just wonder what you're going to do about it."

Maggie stumbled to a halt and faced her, although the shadows made it impossible to see her expression.

"I don't know. It's complicated." Then the car's head-lights flicked on. Although the car was still quite a ways down the road, Maggie could see a little better in the glow of those lights.

"I have a suggestion." Dorcas's eyes looked like amber jewels.

As Maggie gazed into them, she had no trouble be-lieving that Dorcas was a witch. "I'm listening."

"This may sound counterintuitive, but don't go home with him tonight."

Disappointment washed over Maggie at the thought. She hadn't realized how much she'd looked forward to spending another night with Sean. "Why not?"

"I think you know."

She did. Another night in Sean's bed would be won-derful but distracting. She needed time to consider her options without the powerful influence of that strong physical attraction.

She gazed at Dorcas. "Do you have a magic wand?"

"I do, but I didn't bring it."

"Isn't that a *don't leave home without it* kind of thing?"

Dorcas shook her head. "Half the time it gets in the way. I either poke myself or jab someone else. Try carrying an eighteen-inch stick around with you and you'll see what I mean."

"I suppose. It's just that it would come in handy about now."

"Why's that?"

"You could make me disappear."

Dorcas laughed. "Oh, no. That's the chicken way out. You need to face him and resist the temptation. Don't worry. You're up to it."

"Guess I'll have to be." Maggie sighed. "So, if you had your magic wand, could you make me disappear?"

"Maybe, but it's not my specialty, so I never guaran-tee something like that. Sometimes there are glitches."

"Glitches? Like what?"

Dorcas waved a hand in the air. "It's not important. We should probably go." She started toward the car.

Maggie hurried after her. "Do you fly on a broom?"

"On occasion."

"That's wild. Do you have a cauldron?"

"Yes."

"Dorcas, I would love to see those things before I leave. I know you have to keep everything hush-hush. I mean, I can just imagine the reaction if anyone else in Big Knob finds out about you and Ambrose and the dragon and stuff, but I promise not to say a word."

Dorcas glanced over her shoulder. "Then come to dinner tomorrow night. I'll invite Sean, too."

"I, ah, don't know if I'll be here or not." She couldn't plan beyond her appointment with Harold Pierpont.

"Then you can let me know."

"You'll know as soon as I do." Maggie would love to believe that she'd enjoy a cozy dinner with Dorcas and Ambrose tomorrow night, but she didn't think the chances were very good.

Maggie hadn't said much as she drove the rental car along the dirt road toward the main road. Sean hoped that was because she was concentrating on not hitting any ruts.

When they reached the paved road, she put on the brakes and turned to him. "I'm going to spend tonight over at Madeline's instead of staying with you."

He took the announcement like a blow to the stomach. He'd lost her. She wanted her space so she could rededicate herself to the SaveALot cause. She was choosing her job over him.

Well, if that's the way she wanted it, then he had some thinking to do, too. Maybe it was better that she'd tipped her hand now, so that he could decide what to do. After all, he now had the resources to outbid her.

"Then you might as well take me to my truck," he said.

She gazed out the windshield at the deserted road. "I can do that." She sounded unhappy about her decision.

"Hey, don't do this to yourself. If you want to come home with me, I promise not to discuss real estate."

"I know you wouldn't." She swallowed. "But I need some time to figure things out."

So she hadn't decided what to do yet. His impulse was to unbuckle his seat belt, reach across the console and try to convince her to spend the night with him. Given her past response to him, he had a fair chance of succeeding.

But that wouldn't be treating her with the respect she deserved. Although it killed him to keep his hands to himself, he did. "Okay," he said.

She took a shaky breath. "Okay. Tell me where to find your truck."

He directed her to the dirt road where he'd hidden it. "Just stop here. I'll walk in."

She pulled the car over and gave him a tiny smile. "Watch out for dragons."

He managed to dredge up a smile in return. "Right." He longed to lean over and kiss her, but he'd never be able to leave it at that. "I'll probably show up tomorrow morning."

"I know."

He opened the car door, which turned on the interior light. "See you then."

"Sean, thank you for . . . everything."

He glanced back at her. It might be a trick of the light, but her eyes were sort of sparkly, like she might be about to cry. His heart wrenched, but he had no idea how to comfort her. She really did have to figure this out on her own, and so did he.

"Same here," he said. Well, if that wasn't romantic. But if he said anything more, she might think he was trying to influence her decision. He was determined not to do that. "Bye." Climbing out of the car, he closed the door.

He stood there a minute, feeling the ache of loneliness as he'd never felt it before. Then he gave the door a couple of little taps, and she stepped on the gas.

Swinging the car into a U-turn, she headed back in the direction of town. He watched until he could no longer see the car's taillights. There was a very good chance he'd have to learn to live without her. At the moment, it seemed impossible.

Maggie arrived at the property by nine forty-five, halfway expecting Sean to be there, too. Her suitcase and laptop were in the back of the car. No matter what, she wasn't spending another night in Madeline and Abe's sauna of a house.

This morning she'd stopped by the Hob Knob and picked up coffee for herself, Sean, Denise and Harold Pierpont. Despite the obvious conflicts, they could all be civilized about this. She also needed the caffeine after spending a sleepless night at Madeline's.

She'd like to blame that on where Madeline and Abe set the thermostat, but she wouldn't have slept no matter what the temperature had been. Today was too important. And after turning the problem over in her head until she was dizzy, she still wasn't sure what to do.

Gray clouds had rolled in again, and wind buffeted the car as she sat waiting in the drive. A loose shutter banged on the old Victorian. Clouds like that in Chicago meant snow was on the way.

From here she could see the corner window in the parlor that would be the perfect place for a Christmas tree. She pictured the tree decorated with multicolored lights and delicate glass balls, while snow piled up around the house and a thick layer settled on the roof like vanilla frosting.

The postcard image created such a peaceful feeling that she finally had to break out the coffee so she wouldn't fall asleep. She'd finished hers by the time Denise showed up at ten. Getting out of her car, she carried the cardboard tray of coffee cups over to Denise's car and climbed in.

Denise accepted the coffee with thanks and took off the lid to release the steam. "No sign of old Mr. Pierpont, I see."

"Not so far. Sean said he'd probably drive over, too."

Denise sipped her coffee. "You do realize he's got enough money now to make a real run at this thing?"

"So I guessed." Maggie gazed over at the Whispering Forest where it bordered the property. She wondered what Denise would think if she knew that a dragon had been living in those woods for years. A dragon could seriously affect property values in Big Knob.

Last night seemed like a weird dream, but Maggie didn't doubt that it had happened. She'd never forget the moment when Sean had challenged George with nothing more than a pointed stick. Heroes didn't come much braver than that.

"Of course, it's still possible that Pierpont got his geriatric self lost on the freeway," Denise said.

Maggie glanced at her. "Did you ever get in touch with him again?"

"Nope. I tried a few more times but he didn't answer. I guess if he doesn't show we can drive to Evansville and track him down."

And suddenly, the solution came to her. After all the inner debate and the hours of soul searching, the decision was easier than Maggie had thought it would be. Maybe it was seeing the Whispering Forest again and being reminded of that moment when Sean had risked his life for her.

She cleared her throat. "You and Sean can track him down."

Denise blinked. "What do you mean by that?"

"I mean, I'm out of here." Maggie opened the passenger door and fresh, cool air greeted her. She took a deep breath. Yes, this was the right move, the only move.

"Hey, you can't back out now! Your boss will be royally pissed."

"Probably." Maggie knew H.G. would fire her, but so what? Last night she'd challenged a dragon in order to keep Sean from getting killed. Why would she turn around and ruin his precious dream this morning?

Sure, losing her job would impact her finances, but that wasn't nearly as scary as going up against a two-thousand-pound dragon. She'd survive. She wasn't like her parents. Besides all that, a SaveALot next to a dragon's lair made no sense at all. She didn't think H.G. would buy that excuse, though.

Before she lost her nerve, she pulled out her Black-Berry and dialed her boss's private number.

Even on a Sunday, H.G. answered immediately. His tone was uncompromising. "Grady, this had better be good."

"I'm afraid it's not, H.G. I don't have a location for you, after all. I've failed again."

"After all this secrecy, you're coming up empty?"

"Yes, I am."

There was a moment of silence. "Then you give me no choice, Grady. When you come back, clean out your desk." Then the line went dead.

So that was it. She was officially fired. Eventually the reality would set in, but for now, she just felt numb.

"Are you fired?" Denise asked.

"Yep."

"Oh, I get it," Denise said. "You have the hots for Sean, and you want to impress him by giving up both your job and the property."

"I won't be around to find out if he's impressed or not."

"You're leaving?" Denise stared at her. "That makes no sense. Why not stick around and soak up his gratitude?"

"Because I'm afraid it will be mixed with pity. He knew I'd lose my job over this. I don't want him to feel guilty, and I don't want him to feel sorry for me, either."

"I hate admitting this, but I think he really likes you. So what if you lost your job? Get one in Big Knob."

Maggie shook her head. "That's putting way too much pressure on Sean. How do I know if his feelings will last? Didn't you tell me not to become another notch on his tool belt?"

"Yeah." Denise sighed. "But if Sean looked at me the way he looks at you, I'd take that chance."

Maggie considered that for all of three seconds. No, too risky. Sean had made no declarations of undying love. Considering his history with women, he might not even know what real commitment looked like.

She probably needed a little space to sort out her feelings, too. If they had something lasting, it would still be there in a few weeks. Plopping her unemployed self in his lap right now would be a terrible mistake.

"Well, I choose not to take that chance," she said. "I'm flying home and updating my resume."

She intended to find a new job. If they met again, and she hoped someday they might, she wouldn't be some pathetic person with no prospects. Standing on her own two feet financially was important to her, especially after being raised by such luckless parents.

"I hope you know what you're doing," Denise said.

"I do." Maggie stepped out of the car. "And you have a buyer, so you won't lose a commission. Thanks for all your help, Denise." As she started to close the car door, a white Cadillac pulled up behind Denise's car.

"You'd better be damned sure you want to blow this chance." Denise set her coffee cup back in the cardboard tray and opened her door. "I think that's Pierpont. And Sean is nowhere to be seen. You have the inside track."

Maggie was surprised Sean wasn't here yet, but something must have come up. She walked back to the Cadillac as an elderly man with thinning white hair unfolded his thin frame from the driver's seat of the Caddy.

She held out her hand. "Mr. Pierpont?"

"That's me." He wore a black wool overcoat with a plaid scarf wrapped around his neck. "Couldn't find the exit off of Highway Sixty-eight. Had to double back and try again. Finally I saw it, but I swear it wasn't there the first time. Craziest thing." He took off his leather glove to shake her hand. "You must be the buyer."

"I'm Maggie Grady." She gestured toward Denise. "And this is my real estate agent, Denise Woolrich."

"Pleased to meet you both." He shook Denise's hand, too. Then he glanced up at the old Victorian. "Bought this place years ago at auction. Planned to turn it into a house of ill repute." He chuckled.

"Formed the corporation and everything, but I couldn't figure out how to get away with it."

"Lucky for us." Denise glanced at Maggie and rolled her eyes.

"But not so lucky for the male population of Big Knob," Pierpont said. "Sometimes a man needs a sure thing. So what are you planning to do with the place, Maggie?"

"Actually, nothing. I'm no longer interested." She felt a little pang when she said that, but it passed. "You have a buyer here in town, though, and his name is Sean Madigan. Denise can put you in touch with him."

"Maggie." Denise put a hand on her arm. "This is silly. At least put in a bid."

"Can't." She glanced at the house and could swear she saw the glitter of a Christmas tree in the window. "This house belongs to Sean. If you'll excuse me, I have to be going."

Chapter 28

Dorcas threw some freshly ground herbs in the pot bubbling on the stove. Then she glanced over at Sabrina perched on the kitchen windowsill. Sabrina had tensed and was staring out toward the lake, where the wind was whipping up whitecaps.

Crossing to the window, Dorcas scratched behind Sabrina's ears. "See something out there, little girl?"

Sabrina's ears twitched as she concentrated on the lake. Then her tail began to whip back and forth and a low growl rumbled in her chest.

As she stroked Sabrina's soft fur, Dorcas studied the frothy surface of the lake and the wintry shoreline, hoping for a glimpse of what the cat had seen. Was that something dark rising above the surface of the water? Then it disappeared. A moment later she saw it again, three humps looking as if dolphins were swimming across the lake, except that would be impossible.

Then a head emerged, lifting a good ten feet from the surface of the lake. It swiveled to either side like a periscope before sliding back under the waves. Uh-oh.

She turned at the sound of the front door opening.

"Dorcas!" Ambrose sounded upset.

"I'm back here. And lower your voice. You're upsetting Sabrina." The strange creature in the water was upsetting Sabrina far more than Ambrose, but Dorcas was always looking for an excuse to keep Ambrose from bellowing inside the house.

Her husband appeared in the kitchen doorway, his hair windblown from a ride on the scooter. "Maggie's gone back to Houston."

"I know."

"How do you know?"

Dorcas crossed to the stove and stirred her brew. "While you were out putt-putting around on that scooter, I did a quick bit of scrying to check on the property situation. Maggie left so Sean would buy it, which he wouldn't have if she'd stuck around, because he intended to let her have it to save her job. Everything's hunky-dory."

"It most certainly is not. For one thing, she left before we could give her a memory potion."

"Come on." Dorcas sniffed the brew before tossing in a sliced mushroom. "Do you honestly think she'll be telling people she met a witch and wizard, let alone that there's a dragon living in the woods?"

Ambrose unzipped his black leather motorcycle jacket, something he'd bought because he thought the scooter demanded it. "I suppose not. But that's the smaller issue, anyway. The bigger problem is Sean. How can he marry her if she's in Houston?"

"Simple. We'll invite her for a visit in a little while, after she's had time to miss him." She stirred her mixture again. "I assume Sean is back to his old hunky self?"

"Yeah, he looks great, but he's so depressed that the women are leaving him alone. The angst must be nullifying his pheromones." Ambrose took off his jacket and hung it over a kitchen chair.

"Some time apart is not a terrible thing. It'll make

them both appreciate what they've found." She turned down the heat and left the brew to simmer while she cleaned up her utensils.

"What makes you think Maggie will come back?"

Dorcas ran warm water in the sink and added some soap. "She wanted to see my wand, the cauldron and the broom. I promised to show them to her."

Ambrose gasped. "You can't go around doing that sort of thing, Dorcas. We have enough damage control to take care of as it is."

"I can if I show her the equipment before dinner and serve her the memory potion as part of the soup course."

"Serving anyone your memory potion is risky."

"Life is risky, Ambrose." She carefully washed her favorite knife. "Did you check on George?"

"Everything seems quiet in the forest, knock on wood." He rapped on the kitchen counter. "Knowing George, though, he's not going to turn gold in a month. I'll be surprised if he manages it in six."

"That may be just as well. It seems we have a new problem."

"Did Sean blab about the dragon? Or worse yet, about us?"

"No, I'm sure he didn't. He's been too busy dealing with the emotional pain of discovering that Maggie left without saying good-bye. We'll get him over here in the next couple of days and serve him my memory potion. As you can see, I'm making up a new batch."

Ambrose eyed the bubbling pot. "Don't forget the *Amanita muscaria* mushrooms. I remember the time you forgot those. It was a disaster."

"I wouldn't say that. Those two people were only unconscious for eight hours." But she went back to the cupboard, took out the jar of diced mushrooms and sprinkled in about a teaspoon. Something about that ingredient made her forget to put it in, which was sort of funny, since it was a potion to erase memory.

"They were loopy for another five, but never mind. What's our other problem?"

"Take a look out the window. I think the wind stirred up the lake and . . . one of its inhabitants."

Ambrose walked over and peered through the window while he absently stroked Sabrina. "I don't see any—oh, dear Zeus! Is that what I think it is?"

"I'm afraid so."

He turned to her. "Look, we were assigned to take care of George. Nobody said anything about some dinosaur wannabe cruising around in the lake."

"I think it's a lake monster, like they have in Loch Ness."

"Whatever! It's not our responsibility."

"I think it might be, Ambrose. I'm guessing that it's been hiding down there, maybe for a long time, and the vibes from us doing magic caught its attention."

Ambrose stared out the window. "There's a cold front moving in. Maybe the lake will freeze over and trap it for a few months."

"And if the lake doesn't freeze over?"

"Let someone else worry about it."

Dorcas folded her arms. "What happened to those four special words embroidered in the cross-stitch over our bed: *With Harm to None*?"

"*I'm* not going to harm anyone. I can't vouch for that thing. But it's not my problem. Once George is covered in golden scales, we're outta here."

"And in the meantime?"

"I plan to ignore it."

"Then you'd better hope the lake freezes over real soon."

The smell of paint was making Sean dizzy, so he decided to open the balcony doors for a few minutes and air the place out. That's when he realized it was snowing. He stood on the balcony and watched it come down from the twilight sky—big, fat flakes that were already sticking to the trees. By tomorrow morning Big Knob would look like a fairyland.

The timing wasn't exactly right. Christmas was still two days away, but from the looks of this snow, it wouldn't melt in two days. Big Knob would have its white Christmas. He didn't really care, but the rest of the town would be happy about it.

Funny how he had exactly what he'd been longing for all these years and yet he felt so empty. He hoped the empty feeling would let up eventually, but Maggie had been gone for a month and he still ached for her. Once he realized she'd left town, he'd tried calling her cell phone but she hadn't answered.

He'd even tried calling her at the SaveALot headquarters in Houston, only to find out she no longer worked there. He wasn't surprised about that. She'd shot herself in the foot, for some unknown reason. By leaving town she'd made it obvious that she wasn't interested in either the property or him.

He was left to relive the moments he'd spent with her, and he had perfect recall except for that last night in the Whispering Forest. He remembered meeting her there and having great sex while it was still light. But by the time they'd driven away in her car, it had been pitch-dark, which left a gap of time unaccounted for. Strange.

A gust of wind blew snow under the balcony roof, hitting him in the face. He decided to go back in and finish the west wall before going to bed. As he started to pick up the roller, the doorbell chimed.

Expecting Maggie every time that happened was dumb, but he did it, anyway. Walking to the front window, he looked down and saw Jeremy's Subaru parked there. Sean had told Jeremy to stop by sometime and see how the house was coming along, so he must have picked tonight.

Sean headed downstairs and opened the front door. "Hey, what's up?"

"Not much." Jeremy walked in. "I like the tree in the parlor window. Nice touch."

"Yeah, well, it's Christmas. I don't have any furniture in there, but a tree seemed like a good idea. Want a beer?"

"Sure, but you're painting."

"I can paint and drink."

Jeremy laughed and took off his jacket. "All right."

After getting them each a beer, Sean gave Jeremy a quick tour of the work he'd done so far in the kitchen and the downstairs bathroom.

"Looks great," Jeremy said. "So what are you painting?"

"The master bedroom." And he didn't get much company these days, so he might as well relax and enjoy it. "You know what? I'm going to quit for the night. Let me close up shop and we can nuke a frozen pizza or something."

"Sounds good." Jeremy followed him up the stairs. "I'm impressed with how the place looks already. You do good work."

"I should hope to hell. It's how I make my living." Sean walked into the master bedroom and set his beer on the floor while he took care of his brushes and paint roller.

"I heard some news about Annie and Zach today," Jeremy said.

"What's that?" Sean glanced up. Back in high school he'd always thought Jeremy had a crush on Annie, but she'd ended up marrying Zach, a jock who was also her high school sweetheart. They lived in Chicago.

"They're divorced."

"No kidding?" Sean put the lid on the paint can. "That's too bad."

"Yeah." Jeremy didn't sound broken up about it.

"Any kids?"

"Nope."

Sean picked up his beer and wiped his sleeve over the damp spot on the hardwood floor. "I always thought you kind of liked her."

"What's not to like? Everybody liked her. That's why she was voted Dairy Festival Queen. But that was a long time ago."

Taking a sip of his beer, Sean gazed at his friend. "Maybe you should take a drive to Chicago and look her up."

"Nah. She was never interested in me."

"That was then." Listen to him, giving advice to the lovelorn, when his own love life had completely imploded.

"She has her big-city life in Chicago," Jeremy said. "I can't believe she'd ever move back here, and I'm just not a big-city type of guy."

Sean nodded. "I hear you." Sean had debated that issue long and hard, too. In the end, he couldn't picture himself relocating to Houston, and that was even if Maggie had asked, which she hadn't.

"Enough of that depressing subject." Sean started out of the room. "Let's grab some pizza and see what's happening with the Bears game."

Maggie pulled into the driveway behind a Subaru hatchback that she thought belonged to Jeremy. So Sean had company. Well, that might be a good thing. Having Jeremy around would stave off any awkward silences.

The tree in the parlor window brought a lump to her throat. He was settling in, exactly as she'd hoped he would once she got out of his way. She still didn't know what had kept him from showing up to meet

Pierpont on that Sunday morning a month ago, but everything had happened for the best in the end.

Far better that he hadn't been around when she'd decided not to buy the property. He knew very well that would affect her career, and the last thing she'd wanted from him was pity. Now that she had a new job, they could meet as equals, as friends.

Maybe she'd tell him that she'd been right about the mole in the SaveALot corporation. Quite a scandal had erupted in the Houston papers when H.G. had publicly fired his son, and his son had filed a lawsuit against his father. All the dirty laundry had come spilling out. It would be good to be able to talk openly about that with Sean. She'd been so paranoid before.

She was also dying to know what had happened with George. She'd almost convinced herself that she'd dreamed that, but then last week Dorcas had called to invite her to come and check out her witch paraphernalia.

Maggie had planned to visit her parents in Chicago, anyway, so it wasn't a problem to schedule an overnight in Big Knob on her way. Plus it gave her the perfect excuse to find out firsthand how Sean was doing. Dorcas had guessed that she'd want to see Sean but had suggested coming to their house first to freshen up.

Although Maggie had fully intended to do that, she hadn't been able to pass Sean's house without stopping there. Dorcas said Sean hadn't hooked up with anyone, so at least no woman would be living in the house with him.

Knowing Sean, that could change at any moment, and Maggie wanted to touch base with him before that happened. Beyond the satisfaction of seeing him enjoying his house, she had no preconceived ideas as to how the meeting would turn out. If he was the least bit distant, she'd wish him a merry Christmas and be on her way, after she gave him the Christmas/house-warming present she'd brought.

Tucking it under her arm and hoisting her purse strap over her shoulder, she stepped out of the car. Snowflakes gave her moist little kisses on her way to the porch steps. She climbed the steps, which looked newly painted. Two refinished rocking chairs sat to the right of the front door. Now wouldn't be the time to sit there, but she could imagine enjoying that porch in the spring.

A mental picture was all she'd have, though. She and Sean hadn't had time to become more than casual lovers. Trying to make something more of what they'd shared had the potential to embarrass them both . . . unless he'd missed her as much as she'd missed him.

She rang the doorbell and was pleased by the deep chime. He was turning this house into a showplace. Thank heaven she'd had the good sense to withdraw and let him have it. Probably she'd stay only a few minutes before going over to visit Dorcas and Ambrose. They'd offered to make her a bed on the sofa.

Then Sean opened the door, and all her rationalizations went up in smoke. The month they'd been apart shrank to nothing, and her heart beat so fast she had trouble breathing. God, he was gorgeous. Either her memory was faulty or his hottie quotient had increased in the past few weeks.

She wanted him. But more than that, she finally had a name for the emotion she'd been talking herself out of ever since leaving Big Knob. She shouldn't have come, shouldn't have stirred things up again. If he had lost all feeling for her, she might never recover from the blow.

He swallowed. "Maggie."

"Hi, Sean." She struggled to come up with words

when all she wanted was to fling herself into his strong arms. The sound of a televised football game and the scent of pizza told her she'd interrupted his dinner. "You're probably surprised to see me."

"Yes."

"I was . . . that is, Dorcas invited me to visit, and I found this at an art fair, so I—"

"Come in." He stepped back and held the door for her.

Jeremy emerged from the kitchen. "Hey, Maggie! I didn't know you were coming to town."

"Neither did I," Sean said softly.

"It was sort of last-minute." Maggie tried to read Sean's expression, but other than his obvious surprise, she couldn't tell if he was happy or horrified to see her. "I didn't really plan to stay. I just brought you this." She thrust the gift, wrapped only in brown paper and tied with twine, in his direction. "I saw it and thought of you."

"Thanks." Sean took the parcel but continued to stare at her as if she were a ghost . . . or a complete idiot.

She felt more uncomfortable by the second. This had been *such* a bad idea. "Well, you have company, so I'll be going. Dorcas is probably—"

"Don't leave."

"Yeah, you should stay." Jeremy walked down the hall and grabbed his jacket from the coat tree by the door. "I was about to take off, anyway. I ordered my niece's Christmas present online and it isn't here yet, so I need to find out where it is in the system."

That sounded like a convenient excuse to Maggie. She'd busted up their football-and-pizza night, which is what she got for not calling ahead. She'd been afraid to do that, afraid she'd lose her nerve.

She turned to Sean, amazed again at his heart-stopping good looks. "I should have let you know I was coming. I hate drop-in guests because they're so disruptive, and here I am, ruining—"

"Maggie, it's fine."

"Hey, I was a drop-in guest." Jeremy zipped his jacket. "In Big Knob we're all about the drop-in guests."

Sean gazed at her with those beautiful green eyes. "He's right. It's a small town. We don't stand on ceremony."

"That's for sure." Jeremy opened the door. "Catch you later, buddy. I'll be going down to my sister's for Christmas, so if I don't see you before then, have a merry."

"Thanks. You, too."

"Good to see you again, Maggie." Jeremy gave her a salute and closed the door behind him.

In the silence that followed, the sports announcer's voice drifted down the hall. Maggie took a deep breath. "You were eating. I wouldn't want your food to get cold."

The hint of a smile touched his sculpted lips. "It's not like it hasn't happened before."

Heat filled her cheeks as she remembered their first night together and how uninhibited she'd been. She managed a small laugh. "We got a little carried away. Probably the effects of the wine, don't you think?"

"Do you?"

Looking at him, she couldn't imagine how wine could make her want him any more than she did right this minute. She'd better get out of here before she made a fool of herself. "Open your housewarming gift." Once he did that, she could leave.

"Okay." He pulled off the twine and the tape. Then he unfolded the brown paper and pulled out the framed watercolor. "Skunks."

"A family," she said. "Like the ones you saved. I

knew you'd have lots of wall space to cover, and I thought . . . but if you don't like it, you don't have to hang it up."

"I like it." He studied the painting and then looked at her, his gaze soft. "I like it a lot. Thank you."

His tenderness nearly did her in. She'd be begging him to hold her if she didn't make a break for it. "I should go."

"Come in and see the tree first." Without waiting for an answer, he started into the parlor.

Maybe she should do that much. He was obviously proud of it. She didn't know very many men who would buy and decorate a Christmas tree by themselves. Or maybe he hadn't. Maybe several women had helped.

Suddenly she wanted to know that. She unbuttoned her coat and left her purse hanging on the coat tree as she walked into the parlor. The tree, at least nine feet tall, sparkled in front of the elegant window. The room smelled of pine, reminding her of the afternoon they'd made love in the Whispering Forest.

She'd always longed for a Christmas tree this big, but she'd never lived anywhere with ceilings that would accommodate it. "Beautiful," she said. "Did you put it up by yourself?"

"Uh-huh." He laid her framed painting of the skunks under the tree. So far it was the only gift there. "Dorcas and Ambrose gave me the star for the top, but otherwise it was my project."

She noticed several dainty glass ornaments among the more ordinary Christmas decorations. She touched one. "These are unusual."

"My mom's."

Her heart ached for him. Instinctively she knew that this had been exactly where the tree had stood when he'd been a kid living in this house. Considering how much buying it had meant, she wondered how he could possibly have missed the appointment with Pierpont on that fateful Sunday morning.

She touched another of the delicate ornaments, admiring how it caught the light. "Why didn't you show up at the meeting a month ago?"

"I'll answer that if you'll tell me why you didn't buy the property as planned."

Because I love you. She continued to stare at the tree. "Because I realized it meant more to you than it meant to me."

"How can you say that? Weren't you fired over it?"

Finally she glanced at him. "Yes, but I could find another job, which I did, by the way. You could never have found another house. So why didn't you move heaven and earth to get there at ten o'clock and try to outbid me?"

He cleared his throat. "Well, I counted up all the good things I had going on—a job I love doing, a town where I feel at home, friends who watch out for me. You seemed like you were still trying to find your place in life, so I—I was ready to give up the house if it would help you do that."

She was stunned. "You felt *sorry* for me?"

"Not exactly. I—"

"You did! You felt sorry for me. Was that why you had sex with me, too? To boost my confidence?" Her tummy began to churn. She should never have come.

"Hell, no, that's not why!"

"I should have known. No man has ever wanted me like that, so I should have guessed that it was a pity scr—" She gasped as he pulled her roughly into his arms.

"Not even close." He took off her fashionable new glasses and dropped them to the floor with a clatter. Then his mouth came down on hers with such force that it stole what remained of her breath.

Chapter 29

The longer he kissed Maggie, the less empty Sean felt. But he thought it might take many kisses and some skin-to-skin contact before the void would disappear completely. She seemed to be perfectly happy kissing him back, but that didn't answer the question of how long she'd be willing to keep it up.

Finally he had to ask her, which meant they had to stop kissing. It was a sacrifice, but necessary to his ultimate peace of mind.

He lifted his head and gazed into her blue eyes. "Do you love your job?"

"Wh-what?"

"Your new job. Is it great?"

"Um . . . yeah."

"Oh." His hopes came crashing down.

"I mean . . . it's not *that* great."

"Really?" He combed his fingers through her short curls. How he'd missed touching her.

"It's okay."

"Just okay, huh?" His dreams flickered back to life.

"It pays the bills."

Music to his ears. "Then quit."

"Quit? Why would I want to do that?"

He cupped her face in both hands. His heart hammered in his chest as he considered the ramifications of what he was about to say. "Because . . ." Then he thought of something else. "You said you hated drop-ins."

"I sort of do."

God, maybe this would never work. What the hell was he doing? Probably mucking it up. He stroked his thumbs over her cheeks. "On a scale of one to ten, how much do you hate them?"

"Sean, this is a very strange conversation. Why are you asking me about drop-ins?"

"Because if you quit your job and marry me and live in Big Knob, you'll be stuck with drop-ins, and if you hate them, then I don't know if—"

"Marry you?"

He groaned and hastily threw out a safety net to catch his shattered dreams. "I know. Dumb idea. Forget I said anything. I don't know what I was thinking, but from the way you were kissing me, I was hoping that maybe you felt marginally good about us."

"I do."

"Yeah, but that doesn't necessarily mean you'd go for the marriage thing."

"Yes, it does."

He stared at her for several long seconds while that sank in. Gradually he realized that she hadn't turned him down. She had actually, in a manner of speaking, accepted his screwed-up proposal.

But he'd really put the cart before the horse, and he should do something about that. He gulped. "I love you."

Her blue eyes glowed with happiness. "That's nice. I love you, too."

"Oh, Maggie." He had to kiss her some more after that. As he was enjoying the process, he decided they should move away from the tree because their activities were heating up and he'd hate to knock the thing over.

He stepped back, bringing her with him, and heard

the crunch of glass under his heel. Shit. He'd done it again.

In no time she was laughing so hard that kissing became impossible.

"I'm sorry," he said. "I can't believe I did that."

"I don't care." She smiled up at him. "If you still have that taped-together pair, I'll borrow those."

"I have them. I don't need them, but I couldn't stand to throw them away because they reminded me of you." As he looked into her eyes, he still couldn't believe his good fortune. "Could you live here, then?"

"In this house?"

"In this house, in this little town, knowing there would be drop—"

"Drop-ins. I know. It's fine. Kiss me some more, please. Better yet, do you have a bed in this house?"

"Yes, but first I have to make sure you're okay with everything. I know you. You'll want to find a job."

She tried to pull him closer. "I'll find something, maybe working with Denise. Or Dorcas and Ambrose might need an office manager. That would be sort of cool, helping a witch and wizard."

"A what?" He stared at her and wondered if he'd misunderstood.

"That's what they called themselves when they showed up in the woods that last night I was here, the night we met George."

"Who's George? What are you talking about?"

"You know, *George*."

"There is no one living in Big Knob named George. I can vouch for that."

Maggie frowned. "You don't remember George?"

"I know everyone in town, and there's no one here by that name. You must be confused."

She peered at him, her expression puzzled. "Would you excuse me a minute?" She wiggled out of his arms. "I need to make a call."

"Now?" He followed her into the entry hall.

"Dorcas is expecting me any minute, so I need to let her know I'll be late." She pulled a cell phone out of her purse.

"Don't mention any of that witch and wizard stuff." Sean hovered nearby. "I know we talked about Dorcas and Ambrose being a little different from the rest of the people in town, but they're not *that* different." He wondered if Maggie had been watching too many movies.

She punched in a number and held the phone to her ear. "I promise to be careful about what I say. Hello, Dorcas? It's Maggie. I'm at Sean's, and he says there's no one in town named George." She listened for a moment. "Yes, that's what I thought. Anyway, I was wondering—could you use a personal assistant for Hot Prospects, Inc.?"

Now that he thought about it, he could imagine Maggie working for Ambrose and Dorcas. They were from out of town. She was from out of town. They'd get along.

"You could?" Maggie smiled and blew him a kiss. "That's wonderful. Just a sec." She put her hand over the phone. "Will I be staying here tonight?"

Fire ran through his body and settled in his groin. "If I have anything to say about it, you will."

"You have everything to say about it." She returned to her phone call. "I'll see you in the morning, then, okay? Bye, Dorcas." She closed the phone and tucked it back in her purse before turning to Sean. "Now, where were we?"

He ached so much he wondered if they'd make it to the downstairs bedroom. "You were about to take off your coat and stay awhile."

"You're right. I was." She slipped out of her trench coat and hung it on the coat tree.

"Much better." He gathered her close and nibbled on her ear. "Let me give you a tour of the house."

"Okay."

He nuzzled her throat and her breathing quickened. "We'll start with the downstairs bedroom, which happens to be the only one with a bed in it."

"I'd enjoy seeing that."

"Then again, I may not be able to walk that far." He backed her up against the wall and began unfastening the buttons of her sweater.

She moaned softly. "The hall's nice, too."

"Mm." He opened the front catch of her bra and cradled her breasts in both hands.

She arched into his embrace. "Oh, and about George . . . I must have been thinking of someone else. Dorcas said there's no one in Big Knob by that name."

At the moment Sean didn't care if there was a fire-breathing dragon named George living right next door. He was too busy loving Maggie to think about it.

Read on for an excerpt from

WILD AND HEXY

by Vicki Lewis Thompson
available from Onyx
in June 2008.

"I had a chat with our lake monster this morning."
Dorcas Lowell gazed at her companions from behind her black marble desk. How she enjoyed dropping bombshells during Monday staff meetings.

Her husband, Ambrose, and her assistant, Maggie Madigan, recoiled in surprise, as Dorcas had intended they would. Sabrina, the black cat curled in Ambrose's lap, sat upright and blinked, which was as surprised as Sabrina ever allowed herself to be.

Ambrose recovered first, and he was furious. "Look, we agreed you wouldn't—"

"The lake monster speaks English?" Maggie leaned forward in her chair.

"Who cares?" As Ambrose stood, Sabrina leaped onto the polished desk. "You should never have gone there alone. Anything could have—"

"But nothing did." Dorcas stroked Sabrina and smiled at her husband. He was so cute when he was mad. He would never have approved of her going to see the lake monster alone, but she'd known instinctively that was the way to approach the problem.

Ambrose glowered at her. "You might have been killed."

"Nonsense." Dorcas gently extricated her notes from

underneath Sabrina's paws. "Would you like to hear my report?"

Ambrose sat down with a martyred sigh. "Might as well, considering you risked your life to get it."

"I did nothing of the kind." Dorcas put on her jeweled reading glasses and consulted what she'd written. "In a nutshell, Dee-Dee is lonely."

"We can't play matchmaker for a lake monster, Dorcas." Ambrose still had his snit going.

"Why not?" Maggie's voice quavered with anticipation. From the moment she'd learned that Dorcas was a witch and Ambrose a wizard, she'd acted like a kid with a new Xbox. "Couldn't you bring a mate to the lake?"

"Ye gods." Ambrose glared at his wife. "Please don't tell me you're considering that."

"No, sweetie, I'm not." Dorcas turned to Maggie. "Transporting a grown male lake monster here would take more powerful magic than Ambrose and I could manufacture by ourselves."

"But you have connections. The Grand High Wizard was just here this weekend. I'll bet he—"

"He wouldn't do it." Dorcas understood how a non-magical person like Maggie might think that witches and wizards could accomplish anything. "It couldn't be done without somebody noticing. Imagine a creature the size of the Goodyear blimp cruising over the good citizens of Big Knob, Indiana. They'd get hysterical."

"And then we'd have a monster hunt on our hands," Ambrose said. "Once they're alerted to strange creatures in the area, they could easily find George. The only reason they haven't discovered there's a dragon living outside town is because it never occurred to them there was one."

Maggie nodded. "I see your point. I don't want to endanger George."

"Neither do I," Dorcas said, although most of the time she longed to give that silly dragon a kick in the patoot. If he'd paid more attention to his duties as the Guardian of Whispering Forest, she and Ambrose would be off the job and headed home to Sedona. Instead, by order of the Grand High Wizard, they were stuck in Big Knob until George earned his golden scales. That could take months.

"So if we're not going to find Dee-Dee a mate," Ambrose said, "what are we going to do about her?"

"I'm not sure yet." Dorcas tapped her glowing pen against her lips. "She needs more study."

Ambrose's scowl had returned. "Next time I'm going with you, and I'm bringing my staff. Did you even take your wand along?"

"I went unarmed, to gain her trust. And you may *not* come with me next time. This is delicate. Something only a woman would understand."

"Then can I go?" Maggie looked as if she could barely contain herself. A transplant from Houston, she'd asked for this assistant's job and she clearly loved it. She was the only Big Knob resident who knew about Dorcas's and Ambrose's magical powers. Even her husband, Sean, didn't know. He thought Dorcas and Ambrose were psychologists.

"Maybe you can go," Dorcas said. "But let's wait a bit. I wouldn't want Dee-Dee to think I'm gossiping about her secrets. She's vulnerable right now."

Ambrose rolled his eyes. "Nothing that weighs two tons is vulnerable, Dorcas."

"That's what you think. Okay, what else do we have this morning, gang?"

"I have something." Maggie reached into her briefcase, pulled out a folder and shoved it across the desk toward Dorcas. "You both know Jeremy Dunstan. He's a good friend of Sean's." Maggie's eyes sparkled whenever she spoke of her husband.

As Dorcas thought of the match she and Ambrose had orchestrated between Maggie and Sean, she reminded herself that being sentenced to dragon duty hadn't been all bad. The Grand High Wizard's decree had lost some of its sting now that she and Ambrose were using their matchmaking skills on the good citizens of Big Knob.

"Of course I know Jeremy," Ambrose said. "I was just in his Internet café yesterday, surfing the Web."

Dorcas wasn't surprised. The Internet was Ambrose's new fixation. He'd recently created a MySpace page for himself. "Does Jeremy want our help?" she asked Maggie.

"Of course, he wouldn't want it," Maggie said. "But he needs it. I'm sure we can figure out a way to help him without his knowledge."

Intrigue—Dorcas relished it. Smiling at Maggie, she opened the folder and found a neatly typed prospectus for a new matchmaking scheme between Jeremy and Annie Winston, sister of Melody. Melody was getting married next weekend, with Annie as maid of honor and Jeremy as best man. Nice setup.

Dorcas flipped through the contents of the folder. It was a common story. Shy Jeremy had lost out to the football hero, but now Annie and the football hero were divorced. "Jeremy still loves her?" Dorcas asked.

"That's what Sean says." Maggie ran a hand through her short red curls. "I wormed the story out of him this weekend."

Dorcas continued to read. "Annie was voted Miss Dairy Queen the summer before her senior year. What's that all about?"

"It's Big Knob's annual Dairy Festival, which takes place next month," Maggie said. "It's the highlight of June around here, and according to Sean, being elected queen is a huge deal. I'm sure Jeremy was intimidated by that, too."